When Gwyneth returned his gaze, she thought she would be lost in it.

She nearly gasped when Simon went down on one knee before her and bowed his head to her. It was a signal honor to her for all to see and a magnificently submissive gesture that only the least submissive of men could afford.

A breathless moment passed before he reached out and took her fingers in his. As he rose, he put his lips to the back of her hand. She felt his touch all the way up her arm. The effect of his courtly kiss was like a stab to her heart.

Turning her hand, he placed her fingertips on the cuff of his shirt. They began to walk. Gwyneth felt her blood beat faster just to be next to him, as she basked in the glow of his rough-edged presence....

Dear Reader,

Harlequin Historicals welcomes you to another sizzling month of romance. With summer in full swing, we've got four titles perfect for the beach, pool—or anywhere!

From popular author Miranda Jarrett comes another swashbuckling tale set on the high seas—*Mariah's Prize*, her next book in the thrilling SPARHAWK series. In this story, a desperate Mariah West convinces Gabriel Sparhawk to captain her sloop, never guessing at his ulterior motives.

Scottish chieftain Dillon Campbell abducted Lady Leonora Wilton as an act of revenge against the English. But one look into Leonora's eyes and it became an act of love, in *The Highlander* by favorite author Ruth Langan.

In Julie Tetel's stirring medieval tale, *Simon's Lady*, the marriage between Simon de Beresford and Lady Gwyneth had been arranged to quell a Saxon uprising, yet this Saxon bride wants more from her husband than peace.

And finally, if you liked Merline Lovelace's first book of the DESTINY'S WOMEN series, *Alena*, you'll love her second book, *Sweet Song of Love*. When knight Richard FitzHugh was called to battle, he left behind a meek bride given to him by the king. So who was the curvaceous beauty who now greeted him as *husband?*

Next month, our big book selection is *To Share a Dream*, a reissue by author Willo Davis Roberts. Don't miss this moving saga about three sisters who dare to build a new beginning in the American colonies.

Sincerely,

Tracy Farrell
Senior Editor

Please address questions and book requests to:
Harlequin Reader Service
U.S.: 3010 Walden Ave., P.O. Box 1325, Buffalo, NY 14269
Canadian: P.O. Box 609, Fort Erie, Ont. L2A 5X3

JULIE TETEL

Simon's Lady

Harlequin Books

TORONTO • NEW YORK • LONDON
AMSTERDAM • PARIS • SYDNEY • HAMBURG
STOCKHOLM • ATHENS • TOKYO • MILAN
MADRID • WARSAW • BUDAPEST • AUCKLAND

ISBN 0-373-28829-8

SIMON'S LADY

Copyright © 1994 by Julie Tetel Andresen.

JULIE TETEL

has always loved both history and romance, making it easy for her to love reading and writing historical romances. She is from a suburb of Chicago and currently lives in Durham, North Carolina. She has two sons, two careers, at least two points of view, and one husband.

Chapter One

London, England
Late May in the Year of Our Lord 1153

Simon of Beresford knelt over his victim. His broadsword lay a foot away, not far from the one his victim had been forced to relinquish only moments before.

The victim was lying in the dust, looking up at his captor. He was dazed by exhaustion and the fierce sun beating down on the two men. His eyes were glazed with fear. He knew that the face of Simon of Beresford was awesome enough when met upright on the field of battle. He saw it now hovering above him, features set and implacable, and found the sight mortally terrifying. With Beresford's hands around his throat, he felt that he had seen his last.

Simon of Beresford held down his writhing victim effortlessly. "Now is the time," he ground out, "to say your prayers."

The man croaked a pitiful, "Mercy, sire."

Instead of crushing the man's throat, Beresford rose, but not from any generous act of mercy. He said with disgust, "You're an old woman, Langley." He stretched out a hand to help the younger man up. "Never ask for mercy. It's an invitation to death," he instructed. "Even when you're down, you should go after any vulnerable spot you can find."

Langley accepted Beresford's outstretched hand. "I couldn't find any," he complained, brushing the dust off his tunic and shaking himself of the true terror that had gripped him.

"You've learned nothing," Beresford said bluntly. He bent down and retrieved the two broadswords lying on the ground at his feet. He deftly tossed one to Langley. Upon catching it, Langley staggered under the weight of the sword and the strength of Beresford's toss. For a moment, he seemed likely to stumble backward.

Beresford brandished his own broadsword idly, flexing the muscles of his forearm and keeping his wrist supple, while Langley strove to regain his footing.

"I'm tired," the squire said in defense of his clumsiness, "and so would you be if you'd just been ground into the dust."

"You're whining," Beresford countered. "You shouldn't have gone down so easily. You lost the contest in the first minute of engagement with bad sword work. Hold it up, and we'll review your mistakes. Hold the sword up, I said, Langley. *Up!* That's better. And you should know that I'd relish rubbing your nose in the dirt again, so don't give me the opportunity! Now, look here. When I move like this," he continued, not even winded from the recent encounter, "you need to defend yourself like this. No! Not like that, young fool. Like *this!*"

Langley was panting. Large drops of sweat were rolling down his face. "We've...been at this...all afternoon. It's...hot."

"And death is final," Beresford answered. "We'll do this series again, so that I have a measure of security knowing there's a man behind me and not some old woman when next we face Henry's troops."

He forced Langley to move through the series of strokes and counterstrokes, coming at his pupil from the right, from

he left, in a relentless attack. When Beresford was finally
atisfied, he dropped his arm and called an end to it. He
hen subjected Langley to a verbal attack as brutal as his
physical one had been. He turned his back on the young
nan and began to walk off.

Hardly had Beresford turned away before he turned back
gain. Quicker than the blink of an eye, he knocked out of
Langley's hand the sword that the younger man had raised
gainst his master.

Instead of being angry, Beresford was pleased. "Very
ood!" he said with approval. "But next time you come at
omeone from behind, make sure the tip of your sword is at
east at neck level." He flicked a glance over his weaponless
harge, then kicked Langley's sword across the courtyard
nd out of the young man's reach. "Tomorrow we begin an
our earlier," was his curt command as he strode off the
eld of combat, the central courtyard of his town resi-
ence.

Beresford clamped his broadsword under his arm. He was
ripping off his leather gauntlets when he saw Geoffrey of
enlis leaning against a post of the gallery that encircled the
ourtyard. Beresford's harsh features lightened until they
esembled something of a smile.

"What brings you to me this afternoon?" Beresford in-
uired, as he stepped into the shade next to his friend.

"God save you and give you good morrow, Simon,"
enlis returned with characteristic politeness. "I come to
ou with a message."

Beresford handed his broadsword and gauntlets to one of
e attending pages and accepted from the lad a towel and
leather flagon of water stoppered with a bit of hemp.
eresford held up the flagon, silently offering some to his
uest. When Senlis shook his head, Beresford opened the
agon, drank deeply, then rubbed his face with the towel.
eturning the items to the page, he asked with complete lack
concern, "And the message?"

"It's from the king."

Beresford bowed slightly in willing acceptance of the duty that would be asked of him. "Very well. What service is i` that his majesty requires of me?"

"No service, precisely," Senlis replied. "The king—an(Adela, I might add—merely request your presence at th(Tower and charged me to fetch you."

Beresford was surprised. "The king's mistress requeste(my presence?"

"Yes," Senlis said pleasantly. "They wish to discuss som(item of business with you."

Beresford looked down at his blue tunic, which had gon(as gray as his eyes with courtyard dust. "Allow me to chang(my clothing," he said, "and I shall accompany you to th(Tower forthwith."

"There's no time to change your clothes," Senlis tol(him.

"But if I'm to have an audience with Adela, I should—"

"We're to go now."

"But—"

"Now, Simon," Senlis purred, smiling his very charm ing smile, "since when are you concerned about the state o your clothing?"

Beresford had no reason to deny the general implicatio of that question, but he did know that smile. "Since Adel requested my presence," he answered warily, "and I do n(wish to appear before her in all this dirt."

"My sense is that, on this occasion, she will value speed, Senlis countered, "over cleanliness."

Beresford regarded his fair friend, handsome and ele gant as ever. He did not feel a shred of envy in the presenc of the well-dressed Geoffrey of Senlis, but he did begin have a distinct, uneasy sense of trouble in the offing. "A Henry's troops on their way to London?" he asked. thought my men and I had held them off for now."

Senlis laughed and shook his head. "Ever the militar man, Simon!" he commented lightly. "No, they are still the west, but no longer harassing Malmesbury, thanks to you."

Reassured, Beresford asked reasonably, "Then what business would the king wish to discuss with me?"

"I don't know," Senlis said, "and I wish you would hurry so that I may discover along with the others what the excitement is all about!"

It was Beresford's turn to laugh at his friend's frank curiosity. "What excitement?" he asked.

"Your name has been whispered throughout the Tower the day long," Senlis informed him, exaggerating only slightly.

"It has?" Beresford echoed with surprise. He was never, so far as he knew, the object of talk—but he admittedly knew little of court gossip. His brow lowered. "Now tell me, who are 'the others' who wish to stick their very long noses into my affairs?"

"Your audience is to be in the council room," Senlis said, "so the usual barons will be there."

The council room lacked the highly public formality of the great hall and made the business sound friendly. Beresford's brow lightened. "To the Tower, then," he said, abandoning the idea of changing his clothing, which he did not really want to do anyway.

Matching word to deed, Beresford gestured for his horse while asking the attending page to supply him with his hand sword, which he thrust into the sheath hanging from his belt. He called out some instructions to the knights-in-training who were momentarily idle and put the Master of the Armory in charge of the proceedings during his absence. When he had the reins of his piebald steed in hand, he and Senlis left the courtyard by way of the passage above which spanned the main room of the half-timbered upper story of Beresford's rambling house. The porter allowed their access to the sunny street, then shut and barred the door behind them.

Senlis's horse was being held in the street by an urchin. Senlis took the reins and flipped the ragged lad a copper coin. As they swung into their saddles, Beresford said confidently, "The king—and Adela—must wish to discuss the Saint Barnabas Day tourney."

They turned their horses toward Aldgate and the street that would take them to the Tower.

Senlis asked, "But why would they summon you now when the tourney has been long set and is still more than a fortnight away?"

"Perhaps an unavoidable change in the program has arisen that needs to be executed," Beresford ventured.

Senlis shrugged. "Speaking of the tourney, you seemed to be working young Langley hard just now."

Beresford permitted the change of subject. "Not hard enough," he said grimly, "if he intends to acquit himself respectably during the melee."

"But he's reputed to be the best of the younger knights."

"Ha!" was Beresford's response.

They passed by the sign of The Swan, decorated with a bunch of ivy announcing entry to a tavern. Beresford, who knew the local rabble well enough, tossed a brief greeting in English to Daw the Diker and Wat the Tinker, who were hanging about the threshold of the open door, sunning themselves, and properly interested in the passing of two fine knights on horseback. Several more rascals were lounging at the open counter with wooden mugs in hand. Beresford nodded to them as well and moved on without glancing into the shadowy recesses of the establishment, where the poor lighting facilitated the trickery of the professional dicers and improved the looks of the laundresses and tradeswomen who had come to the tavern to pursue a profitable sideline.

Senlis stayed with the subject at hand. "You set your standards too high for any young knight to meet, Simon," he chided, glancing at his friend. "How do you expect them to measure up when you apparently have eyes in the back of your head and can block their blows even when they come from behind?"

Beresford's features lost some of their grimness. He almost smiled. "That was nothing," he said. "I would have been vastly disappointed if Langley had had no fight in him. You see, I goaded him into it."

"But your back was turned, my dear friend!" Senlis exclaimed.

"That was to give him opportunity."

"Well, I did not know that at the time," Senlis said, "and I own to a moment of unease to have seen his sword raised against you with your back turned. However, you recovered with a speed most remarkable—but I suppose you will tell me that you had it planned that way."

Beresford was not going to tell him anything of the sort. He was unused to commenting upon his actions, for the simple reason that it seemed entirely unnecessary to say anything about what was visible to all. Instead, he made a rapid analysis of all Langley's weaknesses and indicated where the young knight needed to improve if he wished to make a name for himself on the field of combat at the Saint Barnabas Day tourney.

They left the commercial avenues and steered their horses toward the protecting wall surrounding the town, which had begun with the Romans. The wall was eight feet thick and twenty-two feet high and had been faced and refaced over the centuries. It had kept out the Danes in six successive sieges, just as it had kept out Earl Godwin more than a century before. However, it had been unable to keep out the great-grandfathers of Simon of Beresford and Geoffrey of Senlis who had sailed with William the Conqueror and put the island kingdom under Norman rule.

As they neared the north bank of the River Thames and the eastern extremity of the perimeter wall, the main bastion of the City of London loomed before them: citadel, castle, palace and prison. Such was the Tower of London.

Above the walls of the fortress rose the central keep, known as the White Tower, its limestone facade blazing candid in the afternoon sun, a potent reminder of the quarry across the Channel from which the stones had come. Beresford and Senlis were greeted expectantly by the gatekeeper and penetrated the fortress's defenses through a wicket in the principal entrance to the castle. Once in the inner ward, they dismounted and were attended by groomsmen in purple-and-gold livery. The two knights made their way to the central keep on foot.

Their passage was accompanied by the comments of various men-at-arms and peers of the realm who, upon sight of the subject of the latest castle rumor, encouraged helpfully, "The king desires to see you, Simon!" "To the council room, without delay!" and "An honor awaits you, Beresford, if the rumors are true!"

Beresford scowled and muttered, "Damn the wagging tongues!"

Senlis laughed. "I hope it's an honor that awaits you, dear friend. In all events, I have the true sense that it will be a surprise!"

Simon of Beresford made no response. He was a man whose instincts were entirely suited to the battlefield, where force and physical skill reigned supreme; he had no talent for the sly caprices of the court. He knew of maces and lances and the bright, shining shield of chivalry; he had no patience for the duplicities of political maneuvering. Though he was generally deaf to the subtleties of court life, his reception at the castle thus far was anything but subtle, and he began to feel uneasy. As he trod the broad, cool flagstones of the wide castle hallways with Senlis at his side, he discarded the comfortable notion that the royal summons had anything to do with an event as straightforward as the tournament; and he did not like surprises, even pleasant ones.

When they turned to enter the council room, he was considering the faint possibility that an honor indeed awaited him. That possibility was slain, however, upon crossing the threshold and perceiving the looks of lively curiosity on the faces of the dozen or so assembled barons when they turned to him. Though not a perceptive man, he knew for a certainty that mischief was afoot.

He was at all times a fearless man. Without hesitation, he stepped forward and faced down each baron in turn. He little realized how his stark presence filled the small yet stately room or how appropriate he looked, hands on his hips, his sword at his side, standing strong and proud beneath the purple-and-gold silken banners of King Stephen's reign, which hung from the beamed ceiling.

He had stepped into the oblong of light that streamed in from one of the long, arched, mullioned windows that broke the masonry walls at harmonious intervals. The summer sunlight, gilding the deep oak planking of the floor and glancing off the aged ash table that occupied center place in the room, fell on Beresford as well. It created a bright aureole around the man who had come to court straight from the field, with his sun-lightened, shoulder-length curls uncombed, his tunic and chausses alive with the honest dirt of physical labor which mingled with the glittering motes of dust dancing around his head and above his shoulders.

His hard gray eyes came to rest on the king and his mistress at the head, opposite him, seated on chairs that were slightly raised on a dais.

Adela said to him, "I am pleased that you were able to come so readily, my lord." She murmured as well a thanks to Geoffrey of Senlis, who had slipped into his seat at the table while all eyes were on Beresford.

Beresford knelt, then rose. "I am always ready to serve you, madam," he said, his deep voice resonant and respectful, "and the king, my liege."

"That, too, pleases me," she said and invited him to take his chair, the vacant one at the foot of the table.

He did so, with a heightened sense of unease at Adela's graciousness, insensibly increased by the sight of the table ceremoniously set with two impressive silver ewers and weighty silver chalices, heavily embossed and chased, one for each person at the table.

Stephen of Blois, King of England, was slumped a little in his chair, a handsome man turned heavy whose one act of decisive courage had won him the throne twenty years before. The king had one or two innocuous words to say to his most loyal knight, then returned the initiative to his capable mistress, Adela of Chartres, seated on his left, who was plainly in charge of the proceedings.

Adela was dark haired and even a little dowdy, despite the grandeur of her raiment, but as canny a politician as Queen Mathilda, who had died the year before. Upon Mathilda's death, it had been widely feared that Stephen would lapse into an inactivity that would surely lead to the Angevin duke Henry's usurping of the throne. However, when Adela stepped in to strengthen Stephen's resolve, her position as surrogate queen in Stephen's court was met with acceptance and even approval.

Adela began to speak to the man she had summoned, yet was able to include all the barons in her gentle conversation. It seemed a disjointed discourse at first, though mellifluous in its delivery, wandering at random over a review of the loyal services that Simon of Beresford had performed for his king.

Beresford let her words wash over him for the first minute or two, nodding, listening, even drifting away for a moment as he tried to imagine the nature of Adela's intentions.

Then he heard her say unmistakably, "And that is why, my lord, I have grown concerned about the loneliness of your present state."

His attention snapped back. "My loneliness?" he repeated, astonished. "I am hardly lonely, madam, I assure you! I live in a very full household, as you must know."

"Ah, but you have been a widower some five years already," she said softly.

"That is true," Beresford answered. "But I fail to see the trend of your argument."

Adela smiled a woman's smile. "You have grieved your dear, departed Roesia long enough—"

"Never a day of it!" Beresford interpolated bluntly, hastening to correct her misimpression.

A titter of laughter went around the table, but Adela admirably kept her composure. She continued smoothly, "—And so bravely. You have been raising your sons without a mother, trying vainly to keep a household in order—"

"My household is in excellent order," he objected, rudely interrupting her again in his continuing astonishment.

"—Managing your many estates alone under great duress. For these reasons, my lord, and principally that of your personal happiness, I am delighted to inform you that we— King Stephen and I—have found you the perfect wife."

Beresford was momentarily stunned, as if he had taken a physical blow. Then, without another thought, he thrust back his chair, causing it to stutter against the floor. Rising, he ejaculated a fiery, *"What?"* He nearly choked in his surprise and anger. He did not bother to address Adela but turned directly to Stephen. "A wife? For *what,* pray? My personal happiness? Tell me that you are joking, sire, and I will forget this outrage!"

A moment of silence fell, as the very room held its breath at the unprecedented insult of a knight to his king. Had these words been uttered by any man other than Simon of Beresford, calls of treason would have been hurled down on his head. Under the circumstances, however, not a baron was disappointed, and they eagerly awaited more.

Adela raised a calm hand and smiled at this trusted knight's outburst, thereby excusing him. "Her name is Gwyneth of Northumbria," she continued, "and she has been recently widowed. Since you are a widower and have experience with both the bliss of the married state and the great loss of it, you are the perfect man to comfort her in her grief.''

Beresford's mouth dropped open. It was hardly necessary to remind anyone present that he had been unhappily married for eight years to an infamous shrew. He had not wished for Roesia's death, but neither had he, in truth, missed her a day since she had died. In fact, he had known a great contentment during these past five years of his unmarried state, a contentment he had not fully realized until this moment. So hapless and befuddled was his expression that several of the barons could not contain their merriment.

Adela took advantage of Beresford's momentary speechlessness by inviting him, in soothing tones, to be seated.

Beresford sat back down but did not bother to rein in his anger. ''I am very far from being the perfect man to comfort any woman in her grief!''

''And she is, furthermore, very beautiful,'' Adela added.

''Then give her to Lancaster,'' Simon fired back, gesturing to the baron on his left, a noted ladies' man.

Adela averted what could have been hearty laughter with her quick response, ''Lancaster is having difficulties just now on his estates, which are in the quarrelsome west. Your Gwyneth comes with a vast tract of land in the north that will need to be managed by a steady and undistracted hand such as yours.''

Beresford's brows snapped together fiercely. ''Then she must be Canute's widow,'' he said. Canute had been a northern supporter of Henry, whose followers Stephen's forces had, almost by accident, recently defeated. Beresford saw the trend, and his analysis was blunt. ''You want my well-trained vassals to do the work of subduing the remaining rebels.'' After a brief pause, he continued, ''My loyalty to you, madam, and to the king are well known, and I am happy to put all my men at your disposal—on the instant!—for the task in Northumbria. It is not necessary to bind me in marriage to assure yourself of my willing help.''

Only by a slight compression of her lips did Adela betray that she misliked having to state her case so openly. "It is not your loyalty that concerns me, my lord. Rather it is necessary to bind Gwyneth in proper alliance, so that Canute's men can be made to shift their loyalty—" she glanced to her right "—to King Stephen."

"Have her wed Fortescue then," Beresford said, flicking his hand toward another baron at the table. "He's a widower with more vassals at his disposal than I have."

Adela's mouth turned down. She said delicately, "The lovely Gwyneth needs a man more in the vigor of his youth, in order to provide her with children, since she is childless." She nodded to Fortescue. "With all due respect to Sir Walter, who has served the king long and well, I wish to honor his long-stated desire to devote more time to his grandchildren."

"What about Northampton?" Beresford said. He tried to call to mind every widowed man of his acquaintance with sizable estates and ample ranks of vassals.

Adela's frown deepened. "It is fortunate," she said, her pleasant tones overlaid with a hint of displeasure, "that Bernard of Northampton is not here this afternoon, my good lord, for it would pain him to hear me remind you that he has been twice married and still has no children to his name."

"And Valmey?" Beresford shifted his eyes around the table and pointed to the man next to the queen. "Everyone knows that he has sired a passel of bastards, and he's not married."

The muffled laughter at this bald comment was not entirely masked by Adela's sedate response. "He is promised elsewhere."

Beresford wished that he had paid more attention to court gossip, for he could have sworn that Cedric of Valmey was currently in an adulterous relationship with one of Adela's favorite ladies. However, since he was beginning to perceive that he was in a losing battle, he did not think it wise to challenge Adela on this tricky point. Even he knew some limits.

Beresford was desperate now to find an acceptable substitute husband for Gwyneth of Northumbria. "Warenne, then," he suggested, flinging an arm at the man next to him, who ducked in self-defense.

The laughter was open this time. "Warenne's wife, Felicia, might object," Adela said, having to bite her lip to contain her own laughter.

Because Felicia Warenne was such a mousy woman, Beresford had forgotten that she existed. His initial thought was "She wouldn't object!" but the general hilarity at the table had put him at a disadvantage. "I beg your pardon, Roger," he said gruffly.

Seizing the moment, Adela said swiftly, "Let us toast your impending happiness then, Simon of Beresford."

The wine was poured and the chalices raised.

Beresford felt a sudden physical restriction, like a cramp in his sword arm. Recognizing defeat, he lifted his chalice and brought it to his grimacing lips. He did not so much drink the wine as filter it through his teeth. It was very bitter.

Chapter Two

At a signal from the king, the barons rose from the table, but they did not immediately leave the council room. Instead, they lingered, speaking of this and that, as was the custom after the conclusion of official business. One or two of the braver barons paused to say a few words to Beresford. The aging Walter Fortescue, along with Cedric of Valmey, who was or was not promised elsewhere, went so far as to wish him well. Lancaster, the ladies' man, had his mind on the Saint Barnabas Day tourney and engaged Beresford on that topic.

Beresford had risen with the others and was accepting their congratulations with very bad grace. He felt a strong sense of injustice and was hungry for prey.

He found it. "Senlis!" he summoned angrily, his tone bringing his good friend's head around with a snap. He strode forward and grasped two handfuls of Senlis's tunic, chest high. Nose-to-nose, he accused, "You *knew*, you cur, and you delivered me into the hands of the king as unsuspecting as a babe!"

Senlis tried to shrug free of Beresford's grip, but to no avail. "I did not know, Simon!" he protested, torn between laughter and alarm. "Truly I didn't!"

Beresford wanted to wipe the poorly suppressed grin off his friend's handsome face. He was within an inch of yielding to the urge when a group of barons overheard the exchange and came to Senlis's aid.

"No one knew," Roger Warenne said, seconding Senlis's assertion.

When Beresford did not immediately release his friend, Lancaster offered, "I thought your summons had to do with some change in the tourney. Why, I was saying as much to Valmey here earlier this afternoon."

Cedric of Valmey soothed slyly. "Yes, in fact, Lancaster assured me that Adela was calling for a change in plans on the field of contest, but instead you have the honor of marrying in service of your king. Why, had I been available to be chosen for the honor, I hope that I would have known my duty and willingly submitted, just as you have."

This distracted Beresford's murderous attention from Senlis, but he still did not release his friend. Eyeing Valmey coldly, Beresford asked, "*Could* Adela have chosen you, then? God's teeth, Valmey, you led the successful campaign in Northumbria! Were you asked first, but declined, pleading a prior promise that might well not exist?"

Valmey quickly held up his hands in a gesture of innocence. "I was not asked, Simon! My guess is that you were the king's first and only choice!" Tacitly declining Beresford's challenge of his "prior promise," he continued smoothly, "And a remarkably good choice it proved to be, as became clear when you encouraged Adela to compare your qualifications, so favorably, to all other possible men of rank."

Beresford was a straight-speaking man, and he hated that Valmey could so deftly bend a man's words to his own purposes, like a skilled smith with hot steel. Beresford would have clutched Valmey's throat in response had not his fingers been already tightly enmeshed in Senlis's tunic. "God's wounds, Valmey! Don't try me too far—!" he began, but was interrupted.

Walter Fortescue stepped into the fray by saying blithely, "Now, there you're wrong, Cedric!" He seemed oblivious to the tension in the atmosphere, and thereby inadvertently reduced it. "Beresford didn't encourage Adela to sing his praises. Not the boastful type, our Simon! Sounded more like he wanted nothing to do with another marriage! Not that I blame him, if I recall his late wife correctly! Well! That's the way *I* interpreted his exchange with Adela, in all events."

Valmey murmured, "I stand corrected," but did not have the look of a man who had erred without purpose.

Fortescue nodded at Valmey and smiled, rather pleased by his own analysis. "Oh, I was surprised when Adela announced that Beresford should wed Gwyneth of Northumbria, instead of allying the poor woman to a man with more liking for the ladies. Not, of course," he said affably, turning to Beresford, "that you're of Bernard of Northampton's ilk and prefer men to women, God wot! We all know about your Ermina. She's a toothsome wench, but you'll have to admit you don't have a soft touch with the ladies, even though you've produced your share of sons. And that's why you were chosen, Beresford—to give sons to Gwyneth. You're the very man to get the job done!"

The amused silence that followed this amazingly insensitive, amazingly accurate speech permitted Fortescue to add, "Now, Simon, do you let go of your friend's clothing, for we all know there's no need to kill the messenger who brings the news."

Beresford's hands had, in truth, grown slack on Senlis's tunic. Now he loosened his grip completely and whirled. "Who should I kill, then?" he demanded through his teeth, ready to fall on Fortescue.

"No need to kill anyone, Simon," Fortescue said simply, "for the news you received is not bad, but good. With this marriage, you'll be doubling your lands."

Beresford was disciplined enough not to brutalize a man twice his age. He balled his hands into fists and thrust them down at his sides. "I've land—and heirs!—to spare!"

"You'll soon have more of both," Fortescue replied complacently. "And I wouldn't complain, if your Gwyneth is as beautiful as Adela says."

Adela chose her moment well. Just then, she stepped up to the group of her most powerful barons, who fell aside at her approach. She did not immediately pursue the subject of Gwyneth's beauty or her land. Instead, she asked Beresford, "Have you had time, my lord, to adjust to your turn of good fortune?" When he hesitated, she glanced over her shoulder at Stephen, who was still seated at the table, now with a court scribe at his side. The king was bent over a curling sheaf of parchment, apparently in the act of applying the royal seal to the document. "Stephen has chosen to grant you an earldom into the bargain. What do you say to that?"

The news that Beresford's coffers would now increase with the earl's "third penny" affected the various barons differently and caused the eyes of several to widen. Valmey's narrowed.

Beresford's did not change, for he could not have cared less about an earldom. However, when Adela smiled and held her hand straight out in front of her in a commanding gesture, he saw how he must answer. He tethered the frayed edges of his temper, knelt and bowed his head over her hand. "I say, madam," he said obediently, "that my good fortune has just doubled."

When he rose, Adela said, "You will now go to meet Gwyneth of Northumbria. She is at present in the great hall, awaiting your convenience, in company of Lady Chester. I would introduce you to her myself, but for the fact," she said, glancing at the king, "that I am needed elsewhere at the moment." She returned her gaze to Beresford. "If you are acquainted with Lady Chester, you might effect your own introduction."

Beresford grumpily denied acquaintanceship with her.

Senlis, who had twitched his tunic back into place, said he knew Lady Chester, and volunteered to make Beresford known to his future wife. Adela smiled and moved away from the group. The barons bowed at her exit and dispersed.

When Senlis turned to Beresford, he had difficulty containing his mirth at the sight of his friend's gloomy, glowering expression. With a foolhardiness that occasionally gripped him, he suggested pleasantly, "Perhaps you'll wish to change your tunic before presenting yourself to Gwyneth—as you wanted to do earlier for Adela."

Beresford returned a black regard that might have slain a lesser man. "Not a chance of it," he grated.

Gwyneth of Northumbria was standing in a slanting ray of sunlight that fell from the high, unshuttered windows of the great hall, hoping the warmth would penetrate her cold skin. She had a few minutes to herself, for Rosalyn, Lady Chester, had just left the room. She breathed an inward sigh of relief for the moment of relative freedom. She was exhausted. She closed her eyes to master the fluttery fear that danced erratically in her stomach, but it eluded her control and rose to flit around her heart and flap painfully at her throat. She felt winded and out of breath.

It was a familiar sensation, being out of breath, but this time it was worse: she felt out of courage.

Where was it now, she wondered, the steady courage that had not wavered during the past fortnight of bloody defeat and terrifying capture. The unfailing courage that had carried her, head high, through five humiliating years of marriage to Canute. The ready courage that she had always taken for granted. The bone-deep courage which she had never before had to name or summon. The plain and simple courage of which she had never before realized that she had been so proud. Where was it, this wonderful courage, and why should it go into hiding now?

She could almost feel the weight and thickness of the stones that separated her from freedom. In her mind's eye, she penetrated the walls of the White Tower and traveled through the inner curtain wall to the outer curtain wall. There her energies faltered, for she knew yet a third wall stood before the deep moat which surrounded the whole. Her courage sank lower.

To raise her spirits, she reminded herself that she had found herself in this situation before and had survived it. It should make little difference that three stout walls of the Tower of London surrounded her now rather than those of Castle Norham. It should make little difference that she was trapped in the main Norman stronghold rather than in the shrieval castle of the Northumbrian Danelaw. It should make little difference that she was promised to a Norman baron she did not know, for he could not possibly be worse than the Danish beast she had wed.

She had been younger then, too, and more tender when she had been taken from her Saxon home and bargained in marriage to Canute to prevent the devastation of her father's estate. She remembered the valor with which she had faced her fate then, and which was so very different from how she was feeling now. Why had she been, as a girl of eighteen, braver than she was as a woman of almost four and twenty?

It made no sense. She had had years of experience in mastering the fear produced by the threats and abuse she had borne from Canute. She knew the signs. Her stomach would flip-flop. Her throat would constrict. She would have difficulty breathing. Yet she had never allowed herself to be overcome by her physical anxiety or to expose her vulnerability. Her courage would always rise up to save her. She would always protect whom she needed to protect, even if it meant further endangering herself. She would always find ways to maneuver around her husband's wretched decisions and would always outwit him in the end.

The knowledge of her successes should be giving her confidence, not draining her of her courage. Unaccountably, the constriction in her throat became tighter.

She drew a painful gasp of air and shifted her glance back to the great hall. Her eyes rose to roam the magnificent rafters, from which hung bright banners that so thoroughly satisfied the Norman taste for symbolic display. Feeling oppressed, she lowered her eyes to survey the impressive length of the hall and the array of noblemen and ladies who were assembling, here and there, for the evening meal and diversions. She attempted to guess whether any man among them was the one who had been chosen to provide her "comfort in grief," as Adela had phrased it.

She picked out a short one, a fat one, an old one, an absurdly young one. They were all possibilities, so far as she knew, for she had been given no information about her husband-to-be, not even his name. She saw a cocky one parading, a tall one gossiping and a clever one, resplendently dressed, watching her through narrowed eyes. She quickly shifted her gaze. It fell on a pair of knights who had just entered the hall and who were standing off to the side, behind the clever one.

She noticed first the handsome one of the pair. He was well formed, pleasing to the eye and had a charming, easygoing smile that he was just then bending on his companion. Interesting. What luck if *he* were the chosen bridegroom. She knew just how to handle such a type.

Then she looked at his companion and her heart convulsed spasmodically. *By Odin!* she swore to herself, invoking a god of her father's father. Indeed, the man was like one of Odin's warriors descended directly from Asgard, with sledgehammers for arms, chips of steel for eyes, molten bronze for hair. His body must have been chopped from the side of a granite mountain, and his features had been fashioned with no other goal than to inspire fear on the battlefield. It was a face only the goddess Freya could love.

Gwyneth glanced away and quickly reassured herself that of the several dozen men in the hall at the moment, it was unlikely that Odin's earthly warrior was the chosen one. Fortunately, her thoughts were given a new direction when

Lady Chester returned to the hall and to her side. Gwyneth saw that her gentle jailer was wearing an expression that gave her winter beauty a crafty cast.

"Well, now," Rosalyn said, "I have just heard that the meeting in the council room has ended and that your chosen husband is Simon of Beresford."

"What should I know about him?"

Rosalyn's slim brows arched. "That he is a most unexpected choice! And that he is a man not known for softness. But more to the point, you should know that he is a widower with three sons." She calculated. "Five years ago already it must have been that poor Roesia came to her untimely end."

"How," Gwyneth forced herself to ask, "did she die?" Her voice wavered, a little pitifully.

Rosalyn laughed. "Did Beresford beat her to death, do you mean? Oh, no! Roesia killed herself, more or less, in a foolish riding accident. But given everything, I am sure that he would have been capable of killing her on any number of interesting occasions!"

At this bad news, the tightness in Gwyneth's throat increased still more. "Do you see him here, then?" she managed to rasp. "That is, you do know what he looks like, do you not?"

Rosalyn's pretty red lips curved upward. "Every woman—and man—at court knows Beresford," she said, somewhat slyly, Gwyneth thought. Rosalyn's black eyes flashed around the room. Then she laughed musically. "Ah, yes! Look straight across. There he is with Geoffrey of Senlis."

Gwyneth glanced in the direction Lady Rosalyn indicated with a tiny toss of her head. Feeling a strong jolt to the nerves, she saw the two knights move forward, the handsome one accompanied by Odin's warrior. She dropped her eyes. Her heartbeat thumped. Her stomach lurched.

"They've seen us now, my dear," Rosalyn purred, "and they're coming our way."

Which of the two men was Senlis, Gwyneth wondered wildly, and which one Beresford? She did not have long to consider the question, for presently the two men stepped into the circle of her downcast vision, and she saw them from the chest downward. The one on the left was standing at his ease, his tunic a fashionable mulberry kerseymere, his chausses and crossgarters neat, his shoes fine and clean. The other stood stock-still before her, as rooted and strong as the Norse world tree, Yggdrasil. The cerulean of his tunic was beaten with dust and dirt and age to a disreputable bruise blue. His chausses and shoes were in such a battered condition that they did not further disgrace his tunic by negative comparison.

The man on the left spoke, and Gwyneth heard his words with a wave of horrified fatalism. "Simon of Beresford," he said, "I have the honor of presenting you to Gwyneth of Northumbria."

Gwyneth felt her throat close completely. She fought for breath.

Upon leaving the council room, Senlis had bent his courtly graces to filing the rougher edges off his friend's demeanor before they arrived at the great hall. The going was not easy, and Senlis was already imagining diplomatic measures to take should the unlucky wife-to-be run screaming from the room at her first encounter with Simon of Beresford in ferociously bad humor.

Beresford only half listened to his friend's cajoling. It was not so much the marriage itself that vexed him but the reason why he had been chosen as the bridegroom. Anger filled his chest to such a degree that at one point he exploded into Senlis's skillful discourse with a bitter, *"Sons!"* His voice was harsh as he strode angrily beside Senlis. "I'm to produce *sons!"*

Senlis's brows quirked expressively. "Is it such a difficult assignment, then, Simon?" he inquired with mock innocence, matching his friend stride for stride. When Beresford's scowl deepened, he added, "A man always needs sons."

Beresford cast a fierce eye at Senlis. He growled, "I'm satisfied with the sons I already have and with the set of my life such as it is!"

"You'll not have to give up Ermina, if that's what you mean."

Beresford had difficulty at the moment recalling the pretty, buxom serving wench, who was, in any case, irrelevant to the conversation. "I mean," he said savagely, "that it's one thing for a king to command a man to raise his sword in honor on the battlefield, and another for him to summon a man to—" Here he described in extremely rude terms exactly what he would raise to produce the commanded sons. He continued inventively in this vein at some length.

With a half laugh at the vivid descriptions, Senlis at last interrupted with the observation that, "We're almost at the hall, Simon. I have no power to cool your temper, but I'll ask you kindly to control your tongue. Adela will not thank me if you cause a riot with your uncourtly language."

Beresford uttered an inarticulate sound of disgust deep in his throat.

"That's better!" Senlis encouraged. "And here we are. Now, smile, Simon! No? Then glower less gloomily, if you please, so that your wife-to-be won't search in vain for something to like."

The moment they stepped into the great hall, Beresford felt insensibly better, in part because he had had a chance to vent his anger so thoroughly, but also because the polished planking beneath his feet and the high beams soaring above his head never failed to impress him with regal majesty and to remind him of his knightly duty. Although his present duty was unusual and he was obeying only grudgingly, he came a fraction closer to accepting it.

"And Lady Chester?" he inquired sardonically, glancing about the room. "Which one is she?"

"I don't see her," Senlis said slowly. He craned his neck, looking this way and that. "Could she have gone—ah, no, there she is, walking toward the ... Well!"

"Well, what?" Beresford asked sullenly.

"Look, my dear friend," Senlis said with a strange note in his voice, "toward the fireplace across the room."

Beresford looked over toward one end of the fireplace. His lip curled. "And is Lady Chester the fat one," he asked with grim satisfaction, "or the wizened one?"

Senlis followed the line of his friend's gaze. He shook his head and smiled. "Neither, Simon," he said. "Look to the other side. You see the woman standing? The dark beauty?"

Beresford considered the dark beauty. "I see her," he said indifferently.

"That," Senlis said, "is Lady Chester. My guess is that the woman standing next to her is Gwyneth of Northumbria."

Beresford shifted his gaze from the dark beauty to the young woman standing beside her. Her face was in profile, for she was speaking to Rosalyn. His eyes widened, and he felt a powerful emotion pass through his body like a lightning bolt. He had never experienced such an emotion and so could not identify it. It was odd and unexpected, certainly. It was strong, too. Its unfamiliarity was strangely tantalizing, but it had a distinctly unpleasant twist to it, like a wrenching of internal organs.

He was looking at the most exquisite woman he had ever seen. Her profile was delicate, with a certain calm strength, her nose straight and finely boned, her lips full. Her skin was a glowing alabaster that, in defiance of nature, was not mineral but floral in quality. Her hair looked like thick, liquid gold spun into filigree braids around her head and caught and curved at the nape by one of those spidery nets webbed with pearls whose correct name he would never know. Her back was straight, her womanly curves were evident and her hands were crossed in front of her. Her long, white fingers were lightly laced.

"Close your mouth, my man," Senlis whispered into his ear.

Beresford mechanically clamped shut the mouth he had not known was open. At that moment, the woman turned her gaze to him. Before she lowered her eyes modestly, he caught a luminous flash of violet.

"Rosalyn is beckoning us forward, Simon," Senlis said. "Come and meet your bride."

Beresford betrayed no reluctance in crossing the hall at Senlis's side. It felt strange, though, this simple walk across the room. He would have felt more comfortable galloping across the tourney field, his lance raised and the raw animal power of his charger working beneath him. He would have known just what to do: strike his enemy down and prepare for the next encounter. In the current case, no similarly clear objective presented itself to him, but from force of habit his stride conveyed confidence and strength of purpose.

When they were standing before the two women, Senlis said, "Simon of Beresford, I have the honor of presenting you to Gwyneth of Northumbria."

Rosalyn returned the courtesy by performing the sleekest of introductions, "Gwyneth of Northumbria. Simon of Beresford."

Beresford mumbled something, he did not know what. Gwyneth of Northumbria said nothing. Beresford noticed that she was taller than he had expected, for the top of her head came to his chin. He glanced down at her briefly, long enough to see that her eyes were still downcast. Feeling as though he were walking into a fire as a test of courage, he stretched out his hand, and she laid hers in it. His fingers closed over hers, and he was almost surprised that he was not burned by her touch. Her hand was cool, even a little cold. He bowed over it, then let it go gracelessly. He had no idea what to say, if anything.

Rosalyn filled the gap. "It is a pleasure to see you again, Sir Simon. The last time we were together was at the feast of Ascension."

If it had been, Beresford did not recall it. A stiff silence threatened to wrinkle the air before Senlis smoothed it over with the bland comment, "I understand that Gwyneth comes to us from the north."

When no response was immediately forthcoming from Gwyneth, Beresford dared to look at her straight on, albeit cautiously. It was left to Rosalyn to supply the account of Gwyneth's journey southward. For the next few moments, Rosalyn and Senlis bandied words, as if it were expected that they should carry the conversation.

During this exchange, Beresford thought he had discovered the flaw in the jewel of his wife-to-be. He relaxed and broke into the banter with the blunt statement, "She is mute."

Rosalyn broke off, her pretty lips parted with a kind of scandalized delight. "Ah, but no, Sir Simon, she is not."

"I see. Does she lack Norman?" He looked down at Gwyneth and saw two spots of pink flushing her alabaster cheeks.

"No," Lady Rosalyn answered.

"Is it English that she prefers?"

"I must suppose that she does."

"Have you heard her speak in any language?"

"Why, yes, of course."

"What, then?" he demanded abruptly. "Is she simple?"

Chapter Three

Gwyneth's anger cleared the constriction in her throat, although she almost choked on that healthy anger as she drew her breath to speak.

"If I have said nothing thus far, sire," she said in a low, clear voice, "it is because I have found that men—in particular husbands—are not partial to women's chatter. In the present circumstance, I sought to please with silence over speech."

Senlis clapped a friendly hand on Beresford's shoulder. "There, you see," he remarked jovially, "she speaks! And very nicely, too!"

"Yes, I speak," Gwyneth said, looking first at Senlis, then bravely at Beresford. Her heart quailed slightly at the sight of him, but she strove to keep her gaze steady. "Perhaps it will benefit you were I to tell you about myself, so that you will understand when I miss a phrase in Norman or fail to find the correct word."

"But, of course!" and "Please do!" Rosalyn and Senlis encouraged. Beresford grunted.

"My father's father was a Dane," she explained, struggling against panic, "so I learned Danish very young, although I grew up speaking English. My late husband, Canute of Northumbria, and his men spoke English, as well, although it was mixed with Danish. The Normans have not conquered northern tongues as thoroughly as they have northern land, so I have learned your language mostly through tutors, but with little practical use. I pray you to excuse any errors I make."

She fell silent again, feeling breathless, nearly exhausted. She did not, however, lower her eyes, but kept them raised and alert.

Rosalyn smiled. "That certainly explains the matter, does it not? Norman, Danish and English. Very versatile."

Gwyneth drew a painful breath. "Only necessary," she said.

Senlis glanced at Beresford. It seemed he needed to step in again to keep the conversation afloat. "You will not have much call for Danish at Stephen's court, but you will find English of great use, especially in Simon's household! Now, as for excusing your errors in Norman, my lady," he said with a gallant bow, "I am afraid you have given us none to excuse!" He referred this point to Beresford. "Has she, Simon?"

Beresford said nothing until Senlis's elbow nudged him into biting off a brief "No."

Senlis smiled charmingly. "Our Beresford is given to silences just as you are, my lady," he informed her affably, "and when he breaks silence, he is a plain-speaking man."

"So I have perceived," she replied.

"Which is, of course, what we all like best about him," Rosalyn offered, insinuating her fingers through Beresford's arm.

"Indeed," Gwyneth said, looking at Lady Chester, who did not immediately release her hold on Beresford. She moved her eyes on to Senlis, then to Beresford. "Plain speaking is a virtue, for then one cannot complain that one has misunderstood you."

Senlis found it difficult to know whether this remark was naive or extremely clever. Either way, he felt it was safe to say, "Well, well, Simon, you are most fortunate, I think, for you are sure to find your lady's speeches as delightful as her silences."

This time a true silence fell, for Gwyneth's eyes had locked with Beresford's. She wished she could breathe better. She wished she could look away from the chips of slate that were his eyes, but she could not, and she saw something unwavering in their depths that caused her to blink first. She hated herself for her weakness at such an important moment and felt her color rise again.

Senlis and Rosalyn were heard to murmur politely, "I have just seen a friend with whom I must speak," and "I promised Warenne that I would meet him soon."

Beresford flicked a glance at their retreating figures much as he would regard disloyal troops abandoning the fray. He was silent a moment longer before ordering gruffly, "We shall walk!"

Gwyneth wondered if he would command a dog to heel in just such a voice or if he would use a gentler tone.

It had been her habit and, in fact, her perverse pleasure never to obey immediately one of Canute's dictates. She had always enjoyed that fraction of a moment when she made her husband think that she was considering his order, as if it were in her power to disobey him, as if the choice to follow his command was a generous act on her part. That moment of artful hesitation had always infuriated the bully-beast Canute, and his powerless fury had always satisfied her. But she did not think that a similar hesitation would serve her purposes now.

She put her fingertips lightly on Beresford's outstretched wrist and nodded agreement. They moved forward, and she looked up at him. She did not know that she was half expecting an apology from him for his initial insult to her intelligence until he foiled that expectation by saying abruptly, "Tell me about the battle."

"About the battle, sire?"

"The one that took your husband's life."

Gwyneth blinked. The man was a brute. She cleared her throat. "A siege was laid to Castle Norham during a fortnight or more." Her voice was low and dispassionate. "

believe that Canute and his men made some tactical blunders. They misjudged the number of the enemy—begging your pardon," she said with a deferential nod, "and did not properly defend the part of a curtain wall damaged by a large petrary. Neither did they adequately prepare to counter the Greek fire." Her free hand fluttered once in a futile gesture. "When the castle was stormed, the capture was successful."

"Given your inexperience with the Norman tongue," he observed, "you have a remarkably accurate military vocabulary."

Gwyneth smiled faintly. "I had much time, during the long journey to London, to hear repeated descriptions of the Norman success, which were recounted, of course, in Norman."

"Tell me about that journey."

Her trip to London had been nothing less than terrifying. "Lady Chester has already described the journey to you," she offered evasively.

He shook his head slightly. "Lady Chester was not there. Tell me in your own words."

"I was treated with utmost respect," she said diplomatically, "and a concern for my comfort was at all times evident."

He let this polite lie pass. "Did you grieve on the journey? You must have lost friends during the storming of the castle."

She fought against her fear of him, of the powerful size of his neck and shoulders and arms as he strolled next to her. "Of course, I lost many. I lived at Castle Norham for five years."

"Did you lose any family members?"

"No."

"You lost your husband."

She looked away. At mention of Canute and husbandly associations, she felt her courage drain away. "Yes, of course, I lost him."

"You had no children?"

"No."

"Are you carrying your husband's child?"

Her eyes flew back to his. The man was *worse* than a
brute. She felt as if she had stumbled painfully, against rock
and some other force, less solid, more dangerous. "No."

"Are you certain?"

She said coldly, "Certain as a woman may be."

He nodded, apparently satisfied.

The topic caused anger to flare within her again. She had
longed for children, it was true, and grieved for the ones she
thought she would never have. Yet she was happy to have
never borne a child of Canute's, for he had regarded the act
of conceiving a child either with dismal disinterest or as an
occasion for brutality. But none of this—her lack of children, her current barren state, her feelings about her late
husband or anything else—was the business of this man—
this outrageous man, this Simon of Beresford, this *Norman*—next to her. She had suffered enough indignities in the
past days and weeks and years. Enough was enough!

With the return of her anger came her courage and all her
well-learned skills of turning disadvantage to advantage. She
quickly composed her features, relying on her long experience of masking anger with complaisance.

Hardly missing a beat, she said, "Well, sire, you have
heard what is most important about me and my life. Now
should like to learn what is most important about you and
your life."

He frowned forbiddingly. "What do you want to know?"
he asked in a far-from-encouraging manner.

"Whatever you think is important for me to know about
you." Her voice held the sweet calm she had cultivated over
the years.

She imagined that he would mention his sons or his late
wife, although she did not know why, in retrospect, she
should have made such a conventional assumption. He said
instead, looking directly down at her, his voice deep and

ough, "You should know that I have just come from an
mportant training exercise on the field and arrived at the
astle unsuspecting, I assure you, of what was to be re-
quired of me."

Gwyneth's mouth nearly dropped open. She did not make
he mistake of interpreting this statement as an apology for
he disreputable state of his dress. Rather, she thought it
anked as the rudest of his rude comments thus far. First he
nsulted her intelligence outright, next he asked directly if
he was pregnant. Then he had the gall to make no pretense
f the fact that he did not want the marriage. This was plain
peaking with a vengeance!

Neither did she want the marriage, but she was not so
oolish as to say so. Nor was she so foolish as to wear her
houghts on her face, especially given the public nature of
his first meeting with her husband-to-be. Ever alert to her
urroundings, she was acutely aware that the courtiers in
heir midst were doing everything possible not to betray their
vid interest in what was transpiring between the most con-
picuous couple in the hall.

She formed her lips into a smile, as if greatly interested in
his news. "And what was the particular training exercise
ou were engaged in?"

"Broadsword."

"I see," she said. "Do I infer correctly that you are de-
oted to training in various forms of combat?"

"Yes."

"And spend much time at the practice?"

"Yes."

She read in his face the impatient question, *Is there any-
hing else you want to know?* Although naturally offended,
he had never intended to probe into his personal life, and
ow turned the conversation to more neutral matters.

"Well, then, since I am new here, you could perhaps help
e in identifying some of the people I am to live among. We
hould be as interested in them as they apparently are in us."

Beresford seemed surprised. "They are?"

"And making such worthy attempts to hide their inter-est!"

Beresford glanced around the hall. Heads quickly turned away. His already scowling expression deepened, and he muttered something to the effect that people should mind their own affairs and leave his life to him.

"Oh, I agree," she said lightly, "but the interest in us is, unfortunately, most understandable, don't you think? And it's all the more reason for us to take advantage of looking at them, while they are looking at us. So, then, sire, who might that man be? There, across the hall from us."

"That's Walter Fortescue."

"What should I know about him, pray?"

"That he's too old for the tourney field."

"I can see that, sire," she said. When no further descrip-tion of Fortescue was forthcoming, she shifted her gaze and asked, "The man to Sir Walter's right? Is he known to you?"

"Roger Warenne."

"Roger Warenne," she repeated, committing the name to memory. "And what should I know about him?"

"He's an indifferent swordsman," Beresford replied. After further consideration, he added, "He's married to a woman named Felicia."

"Ah! I shall look forward to meeting her." She bit her lip. Her eye next fell on the man she had earlier decided must be a clever one. He was not looking at them at the moment, but she recalled that just before Beresford's arrival, he had sur-veyed her through narrowed eyes. "Who is that?" she asked. "The handsomely dressed man standing by the far door? I saw him earlier, just before you arrived."

Beresford frowned. "That is Cedric of Valmey."

She had to swallow her gasp of dismay. She knew Val-mey's name from the siege of Castle Norham, but she had never seen the man responsible for destroying her life, for he had left to his men the task of gathering the spoils, of which she was a part.

"What should I know of Cedric of Valmey?" she asked calmly. When her question yielded nothing but silence, she added, with a touch of irony, "And how is he on the tourney field?"

"Well enough."

She interpreted that as high praise. Since she did not think further inquiries about male members of the peerage would produce any comment beyond an assessment of their marshal abilities, she turned her interest to the ladies.

With her eyes roving, she remarked, "I know, of course, Lady Chester. Yes, there she is. She told me that her husband is very ill. Do you know anything about his condition, sire?"

Beresford looked as if he were having difficulty remembering who her husband was. "I believe you must be speaking of Godfrey," he said at last. "I have not seen him in an age."

"Was he not at the feast of Ascension with his wife, the occasion she mentioned to you?"

The vagueness of his response to this did not encourage her to pursue the question. She said, "Well, I am very sorry for her. Ah, she has just joined Sir Cedric, and they are speaking most intensely! There, you see, I am already becoming familiar with the court. Now, next to them, sire, off to the left, can you tell me who is the woman with the dark hair and green bliaut?"

Beresford considered her. "I've never seen her before."

"Well, then, the woman to whom she is speaking— Do you know her?"

"She looks familiar," Beresford admitted.

She tried several more ladies before she received a positive identification. "Oh, that's Johanna," he said. "She's been around forever."

Gwyneth laughed, for Johanna was a young and lovely woman. "She is not old enough, I think, sire, to have been around forever," she said.

She glanced up at him, and caught an interesting angle of his face. She followed the thick column of his neck up the sharp plane of his jaw to his nose, which was surprisingly straight and well defined in profile, and down to his lips, finely cut but held hard and uncompromising. She wondered fleetingly how he might look with a shave and his hair trimmed. Or even a smile? The thought intrigued her.

She decided to take a chance. "I have commended you for your plain speaking, sire, and I am sincere," she said. Her tone and expression artfully blended admiration and teasing. "However, the point of plain speaking is to be always truthful! In the case of Johanna, you have not been truthful, merely rude."

The expression in his eyes slew any possibility that his looks would improve with trim hair and a shave. She doubted even that his lips knew how to curve into a smile. Her heart beat spasmodically in anticipation of what he might do in response to her impudence. She braced herself, but did not flinch.

"I have known her for most of my life," was Beresford's rather mild response to her remark. "Johanna is kin to me, related through my father."

Gwyneth breathed a sigh of relief. "Which does not translate, you will agree, sire," she continued, bravely staying her course, "into her having been around forever. Say better, 'I have enjoyed her acquaintance for some years.'"

"I have enjoyed her acquaintance for some years," Beresford repeated, rather more, she believed, from astonishment at her instruction than from obedience.

"Very good!" she approved, impudent still.

His eyes held hers, assessing this time, as she imagined he might size up an opponent across the field of tournament. "I will remember your advice, ma'am," he said slowly.

She felt breathless again. Since she could not easily read his tone or his expression, she thought it prudent to move along. "And those ladies?" she asked.

She nodded toward the far end of the hall, toward a group of three old women. They were standing off by themselves, and their rather strange figures, darkly clad, were framed half in the light of the hall's high windows, half in shadows, lending them an eerie aspect.

"The three crones?" he queried. Cutting his gray eyes back to her, he added, his heavy brows lifting slightly, "If you will permit me the term."

Gwyneth nodded graciously. "I will certainly permit you the term," she said, "and will license you to say that *they*, at least, have been around forever. They might well demand that you venerate them, for if you do not, they may withdraw their protection and cast an evil spell on you."

Beresford's brows rose higher. "What makes you say that?"

Gwyneth gave her head a tiny shake. "No reason. It just came to me, that's all."

It was just as well that a courtier made so bold as to accost them then, introducing himself to Gwyneth and congratulating Beresford. Others, having stayed away for as long as they could possibly contain themselves, came too, eager to see close up the titillating mismatch of the beautiful captive and the ugly bear. Soon Gwyneth and Beresford were swamped with well-wishers. Thus was she relieved of the effort of maintaining difficult conversation with him, although she was now confronted with the equally difficult task of sorting through all the new names and faces.

Gwyneth did not again notice Beresford until the moment he abruptly quit her side, with the minimum of a bow and no words of valediction. As she briefly watched his exit, she felt an angry satisfaction that, even in retreat, he had given her no cause to soften her opinion of the rude, rough oaf, senseless chunk of a man she was to wed.

Senlis was lying in wait for Beresford when the latter strode out of the hall, and he fell easily into step beside him. As they proceeded down a long passage, he informed his friend, "Adela has requested that I take you to the vestiary to find you a suitable tunic to wear at this evening's supper. She thinks there is not enough time for you to return to your house now."

Beresford looked at his friend skeptically. "Did you drop a word in her ear about the state of my clothing, my dear Geoffrey?"

Senlis held up his hand, as if taking an oath. "No, I did not, Simon. May I say that it was not necessary to do so! In any case, Adela was the one who insisted that you be presentable when the toasts are made." He let drop this triviality and came straight to his point. "Ever the reluctant bridegroom?"

Beresford had a succinct answer to that. "Bah!"

Senlis regarded his friend with surprise. "What was the problem?"

"Too many people," Beresford complained. "A man could suffocate in such a crowd."

"Ah, no, I mean before the well-wishers accosted you. Your exchange with Gwyneth looked to be going rather well, from what I could see. She wore no look of undisguised horror."

Beresford grunted. "I suppose I said all the wrong things to her after you left."

"No, no, no, Simon!" Senlis reassured him. "You said all the wrong things to her *before* I left! You certainly could not have become more tactless afterwards." At his companion's silence, Senlis checked his step. "*Could* you have become more tactless? God's blood, Simon, what did you say to her?"

Beresford scowled. He latched onto the defining moment in their exchange, during which something seemed to have hung in the balance, but he did not know what. "She did not like what I had to say about Johanna."

"What on earth could you have said about your cousin?"

"That she has been around forever."

"And what did Gwyneth object to in that remark?"

"She said that Johanna was not old enough to have been around forever."

Senlis admirably suppressed his smile. "Very true!" he agreed lightly. "But that is only a mildly offensive remark, Simon, even by my standards. What else did you say that Gwyneth objected to?"

Beresford had a sudden vision of violet eyes and felt an alien sensation pass through him—a bout of weakness, perhaps, or the sigh that comes with the ethereal effect of a fragile line of poetry. He said harshly, "I was not able to determine whether she grieves for her husband."

Senlis nodded in understanding. "That would be difficult to determine in all events, I think, Simon."

"On the other hand, I was able to determine that she is not carrying his child."

Senlis's expression fell comically. "You *what?*" he demanded.

"I discovered that she is not carrying her late husband's child," Beresford repeated.

Senlis asked slowly, "And did you discover such a thing, mayhap, by asking her?"

"How else was I to know?"

Senlis's oath was inventive and profane. "There are a hundred and one ways to discover the answer to such a delicate question without asking the lady herself!" He delivered several more irreverent phrases, shook his head, then asked with some exasperation, "And this line of inquiry came after your unfortunate remark about Johanna?"

"No, it came before."

"Gwyneth was still speaking to you after that?" Senlis asked, amazed. He took a moment to absorb that information, then uttered a pithy, "Well! I did not know at first whether your Gwyneth was not, perhaps, too..." He did not complete his thought, but said, "Instead, it seems she has great fortitude, for throughout the entire conversation, her face betrayed nothing but serenity from what I could see. Or perhaps," he continued reflectively, "she did not properly understand you. Could it be, as you first suspected, that she is simple?''

"Ha!'' Beresford said, almost bitterly. He was a man who could recognize his mistakes.

"Well, Simon,'' Senlis said, "you seem to have made a mess of it.''

"How so, Geoffrey?'' Beresford challenged. "What is so wrong with what I asked? You think that I was going to let Stephen—or Adela—maneuver me into accepting a woman who was carrying the brat of one of Henry's followers? Is that what you think?''

Senlis thought many things, but he cut to the heart of the matter. "I think she is the most beautiful woman I have ever seen.''

Beresford stopped dead in his tracks and grasped the tunic of his friend, as he had earlier in the council room.

Senlis still dared his flippant tones. "Ah, no, Simon! Let me tell you, since you are in dire need of a lesson in manners, that it is very bad form to threaten the life of a good friend twice in one day! And while I am about the grand task of trying to tame you into near-human behavior, allow me to put a word in your ear. Subtlety— Do you know what it means?''

Beresford pulled himself together. The poetic feeling had passed. So too had Senlis's flippant mood, judging from his face when Beresford did not release him.

"Shall you put words in my mouth and teach me to speak just as my wife-to-be has done?'' Beresford said in none too pleasant a tone. "I do know the meanings of some words, my friend, and I will now indulge my penchant for plain speaking. A threat is a violent action that is not necessarily acted upon. Permit me to tell you that I never threaten.''

Chapter Four

Adela sat straight in the chair in her solar and did not reveal her satisfaction at the news she was receiving from her councillors, with whom she met every day just before supper.

In the year since she had unofficially succeeded Queen Mathilda, she had made few political mistakes, for the simple reason that she could not afford the luxury of making them. Stephen's hold on his throne was being weakened from within by the increasingly quarrelsome earls of the realm and threatened from without by the Conqueror's great-grandson Henry, who had his eye on the English throne and his feet on English soil. Adela had room only for wise decisions. She would have been greatly satisfied if Cedric of Valmey had agreed to marry Gwyneth of Northumbria, but he had turned the idea down flat. Adela did not press the issue, knowing that Rosalyn, her most reliable source of information, would object.

She thought she had recouped brilliantly in choosing Simon of Beresford as Gwyneth's bridegroom. It was true that Beresford had taken badly to the idea, but Adela had reckoned on his displeasure and had calculated to temper it, if necessary, with the bestowal of the Northumbrian earldom.

Although she knew that Beresford's elevation would be viewed with envy by several of the barons, she also knew that the grumbling could not be too great, for Beresford's loyalty was well known and his reward justifiable. From the reports she was receiving, she was reassured that Beresford's new honor was being met with general approval in the castle. Adela had good reason to be pleased with her day's work.

She was pleased, as well, when Gwyneth of Northumbria was announced at the queenly bower and ushered into the room by two ladies-in-waiting. At her entrance, Adela summarily dismissed her councillors, rose from her chair and moved forward.

"Thank you for coming, as I requested, my dear," she said, her hands outstretched to grasp Gwyneth's. "Let me look at you." She stood at arm's length. "Very lovely. Yes, very lovely. Perfect for this evening."

Adela, indeed, approved of Gwyneth's appearance. The young woman had left Northumbria with little clothing, so Adela had provided her with a dark blue kirtle, over which she wore a light blue linen bliaut that laced at the sides and fit closely to her hips, flaring out below. The pretty woven-leather belt that Gwyneth had passed twice round her waist and knotted in front was her own, but she had no jewelry, nor did Adela intend for her to wear any until she remarried. Particularly satisfying was the change in Gwyneth's hair. Adela had provided her with a plain circlet and a small round veil as a replacement for the snood, and this proper headdress made the young woman look less Norse and more Norman.

Gwyneth thanked her hostess modestly for the compliment while Adela led her to a wide window seat piled luxuriously with pillows and cushions. "Lady Chester has already informed me," Adela said, "that your initial meeting with Simon of Beresford went exceeding well. Now I would like an account of the event from your lips."

"It went very well," Gwyneth agreed in her lilting accent. "But as for a precise account, I would not know where to begin."

"You might begin by telling me whether you are in any way displeased with your husband-to-be," Adela suggested gently. To the nearest lady-in-waiting, she requested that two cups of wine and a bowl of nuts be brought, then she drew Gwyneth down next to her on the gaily striped cushions. Lowering her voice in a conspiratorial tone, she said, "The matter is not cast in stone until the wedding vows are spoken, you know."

She saw Gwyneth pause a moment before replying demurely, "Displeased with him? No, madam."

Adela smiled encouragingly. "Are you pleased by him, then?" she prodded.

Gwyneth lowered her thick, blond lashes. "I am pleased to accept your choice of husband for me," she replied, ever demure.

This was not the response Adela was angling for, and she wished she could have seen into the young woman's eyes. "Very proper," she confined herself to saying. Hoping to coax Gwyneth into revealing her feelings, she ventured, "Simon of Beresford has many fine qualities."

"Oh, yes, I am sure that he does," Gwyneth replied.

"He is strong and rich," Adela continued, "although he is not one to display his wealth." She paused long enough to take a cup of wine from the tray held by the lady-in-waiting and to gesture invitingly toward Gwyneth. "And he is kind."

Gwyneth took the cup and raised her eyes. In the benign light of the dying day, Adela found herself looking straight into a limpid, limitless violet that told her nothing of Gwyneth's thoughts.

"I have seen that he is strong," Gwyneth said sweetly, "and I believe you when you say that he is rich. However, I have too slight an acquaintance with him to know yet whether he is kind."

Adela laughed once, musically. "You may as well state that his manners are harsh and that his social graces are few!" she said humorously, switching tactics. "Such a man

is our Simon! But I assure you that he is honorable and that
beneath his ragged manners beats a warm heart.''

Gwyneth nodded acquiescently, and Adela felt the first
stirrings of dissatisfaction with her day's work. "But you
are not drinking, my dear,'' she said, noting Gwyneth's un-
touched wine. "It will relax you after the excitement of the
day.''

Thus commanded to drink, Gwyneth obeyed.

"Now that I have mentioned Beresford's rather blunt
ways,'' Adela continued, keeping her tone light, "I must say
that they were in full evidence earlier today in the council
room. A number of barons were present when I bestowed
upon Sir Simon the privilege of marrying you, and in his
surprise, he reacted without thinking!'' Her voice was co-
zily confidential. "You, dear Gwyneth, know how rumors
can scurry throughout a castle, becoming more distorted
with every telling. The ones circulating about Sir Simon that
so closely concern you are bound to come to your ears, and
I did not want you to be distressed, my dear, if you were to
hear that Sir Simon was not happy with the match.''

Gwyneth replied with an openness that gave her words the
ring of truth. "You need not worry about untoward rumors of such a nature coming to my ears, madam, for Sir
Simon told me himself that he was against the marriage.''

Adela was mightily displeased by this information, but
had enough experience not to show it. She had not thought
it necessary to speak to Beresford alone before he met his
bride, figuring that Gwyneth would win him over with her
beauty. She did not know what ailed the man, but she made
a mental note to meet with Beresford immediately before
supper.

Before replying, she fortified herself with a leisurely sip
of wine and encouraged Gwyneth again to do the same.
Then she set down her cup and matched Gwyneth's openness with a pleasant candor of her own. "Our Simon,
again!'' She shook her head in affectionate dismay and
chuckled. "I shall make a point of having you visit Beres-

ford at his home in town tomorrow. You will have a very different impression of him when you see him in his element. Your feelings will undergo a measurable change for the better.''

Adela paused. The young woman's obvious retort would have been, 'Ah, madam, it is not *my* feelings about the marriage that need to improve, but those of my husband-to-be, who has expressed his displeasure at the match.'

Instead, Gwyneth said nothing. She merely nodded. Adela waited another moment for a response, and when Gwyneth glanced at her modestly and expectantly, as if waiting for the next topic, Adela felt her dissatisfaction grow into frustration. For all her skill at eliciting valuable information from the unsuspecting, Adela was baffled by Gwyneth. She could not determine whether the young woman was remarkably docile or exceptionally smart.

Adela sensed that her plans could go awry if she did not realize them soon. ''Everyone will feel better, I am sure, when the date for the wedding is set,'' she said with a smile. ''I will have it announced at supper this evening, when the toasts to your happiness are made.''

So saying, Adela rose, thereby bringing the brief conversation to its conclusion. She touched her hand to her forehead and said, ''Ah, but I have just bethought myself of a task left undone.'' She turned toward one of her ladies. ''Marta, I pray you, escort our guest to the hall for supper.'' Turning back to Gwyneth, she said, ''I will follow shortly. You will understand if I am unable to accompany you there myself just now, won't you, my dear?''

Gwyneth understood perfectly. She had held no illusions before the summons to the king's consort's solar, and held none now. When Adela had opened the discussion with, ''The matter of your marriage is not cast in stone until the wedding vows are spoken, you know,'' Gwyneth had not been deceived into thinking that she had the power of refusal. When Adela had brought up the little matter of the

rumor circulating that Simon of Beresford was not well
pleased with the match, Gwyneth had grasped the true reason she had been honored with an invitation to the private
chambers: Adela had wished to forestall a potential scan-
dal and avoid an openly unwilling bride. Gwyneth had
seized upon the occasion to reaffirm Beresford's opposi-
tion to the scheme, and although her ploy might not undo
the match, she was not sorry to have tried. Not for anything would she have revealed her own fears for her future,
for she had lived with Canute too long to ever expose weakness. And her tongue was *never* loosened by strong drink.

Accompanied by Marta, Gwyneth arrived back at the
great hall, where preparations for the lighter of the two daily
meals were going forward. Even in this warm weather, low
fires mulled on the hearths of the wide fireplaces that faced
one another across the length of the room, chasing any chill
and damp. Pages were setting up the trestle tables and
benches and arranging the silver spoons and cups of horn.
Servants with bronze ewers circulated throughout the hall so
that the nobles could wash their hands.

Upon stepping into the activity, Gwyneth felt a calm that
came from knowing the worst of her fate. A glance around
the room confirmed that Beresford was not there. She did
not have a moment to feel at a loss in this gathering of
strangers, for several women came up to her, friendly and
curious. She had hardly been introduced to them and begun to receive their congratulations when a man joined the
group, smooth and smiling, and somehow she found herself separated from the women and alone with him.

"You are Cedric of Valmey," she stated. The handsome
man, dressed in a rich burgundy tunic that enhanced his
dark good looks, was standing too close to her, and she took
a discreet half step away from him.

He bowed and said, "You flatter me, Gwyneth of Northumbria."

Since she had earlier perceived him to be a man who
would think himself irresistible to all women, she did not

bother to deflate him by saying that she was hardly likely to have forgotten the one responsible for her captivity. She also refused to blush or simper in apparent confusion. "I did not mean to do so, sire," she said. She regarded him steadily, a disconcerting trick, she had learned, that sometimes put overbold men at a disadvantage.

Not Cedric of Valmey. "Then, perhaps, madam, you accuse me."

She knew that it was wiser to preserve a respectful silence than to respond.

Valmey sighed with a smile. "Perhaps you know that I led the attack on Castle Norham. It is natural for you to hold it against me, but in sooth, it could have been any knight present who did the deed." He waved the topic away and continued, still overly solicitous. "Because I wish to give you a much better impression of me, I have come forward with the rest to offer my congratulations to you."

"I thank you."

"And to complain," he continued with a sly, sensuous, teasing smile, "that Simon of Beresford received two remarkable honors today."

Gwyneth looked at him questioningly.

"The second remarkable honor being, of course, the fact that he is to marry you."

"And the first?" she demanded.

"He has received the earldom of Northumbria, in addition to your hand and your land," Valmey informed her.

Gwyneth lowered her lashes. Beresford had not mentioned the earldom, and neither had Adela. Was Valmey telling her this now to suggest that an additional honor had been necessary to overcome Beresford's obvious reluctance to the marriage? Or was it, rather, that Valmey was jealous, since the land should have been his by right of conquest? She replied, "It seems a proper honor to bestow on him, under the circumstances."

"Under the circumstances," Valmey repeated.

"What circumstances?" asked a voice at Gwyneth's side. She turned to find Geoffrey of Senlis standing there. "But let me guess!" he said.

Gwyneth greeted him and said, "We were just discussing the appointment of Simon of Beresford as Earl of Northumbria."

Senlis bowed. "An excellent appointment," he said approvingly, "and unlooked-for on Beresford's part, I can assure you!" He gazed frankly at Gwyneth as he continued, "Simon has never sought honors."

Gwyneth perceived the merest hint of tension in Cedric of Valmey and wondered whether Senlis's comment was less for her benefit and rather more for Valmey's. "You mean that he is modest," she said.

"I mean that, too," Senlis said, his eyes twinkling.

Gwyneth riposted, "I refuse to credit, sire, that as Simon of Beresford's friend, you are suggesting he is unambitious."

Senlis laughed. "I did not mean that, my lady!" he disclaimed instantly, stepping back and putting his hand over his heart.

Cedric of Valmey smiled at the good-natured raillery, but the smile did not reach his eyes. When he murmured his excuses, Senlis said affably, but with an undercurrent of challenge, "What, Valmey, you are leaving us?"

With equal affability and challenge, Valmey replied, "I shall return when I may have Gwyneth of Northumbria to myself."

Gwyneth supposed that she was to feel flattered, but she did not. She had no doubt that Cedric of Valmey was a rat, and not just because of his sacking of Castle Norham. He was a handsome rat, but a rat all the same. She turned to Senlis. He was handsome, too. But he was not, she thought as she looked into his fine eyes, a rat. She felt a kind of relief in his presence that she had not experienced since coming to the Tower. Perhaps it was his blue eyes and blond hair, which made him seem so very familiar to her. For the second time that day, she thought how much easier her life would be if *he* had been the chosen bridegroom.

He extended his arm. She laid her fingertips lightly upon it. He invited her to stroll and she accepted prettily. He spoke easily of this and that. He regaled her with an inconsequential story or two. He sketched for her the foibles of those present in the hall and mapped their family ties to those who would be presently joining the evening's festivities.

The context thus existed for Gwyneth to ask casually, "And Cedric of Valmey? He is not married?"

Senlis shook his head. "No, my lady." He smiled charmingly. "Promised, however, I think."

Gwyneth let the subject pass. "And to whom is that man married— Ah, I believe he is the Earl of Exeter?"

"Very good! You have a head for names, it seems. Exeter is married to Catherine of Kent, and I perceive," Senlis said, with a glance at her, "that marriage is on your mind."

She returned his look and admitted, "I suppose that it is."

"It's very understandable," he replied, "but if you are determined to pursue the subject, I think you would find it far more interesting to ask about *my* marriage plans."

Gwyneth entertained the rather attractive thought that Geoffrey of Senlis might be flirting with her. "Well, then, sire," she said, deciding to oblige him, "what are your marriage plans?"

"I have none!" he answered. "Like Valmey, I am unmarried. Unlike Valmey, I am promised to no one."

"Oh? You are, perhaps, too particular?"

"No," he said, shaking his head sadly, "too poor!"

"Some woman will take such a well-set-up man for preference."

"It's a lowering thought to be loved for one's face."

"You'd rather be loved for your land?"

Senlis cocked his head and looked down at her. "No," he said slowly, "you are not at all simple."

She glanced quickly at Senlis, then away, startled by this reminder of her initial, disastrous encounter with Simon of Beresford. She raised her eyes and was startled again, for suddenly Beresford stood in front of her. She felt a stabbing sensation somewhere in the region of her heart. With the part of her perceptions that were still functioning normally, she noted that he had been cleaned up. Someone had taken a razor to his face with not indifferent results and had tried to bring his hair into order. His tunic, though far from stylish, was clean and in good repair. For all these improvements, he looked not one whit less formidable.

Beresford's slate glance had struck his friend and stopped. "Geoffrey," he said pleasantly, but something in his tone sounded distinctly unpleasant to Gwyneth, "thank you for attending to my wife-to-be while I was speaking with Adela."

"You are most welcome, Simon," Senlis replied, with an elaborately polite gesture, then threw out an appetizing morsel. "We were discussing, in fact, the very subject of marriage."

Beresford did not bite. He had come to escort Gwyneth to supper and said as much. He took possession of her hand and began to lead her to the head table without so much as a by-your-leave. The maneuver was adroit, and Gwyneth had the notion that he must have relieved many an enemy of his weapon in a similar way. She also saw that his customary rudeness could work to his advantage, for there was nothing in his manner to make her think that he was angry or jealous or otherwise moved by her conversation with Senlis. He was simply being Simon of Beresford.

So why did she feel just the tiniest grain of guilt? There was no reason, of course, for she owed Beresford nothing. She decided that she was merely irritated at having her conversation with a charming, handsome man rudely interrupted. The self-righteous thought gave her courage.

They arrived at the head table and sat down, having exchanged the kind of pleasantries two people would say to one another as they sought their seats. Gwyneth acquainted herself with Walter Fortescue on her left. Beresford withdrew his knife from the leather sheath at his belt and laid it on the table between the trencher and cup that he and Gwyneth would share. They were honored this night to be placed at the table on the dais, which was under the central vault of the hall. They were not, of course, directly next to the king and his consort, but Gwyneth was seated close enough to receive a tasty morsel from Stephen's knife, if he cared to extend one to her.

She turned back to Beresford at the same moment he turned toward her. It had seemed to her that he had been avoiding looking her way, but now he was staring fixedly at her.

Surprised by the intensity of his gaze, she thought it necessary to say something. "I will be visiting you in your home tomorrow, sire," she said, imagining this to be an acceptable topic of conversation for the meal. "Adela is arranging for my escort."

He did not say a word to this, but simply continued to stare at her a moment longer. Then he grunted and looked away. She assumed he was not terribly interested in her visit, but at least he had registered the information.

Then the royal sign was given to the servitors to begin the procession of dishes, the lamb first, and fish fresh from the sparkling waters of the Thames. The rest of the company sought their benches at the other tables formed in a U-shape around the room. The serving of the food necessitated some words being exchanged between Beresford and Gwyneth, for it was the gentleman's role to choose the tender bits for his lady. He was attentive to her, but just ordinarily so, and the conversation they exchanged was equally ordinary.

When they had settled into the rhythm of the meal, Gwyneth's gaze fell on the three weird women she had noticed earlier. Something prompted her to turn to Beresford and say impulsively, "I pray you, tell me about your sons."

He had just skewered a bit of meat on his knife when she made her request. He nodded readily and invited, "What would you like to know about them?" He offered her the dainty bit from his knife.

Before accepting it, she said, "You may wish to begin by telling me their names and ages."

Beresford obliged her. "Elias is fifteen, Laurence is thirteen, Daniel is ten, Benedict eight and Gilbert six."

She had accepted the meat and was chewing as he spoke. When he was finished, Gwyneth pronounced the meat to be delicious, then said in some puzzlement, "Lady Chester told me you had three sons."

"Why, no," he corrected, "I have five."

She swallowed and said mildly, "Lady Chester is, apparently, misinformed."

His brow lowered, then cleared. "I have three sons by Roesia, my late wife," he said. "Perhaps they were the only ones she was counting." He added as a point of information, "Elias, Laurence and Daniel have long been in training. Laurence and Daniel are under the tutelage of Valentine, Roesia's brother, while Elias serves already in Fortescue's household. Benedict and Gilbert still live with me, although Benedict should be leaving soon."

She had nearly choked. She was hardly shocked that a man would have natural children, only that he would acknowledge them at this particular time and in this particular setting. She felt it like a slap in the face, then reconsidered. It was an adjustment for her, this man's brute honesty which he applied equally to himself and to everyone else. After the feints and lies and dissemblings of Canute, she did not know how best to approach Simon of Beresford to protect herself from his power over her.

Right now, she did not need to protect herself from him, only to maintain conversation and a shred of dignity. Her best course at the moment, she decided, was simply to humor him. If the topic of his sons entertained him, entertain him she would. She calculated that Elias, his oldest son,

must be a product of his coming-of-age. She inferred that
Laurence and Daniel were two of the legitimate sons by
Roesia and decided to take a chance at determining the
third. "And Gilbert will also be joining Valentine's household?" she asked.

Beresford confirmed that this was so, allowing Gwyneth
to infer that eight-year-old Benedict was the second natural
son.

When the topic of his sons had been rather fully explored, Gwyneth asked, "You have no daughters?"

He looked down at her and said flatly, "One was still-
born and the other died on the day after her birth."

"I am sorry to hear it," she managed.

"That is the way of the world," he said without emotion.

Their eyes locked, and her heart beat faster. His utter indifference shocked her. It was at that moment that the king
stood up from his chair. The main dishes had been served,
and an appropriate point in the meal had come for an-
nouncements.

The king raised his cup to the hall and said, "I have the
great pleasure to announce this evening the impending union
of Gwyneth of Northumbria to Simon of Beresford."

Cups were raised in response. Congratulatory comments
were called out from the floor. Several rounds of toasts were
offered. Enough heavy wine had been drunk for the comments to become suggestive, but conventionally so.

The king recaptured the initiative. He extolled the virtues of Simon of Beresford, which, he stated, were not necessarily seen but always felt, and contrasted Beresford's
invisible virtues to the highly visible ones of Gwyneth of
Northumbria. Since this contrast was met with general approval, he went on in this style for some time, then finally
mentioned the Saint Barnabas Day tourney. After pausing
for the raucous reaction to this long-awaited event to die
down, he mentioned the difficulties of planning a wedding

that might interfere with the tournament, not forgetting the feast of Trinity, which was almost upon them.

He came, at last, to his point and said, ''We shall celebrate the marriage of Gwyneth of Northumbria to Simon of Beresford five days hence.''

Five days! Gwyneth's immediate thought was that her ploy of mentioning to Adela Beresford's displeasure with the match had worked in reverse. Instead of making her reconsider the marriage—which Gwyneth had not truly thought she would do—she had pushed the wedding as far forward as she could. Gwyneth had to will herself not to look at the king's consort, for she feared betraying herself with an accusatory look. Instead, she composed her features and turned toward her husband-to-be.

Beresford had swerved his head to her, evidently as dismayed as she was. At his openly uncomplimentary reaction to the imminence of their marriage, she felt a strong feminine pique overcome her own displeasure and her fear of him. She saw many horrible possibilities for her future in the Norman court unfold in her mind's eye and thought that he might as well beat her in public now, for all the respect she would ever receive if it was clearly seen that he did not want her. She preferred a quick and bloody end to a slow and bloodless death from shame.

She did not flinch from the look in his eyes, but smiled at him agreeably. What she said was at great variance with her serenely beautiful expression, however.

''If you insult me now with a display of displeasure at this match,'' she said so low that no one else could hear, ''I will kill you, Simon of Beresford.''

Chapter Five

Beresford had no idea what she meant about him insulting her, but ignored it, for here at last came a turn in conversation to which he knew how to respond; and he was unexpectedly charmed by her expression of feminine blood lust. It sounded so different to him from Roesia's whining and wheedling, designed not to challenge him with her strength but to irritate him with her weakness. By contrast, Gwyneth's statement was strong and sure, and startling, coming as it did from so delicate a woman.

Although he was not well versed in courtly ways, he did know what to do. He was aware of her and of his audience and could play to both differently. Looking into her eyes, he took her slim hand and weighed it lightly in his palm for a moment, as if testing the balance of a finely wrought dagger. "Would you kill me with poison or a knife, I wonder," he said for her ears only, "or would it be with your bare hands?"

These words of male challenge tasted strangely appetizing on his lips when said to a woman. Without giving her a chance to respond, he turned her hand over and put his lips to the white skin of her knuckles. Beresford's gesture, seemingly more affectionate and respectful than it was graceful, brought hushed "oohs" and "aahs" of approval from the hall.

He released her hand and asked, "Shall I live, my lady?"

"For now," she whispered back.

Next he reached for the horn of wine that sat between them and drank from it. When he handed it to her, he turned the cup so that the part of the rim that had touched his lips was toward her. She was left with no choice but to put her own lips where his had been and to drink from the cup. He felt the satisfaction of having maneuvered an opponent into a defensive position on the field and was momentarily pleased.

Scattered applause broke out. Along with shouts of congratulations and encouragement came friendly abuse, which he deflected with return comments of a similarly ribald nature. When the moment had passed, he looked down at Gwyneth and saw her lashes lowered and her cheeks tinged with pink. He could not determine whether she was angry, embarrassed, chastened, vexed or merely warm from the wine. When she did not counter him challenge for challenge, it seemed to him that she had gone into a retreat that he did not know how to flush, and his confidence in the turn in conversation ebbed. He felt himself floundering again, as he had moments before when she had spoken to him about his children and he had not known what to say to her, beyond the obvious and uninteresting.

The evening had begun badly and was getting worse. Before supper, he had been drawn aside by Adela and given instructions that had puzzled him as much as they had angered him. She had told him that he was not to indicate again to Gwyneth that he did not desire the match, and he was annoyed when she rejected his denial that he had said anything of the kind. To his further irritation, Adela had suggested topics suitable for discussion during the meal, having to do with such inscrutable activities as needlework and household management. However, he had never known Adela herself, or Queen Mathilda before her, to speak of needlework, and so he decided that she had made an incomprehensible attempt at humor.

Thus, even before the meal, he had already been puzzled, angered and irritated. The moment he had sat down next to Gwyneth and really looked at her, he had been struck dumb and had not had the faintest idea what she said to him, thereby aggravating his puzzlement, anger and irritation. To these unsociable emotions was added an increasing clumsiness as he tried to keep in mind Senlis's earlier recommendation of "Subtlety!" He had realized, once the meal was underway, that he did not have a clue about what Senlis meant. And thinking of Senlis, particularly of him strolling so companionably with Gwyneth before the meal, Beresford was gripped by a violence he could not deny, but was not yet fully prepared to understand.

He was at a loss for a few moments after the applause and congratulations and friendly abuse ended. He looked out over the hall, feeling strange and unpleasant emotions crawl around inside him, until by chance his eyes fastened on the three weird women who had formed themselves into a circle in a far corner.

He turned to the beautiful, confusing creature next to him. "So I am safe from your wrath for now," he said, and asked idly, "but am I safe from the evil spells of the three crones?"

Gwyneth looked up at him in surprise, and then followed the direction of his gaze. "Yes," she said slowly, "for I think that you are more protected than threatened by the Norns."

He frowned. "The Norns?"

"That is what the Danes would call them," she said, shifting her eyes back to the women. "I do not know the word in Norman, or whether such a word exists."

Interested, he demanded, "Who—or what—are the Norns?"

She raised her eyes to him, and he allowed his gaze to be drawn into her violet pools. "They are the wise women who tend the world tree, Yggdrasil, which, according to Norse legend," she said, "holds our world in place. The Norns also decide the destinies of all creatures, mortals and gods alike."

"Gods?" he scoffed, with an edge of reprimand in his voice at her blasphemy.

She lowered her eyes modestly and said, "I hope that I am a good Christian, and I assure you that the Northumbrians came to the true religion long ago. However, before the one Christian God was made known to us, there were other gods that ruled heaven and earth, and other creatures, too, that inhabited it."

"Other creatures?"

"Elves and dwarves and such."

He waved dismissively. "And the gods?"

"There was Odin," she said, "who created the earth and sky."

He shook his head. "The Father of the Trinity was the creator of the universe."

"Yes, of course," she acknowledged, "but Odin was different, for he was not part of a trinity. He was the father of all other gods, and he was married to the goddess Frigg." She seemed to know to fill the silence, and he was pleased to permit her to. "Odin slew a giant and made the earth from his flesh," she went on, "the mountains and rocks from his bones and teeth and the rivers and seas from his blood. He made the dome of the sky from the giant's skull and tossed his brains in the air as clouds. He then fashioned the first man from an ash root and named him Ask and took an elm root for his wife, Embla." She added, "Odin was an Aesir, or warrior god."

He looked away from her then. "A warrior god," he repeated, considering. Although he was in no danger of believing a pagan account of the world, he thought Odin's work a reasonable way to begin a universe. He stretched out his hand to fiddle with the cup of wine, turning it this way and that, keeping his eyes fixed on the play of light on the ruby liquid. His curiosity caught, he asked, "Were there other warrior gods in addition to Odin?"

"Oh, many!" she assured him. "Perhaps the most interesting to you would be Thor, the thunder god, who was Odin's eldest son. He was huge, even for a god, and incredibly strong. He had wild hair and a beard, and a temper to match. His main weapon was a hammer, and he had a belt that doubled his strength when he buckled it on and iron gauntlets that allowed him to grasp any weapon."

He was rather entertained by her account of this Thor. He slanted his eyes to Gwyneth. Her cheeks, he noted, had faded to their customary immaculate ivory. He could not interpret her calm any better than he could her flush. He knew only that he wished to hear more.

"Thor sounds a fearsome fellow," he commented.

"In a way, but he was also trusting and good-natured and the most popular of the gods," she replied. "His symbol was the oak tree."

It made sense to him. He nodded approvingly.

"The warrior gods lived in a great hall called Valhalla," she continued, "the walls of which were made of golden spears and the roof of golden shields. Some of the earthly warriors slain in battle were chosen to join Odin in Valhalla, where they would feast and make merry every evening."

"But so many men are slain in battle," he pointed out, still fiddling with his cup as he listened. "How did Odin choose among them?"

"Only the bravest were chosen, but Odin did not select them. That was the work of the Valkyries, the female warriors—"

His eyes cut to hers, his brows raised.

"Yes, female warriors," she repeated, with the hint of a challenge.

His eyes rested on her a moment longer. He was having difficulty imagining a female warrior who was not beautifully fair and deceptively delicate. With cautious interest, he asked, "What were they like, the Valkyries?"

"They were magnificently strong," she told him, "and swooped over battlefields on horseback, directing the fighting. They had frightening names like Raging Warrior and Shrieking and Shaker. They chose only the bravest heroes for Valhalla, as I have said, and it was common for a man chosen to die to see a Valkyrie just before the fatal blow."

He scanned in mental review the decisive moments of battles he had fought and noted with satisfaction that he had never seen a Valkyrie. He was as loyal to his God as he was to his king, but when it came to beliefs that governed his warrior's life, he was tolerantly eclectic. Since he admired the Norse fighting ethic, which he knew he himself had inherited, he thought their beliefs highly worthy of consideration. As much as the prospect of Valhalla appealed to him, he decided to make every effort in future to elude the grasp of a Valkyrie, should ever he see one coming toward him on the battlefield.

He grunted meditatively and took a sip of wine. Gwyneth interpreted that as a sign to continue. "The Valkyries also worked as Odin's servants," she said, "and served food and drink to the warriors in Valhalla, who returned every evening after a day's adventure."

He grunted again, and Gwyneth obliged him by beginning to recount heroic deeds of the Norse gods. As she told him of monsters and magic horses and magic rings, he relaxed on the bench and was lulled by the lilt of her low voice. He listened, caught in the rhythm of her hesitations as she searched for a word in Norman. He listened, hardly conscious of the fact that his gaze had fallen on her right hand, resting on the table next to him.

His ears were full of the death of Odin's son and of the tricks played by Odin's blood brother, Loki, the mischievous giant god. His eyes traced the graceful crook of each of her long, white fingers to the curve of their pretty nails, and followed the outline of the back of her hand to her slim wrist, over which fell the soft folds of the finely braided sleeve of her kirtle. It was an exquisite hand, and he decided that the seductively morbid emotions it evoked in him as he contemplated it must be due to the dark and compelling stories she was telling.

She had turned to the tale of the god Tyr, the bravest and most honorable of the warrior gods, the one with the most integrity. Beresford listened in horror to the story of how Tyr lost his hand, and murmured with a fellow feeling of relief over the fact that it had been the left hand lost, not the right.

After a moment, Gwyneth said, "Tyr's wife was glad, too, that he could still fight."

"Tyr's wife?" he queried. He frowned into his wine. "Was she a Valkyrie?"

She laughed gently. "No, she was not a warrior, but from a different race of gods, thus making her a . . . foreigner to Valhalla. She was not afraid of violence, but did not approve of it. She was not physically strong, but her understanding was great."

"Why did he marry her?"

"The marriage was arranged by Odin to bring a peaceful element to Valhalla, and he arranged the marriage with one condition: that Tyr was never to raise a hand against her or harm her in any way." She paused. "Or else."

He met her gaze. "Or else what?"

"Or else Odin would have the Norns withdraw their protection from him."

"Did Tyr lose his hand because he did not treat his wife well?"

She smiled. "No, he lost it in an act of great courage, and because of his bravery, the Norns agreed thereafter to protect him. Unless, of course, he did not treat his wife well."

"And what happened to him?"

Her smile deepened. "Why, nothing. Tyr always treated her well, and the Norns continued to protect him."

It was a smile she had given him—a very lovely smile, but just a smile, nothing more. Still he felt the effect of it like a deep wound in his breast and had the vague notion that he had been tricked into lowering his sword and shield to receive the thrust of a slender lance. He was momentarily stunned and reinforced himself with a sip of wine. He did not like what had just happened to him, and he would take care that it did not happen again.

He mentally lowered his visor against her. Only then did he dare look at her again. "It is a fascinating tale you tell, my lady," he said. He glanced over to the corner, now empty, where the three weird women had stood. "The crones are gone," he said by way of closing the subject, "and so are the Norse gods." As his gaze traveled over the hall, he saw Cedric of Valmey, who had caught him before the meal and requested a meeting. He added, "There is someone I must see now."

So saying, he rose from the bench without further excusing himself. As he left her, he had the fanciful thought that he should be ready to fend off a Valkyrie. He looked furtively about him, but saw no signs of warrior women. However, just at the limit of his vision, he perceived a very different image that made no sense to him. It seemed to be a plump baby boy who had wings and could fly. He easily banished this absurd image and continued to stride across the hall toward Valmey, feeling increasingly better the further he was from the table.

Gwyneth watched him walk away. She wasted no time being offended by his abrupt withdrawal. She was rather more interested in evaluating the effect of the risk she had taken by inventing a wife for Tyr—a weak and peaceable wife, no less. Simon of Beresford was blunt, not stupid, and he had not missed her point. She deemed it counterproductive to be overly obvious, and had decided not to declare that Tyr was supposed to be a faithful husband as well as a gentle one. If she had to choose one indignity to protect herself from, it would be from a husband who beat her. She could more easily accept a husband's roving eye and any natural children that might result, which Beresford seemed to produce with ease.

All in all, Simon of Beresford was a difficult man for her to judge. He was certainly not a companionable and comfortable man, like Senlis, for instance. Nor did he seem to be, as she had first feared, as dismally predictable as Canute. He had frankly surprised her with his reaction to her threat on his life. Canute would have breathed fire or pouted sullenly, but in either case, he would have backed down and grudgingly fulfilled her request for a show of public respect, although he would have later made her pay for that direct challenge. Beresford had managed both to fulfill her request without backing down and to disarm her. The moment he had looked into her eyes and put his lips to her fingers, she had felt her breathlessness overtake her again. She hated to think that her reaction was from fear; she hated to think that it was from anything other than fear.

And she was feeling rather breathless again, just now, from the cool way he had looked at her upon rising from the bench and leaving her. Perhaps she *was* offended by his graceless exit, and her fluttery feeling resulted from renewed anger at his boorish behavior.

She did not have more than a moment to examine her feelings, however, for Walter Fortescue was saying into her ear, with avuncular affection, "It's a splendid match, my dear, and I hope that you are pleased."

Out of the corner of her eye, she kept track of Beresford's movements. She saw him meet with Cedric of Valmey, and then walk away with him. She registered that piece of information quickly, then turned and smiled at the elderly courtier. "Yes, splendid," she agreed modestly. "I am honored by the match."

"Quite right," Fortescue said approvingly. "It's splendid. Why, I was saying as much to Simon this afternoon, just after Adela announced her plans for him. We were all surprised. Oh, yes, and Simon most of all! But I can see that he's come around to the idea. Oh, yes!"

"I am pleased to know that the match suits him as well as it does me."

"Well, he's doubled his lands, as you know," Fortescue continued, with all the candid eccentricity allowed a man of his age and status, "and was given an earldom into the bargain! I should say he would be pleased! But, then," he reflected, "Beresford is not one to seek worldly advancement. His pleasure in the match, I am thinking, must come from being allied to such an extraordinarily charming young wife!"

Walter Fortescue seemed likely to continue in this vein for some time. Because maintaining a polite and patently false conversation such as this was as simple for Gwyneth as setting a plain stitch, she was able at the same time to observe the after-dinner mingling in the hall. With the part of her mind not engaged in making conversation, she applied herself to putting the names she had learned earlier to faces. She was exceptionally skilled at interpreting the most minimal gesture, the casual nod, the hasty glance, because her personal well-being and that of her immediate retinue had depended so desperately on her ability to read the mood of the men at Castle Norham.

This evening, as she unassumingly scanned the hall and felt its pulse, she quickly determined several friendships and several enmities. She noticed that Johanna, Beresford's cousin, was flirting prettily with a man Gwyneth recalled as Lancaster. She noticed that Beresford had left the hall. She noticed that Valmey had left, as well, presumably with Beresford.

In fact, little escaped her notice. During her lengthy, inconsequential conversation with Fortescue, Gwyneth also learned that Rosalyn enjoyed an easy relationship with Adela, for she had come to the head table and spoken familiarly with the king's consort, chatting and laughing. She saw that Valmey returned to the hall, but not Beresford. She watched as Rosalyn left the queen's side and crossed the hall to intersect, as if by chance, the path of Valmey. Although they did not appear to exchange more than a greeting, she noticed that the baron checked his step slightly to put a word in Lady Chester's ear, and she noticed that Rosalyn nodded in understanding. Then Adela rose from her chair and headed in Rosalyn's direction.

It was as if Gwyneth had seen a web of intrigue woven before her very eyes. She did not pause to reflect on the nature of the intrigue, but she knew she had to act swiftly. To Fortescue, she declared her desire to catch a breath of fresh air, and the elderly courtier was kind enough to offer his arm to escort her outside. She promptly accepted.

They rose from their bench and made their way in the direction Adela had taken. Fortunately, her progress through the hall was very slow, due to the fact that this important woman had to stop and speak with so many people. Thus, Gwyneth was able to anticipate her direction by going to the door under whose barrel vault Rosalyn had just passed and which led, as she recalled, to the staircase.

Indeed, she and Fortescue came upon the circular staircase at once. He suggested that they go down for a turn in the pleasance in the courtyard below. Gwyneth had no interest in the garden and cocked her ear to determine whether she should descend or ascend. She knew that below the great hall was the guardroom. The floor directly above held the sleeping chambers. This staircase led as well to the square tower above the chambers. She hesitated, then made her choice by instinct.

"But I would far prefer to be high above it all just now, Sir Walter," she said with a suggestive sigh.

"To the battlements, then, my dear," he replied chivalrously.

With Fortescue behind her, she held her skirts in one hand and placed the other on the central stone column of the stairs, which fanned out like a snail's shell to the stairwell wall. At the dormitory floor, she listened, heard nothing and kept climbing. She arrived at the fourth floor and stood a moment on the landing before deciding whether to mount the adjoining stairs, a straight flight, to the exterior of the castle. She nodded to the sentry at the head of the steps, who regarded them impassively. She wished to ask him if another couple had just come this way, but decided against revealing her motives to Fortescue.

Following her instincts still, she sensed they should go outside. "Here we are, then, Sir Walter," she said, linking arms with him now that they could walk side by side up the stairs to the battlements.

They walked out into the soft, smoky blue evening. When they walked past the crenels that cut the wall at regular intervals, she could see a long way over the city of London to the outlying fields, plowed straight as arrows pointing to the thick woods beyond.

Around a far corner, she thought she saw the train of Rosalyn's gown disappear. She tried to quicken Fortescue's step. Behind her, she heard Adela greet a sentry as she made her way along the battlements. She had no clear idea yet what was happening or what she would do about it, but she knew that she was wise to be here, to protect whatever her interests may be.

They proceeded around the far corner Rosalyn had taken, and she was lucky enough to find an empty corner in which a sentry would stand. She drew Sir Walter into it with her and paused as if to admire the remarkable view of the surrounding countryside afforded by the arrow slit in the thick stone wall.

When she turned back toward the interior battlement, she was witness to a remarkable scene. Ten feet ahead there was a break in the height of the battlement, joined by three steps. Beresford was about fifteen feet away, striding toward the steps, and Rosalyn was moving toward him from the other direction. When she came to the steps, she stumbled artfully. Beresford rushed forward and caught her before she fell, and suddenly he was holding her in a most intimate embrace. Rosalyn lifted her head to Beresford and seemed to invite a kiss.

Gwyneth had but the flash of a second to consider the implications of this little scene. It was certainly possible that Rosalyn was the woman of Beresford's current interest. Since it was well known that she might soon become a widow, Beresford's anger at his forced marriage to Gwyneth might thus be given a plausible explanation. But was this an amorous passage-at-arms and did Beresford desire it? Given Rosalyn's trick, she was inclined to doubt it.

Just then Adela rounded the corner in front of them, to see Rosalyn in Beresford's arms, and Gwyneth saw Adela's back become rigid.

"What is the meaning of this, Simon of Beresford?" Adela demanded.

Gwyneth emerged from the shadows, gesturing behind her to Walter Fortescue. "We all of us needed a breath of fresh air, madam," she explained, as if the two couples had arranged to come together, "and my lady Rosalyn lost her footing on the step. Sire Beresford was so quick as to catch her and so prevent her from turning her ankle."

Three faces turned toward Gwyneth. The queen's look of displeasure was replaced by one of relief to see Gwyneth present. Beresford was clearly dumbfounded, and Rosalyn was unable to conceal the malevolent look of a conspirator foiled that sprang out before she smoothed her face into a pleasant mask.

"Why, yes, that is correct, madam," she confirmed. She moved away from Beresford, who released her immediately. "I lost my footing."

When Rosalyn turned to look over her shoulder, Gwyneth did not think that she had made an enemy so much as discover that she already had one.

Chapter Six

The next afternoon, Gwyneth was escorted by a litter with several ladies-in-waiting accompanied by two soldiers, through the streets of London to Simon of Beresford's house. The sun was shining benevolently, and a good night's sleep had taken the edge off her fear for her future. The colorful journey, the first through the streets near her new home, helped to raise her spirits. She saw craftsmen at their benches, young students in the schools, priests at their devotions, apprentices practicing archery, ladies at their spinning wheels and well-kept public cook shops with their savory meats roasting on outdoor spits. When she passed by the sign of The Swan decorated with its ivy, she was beginning to feel almost cheerful about the prospect of living in such an industrious environment.

Thus, she was not entirely prepared for what was to greet her once she entered Beresford's home. Passing through the portal and coming upon the central courtyard, she beheld what she initially reckoned to be a legion of men, most lounging about and regarding with interest the drama unfolding in the center of the yard. That drama consisted of vigorous training exercises, in the very center of which was her husband-to-be, and this is what held her initial attention. Then she took in the structural details of the house, blinked in disbelief and looked back at the knights-in-training. Her eyes flitted again to the upper story of the house moved up to the roof, then down to the gallery in whose shade she stood. She hardly knew where to look next, for she was having great difficulty reconciling two wildly different impressions.

Never had she seen a man more graceful in combat than Simon of Beresford. Never had she seen the house of a nobleman in more graceless disrepair.

In the center of the yard, drenched in brilliant sunshine, Beresford stood with shield and sword engaged, clearly commanding the activity. He seemed to be giving most of his attention to one young man who looked strong and fit but entirely incapable of keeping up. Beresford would stop occasionally to show him a movement and work through the series several times before surprising the young combatant with an unexpected attack. His teaching was methodical and masterful.

Then Gwyneth gazed again, aghast, at the state of the house that surrounded her. The gallery sagged in various places, and slats were missing from the balcony railing like gaping teeth, along with those of the railing of the exposed staircase, which did not look safe to use. The posts holding up the whole were scarred and half were probably rotten. There was no doubt about the rotten state of the shutters of the rooms of the upper story, and each seemed to hang on one hinge. The eaves sagged in sympathy with the gallery, various roof tiles were missing and the courtyard, whose proportions were undoubtedly generous and lovely, was beaten to dust, fine clouds of which drifted over everything. The whole had obviously not been cleaned in years.

Beresford had apparently become disgusted with his pupil, for he knocked his sword out of his hand and called to an older man, an obviously experienced knight, to work through the movements with him. Now Gwyneth saw the full range of Beresford's skill, and as much as she abhorred the violence of the exercise and of the world that made such exercise necessary, she realized that Beresford's sword work approached beauty.

She gasped at the decrepitude of the rain barrels off to her left, and was even more outraged by the ragged state of the two unattended boys playing around them. She caught a whiff of something foul emanating from an unseen corner. However, she did not have a moment to investigate what household horror had produced it, for Beresford had been made aware of her arrival by one of his men and had called a momentary halt to the combat. The sound of his commands brought Gwyneth's head around, and she saw him narrow his eyes against the sun to focus on her in the shade of the gallery. His expression registered recognition, then mild interest in her appearance at his home. He handed his sword and gauntlets to the knight with whom he was sparring, indicated what he wanted the men to do, then gave the signal for everyone to continue with their business.

He strode first to the stone well not far from the rain barrels and poured several quick ladlesful of water over his head, which he shook once. He called to a page to toss him a towel. By the time he arrived at Gwyneth's side, he had wiped his face dry, but his sun-streaked hair was still spangled by dripping sweat and water. He was incredibly dirty and disreputable, but so thoroughly in his element that Gwyneth judged him, incongruously and to her own amazement, elegant.

"I did not know you were coming," he said by way of greeting.

She came to her senses and met his hard, gray eyes. She saw no profit in reminding him that she had informed him last evening of this day's visit. She swallowed the insult to her pride at his contemptuous welcome and curtsied respectfully. "God save you, sire. Adela recommended that I make myself acquainted with my new home."

From the look on his face, Gwyneth would have sworn that her words reminded him of something else he had forgotten, namely that she was to become his wife. He recovered enough to say, "I see." He peered around her at the company in which she was traveling, and frowned. "And for this visit you needed an entire retinue?"

"I could not travel alone through London," she explained calmly, making a continuing effort to restrain her indignation at this insulting reception, "and was pleased to accept the escort that Adela provided me."

He grunted, then asked, apparently recalling some precept of civility, "Have you had dinner? May I offer you a cup of wine?"

She hastily declined any offer of food or drink, her stomach shrinking from accepting anything from Beresford's kitchens. But she was mindful of the others of her retinue, whose tastes might be less fastidious, and consulted their wishes. While the requested water from the well was being fetched, she turned back to Beresford and declined, in advance, any further forced gesture of hospitality from him.

"I see that you are engaged in your work, sire," she said pleasantly, "and can assure you that it is not necessary to interrupt your exercise to show me about. You need only send me your housekeeper and she will attend to me well enough, I am sure."

Beresford liked the first part of what she said about not interrupting his exercise. He had passed an excellent morning and afternoon in combat and had no desire to stop now. The physical release had been very effective in draining the disaster of the previous day out of his body. It was the second part of what she said about a housekeeper that stumped him.

After he had looked about him and muttered, "Housekeeper," several times, as if attempting to conjure up a mythical creature, Gwyneth tried to put an end to his puzzlement.

"You need only send one or two of your serving women to assist me in my tour," she said calmly. A momentary silence prompted her to ask, "You do have women in your employ, do you not, sire?"

"Yes, of course I have women in my employ," he said confidently, although a slight raising of his brows seemed to suggest, "At least, I think I do!" He turned away from Gwyneth and said to the nearest page something that sounded to her remarkably like, "Go to the kitchens and see if you can find any women. If you do, send one of them here at once." Then he added some further instruction, rapidly spoken, that Gwyneth did not catch.

The page ran off. Beresford looked at Gwyneth, feeling impatient to return to his day's work. She looked at him, hard and handsome in his way, and was caught between two radically different emotions. She drew a breath and took control of herself and the situation. She had decided that she would not allow the ladies-in-waiting from the castle to accompany her on her tour of the premises. She was sure that the vile condition of Beresford's house must be widely known, but she did not wish for the humiliation of fresh details to be spread in court. What could be seen from the gallery was bad enough.

"Well, my lord," she said, "if you would have a bench brought around for the ladies, they may remain here and watch the training in company of the two castle soldiers who, I am sure, are eager for you to take the field again."

Beresford found immediate favor with this suggestion and had her request for the bench quickly fulfilled, whereupon Gwyneth assured him that he need not wait for the arrival of the household women. With a nod, he turned again to his training, working his shoulder muscles as he strode toward the fray, eager to wield his sword.

Presently, Gwyneth saw a lone woman emerge with the page from a far passage diagonally across the courtyard. This passage led, no doubt, to a second courtyard, around which would be arranged the stables, the servants' quarters and the kitchens, which would communicate with the main part of the house from behind. As the woman approached, Gwyneth saw that she was a slattern, though a pretty one. Dressed as she was, in a sluttish skirt and shirt, her virtue seemed to hang by a few threads. From the comely young woman's expression, it was clear she was put out. Gwyneth reckoned that she should well not be pleased to have another woman bear witness to such an ill-kept house. Gwyneth guessed that she had heard the news of her master's impending marriage and was, furthermore, displeased to have a new mistress—or any mistress at all.

This was confirmed by the young woman's palpably insolent demeanor. "Give you good day," she said curtly in a version of Norman. "My name is Ermina."

"Good morrow to you, Ermina," Gwyneth said in English, making the young woman's eyes widen in surprise. Ermina's attitude held no challenge for Gwyneth. She said authoritatively, "You know who I am and where I come from. You should also know, then, that I prefer English to French. In this case, I think it better to use English so that no misunderstandings may arise between us."

Ermina said, "But your English sounds different."

"That is because I come from the north. I confess that your English sounds different to me, but it's completely understandable, which is the essential point, is it not?"

Ermina cast a wary glance at Gwyneth from sultry brown eyes. "Yes, my lady," she said sullenly.

"Now, are you the woman in charge here?" Gwyneth inquired.

"In a manner of speaking," she replied with a careless shrug.

Gwyneth did not hesitate to put the woman in her place. "Then we may begin my inspection of the house with the chambers in the upper story and descend, in due course, to the foul corners of the gallery."

Ermina was brazen enough to say, "I'm to show you around the back courtyard." Her disrespect was obvious. "The master's wishes."

So that was the extra order that Beresford had conveyed to the page. Gwyneth smiled briefly. Beresford wanted her out of the way, did he? "I have neither time nor stomach today, I fear, to brave the kitchens or the stables. I wish to begin with the main living quarters. Pray follow me to the stairs.''

Gwyneth did not look back as she set off with a determined step toward the unsound staircase that led to the upper story. She knew that Ermina was following her, and she used all her instincts to gauge the climate of emotions that emanated from the young serving woman. It was a complex composition, Gwyneth decided, and she would need further interactions with her before determining how best to dispel the woman's mood or to turn it to her own advantage.

Having circumvented the activity in the yard by way of the gallery, they arrived at the staircase. Gwyneth lifted her skirts and tried the first step. She was rather surprised when it held her light weight. She put her hand on the rail and tested its strength. It had an unstable, elastic feel, but seemed usable.

With Gwyneth present in his house, Beresford was distracted from his practice, as if a mote of dust clouded his eye. He blinked to be rid of it, then blinked again as he looked over at the spot where Gwyneth had stood. She was gone. His narrowed eyes quickly scanned the gallery and then popped open when he saw her at the bottom step of the stairs, accompanied by Ermina. Why did the page have to find *that* woman? He breathed a savage Saxon epithet, imagining the havoc that Ermina might wreak, after which—worse thought!—he wondered if Gwyneth would make it past the broken third step, which he from long habit knew to skip. Too late! He saw her stumble and nearly fall, saved only by her grip on the rail. Resigned, he threw his sword down, nearly maiming the man nearest him. He quit the field for the second time, fending off a blow with his shield as he did so.

He crossed to the staircase in a few long strides, bounding up the first few stairs, which groaned under his weight. Brushing past Ermina, he cocked his head and gestured her away. He caught Gwyneth at the small of her back and fairly propelled her upward, over the treacherous second-to-last step.

Upon stumbling on the third step, Gwyneth had remarked to Ermina that the house did not look as if it had been touched in five years. She had just received the rather snide rejoinder that it had been much longer than that when she heard the ominous sound of wood giving way and had the horrible thought that the stairway was about to collapse. Then the scent of male sweat and two powerful hands engulfed her, and the next thing she knew she was standing in relative safety on the balcony. With her heart beating erratically, she looked, astonished, into the gray eyes of Beresford.

"I've decided to accompany you on the tour of this part of the house," he said gruffly. "If I had known you wished to visit here first, I would have done so from the beginning." To Ermina he said, "You may go now."

Gwyneth stepped away from him, and he quickly dropped his hands from her waist. "It is not necessary for you to accompany me," she stated evenly, trying to regain her composure after the shock of his rough, protective touch, "and I think it important to be accompanied by at least one of your women." She told Ermina in Norman, "You may stay."

With her large sultry eyes, Ermina consulted her master. Beresford was out of his depth, but he was in his own home and would be damned if he was not in charge. Effecting what he thought was a pretty clever compromise, he gestured ahead of him, vaguely indicating a far door to his right. To Gwyneth he said, "You will probably wish to visit the mistress's quarters, above all." Then he turned to Ermina. "Run along ahead and straighten up, if need be."

Ermina obeyed.

It seemed to Gwyneth that Beresford was still trying to get rid of her quickly. She would have none of it. She took a step in the opposite direction. "Yes, I will want to visit the mistress's quarters," she said. "But first I would like to visit the solar, which, if I gather correctly, runs above the passage over the main entrance, opposite us."

He confirmed that this was so.

She looked up at him. "If we visit there first, Ermina will have more time to set the mistress's room to rights, if need be."

Beresford shrugged. He did not really care about the condition of the room, but wanted Ermina as far away from Gwyneth as possible. He proceeded to lead Gwyneth to the solar. After he had mounted his strong guard against the effect she seemed to have on him, he began to entertain the suspicion that she was deliberately trying to annoy him by opening every door and poking her head inside, thus making their progress around the balcony over the gallery excruciatingly slow.

Gwyneth was not trying to annoy him with her inspection of his house. As she looked into chamber upon chamber of unswept filth, she was attempting to discover the true extent of the neglect. She was also taking her time in order to brace herself for any truly nauseating experience. Finally, they arrived at the solar, and Gwyneth opened the door, half fearing to be overcome by some stench. Instead, the room looked merely unused, rather than abused.

She stood on the threshold but did not enter. It must have been a beautiful room once. Its generous space was in proportion to the general plan of the large house. The walls were paneled and the exterior one boasted the extravagance of three pretty windows of thick, leaded amber glass. Most of the panes were broken, of course, and stuffed with rags or simply gaping. Half the shutters were gone as well; the other half might best be used for kindling. The design of the limestone fireplace was impossible to discern for the soot staining it. The hearth was choked with ashes. The state of the fireplace gave her a fair estimation of what must be the state of the kitchens, for she guessed that this hearth stood back-to-back with the fireplace in the kitchens sharing the chimney.

In the center of the solar was the only piece of furniture, a trestle table, with the benches stored atop it. The rushes on the floor had long since decomposed and smelled merely stale, not rancid. She thought that it might be used now as a storage room of some sort, for she saw what she thought was an old mattress shoved in one corner, the straw stuffing exposed at crazy angles.

She closed the door and, standing beside Beresford, looked up into his face. Despite herself and the outrage that surrounded her, she was aware of the pulse of this strong man who could wield a sword with terrifying beauty. She was aware of his sweat, too, and its fresh quality. He was not, by Odin, clean in his household habits, but he was at least clean in his bodily habits, for his scent was not that of rank male sweat unwashed for days. It was that of a healthy man hard at work.

He looked down at her, still surprised that she had come to his house and puzzled by her desire to open every door of the living quarters. He was amazed that so ethereally lovely, so seemingly frail a woman would have such a visceral effect on him.

She broke their locked gaze by looking away, and said, "I gather that you do not use the solar these days."

"Certainly it is being used," he said. "My sons have it for their bedchamber."

Her eyes flew back to his. "Their bedchamber?" She frowned. "That would be Benedict and Gilbert, no?"

"That's right," he said. "They're down there, playing by the rain barrels."

Gwyneth spotted the two boys below, who, she would have sworn, were urchins off the street. She looked determinedly away. Maternal anger shot through her. She took a deep breath and closed her eyes. When she opened them again, she had summoned a noncommittal smile. She said pleasantly, "Shall we continue?"

They proceeded along the adjacent leg of the balcony to the mistress's chambers, where Ermina was making a half-hearted effort to put the dusty, musty wreck to rights. Gwyneth actually stepped into this room. Beresford, thinking that she would next inspect the master's chamber, quickly entered his own room to pick up any clothing that he might have left here and there over the last day or two. As he snatched up several piles and tried to think of places to stash them, it occurred to him that perhaps he had let his chamber go more than just a day or two. He also made an effort to arrange the wild disorder of bedclothes, with not the most expert results.

Gwyneth was still next door, looking about her at the dismal state of her future bedchamber and trying not to fall into a pit of black despair at the age and depth of the dirt. The window giving out onto what she guessed was the secondary courtyard was boarded shut, as was the window to the balcony. The shutters were gone. Ermina flicked a limp dust cloth ineffectually at the cobwebs in one dim corner. In another corner Gwyneth spotted an interior door covered by a ratty curtain, which evidently led to the master's chambers. Through the door she could hear the sounds of Beresford's movements.

The bed occupied the whole of the long wall. Its frame looked sturdy, but Gwyneth guessed that the mattress needed a month's airing, while the bed curtains were beyond cleaning and needed to be burned. Beside the bed was a chair, a minor luxury except that it sat at an angle, missing one leg. The whole of the room cried out for a scrub brush, lye and a great flush of water.

The carved chest beside the door to the balcony captured her interest. She bent down in such a way as to avoid having her knees come into contact with the floor, to inspect what might be within the chest in the way of linens. There were some moth-eaten remnants of what might have been blankets, but as she gingerly picked them up, they crumbled at her touch. In her excavation, she came upon the curiosity of a little mirror encircled by a badly tarnished silver frame. She held the mirror up and looked into it. Her attention was not captured by her own image, which she had only rarely seen, but with the scene that unfolded behind her.

Ermina, seeing Gwyneth's back turned, had dropped her pretense of cleaning and had gone to the door that led to Beresford's chamber. In the reflection, Gwyneth saw her lift the curtain that separated the two rooms in the manner of a whore lifting her skirts. She heard Beresford's movements momentarily halt, and she saw Ermina strike a pose that even in the dim light Gwyneth had no difficulty interpreting. She was left to imagine the gesture Beresford made in response, for Ermina let the curtain drop with a huff, but not before she had sent Beresford a bold, pouty look of purest desire.

Gwyneth thought, *But of course!* She put the little mirror back in the chest, closed the lid, and rose from her position. She left the chamber to stand on the balcony and wait for Beresford. She did not even look into his chamber through the open door. She was considering, in a vague sort of way, the visible desire of this strumpet for the man she herself was to wed, when Beresford was suddenly next to her on the balcony.

He asked, "Do you wish to see my chamber now?"

Gwyneth composed her face and looked down modestly. "It would not be proper, sire."

Beresford was vexed that he had been put to so much bother with the piles of clothing for nothing and was prevented from commenting rudely on her intrusion in his household only by the appearance of Ermina on the balcony.

Gwyneth reappraised the maid in relation to Beresford and felt the force of Ermina's dislike for her down to her toes. She was unmoved, however, and asked the woman to fetch a broom and begin sweeping the mistress's chambers at once. When Ermina replied cheekily that there was no broom at hand, Gwyneth informed her that she had seen one in a room off the balcony, third door on the right. When Gwyneth again asked her to get it, Ermina turned to her master. Beresford gestured with his head that she should fetch the broom.

"Thank you so much for your time, my lord," Gwyneth said when she had gone. "Ermina will spend the rest of the day cleaning my chamber." She smiled, cool and confident. "And I will find her a position in another household before I move in."

"A position in another household?" Beresford repeated blankly. "Why?"

"What would you do with a knight-in-training who did not live up to your standards?"

Beresford looked around him, frowning, wondering whether the house had not become a little disheveled in the last year or two. He was honest enough to say, "I would have him turned off."

"Exactly," Gwyneth said. "Ermina is most unsuitable, in every way, and she shall not be here when I am mistress. Of course, until then, I have no cause or reason to interfere with your arrangements. For the next four days, she may stay here and do for you what she has always done," she added pointedly.

She asked Beresford to escort her to the door. Not many minutes later, she had left with her ladies and the two soldiers, leaving him to wonder, *How did she do that?* He could tell from the inflection in her voice and the expression on her face that she knew exactly what Ermina had always done for him. He was amazed, because just as the maid had conveyed to him the offer of her body, he had been able to see from his chamber that Gwyneth's back had been turned away from them and that she was bent over Roesia's linen chest. He considered the unsettling possibility that all women naturally knew these things. Then he remembered that Roesia had never seemed to know about his casual women and had not seemed to care. Or perhaps, he

suddenly realized, it was rather that he had not cared if
Roesia knew and did not know if she cared.

But Gwyneth ... It might well have been some feminine
notion of housekeeping standards that caused her to turn
Ermina away. And it might well have been coincidence, the
evening before, that had brought her with Fortescue to the
battlements at the very moment he had caught Lady Chester in his arms in full view of Adela. The way Rosalyn had
looked up at him at just that moment had given him pause,
and it would have put him at a disadvantage with Adela if
he had given in to the impulse to take advantage of what she
was so plainly offering him. When he had considered it later,
it had seemed, in fact, that Rosalyn *wished* to put him at a
disadvantage with Adela, if not also with Gwyneth.

He shook his head and decided that none of it was worth
thinking about. None of it. Not Rosalyn. Not Ermina. Not
Gwyneth. He was in his home, in command of his men, and
he knew what he had to do to release the energies shooting
through him.

He walked back on to the field where the men, in absence of their leader, had become slack in their exercises. In
any case, they had been rather more interested in witness-
ing the progress of the threesome on the balcony.

Beresford bent down easily and retrieved the sword he had
earlier relinquished. He slashed the air several times, flexed
his shoulders, then smiled at the circle of very dirty, sweaty
men.

"Any takers?"

Two young men were foolish enough to try their skill
against him and were fortunate to end the encounter still
able to stand, although their self-respect was severely
drubbed into the dust of the disreputable courtyard.

Chapter Seven

Over the next four days, Beresford spent a good deal more time at the Tower than he was used to spending or even cared to spend. He did not understand how a vital man in his prime could pass day after day within doors, or at least within castle walls, talking, eating, strolling, politicking. Certainly, there was tournament practice in the yard before the lieutenants' lodgings, but it lacked scrappiness, and he thought it pretty tame sport.

However, crossing swords with the castle guard was a good deal more entertaining than being cornered in the great hall by any number of court ladies whose names were a jumble in his brain. It reminded him of the period following Roesia's death, when it had seemed that every woman, known and unknown to him, had something to say to him or do for him. Of course, he was accepting congratulations now and not sympathy, but the unpleasant parallel between the two occasions—Roesia's funeral and his marriage to Gwyneth—struck him forcibly. Mostly, he found it all boring, except for those times when he was just plain aggravated by the teasing of many of his oldest friends, who had taken an unprecedented interest in his personal life.

He suspected that this interest stemmed principally from the particular attractions of his wife-to-be. He did not suspect that his own perceived distaste for the marriage had contributed to the interest in her, nor did he guess that testing the limits of his potential jealousy added piquancy to the pursuit. Whatever else he did or did not guess, he had determined not to let Geoffrey of Senlis out of his sight when Gwyneth was near.

As for Gwyneth, during those four days, he saw her on occasion in the course of his normal movements through the castle, but never privately; and he spoke to her not at all apart from public moments at mealtimes. He found these occasions most unsatisfactory. Since the announcement of their betrothal, they had had to continue to sit at the head table, which not only constrained their conversation, but made them targets for an endless stream of well-wishers and for all sorts of other courtly annoyances.

On the last evening before their wedding, as supper was coming to an end, he became aware that some fool minstrel was standing before him singing of an even more foolish man who languished with love for his lady. Beresford's impulse was to relieve the fool of his lute and crush that instrument of mawkish torture in his bare hands, but it occurred to him that such an efficient action might be deemed "unsubtle." He considered instead explaining kindly to the fool that the musical drivel was giving him a stomach cramp as he was trying to digest his meal, but decided that the minstrel was really so bad that he deserved no such explanation.

Beresford settled for the direct command to the fool to go away, accompanied by a gesture that dismissed him to the other end of the table.

This brought Gwyneth's head around, and he looked at her, expecting to be thanked. She did not thank him, but merely arched one brow, as if somehow amused. He guessed that, all in all, she was pleased he had sent the musical idiot away.

"He's gone," Beresford said, feeling self-satisfied.

"Yes, and it was very considerate of you," she replied, "to send the minstrel to the other end of the table. I believe that he was performing the king's favorite song."

She suppressed her desire to laugh out loud at the expression on Beresford's face as he assimilated this news. After a moment, he said, "Did you wish to hear the song, my lady?"

Gwyneth shook her head, smiling, for she was in a strangely equitable mood this evening. "I heard it once yesterday and once the day before, and I'm sure I'll have another opportunity at tomorrow evening's festivities."

At this mention of the morrow's celebrations, Beresford grunted. Then, suddenly, he rose from the bench and looked down at her. He said, "Come."

Gwyneth blinked at his abruptness and wondered, despite his plain words, what exactly he might mean. He had not once sought out her company or requested to see her alone at any time since first meeting her. "Leave the hall?" she asked cautiously.

He looked around. "It's crowded in here. I thought we might go outside." He stretched out his hand to help her up from the bench.

She laid her hand in his and asked, "Do you wish to take a turn on the battlements?"

He bit off a hard laugh that held a trace of self-mockery. "No, not the battlements," he answered, drawing her to her feet. "I'd rather go down to the yard."

"Ah, the pleasance, then," she said, standing. But he did not seem to have had the gardens on his mind. It would have amused her to learn just where he had intended taking her. The archery pit? The slaughterhouse? But she did not choose to put him on the spot.

His expression became bemused, then a little fixed. "Yes, to the pleasance," he said at last. He let go of her hand, gracelessly, as usual. He extended his wrist—grudgingly, she thought—to escort her out of the hall.

They stopped first at Stephen's chair, as was proper, to excuse themselves from the king's presence. Stephen bestowed on them an absent nod, after which they made their way through the hall, stopping frequently to respond to the variety of greetings directed their way. They encountered, among others, Johanna, Beresford's cousin, whose acquaintance Gwyneth had cultivated during the past days.

Johanna was, in part, responsible for Gwyneth's equitable mood this evening. After she had left Beresford at the door to his house four days earlier, her opinion of him had sunk so far into the ground that she had thought it likely to remain there forever, deeply buried. However, earlier this very afternoon, she had been startled to see Beresford across the hall bending down on one knee, listening attentively to a little girl who could not have been more than five years old. Everything about him had seemed graceful and courtly.

"That's little Cristina, a second cousin of mine," Johanna had said, "and of Simon's."

Gwyneth had erased whatever expression she had been wearing at the sight of Beresford so engaged. "Your family is large and extended, it seems," she had remarked conversationally, unable to take her eyes off the sight of Beresford kneeling before the girl.

"Yes," Johanna had said, "although very few of us are at court, as you know." She paused and added, "Cristina adores Simon, for she thinks him a source of indulgence for her every whim and passing thought."

"And is he?" Gwyneth had asked, glancing at Johanna, surprised and skeptical.

"Of course, else Cristina would not think of him in such terms."

Johanna had not belabored the point, leaving her intrigued by this very different glimpse of her future husband.

At length Gwyneth and Beresford made their way through the crowd and reached the arched passage by which they would exit. With a humorous turn of mind, Gwyneth imagined that Beresford, from the way he exhaled gustily when they arrived at the stairs, had had enough of the parting chitchat. He ushered Gwyneth in front of him so that she could precede him in the descent.

"You have not returned to my house this week," he said suddenly to her back.

Her right hand gripped the newel column of the winding stairs. The cool stone felt good against her palm. With her left hand, she lifted her skirts to her ankle. "No," she answered, keeping her eyes on the tricky stairs as she stepped down, "I have been able to conduct all my household business from the castle."

"I know."

At his tone, she permitted herself a smile, which he could not see. She had refused to return to Beresford's wreck of timber until she was officially mistress, and so had persuaded Adela to provide her with couriers so that she could work effectively from afar. She had not accomplished much beyond retrieving a few items from Beresford's house that needed her attention before the wedding. Her greatest administrative accomplishment was, of course, the arrangement of Ermina's new employment, which would begin on the morrow. Was the pretty slattern's removal from Beresford's convenient use the cause of his slightly aggrieved "I know"?

She said, without turning around, "I hope that my couriers did not trouble you too much in your household routine."

"They did not trouble me, in any event," he replied, "because I have spent much of my time at the Tower in the past few days, as you may have noticed."

She paused and said, "I have noticed."

"And I am to spend the night here tonight."

She made the mistake of stopping and turning around to look at him. It was a mistake because she was two steps below him and had to look up. She had always used her height to advantage with Canute, with whom she could speak on eye level, but since Beresford was taller by a head to begin with, she felt a double disadvantage at her position on the stairs. He had been about to take the next step down. The muscles of his thigh were flexed in definition below his tunic. The lower edge of the tunic grazed her breast when she turned toward him.

She felt an unexpected spark at this breath of contact. What was Beresford telling her? she wondered. That he was not going to make free with Ermina on the eve of their marriage? She looked into his eyes but did not find any answers in their cool, gray depths. Instead, she felt his strength as he stood above her on the stair and saw a man who could wield a sword with beauty, who could bend gracefully before a little girl and who could obviously satisfy a desiring woman. She felt herself blush, and turned around to continue her descent.

"That will save you much trouble in the morning," she commented, stepping down and away from him, "to be already here at the Tower."

"It will save me much trouble this evening as well."

"Indeed?" she replied. "How so?"

"If I am here, I may see to those items that require my attention," he answered offhandedly.

"Naturally," she said, then pressed, "Is it some piece of court business that requires your attention now?"

"In a manner of speaking."

Her ears pricked up, but before she could think of the most effective angle from which to respond to this provocative comment, he continued. "And the hall is too crowded for the kind of conversation I want."

She had arrived at the bottom step. Beresford was just behind her. "It is?" she asked.

"Yes."

"And what kind of conversation do you want?" she dared to ask when he drew even with her.

They walked through the shadowy passage and emerged into the soft twilight of the open yard. Beresford greeted the guards whose paths they crossed. He and Gwyneth began to angle around the White Tower and back to the Wardrobe Tower, behind which lay the gardens.

"A private one, above all," he replied.

He did not extend his wrist to her, and she guessed that he saw no further need of formality. She was in a mood to excuse him the lapse. She slanted him a glance. "A private one suitable for the pleasance?"

He shrugged. "Not unsuitable for the pleasance, I think."

She pressed further. "The court business that requires your attention this evening," she stated in summary, "concerns a private conversation with me that is not unsuitable for the pleasance."

His tone and his expression registered mild surprise. "Have I not just said so, ma'am?"

She lowered her eyes modestly and sketched a curtsy that was both ironic and coquettish. "I beg your pardon, sire. Lest you think me simple," she said, yielding to her mood and risking a reference to their very first meeting, "I had reckoned you to be the advocate of plain speaking, and I wished to match you on your own terms."

He cocked a heavy brow and warded off her delicate thrust with a heavy parry. "If you are willing to match me on my own terms, then I need not fear being unsubtle during our private conversation in the pleasance."

He stopped then, turned toward her and bowed as he would before an opponent. The spark in the air became a definite charge, as if flint had struck flames against silk. Gwyneth was caught off guard.

To regain her composure, she asked coolly, "Is there a particular topic that you wish to pursue unsubtly and in private?"

"Yes," he replied. "I wish to pursue a topic we broached at the supper table two nights ago with Fortescue."

At this tantalizing moment, they were interrupted by a threesome of castle hounds bounding up to them. The dogs dashed around Gwyneth and Beresford several times, barking high, earsplitting notes, and Gwyneth would have been afraid if Beresford had not known just what to do to bring the beasts to order. Once he asserted his authority, Beresford was apparently deemed worthy of receiving a branch that the leader of the pack seemed to want thrown for him. Beresford obligingly laid hold of one end and tried to pull it from the hound's ferocious jaws. Gwyneth knew a moment of fear when, instead of releasing the branch, the hound threw himself into a tug-of-war with the strong master, growling menacingly and wagging his tail furiously. The next moment, she perceived that Beresford was enjoying himself as much as the hound. Somehow he wrested the branch from between the flashing white teeth and entered into the game as heartily as did the hound.

While Beresford sparred with the bloodthirsty dog, Gwyneth had a moment to review the various topics discussed two evenings ago at the supper table with Walter Fortescue. She could think of no topic remotely interesting or needful of private discussion.

Since Beresford was so evidently a man of action and not words, she could not imagine why he would wish for a private conversation with her. The thought crossed her mind that he intended no conversation at all. She recalled that Fortescue had had a habit at supper of succumbing to prattle concerning the excellence of the match Adela had arranged. Was it two nights ago that he had pronounced Gwyneth and Beresford to be perfectly suited and insisted that they would enjoy a wonderful, loving relationship?

Her equitable mood was suddenly disturbed by a new emotion. Was Beresford's purpose in suggesting this private moment together to try a little lovemaking in the gardens? Did he mean to sample in advance something of the nature of the relationship Fortescue had predicted? She indulged her imagination by picturing a tender scene in the gardens, under a leafy arbor, surrounded by flowers, her hand in his. Then she remembered that he had made explicit his intention to be unsubtle, and imagined a more intriguing possibility—Beresford's arms coming around her, his head bending toward her....

She caught these wayward thoughts up short. This was not an intriguing scene, by Odin! It was, however, a reas-

suring one. She prodded her little fantasy to continue. She
realized that she needed reassurance concerning the greater
intimacies that he would be allowed on the morrow. She
even acknowledged wanting that reassurance now, this evening, while she felt slightly inclined toward him. Well, not
inclined exactly. Tolerant, perhaps. Curious, too, in a normal sort of way.

Beresford flung the stick wide, sending the hound
bounding off and yapping boisterously. He returned to her
side. She looked up at him and was startled by a new perception of him as a suitor. She was aware of a change in
him, an easiness, as if the vigorous exercise had worked off
the rough edges that were often so evident in the great hall.
Not that all his rough edges were gone, but those that were
left he wore well. They fit him, were a part of him, gave him
texture, made him interesting. She lowered her lashes.

"To the pleasance," he said over his shoulder.

At the sound of his voice, and her image of what might
happen in the gardens, her breath caught in her throat.
"Oh, yes," she gasped. She was surprised that she should
have such a reaction, since she was feeling so benignly disposed toward him this evening. She wondered whether she
still feared him. As they walked toward the bakery and
crossed under the pigeon loft, she attempted a painful
breath but did not quite succeed.

She knew that her only course now was to confront the
possible cause of her fear. "And the topic, sire," she managed, rasping a little with the effort to speak, "that you
wished to pursue? The one that was broached two evenings
ago with Sir Walter?"

He nodded. "It concerned the position of Henry's forces
after his defeat against Malmesbury."

Completely diverted, she was able to take a full breath of
air, but her throat still felt tight. She attempted to retrieve
the threads of that conversation. "You and Sir Walter were
discussing how Duke Henry's forces had taken the town by
assault but had failed to storm the castle."

"That's right," Beresford agreed, "and we mentioned how Henry's cause was further compromised when Stephen's forces came to Malmesbury's aid."

"In which action you and your men took part, I believe," Gwyneth commented. "Then, after that, you and Sir Walter spoke of those earls once loyal to Stephen who were transferring their allegiance to Duke Henry or, at least, refusing to fight him more recently at Cirencester."

"Yes, the traitors Cornwall and Hereford, to be precise." Beresford looked pointedly at her.

Gwyneth noted his look and was puzzled. She had not commented on Cornwall or Hereford or Duke Henry, for that matter. She said, "As I recall, I did not take much part in that conversation."

They had passed the beehives and fruit bins and were in front of the gardening sheds. Gwyneth was a half step ahead of Beresford, and at the garden's portal she halted. Beresford's left hand went around one side of her to unhook the latch, and his right hand went around the other to push back the iron grille. For a brief second, she was within the circle of his arms.

He said, "And your lack of participation in that conversation is the very topic I wish to discuss."

She blinked up at him. "It is?" she said, not understanding his drift. "You mean I should have had some opinion of the military strategy involved in that campaign?"

"No, I mean that I wish to know where your loyalties stand with regard to the rightful King Stephen and the usurper, Henry of Anjou."

She looked away. The spurt of anger that coursed through her quickly cleared the constriction in her throat. She drew a deep and easy breath and rapidly adjusted to the absurd and unexpected topic. The gate had swung open, and she stepped into the garden, which was fragrant with the herbs that had seasoned their supper: mustard and parsley and cumin, fennel and coriander and anise.

"My loyalties, sire?" she replied lightly, turning down the first path that presented itself. Beresford was behind her. "You know that my late husband was one of Henry's supporters."

"But he is dead and you are not—" Beresford began.

"Ah, yes! You promised to avoid subtlety!"

"—And I am more interested in your loyalties," he continued, "than Canute's."

"But you should know the whole of my background. My father was for the empress," she informed him testily, "who was, as we both know, the Conqueror's granddaughter, the first Henry's daughter and Duke Henry's mother. If there was a usurper to the throne, it was Stephen twenty years ago."

"This point of contention, of course, is what the squabbling is about," Beresford said placidly.

Gwyneth did not understand his calm. She was further confused by what she thought was a gleam of humor in his eyes. "Some call it a civil war," she said with haughty dignity.

"So you consider yourself a supporter of the young Henry," he said, "despite Stephen's legitimate claim on the throne these past twenty years."

She found it strange to be forced into a declaration, for as a powerless Saxon woman in Norman England, she had considered political loyalty to be little more than an expedient of survival. However, if Beresford wished to discuss political principles, she was happy to oblige.

"Because Duke Henry is the lawful heir to the kingdom, I could hardly consider myself anything else!" she replied. In some pique, she added, "And I can hardly imagine any discussion less pertinent on the eve of our marriage!"

At that, he put one hand on her shoulder and turned her toward him. With his other hand, he caught the tips of her fingers and weighed them in his palm. His tone and his words were as blunt as the hilt of a sword. "Since we will soon be sharing a bed, I'd like to know with whom I have to deal."

Gwyneth felt a thrill of shock down to her toes and surged with a delicious desire to wring his neck. On second thought, she decided she would prefer to draw blood. "You might consider checking me every night for knives," she said through her teeth.

"I will," he replied, "so that I may sleep without an itch between my shoulder blades."

She nearly strangled, this time not in fear but in fury. She was aware of the pungent, bracing combination of herbal scents that surrounded her, of the rough edges of the bristly man who held her. She was aware of his hold on her, which, she was determined, would not arouse her by its very lack of seductive intent.

A truly masterful retort sprang to mind, and she opened her mouth to speak. However, she was never to utter her sublime opinion of his crudeness, which he would have been too oafish to appreciate anyway, because they were interrupted by none other than Geoffrey of Senlis.

"There you are, Simon," Senlis said, coming upon them where they had stopped, abruptly, in the middle of a pathway. He bowed politely. "And Gwyneth." He must have perceived some tension in the air or in the way they were facing one another, for he ventured, "But perhaps I come at a bad time?"

"Not at all," Beresford said, dropping Gwyneth's hand and moving a step away from her.

Gwyneth murmured, "Sire Senlis," and left it at that.

With a brow inquisitively arched, Senlis looked from one to the other but wisely did not comment. He said merely what he had come to say. "I've been looking for you for some time. The king has asked for you, Simon, and you are to report to him anon."

"Indeed, Geoffrey?" Beresford replied with heavy irony. "The king wishes to speak to me? At this very moment?" He looked from Senlis to Gwyneth and made no movement to leave the gardens. Instead, he folded his arms across his chest, in rude rejection of his friend's message.

Gwyneth was angry with Beresford all over again. Although he did not want her, he did not want any other man to be with her—and he was embarrassingly obvious about it. How she would have preferred to stroll in the gardens with the handsome Geoffrey of Senlis!

Senlis must have similarly understood the implications of Beresford's reaction, for he bent his head toward his friend's ear. "I am to accompany you to the hall, Simon," he said in a placating voice. "Gwyneth may stay here, unattended, if she likes, until you are free to return to her side."

Beresford's brow cleared, and he nodded. Then he turned on his heels, and without another word, left the gardens with Senlis.

Gwyneth glared at his back, fuming over his manners, his treatment of her and his unsubtle, blunt ways. When she attempted to cool her anger, she discovered that she had no real desire to be calm but rather wished to give her anger room to roam. So Beresford had not envisioned an episode of lovemaking in the gardens, but had wanted to discuss her political loyalties! She should have guessed his intention was to insult her rather than to woo her! She should have guessed he would be looking out for his own safety in bed rather than her pleasure!

Without being aware of it, she had wandered down a path that took her from the neat rows of herbs to the flowers. She did not know how long she had been alone, but it was enough time for the rankling to have smoothed out and for some of her earlier equitable mood to have resurfaced. Yes, she thought, more reasonably now, she should have guessed that Beresford would behave true to form, for the gardens, the hall and his home were all one to him: a field of combat. Staring down at the fragile bud of a rose ready to bloom, she realized that it had been a mistake to allow her pique to be so evident. Not that Beresford was discerning enough to have noticed!

She was calm now, calm enough to handle his eventual return—that is, if he had the courtesy to return to her. When she heard the fall of a foot behind her, she smiled inwardly.

She was doubly glad that she had composed herself when she turned around and saw who was there, bowing before her.

"Cedric of Valmey," she stated in greeting.

Chapter Eight

She did not like Cedric of Valmey, but made every effort to keep the dislike out of her voice. She felt a trace of apprehension at being alone with him in the gardens. The situation did not occasion fear, but she knew that she would have to tread very, very carefully.

Valmey straightened, took hold of one of her hands and grazed the backs of her fingers with his lips. She resisted the impulse to snatch her hand away and allowed it to rest in his light grip, which lasted a moment longer than was seemly. He gazed at her with liquid brown eyes in whose depth flickered tiny flames that promised more.

"Gwyneth of Northumbria," he replied languidly.

"Soon to be of Beresford," she reminded him.

"Oh, yes," he said. "On the morrow, in fact." He was hardly put off by her reminder. Instead, he extended his arm in silent invitation that they stroll together.

Gwyneth thought it more dangerous to refuse than to accept. She placed her fingers on his wrist, making sure she touched only the cloth of his sleeve. They were surrounded by the fresh, leafy scent of tight, unbloomed roses and the springtime promise of peonies, lilies, lavender and marigolds. With a wrinkle of irony, she was aware that here was her opportunity for lovemaking, if she so desired it. Her immediate objective, of course, was to find a way to avoid such a scene, without offending Sir Cedric.

She decided to take the offensive. "The preparations for tomorrow's wedding have been going forward at such a pace these past few days, sire, that I welcome this moment of evening repose." She glanced up at him guilelessly. "A moment when no demands are made of me."

He nodded and said merely, "I am happy to accompany you in this moment of repose."

"How kind of you," she said. "Until a few moments ago, it was Beresford's task to accompany me." She did not think she was overdoing it to look up at him and to flutter her eyelashes. "Did you know that he was just called from my side?"

At his hesitation, Gwyneth wondered whether he had engineered the request from the king for Beresford and Senlis to return to the hall. Valmey effectively hedged with the statement, "But he is not here now."

They passed currant and raspberry bushes dotted with hard, green berries. Gwyneth stretched out her free hand to graze their springy tops. "No, he is not here now," she agreed simply, "but he is due to return at any moment."

Valmey became bold. "Is that what you wish, my lady?"

Gwyneth remained modest. "Of course, a good wife wishes for her husband."

"And you are a good wife?"

"I mean to be."

Valmey switched tactics and played into her statement, rather than against it. "You must be well pleased to be marrying a man of such riches and renown."

"I am."

"One so accomplished on the battlefield."

"It is a comfort."

"One so constant."

"Above all."

"And so compassionate."

"A true knight," she said. "I do not ask for more."

Valmey paused. When he spoke again, his voice teased her on the edge of flirtation. "I confess, my lady, to an envy of Simon of Beresford."

"You have confessed that once to me already, Sir Cedric."

He paused again and his brows rose, not in inquiry but in slightly exaggerated surprise. Then he smiled. He shook his head. "No, my lady," he contradicted, "on the previous occasion, I merely registered a complaint that Simon of Beresford had received two remarkable honors in one day."

She felt the check. Valmey was not, apparently, a man who repeated himself. "Now you come to confess to me your envy. Is it because of Beresford's elevation to the earldom?" she asked. She had not forgotten the possibility of Valmey's jealousy.

The baron's smile was intimate, even secretive. "I've riches and titles enough, so I do not begrudge Beresford his earldom, my lady."

She had not been fishing for compliments. She did not want one now. She turned to face him. Her expression was direct. "It is good for you to recognize the sin of envy—whatever the reason—so that you may confess it and exorcise it from your immortal soul."

She saw Valmey's seductive brown eyes narrow slightly, but he recovered nicely. "I thank you, my lady, for considering the heavenly fate of my immortal soul."

"You are most welcome."

Valmey smiled graciously. He knew when to retreat.

They had come upon the tiny orchard. Songbirds fluttered from pear to apple to medlar tree. Arching between the higher branches of two leafy trunks, grapevines had met and married, creating a filigreed canopy that shaded a pretty stone bench beneath.

"I cannot help but wonder," he said, coming to a stop under the arbor, "whether, among all the qualities we have just enumerated for Simon of Beresford, a knowledge of the gentler arts is included."

Gwyneth was turned so that the backs of her knees were against the stone bench. She did not immediately respond and, in fact, knew not what to say that would be neither transparently false nor patently silly.

Valmey pressed his advantage. "I wonder whether he can turn a phrase—" here he picked up her hand and turned it, tender palm up, in his "—as easily as he can turn his sword against an opponent."

Gwyneth had no doubt about Valmey's present intentions, although she was not sure of his overall purpose. Did he wish to enthrall her or embarrass her? Did he wish to seduce her or merely arouse her desire for him? Was he motivated by an amour propre that would not allow any woman to escape his spell, or was this little scene intended to do some kind of damage to Beresford? And what was his relationship to Rosalyn, Lady Chester? Was he in love with her, or was it simply connivance between them?

She strained away from him, a little awkwardly, for her knees threatened to buckle against the bench. She turned her head and softened her gesture with diffidence. These tactics gave her just enough time to formulate the perfect reply that would keep Valmey guessing and at a distance.

"Sir Cedric . . ." she began in a tone mixing modesty and mild reprimand.

Beresford had listened to the king's request with puzzlement. He was being sent to the Bowyer Tower in the outer ward, on the opposite end of the grounds from the queen's gardens. He was to discuss with the castle bowmaker the various weapons that would be needed for the Saint Barnabas Day tournament. Because he was not in the habit of questioning the usual royal commands—only the unusual ones that concerned, for example, his marital status—he did not say that he had spent a good deal of time lately with Master Bowman discussing precisely that. Causing Beresford further puzzlement was the king's request that Senlis go to the Flint Tower, the most dank and noisome dungeon in the entire fortress, for some equally frivolous errand.

It was not until Beresford had left the White Tower for the second time in an hour, crossed before the lieutenant's lodgings and greeted his cronies that the wiliness of the scheme dawned on him. Senlis, you clever dog! was his immediate thought. You must think your old friend Simon is stupid!

He reversed his steps and headed back toward the pleasance, fully expecting to find that Senlis had stolen the march on him. He was not about to be outfoxed by Geoffrey at this stage of the game. Oh, no! Not when he had arrived at so interesting a point with Gwyneth!

For it had been interesting, that moment when he had understood that the light, tight tone in her voice and the pink flushing her cheeks bespoke anger. Yes, she had been angry at him, angry enough to threaten him—verbally!— with knives. In the context of their bed, too. He had really enjoyed that. It had made him want to take Gwyneth and leave the bland confines of the gardens to find some wilder place to explore the possibilities of his enjoyment. The riverbank, perhaps, just beyond the Iron Gate and below the pile of stones that made the outer wall. He knew a place, deep in a tangle of bramble bushes rampant with wild honeysuckle, where earth slipped down to slick stones. It was an inspiring thought: rock above, rock below, thorny green branches trailing above, female flesh around him and indulging in his most favorite and inventive position. It was an inspiring thought, especially imagining himself surrounded by the flesh of a woman who had threatened him with knives.

As for that threat, he could not have said for a certainty, but he was almost sure that she did not care about politics. Of course, she was a supporter of the Angevin duke. As she herself had said, how could she be anything other? But she had not taken a real interest, a *man's* interest in the issue.

That was it—she had acted like a woman. Huffy, sort of. Cattish. He had found her behavior rather amusing.

And most reassuring. He had not intended to pursue the subject of politics when he had invited her to leave the hall after supper. He had not intended anything in particular, in fact, until they had been making their way through the throng of extremely tiresome well-wishers. One moment he had been looking down at Gwyneth, seeing her smiling at his cousin. The next moment he had looked up unwarily and seen, just at the limit of his vision. There it was again; the ridiculous image of the plump baby boy with wings that had hovered before his eyes several evenings before, when he had been on the lookout for a Valkyrie.

He did not understand it at all, for he was never given to fanciful imaginings. It was a most harmless image, the most harmless imaginable! And yet he had felt threatened and somehow a target of it, as if the baby boy were carrying a bow and arrow. He had felt unwontedly weak, and he had been shaken by the notion that he might, for the first time in his life, succumb to the ague. Then he decided, more plausibly, that a Valkyrie had disguised herself and was warning him about something—he figured, given his reputation, that the female warriors would be disposed to treating him specially. He had no idea what that warning might be, but it occurred to him that a reasonable man would make sure that he was not marrying an agent of death.

Well, he was not going to worry about an open threat with knives. Not from Gwyneth, at any rate. He was a man who knew what and what not to fear.

On the other hand, and more to the immediate point, the passage in the garden had made Gwyneth seem less fragile, more physical. Less ethereal. More of flesh and blood. More of the riverbank.

He arrived back at the gardens and found his way through the herbs and flowers to the orchard. Through some branches, he saw Gwyneth's skirt. He approached just as she leaned away, her head held to one side. He saw Senlis

from the back, bowing low over her hand, so that his head
was blocked from Beresford's vision.

Too many impressions came to him at once for him to be
able to sort them out completely. He saw that the expression on Gwyneth's face and the lines of her body suggested
maidenly modesty, but he was aware that on some other
level she was displeased. He heard her say, "Sir Cedric,"
with an inflection that warned of trouble, but that interesting perception of her tone was obscured when the name itself registered in his brain, causing him to frown. At the
same time, Gwyneth glanced up, apparently hearing his approach. He thought she looked rather relieved to see him,
but his thoughts were still preoccupied. He had been expecting Senlis. Could the man instead be Valmey?

He asked aloud, his surprise evident, "Valmey?"

The man's head came up and around, and Beresford was
indeed looking into a pair of dark eyes that did not belong
to Geoffrey of Senlis.

"Simon," Valmey soothed. He released Gwyneth's hand,
but none too quickly. "You have returned, as your bride
predicted."

Of course he had returned, but he did not bother to state
the obvious. Instead, he simply jerked his head to the side,
indicating that Valmey should leave.

An infinitesimal pause was all it took for Valmey to bow
his head in acquiescence and to excuse himself in soft,
flowing words. Upon departing, he cast a meaningful,
sideways glance at Gwyneth.

After a moment of charged silence, Beresford observed,
"It seems I arrived just in time."

It took all of Gwyneth's self-control not to say tartly,
"Did you think you were saving me from Geoffrey of Senlis, perhaps? Or do you not know by name the rats who in-
habit the Tower?" Instead she said, as calmly as she could,
"I must suppose you did, sire. However, I thought to have
the situation well in hand."

"Ah!" was all Beresford said.

Did she detect a smirk on his face? Did he think her so defenseless? Was he indeed so devoid of jealousy? For all he knew, Valmey *could* be a rival. Well, she was not going to stand idle under a perfectly charming arbor in the soft evening twilight laced with the cooing sounds of nesting birds. Oh, no. She was not going to wait for Beresford to whisper sweet nothings into her ear and make tender advances! He was as likely to insult her with more inappropriate questions.

"Shall we . . . ?" she said coolly, making obvious her desire to leave the pretty spot.

"Any suggestions about where to go?" he asked.

She looked at him. His brows were raised, his gray eyes were lit and he was smiling, a little lopsidedly. She felt perversely angry at his lighthearted calm—or was it rather lighthearted expectation? No matter, for she was blind to the fact that he had—finally—propositioned her. She replied, with a studied lack of emotion, "To the hall, if you please. I do not wish to remain in the gardens."

The seal was set on her irritation when Beresford shrugged and said, "Fine with me. I didn't want to come here in the first place."

"Your hair, my dear! It is finally dry, but your braid has escaped its pins again! How will we ever set the circlet straight so that it stays in place?"

"Don't move. Now, don't. Ah, see now! You've upset my stitch on your hem. I'll have to begin again. Don't move. Don't move, I say!"

"Your other slipper! Now where can the little squirrel have gone? Did it scamper off?"

"If you don't lift your arms, I cannot tie your bliaut. The gold becomes you, I think, but I am not partial to the red kirtle. Ah, well. You are a beautiful bride, by anyone's measure!"

"Sir Simon will swoon!"

"Before or after he comes to his point of points?"

"From what I hear of him, he will not swoon before! He's a man who sees his duties through!"

"Stop laughing, you silly ducks! The hem again, my dear! There, now. You are standing still for once! 'Tis a pity you did not work as diligently these past few days on your own gown as you did on Beresford's tunic!"

All the fussing produced the paradoxical result of calming Gwyneth's nerves. The pinching, the poking, the hemming, the braiding contrived to impress upon her the reality of the event. To be sure, being sold to some man not of her choosing was reality enough for her. What was not real was her purely feminine pique of the evening before. Upon rising this morning, she had decided that it must have been something she ate. She had no reason to fear Beresford. Or, at least, she had no reason to believe that she would not be able to face down her fear of him, just as she had always faced down her fear of Canute.

Then she saw him. By the time her dressing was completed, the sun had climbed high enough in the sky for the bride's party to descend from Adela's solar. They were to meet the groom's party in the yard before the White Tower, so that everyone could proceed together to the Chapel of Saint Peter.

She hardly recognized him at first, so noble did he look and worthy of his rank. His curls were tamed, and his hair was neatly cut to just above his shoulders. Shapely now, his locks no longer fought with his irregular features but framed them, emphasizing their strength, the cut of his jaw and the thick column of his neck. He was neatly, even resplendently dressed in a tunic the deep blue of the summer sky, emblazoned with the Beresford shield, a per chevron field of argent and azure surmounted by a castle with two towers in sable. What drew Gwyneth's eyes was the cut of his shoulders from which the tunic fell, side slit to the waist, where it was caught by a wide leather belt, from which hung his sword.

She looked away quickly, not wishing to spoil her calm mood with any unsettling thoughts.

It was just as well. If she had seen his expression when his eyes fell on her, she might have felt a good deal less calm, for he gave her a brief but unmistakable look of desire and displeasure.

In truth, Beresford was in no good mood. He did not like all the fuss and he could not remember any of it from his wedding to Roesia, thirteen years before. He had disliked having the barber attend to him during his bath this morning, hated for someone else to shave him and did not think he needed his hair cut so urgently. Of course, he could hardly refuse the barber's services, once he was there. He spared himself the indignity of having the man open his mouth to check for rotten teeth by informing him, none too politely, that his teeth were all there and in good condition. It was just as well that Beresford did not know it was Gwyneth who had ordered the barber to his chamber.

He guessed, however, that she had attended to his tunic, for he knew that she had sent castle couriers to his house to retrieve a trunk of his old clothing. When the tunic had been presented to him at his bath this morning, he recognized it as one he had put away years ago, it being too ceremonial for his taste. Once having donned it this morning, he decided he liked the feel and weight of the fabric and thought it perfect now for daily exercise. He was amazed at the excellence of its condition. He suspected that Gwyneth had refurbished it a little, but completely underestimated its original state of disrepair. His chausses and shoes, however, being new, were not at all comfortable, and his demand for his old ones had yielded nothing but baffled looks from his attendants. Nor could they tell him where these new items had come from.

He had had more pairs of hands touching him this morning than in any battle he had ever fought, and as if that was not enough, there was still the wedding to endure. Even as a mere spectator, he was bored unbearably by these tedious ceremonies. As one of the main participants, he was bound to be irritated, as well.

Then he saw her. Each time that he saw her was like seeing her for the first time. Each time was associated with a strange and wonderful pain. Seeing her this morning in the yard before the White Tower, he could not have said whether her dress was blue or red or green or a jester's motley. He knew only that she was the most beautiful woman he had ever seen. The pain was there this time, too, and it was physical. His eyes hurt from the way she seemed to shimmer in the sunshine.

The men came forward to meet the women. Gwyneth's hand was placed in Beresford's. She glanced up at him cautiously, and was satisfied that, for once, he did not discredit her. He looked down at her and tried to shake off his uncertainty about the nature of possession, for she was soon to belong to him, though not in the way that his sword or his horse belonged to him. He had a vague, unsettling sense that she would belong to him more in the remote and mysterious way that the stars belonged to the sky. He felt at a loss that he would never truly possess her.

The wedding party moved through the inner ward, which was alive with ordinary activity, this day being a usual workday. Pitched among the wooden structures of the ward were tents and awnings, gaily painted and surrounded by the numerous servants of the court, the piemakers, fishmongers and others from the city who had come in the hope of obtaining an order for their wares. These tradespeople spared a glance and then a second glance for the beautiful bride; they called out proper encouragement for the groom. The wedding party passed not far from the kitchens, which were busy with the wedding-feast preparations. The yard outside was gamey with poultry and pigs still awaiting the attention of the butcher and the cook.

The party arrived at the chapel, solid and square towered, and halted before the doors set under the heavy stone porch. Performed there was the most important part of the marriage service. For all to hear and see, Beresford named the dower he bestowed on Gwyneth and presented her with a ring and a gift of silver coins, his pledge to her, his *wedd*. She accepted these and stated what she would give him in return, and after the exchange of vows, the party moved inside for the celebration of the nuptial mass.

The moment he entered the cool interior of the chapel, Beresford suddenly felt the weight of the stones and the tradition and the ceremony press down on him and fasten around him like bonds. He would have vastly preferred to have been outside in the sunshine or even in the rain, if it came to that. In the fresh air, in any case, where a man could breathe.

He led Gwyneth to the altar, past the tombs with their recumbent effigies, past the statues of Saint Etheldreda and the Virgin Queen, past the stone fonts. They stopped before the altar, where stood the earthly interpreter of the Heavenly Father. The light of stained glass was behind him, falling forward. Beresford felt the bonds tighten, as if his shield was cinched too tightly across his chest and shoulder. He took a deep breath and worked his shoulder muscles, but could not loosen the strap that was constraining him.

The stained glass lent the woman at his side an aura of mystery. It divided her into cold, brightly colored fires. One cheek moved in and out of a pool of grape violet as she stood and kneeled, then stood again. Her brow flowered green and gold. Rose red stained her pale neck and chin and mouth. Berry red stained her kirtle, deepening its crimson. Eyelids were purple shadowed. The gold of her bliaut glittered with turreted purple ridges. Dust danced in a shadowy halo around her shining head, like black motes in gold. He felt himself yearning, but he did not know for what.

The ceremony continued, wafers, wine, and words spoken. She turned her head through the rainbow. She lifted her lips, rose red, now berry red, to accept his kiss.

When he put his lips to hers, the alien sensations fled. He touched not cold, colored glass, but warm flesh. The strap that had been constraining him fell away, like old twine yielding to light pressure. He knew exactly the way he would possess her.

Chapter Nine

The kiss would ultimately unknit the fabric of Gwyneth's calm, but so slowly that she was hardly aware of it until it was too late in the day to make whole again her self-possession.

When he gave her the kiss she had wanted the evening before, but with none of a lover's reassurance, she was still too absorbed in performing her part of the public ritual to notice its effect on her. When their lips parted, they knelt for the last time, bowed their heads and had a cloth stretched over them, thereby ending the ceremony.

They rose together and left the chapel, the wedding party in their wake. Outside in the yard they accepted congratulations for a good length of time, during which it seemed to Gwyneth that Beresford was abrupt to the point of rudeness to one and all. If anything, his customary lack of sociability bolstered her calm rather than unsettled it, for it kept her properly primed and on her toes to the point that she was unaware of any other effect he was having on her.

Nor did she notice any change in her temper or her feelings toward him once they returned to the great hall, where fresh rushes had been strewn and garlands hung for the occasion. The atmosphere in the hall was clearly marked by festivity. The pages were falling over one another in their busyness, the tumblers and acrobats were warming up in the corners, the minstrels were already strolling, the tables were spread with food and groaning under the quantity of dishes and the air was thick and sweet with the scents of savory fare. They took their places on the raised dais.

When she made a conversational remark to him about the decorations, she received a blank look. Then he shrugged and said something to the effect that it was not so bad being in the hall on a bright day such as this with the sun streaming in through the unshuttered windows. He went on to imply, though, that regardless of the weather, he vastly preferred to be out-of-doors. Since he made no effort to hide his dislike for the hall, even on this, his wedding day, she tallied his comment as his first insult of their wedded life. Because they had been married nearly an hour, she wondered, with perversely satisfying irony, what had taken him so long.

Nor did she notice any change in him once the feasting had begun. She had already determined that Beresford liked his food plain, and feast or no, today was no exception. She noted that he partook liberally of the roasted haunch of oxen and the boar's head in aspic and the venison in broth. However, he shunned the more delicately prepared swans, capons and peacocks, as well as the fowl that had been plucked, farced and replumed for display; and he regarded as apparently inedible the doves and larks in pastry shells latticed with braided dough and glazed. His taste for sweets was similarly austere. He passed over the frumenty, marzipan, compotes, honey pastries, candied almonds, jellies and custards, but indulged heartily in the season's first strawberries, without the cream. The amount of wine he consumed was moderate.

During the feast, no occasion for private talk between them presented itself—nor would she have expected it or even sought it. Woven throughout the various toasts, the conversation ran merrily at the head table, which was crowded at all times with a changing array of people, and where many topics and jests were kept aloft, like so many jugglers' balls.

At last the crowds around the head table thinned, the quantities of food diminished and a lull came over the hall. Gwyneth was speaking quietly with Felicia Warenne. At Felicia's significant nod, Gwyneth turned to Beresford. He was conversing idly with Lancaster, the ladies' man who had taken to hanging about the bridal couple, and with Roger Warenne.

The minstrels strummed the opening phrases of a chaconne. Several times. Gwyneth waited patiently, and then was miffed when she realized that Beresford, the dolt, was oblivious to the groom's duty. It was left to Adela to rise from her chair and, before the eyes of everyone in the hall, to drop a whispered word into Beresford's ear.

At this prompting from Adela, Beresford got up and extended his hand to Gwyneth, who accepted it. The expression on his face when he looked down at her told her everything she needed to know about her husband's opinion of dancing with his wife.

As they walked out to the center of the hall, Gwyneth said to him, very sweetly, "You may not wish to dance, my lord, but others who do enjoy it cannot begin until we have opened the activity. So please console yourself with the knowledge that you are performing a public service."

Beresford's response to this wifely reprimand was a noncommittal grunt. His dancing confirmed that his particular grace was better suited to the battlefield. When the dance was over, he would not be persuaded into another, no matter which lady encouraged him. On the other hand, he did not object to any man who applied for the bride's hand in a dance. The line for that honor was indeed long. At the head of it stood Lancaster.

Much later, she was to realize that the seeming normalcy of Beresford's behavior toward her since the wedding kiss had dulled her to the subtle signs of change that had been in the air between them now that they were man and wife. At the opening of the dance, when he had turned toward her and they had joined hands, she had felt strong and sure of herself and thought she knew how she would handle him. It was a moment of arrogance and miscalculation, for something inside her had already tilted and her calm had begun to unravel, like thread off a carelessly held spindle. She resisted her attraction to him because she was more comfortable in her anger over his lack of desire to dance with her. Just as she had resisted the effect of his kiss in the chapel, attributing its fearful beauty to the slanting rays of crimson, cobalt and canary that had fallen on him from the stained-glass windows, when his lips had touched hers briefly, but with demand.

During her second dance with Lancaster, she looked around the hall and chanced to see her husband off in a corner, speaking with the three weird women. No, not speaking with them precisely, she realized as she swiveled her head to keep him in view when the dance took him out of her line of vision. Was it possible that he was dancing with them? No, he was not dancing with them, either, she could see, turning her head again. But what were they doing?

Gwyneth saw that the three weird women were dressed in pink and mauve and purple, and they had joined hands to make a circle. In the center of the circle stood Beresford. Instead of appearing awkward or bufuddled by the circumstance, he looked perfectly natural there, straight and tall and grounded. Rooted, almost. From the glimpses she could snatch—she did not wish to make her interest in her husband crassly obvious—she put together the oddest picture of the three women closing the circle around him and then expanding it, as a flower unfurling or a pupil dilating to embrace the dark. Once. Twice. Now three times.

Then her own group of dancers drew into a circle, and she had to face into its center, away from Beresford. The next time she looked for him, he was no longer in the corner with the three women. She glanced this way and that, under her lashes, looking for him and feeling a little shameful for doing so. She felt even worse when she spied him at the moment when Rosalyn caught his attention and stopped him.

She watched as Beresford responded to the snow-skinned beauty with characteristic brusqueness. She watched as Rosalyn returned some comment with a provocative arch to her eyebrow and a very pretty smile. She watched as he nodded in response, wearing a half smile, and walked on, his parting comment apparently causing Rosalyn's chill beauty to warm several shades.

Gwyneth was beginning to perceive some new dimension to Beresford. Perhaps it was the look on his face when he had spoken to Lady Chester or the way he had inclined his head toward her, but suddenly Gwyneth became aware that though he might be brusque, he was also deft. It looked as if he had disarmed Rosalyn and slipped under her guard, all without too much trouble. Then he casually presented his back to her, the victor's prerogative.

"I am so glad you agree with me, my lady," said the voice at Gwyneth's side.

Calm and confidence! she admonished herself before turning, with a placid smile to see Geoffrey of Senlis. She did not know how long he had been there or how long he had been speaking to her. Nor did she know to what she had just agreed, and she hoped it had not been either idiotic or improper.

"And why should I not?" Gwyneth replied, thinking this answer safe enough.

When Senlis made some response, Gwyneth answered again at random, for despite her best efforts to concentrate on the man at her side, her thoughts remained on the little scene she had just witnessed. She was wishing dearly that she could see Rosalyn's face right now in the wake of Beresford's snub.

Senlis said something else. Gwyneth responded automatically, all the while seriously wondering whether trimmed hair, a decent shave and a clean tunic could really do so much to alter a man.

"You think not?" Senlis asked, with an inflection of surprise.

Gwyneth realized that she had spoken amiss. She tried to recall the statement to which she had just responded, but failed. "Well, I mean, of course, that I rather think so!" she said, striving for a touch of carelessness as she reversed herself.

"I understand your confusion," Senlis said humorously, with a nod toward the head table, "and freely admit that your husband's glowering expression when he looks at us does not necessarily betoken anger any more readily than it does amusement."

The words *your husband* caught her attention, and she was able to focus now fully on Senlis. Because she found herself as Geoffrey of Senlis's partner in a courtly couples dance, she quickly pieced together the idea that their conversation must have turned on the question of whether Beresford would object to Senlis's dancing with her. She had no real idea whether he would object, but she was determined *not* to look over at the table where he was apparently seated and again looking at them.

She recalled dancing with the handsome and most graceful Geoffrey of Senlis earlier, and tried to remember whether this was the second or, perhaps, even third time that she had stood up with him this afternoon. It occurred to her that if this were the third time, Beresford might have true cause to object. She had already decided not to dance a third time with Lancaster, for fear of breaching propriety. Perhaps the question of a third dance had been Senlis's concern when she had not rightly been attending to him.

The little pang she felt at the thought was not guilt, but defiance. If Beresford would not dance with her at their wedding, he would have to watch her dancing with other men. Unfortunately, and somewhat inexplicably, she was not enjoying the dance as much as she would have liked, although Geoffrey of Senlis was a charming partner and kept the conversation light and amusing.

When the last wistful note of the lute dissipated in the air, Senlis escorted her to the side of the floor. She was surprised to find Beresford there on hand, ready to take her arm in his. He thanked Senlis curtly for having taken such good care of his wife. Then he drew her away without further discussion or explanation.

Gwyneth realized now that the strange and colorful threads of her emotions had fallen off their spindle and were all confused. She did not know whether to be angry or merely vexed by Beresford's peremptory behavior. Or even, oddly, flattered.

"How do you know that I do not wish to dance again?" she asked her husband.

His gray eyes met hers. "I don't."

"Am I to infer that you do not care whether I wish to dance again?" she asked.

"You are," he said bluntly, but caused her to lose a bit of her anger when he added, "Sit with me."

It was stated as a command, but Gwyneth, slanting him a speculative glance, was just able to hear it as an invitation. She acknowledged privately that she no longer cared to dance and so could allow herself to accede to his wish because of her own tiredness rather than his uncivil request, if request it was.

"All right, then," she said. When she heard the grudging acceptance of her own words, she amended, "I will be pleased to sit with you, my lord."

He confined himself to a nod in response. However, the equally speculative glance he returned to her suggested that if he were a different kind of man, he might have said something flirtatiously ironic.

Gwyneth was fully aware of the change in Beresford, a change similar to the satisfied easiness she had noticed in him the evening before, after the vigorous game of fetch with a castle hound. This evening he had much the same easiness, as if he had just engaged in some satisfying sport. However, to her he had the look of a man who was not yet fully satisfied, one who was still ready for more. The effect struck her now as dangerous. In the split second their eyes met, she thought he looked as dangerous as an unsheathed sword, one that had lately sunk itself deep into human flesh. One that had been wiped clean of blood and that gleamed dully in the satiny afterglow of a whetting by human viscera.

"We'll go back to the head table," he directed, as he began to lead her around the edge of the dancers toward their places.

She cleared her head of its violent fancy. "Yes, of course," she said, drawing a quick breath. "Conversation would be very welcome right now." His inarticulate response did not encourage her to suppose that he intended entertaining her with dazzling conversation. She added provocatively, "I imagine that you, too, sire, have been absorbed by the most exciting topic of talk today."

Beresford looked mildly surprised. "The most exciting topic?"

"The Saint Barnabas Day tourney, of course," she answered. "Have you yourself not been discussing it throughout the afternoon?"

"I have," he replied, "but I did not imagine that the tourney would serve as a topic of talk, particularly today."

"Have you never noticed," she said, "that few topics are more pleasant to discuss at a festive occasion than the prospect of yet another festive occasion?"

Only a slight lightening of his harsh features indicated that he appreciated her observation. "True," he admitted, "but I had no idea that anyone save a few of us would care, for instance, about the particulars of the role of squires on the tournament field."

"Oh, I did not say that talk had run to the particulars," she replied. "Most people seem interested to know how many jousts there will be and whether the day will be fine."

Beresford frowned. "To discuss the weather is idle, and there will be the usual number of jousts." He waved these considerations away with an impatient gesture. "Of greater importance is the nature of the tournament procedures that many of my fainthearted companions wish to see written into the statutes.''

"Do you mean the procedures concerning the role of squires on the tournament field?'' she ventured.

"That and other things.''

"Such as . . . ?''

He looked down at her. "It goes without saying that no animal should suffer death or pain, and for even the accidental wounding of a horse, a penalty should be imposed.'' His gaze was steady upon her when he continued, "Is this, then, my lady, the kind of talk about the tournament that interests you?''

They had almost arrived at the head table. She had the indefinable sense that he had called her conversational bluff. In any case, she felt that she had just been challenged. It was not the first time that she, who had talked circles around Canute, had not easily gained the upper hand in conversation with Beresford, and she was inclined to refine her opinion of him yet again. She decided that, while he was always plainspoken, he was not always blunt.

She had no interest whatsoever in tournament regulations. However, she answered him with a bright, "That is exactly the kind of talk that interests me,'' to salute, in effect, the sword he had raised to her. She then realized that she had left one duty undone during the past several rounds of dancing. Because she felt at a strategic disadvantage, she decided to use the excuse to give her time to regroup her forces. She checked her step, and Beresford's halted accordingly.

She smiled. "Before we can discuss the topic in detail, I find that I must excuse myself from the hall for a short time. If you will pardon me, sire . . . ?''

Beresford's brow lowered. "Why?''

Gwyneth blinked. He was not *that* obtuse, surely! If she had been with Geoffrey of Senlis, she would have flashed him a little smile and said, "A *preux chevalier* does not ask a lady such a question.'' Instead, she dared to be as blunt as

Beresford. "Because I have consumed much liquid in the
past hours, you see, and..." she began, but chose in the end
to leave her thought delicately unfinished.

Beresford's face lightened. He was hardly embarrassed by
her reference to body functions, and his response was entirely commonsensical. "Well, why didn't you say so in the
first place?"

Why not, indeed! Gwyneth wondered to herself as she left
the hall to seek the garderobe. Although momentarily
amused by him, she wondered how she was going to keep
alive her interest in the topic of tournament statutes upon
her return to his side. Quite by chance, she was given a dis-
turbing reason to wish to discuss with Beresford tournament regulations, particularly those concerning the role of
squires on the field.

It came on her way back to the hall, a few minutes later,
when she caught a snatch of low conversation coming from
a shadowy alcove by the main staircase. She thought she
heard the whispered words *the loving bridegroom* ironi-
cally spoken, but could not have said for a certainty. With
her heart beating uncomfortably, she stopped her steps and
flattened herself into another scallop in the wall next to the
alcove. She did not experience a moment's qualm about
eavesdropping, for she guessed that the woman who had
spoken the words was none other than the beautiful, un-
trustworthy Rosalyn, Lady Chester.

Gwyneth's guess was confirmed with the woman's next
words. "Do you think it so necessary, then?" Rosalyn asked
of the person with whom she was sharing the alcove.

Her companion's reply was soft and smooth, his voice
clearly recognizable. "Indeed, I do," replied Cedric of Valmey. "You may consider yourself responsible for the necessity of it."

Upon hearing this gentle reproach, Gwyneth felt the
charge in the silence. She could well imagine the arch to
Rosalyn's fine brows when she challenged with sweet skep-

ticism, "You consider me responsible, my love? I was not, after all, the one who threw away the initial opportunity."

Valmey's laugh was attractive and evil and unrepentant. "Surely you do not hold against me a decision that was intended to demonstrate my constancy to you."

"Was it?"

"Do you doubt the evidence of your eyes?" he chided.

"When you turned the opportunity down, you did not know what you now know."

"Given what I know now, you would not have been pleased with the situation, I think."

"It might have proven interesting," Rosalyn countered.

A pause. Then, "Perhaps, but we wander from the issue. As I was saying, your little scheme—as intriguing as it was—fell far short of its goal. As a result, your failure has made more drastic action necessary."

"Yes, but—"

"No buts," Valmey replied with a hint of steel beneath the velvet tones, adding slyly, "unless you have had a change of heart, my love."

"I have not."

"Well, then, my plan is simple and has the added merit that neither of us needs to raise a hand against him."

Rosalyn's next words caused Gwyneth's heart to jump to her throat. "Very true," she said, "but a knight's squires are, as a rule, loyal to their master, particularly to a knight of such great repute."

"The great repute of a knight does not always mean that he treats his squires...equitably. You should know that I enjoy an easy relationship with Breteuil, to name but one. Then again, there is..."

Gwyneth did not catch the second name. Valmey had either lowered his voice or turned his head away. His next words were muffled by the rustling of their clothing, as if they were about to return to the hall. Her heart fell to her stomach, and she was suddenly anxious that she would be discovered in her hiding place. It was too late for her to do anything now except hold her breath and tug her skirts back out of sight. Fortunately, Rosalyn and Valmey left their alcove without indicating that they were aware they had been overheard.

Gwyneth remained a moment longer, attempting to steady her jumping nerves and absorbing the depths of the treachery of Cedric of Valmey.

She did not know exactly who or what Valmey and Rosalyn had been talking about, but she had more than enough to discuss with Beresford when she returned to his side at the head table a minute later. With genuine interest now, she asked her husband to explain the role of squires on the tourney field.

"I agree with the regulation," he answered, "that no earl, baron or knight should have more than three squires attending him. I also accept that no one is to assist a fallen knight except his own squires, under penalty of three years imprisoned." The look in his eyes was unreadable or, at least, ambiguous to Gwyneth, and she thought that he was either challenged or amused by her interest in the unfeminine topic. "However, other than taking every precaution not to permanently injure an opponent," he continued, "I see no reason to constrain an event that works best with fewest regulations." He proceeded to outline for her some of the rules to which he was opposed.

She nodded and agreed and encouraged him to elaborate. At one point, she said conversationally, "But let us return to the subject of your squires. Did you say that you are entitled to three on the field? What exactly are their duties?"

Beresford told her how they cared for the knight's weapons and his horses and provided food and drink between jousts. It was her hope that he would mention his squires' names, but he did not. So she asked directly, "And which, among your squires, are your favorites?"

"Langley," he replied without hesitation, "although he still needs practice with the sword and is inclined to whine." He lapsed into silence.

"No others come to mind?" she prodded.

He shrugged and tossed out a few names haphazardly.

She deftly caught one of them. "Breteuil?" she echoed slowly, trying to form her mouth around the strange vowels. "It is a difficult name for me."

Beresford's face relaxed into a faint smile. "You had better get used to it, for it is common enough at court."

"Indeed?"

"It's a large family, the Breteuil."

"But among the young squires are there so many?"

"A half dozen," he replied indifferently.

Gwyneth made a mental note to discover who among the other knights had a squire named Breteuil. With one part of her mind, she kept up a light conversation with Beresford on the relatively safe topic of squires. With the other part, she bent her thoughts to the troubling problem of the threatening words Valmey had spoken to Rosalyn in the alcove. Thus, she was unprepared for the inevitable moment when Beresford turned to her and said, "It's time."

She dared to look at him. She saw a plain-speaking man who insulted her and ignored her and kissed her with unexpected effect. She saw a rough-edged man who had the ready look of an unsheathed sword. She saw a hard and handsome man who did not attempt to disguise his determination or his desire.

She realized belatedly that she had been careless with her courage, for it seemed to have deserted her. "It is?" she managed.

Chapter Ten

He looked out over the revelers in the hall and knew that he had waited long enough. "It is." He turned back to her. "The rest of what I have to say about tournament regulations turns on technicalities."

She took a sip of wine and cleared her throat. Her voice was tight. "What you told me was most useful and interesting."

He caught a flicker of some emotion in her eyes before she lowered her lashes again, but he could not identify it. Nerves? he wondered. Or modesty? He was dimly aware that a young woman might feel nervous or modest on her wedding night, but since he had no experience with skittish virgins, he suddenly perceived the great advantage of Gwyneth's widowhood.

"I've no wish to dance," he continued. "And you, my lady?" Her head was lowered now, so he could not read her expression. She shook her head in agreement with him. That much, at least, he could interpret. "No, no dancing," she said. Her voice was very low and seemed to rasp.

He rose from the bench and took her hands in his. He was pleased that this occasion did not call for subtlety. "If the dancing holds no further appeal, and we've exhausted the present topic of conversation," he said, drawing her to her feet, "I propose we proceed to the next part of the evening."

She rose with him, unresisting. Good enough, then, that she accepted so easily what was before them. When he placed her hand on his wrist and turned to leave the table, she whispered, "Should we not signal Adela?"

He was never in the mood for trivial courtesies, even less so this evening. "She'll know where we've gone."

"No," she said, her voice still soft and ragged, "I mean so that she can arrange the final ceremony of the day."

He had conveniently forgotten about the bedding. He recalled it now from his marriage to Roesia. He had no objection to the ceremony; he even understood the various reasons for bedding the naked bride and groom in the presence of ladies and gentlemen of suitable rank. The public nudity insured that neither party could later object to some defect or deformity in the other. The presence of a large number of eyewitnesses in the bedchamber reduced the possibility of appeals for annulment, although the couple would certainly perform the actual marriage act alone. The stripping of the sheets in the morning to display the spot of the bride's blood proved that she had been a virgin. It was a practice that made sense in most cases.

But not in this case. "We don't need it," he said. Since he had already determined that the occasion did not call for subtlety, he ran an openly assessing eye over her. "You look to me to be a healthy woman in all respects." He continued bluntly, "I've every intention of consummating this marriage, and as a widow, there is no question of your virginity." To clinch his arguments, he added, "Since you, my lady, have no family to object to me, I cannot imagine what purpose the bedding would serve for a marriage that was arranged by royal decree."

He saw the color drain from her face to leave it purest alabaster, then return to tinge her cheeks palest pink. She said nothing, only nodded. He was pleased to think that she found his arguments reasonable and not worth refuting. Then he called to a page, who trotted up and, upon receiving rapid instructions, trotted off to obey them. At that point a thought occurred to him. "Do you need any of your women to attend to you?"

She shook her head.

As they left the hall, he was further pleased that his wife was not a slave to empty ritual and that she did not intend to admit giggling serving women into their chamber on their wedding night. At the same time, he was slightly puzzled by her continuing silence. With her head held high and her eyes fixed straight ahead, he could not determine whether she was reluctant to leave or as happy as he to be quit of the throng. Whatever the state of her emotions, he knew that she was not angry. Her anger he had experienced with great delight in the gardens the evening before, when she had threatened him verbally with knives.

He was curious. When they were near the exit, he asked abruptly, "Did you wish to remain, my lady, at the celebration?"

She shook her head again quickly, glanced at him with a "no" in her eyes, then looked away again.

"You're content to leave?" he pursued. He looked over his shoulder at the revelry in the hall, then down at her.

She nodded. "Yes, it is time, as you have said," she answered, but her voice sounded as if the words came with effort.

He glanced back over his shoulder, for he had caught Geoffrey of Senlis's eye just before he looked at Gwyneth. Senlis had been watching them depart, and when Beresford looked back at him, the baron bowed deeply. Perfectly understanding the message Senlis conveyed to him, Beresford's eyes narrowed to a gleam of gray, and he smiled.

He was still smiling when he ushered Gwyneth through the passage that led from the hall to the staircase. He was smiling when she removed her fingers from his wrist so that she could grasp the newel post of the staircase with one hand and lift her skirts with the other. He was smiling when his thoughts ran far ahead to riverbanks and bramble bushes and a beautiful woman in his arms.

He had forgotten his initial outrage against this marriage of political convenience. The cramp that had come over him at the very thought of marriage. The strange pain the sight of her always caused him. The invisible bonds around his chest when he had stood in the chapel during the wedding mass. He remembered only the unlacing of those bonds when he had kissed Gwyneth for the first time, drenched in the chill fires of bright stained light.

That was it, then. He had been wanting to kiss her throughout the festivities but had not found a moment alone with her. Certainly he had enjoyed touching her hip and her arm and her shoulder when they danced, but the enjoyment had not been satisfying enough for him to wish to make a fool of himself twice on the dance floor. Besides, he did not know why he should waste his time with such an annoying activity as dancing when what he wanted to do was hold her and kiss her and sink himself into her.

She was ascending the stairs ahead of him, and her hips were at eye level. He admired her movements. Perfect swing. Perfect curves. Perfect opportunity. He reached out and put his hands on her waist, bringing her to a halt. He advanced until he was only one step down from her, and turned her so that she was facing him. He moved with his customary speed, and Gwyneth was caught off guard. In turning, she almost lost her footing on the smooth stone, but he was as steady as he was quick and easily absorbed the force of her full weight against him.

He saw the surprise on her face before he caught her. He liked the flash in her eyes that followed. It was irritation or, perhaps, a dislike of being surprised. It reminded him of the look in the eyes of an unwary opponent he had outmaneuvered.

They were eye-to-eye, nose-to-nose, mouth-to-mouth. His hands had come to rest on her hips. One of hers had fallen on his shoulder. The other rested against the newel post for support. She exhaled a tiny gasp.

"That was dangerous," she chided when she realized that she was not going to fall and that she was secure in his grip.

"Let's hope," he said.

Then he placed his lips on hers. He relished the sense of danger in drawing her to him so that she was nestled against him. He delighted in the feel of her breasts against his chest, her hips flush with his. He reveled even more in the fact that she was level with him, their heights equalized. It increased his sense of being engaged with a most worthy opponent, an opponent to challenge, to fear.

When he had set eyes on her for the first time across the great hall, he recalled, he had imagined himself galloping across the tourney field with his lance raised and his charger beneath him. When she had spoken to him of the Norse gods a few evenings ago, he remembered lowering his visor against the effect of her stories and her smile. Now he was happy to strip off his armor and engage in hand-to-hand combat, a gentle art that took skill and perception and an ability to respond move for move, advance for advance, stroke for stroke. He was eager to wrestle her to the ground, to roll with her on the earth, to best her, to have her best him.

He took the hand she held against the newel post and placed it on his shoulder. Now she was holding him as intimately as he was holding her. He moved a hand up to her full breast, which fit his hand much like the hilt of the magic sword, Gungnir, must have fit Odin's grip, judging from the stories that Gwyneth had told him. He moved his hand back down her body to the curve of her hip. The gesture felt familiar to him, as if he were sliding his palm over the rim of his shield to polish it. Better than a magic sword, better than his shield, she was the most beautiful woman he had ever seen, and he was holding her hips against his.

With his kiss, he prodded and sought and was initially disappointed. He wanted more from her. He wanted her engagement. He wanted her response. Her anger. Her fire.

He trailed his mouth from her lips to her ear. He spoke as he would to bait a hesitant opponent. "We can always return to the hall to finish our discussion of tournament regulations, if you like."

She drew her head slightly back to look at him. The glint in her eye was distinctly speculative. "To inform me of the technicalities?"

"To bore you with them, yes," he said. His hands left her hips and came to meet hers on his shoulders. He slid his fingers between hers. The cool appraisal in her beautiful eyes inspired him mightily. She had not misunderstood.

She drew a deep breath. "Why should I wish for you to bore me with the technicalities of tournament regulations?" she asked. Her voice was low and lilting and completely clear of its earlier obstruction.

"If you are not quite ready—" he drew her toward him and licked her lips, once, lightly "—for this." He kissed her.

When he finished, her face was flushed, and not, he was pleased to note, with embarrassment. "Well, now," she said. "We've agreed that it's time, and that's that." She gave him a slight push, causing him to teeter, and thereby disengaged her fingers from his. Without waiting to see whether he lost his footing, she turned smartly and gracefully on the steps and began to mount them again. The swish of her hips just then was especially appealing.

His smile was very broad as he followed her up the stairs. It had not faded when they arrived at the door to his chamber, where the page was standing ready to bow them into the room. He dismissed the lad, and after Gwyneth preceded him into the chamber, he shut the door behind him with a great deal of anticipation. He was satisfied by what he saw around him.

He had ordered that a low fire be lit to take the damp and any chill from the room. He walked toward it to stir the embers. On the floor next to the hearth was the tray he had requested, on which sat two goblets of wine, a silver ewer and a bowl of fruit. The shutters of the high window to the exterior were half-closed, filtering the pastel glow of the dying day. Below the window, filling half the room, was the large bed, the covers of which had been turned down invitingly. The bed would serve the purpose, of course, but he was thinking that clean, crisp sheets were a poor second to the pleasures to be found on a riverbank.

He turned his back to the warm coals and saw Gwyneth standing in the center of the room. He reached out his hands, beckoning to her. She came forward obediently, her features composed, her eyes upon him, unwavering. The veil held by the circlet on her head fluttered gently as she walked, creating the effect of a gossamer halo or a transparent butterfly wing.

"You'll be warmer here when you undress," he said.

Her voice was low when she replied, "I'm not cold."

"All the better then."

When she was next to him, he dropped his hands to unclasp his belt. He let it fall to the floor, and his sword clattered beside it. His desire for her was flowing easily throughout his body. It was strong, but he was in control of it. Even so, he saw no need to wait for his satisfaction, and he intended to make full use of the long night ahead of them.

He pulled his tunic over his head and let it fall atop his belt. His shirt came off next and was added to the drift of clothing. He deftly undid his crossgarters and every other clasp that held him together. Shoes and chausses were cast aside, and he was naked before her, ready and rigid with husbandly intention.

He saw that Gwyneth had made no progress with her clothing beyond moving her right hand to the wrist of her left, where she was pulling at ties, rather ineffectually, it seemed to him. He made an impatient noise deep in his throat and moved toward her. He raised his hands to help with the absurd complexities of feminine apparel, but before he touched her, she looked up, and he saw deep in her violet eyes a start of surprise and another, darker emotion.

Her eyes lowered quickly. When his hands came down on her shoulders, she flinched.

It was an involuntary reaction on her part, he knew. And it was so minimal that he might have missed it, except that he was too well experienced in the precise moment of hand-to-hand contact on the field where the world came into the sharp focus of kill or be killed. He was also well experienced in adjusting strategies to varying goals, understood vulnerability as only a strong man could and distinguished sharply between harm and pleasure. He raised her chin. Her lashes fluttered up. He was not entirely surprised, but was truly impressed by the look of stout defiance deep in her violet eyes. He saw now that she was afraid of him but had so masked her fear that even he, who could smell the faintest whiff of it, had not sensed it.

The situation was plain. It was equally plain what he was going to do about it. He knew how to preserve her dignity, and he wanted to rouse her desire. He did not say bluntly, "You have no need to fear me." He did not say pityingly, "You've been abused." He did not say chivalrously, "If Canute of Northumbria were not already dead, I would kill him."

What he said was, "You have properly forewarned me, my lady, and I'm unarmed, as you see." He looked down at himself, unashamed of his nakedness and his naked desire. "You'll understand that I need to check you for knives."

He liked the shift of emotions in her eyes as she registered his statement, and the color that came to her pale cheeks. He was aware of the rise and fall of her breasts not far from his chest as she took a deep breath. He raised his hands slowly and deliberately to her head and removed the circlet. He turned slightly to toss it atop the pile of his own clothing. The veil followed, billowing softly in its descent.

He touched the braids knotted at her nape. She seemed to relax, and he spread his fingers through the knot, loosening it. Then he partially combed out her braids with his fingers and permitted himself an "Ahh" of satisfaction at the feel of her hair in his hands. He leaned forward and pressed his lips to her neck. He murmured, "No knives here that I can see."

He raised one of her arms so that he could untie the laces that held together the front and back panels of her bliaut. This overshift soon fell into a puddle at her feet, and then there was only her kirtle and the laces of one sleeve left to undo. He continued as if searching for hidden weapons. He commented, "Only curves. No sharp points." He held up her wrist to unlace her sleeve. When the laces were free, he pulled the kirtle over her head, causing her hair to tumble and tangle in disorder down her back. He tossed the gown atop the circlet and veil.

She stood before him in her light shift, the outline of her body visible beneath the transparent cloth. He had become impatient. He thought that undressing her was as much a waste of time as dancing with her. He eyed the neckline and knew that he could strip it from her with the force of one finger.

She must have read the look in his eyes, for she rasped quietly, "Don't rip it." She paused and met his eyes. "Please." Her hands came to the ribbon at her breasts, and she began to fumble with it.

He reined in his impatience. He lifted his hands to hers and pulled the ribbon. As slowly as he was able, he pushed the shift from her shoulders so that it lay with the bliaut at her feet. His eyes swept her naked beauty. His hands did the same. He paused to reconsider his predilection for hips and caressed her breasts at length, marveling in their shape and feel. He bent to kiss their tips. He swirled his tongue over milky pink roses and sucked gently. He had the errant, unworthy, wholly delicious thought that he had been too hasty in denying the need for the bedding ceremony. He would have dearly loved to see the look on Senlis's face upon beholding Gwyneth's body. Still, he hardly needed or cared for the approval of a male audience to know the value of what he was holding and touching, kissing and caressing.

He placed her hands on his shoulders, ran his palms from her armpits down her sides to come to rest briefly on her hips, then continued over her buttocks. He pressed her to him, groaning in anticipation. He leaned into her farther, traced the backs of her thighs to the tender underside of her knees, then back up and over her spine to her shoulders and across her arms, which were stretched around his neck. His hands held hers, his elbows raised and propped on her shoulders.

He nuzzled both sides of her neck. Then he bent his lips to hers. "So far, I've discovered no fearsome weapons concealed on your person," he said, "but I've one last place to look." The kiss she gave him was almost what he wanted. "Can you guess where?" he asked.

She blushed and shook her head.

He moved against her, nudged her legs apart with his knee. He dropped his arms to her waist to support her. "Afraid to guess, my lady?" he said, frankly taunting.

She gasped, but met him taunt for taunt. "Show me."

He did. He dropped down on his knees before her. He bent his head to place one cheek, then the other, against her abdomen, and stretched his neck against the fine triangle of curls at the apex of her thighs. Involuntarily the thought, *daughters,* came to him, and he was pleased. He raised his head so that his lips and nose were at her waist. He was intoxicated by the feel of her skin and her scent. The top of his head grazed the full curves of her breasts, then he rose to his feet and moved one hand behind her, boldly splaying it over her buttocks. The other hand he placed delicately, but unhesitatingly, at the front of her thighs. He pushed his fingers between them, gliding them over her, pausing a moment at the opening that existed for him. He found it dry.

He perceived another problem now, a different one than he ordinarily encountered, for he had never had experience with unwilling or unready women. His own desire was surging and might have, under other circumstances, lost its direction in frustration and found outlet in violence; and if he had not already been attuned to her fear, he might have determined that her coldness was the one flaw in the jewel that was his wife. However, this night he felt protected by the Norns. He had been blessed by the three weird women, guided by them, inspired by them.

Again, he knew just what to do. He kissed her sweetly. He lifted her in his arms and carried her to the bed. "I'm reassured that no sharp knives await me," he said, "but there may be other dangers in store for me there." He laid her down on her back upon the bed and stretched out next to her on his side. He arranged her legs so that her knees were bent, her feet flat on the bed and near her buttocks, her legs spread a fraction. "I need for you to clarify a story."

"A story?"

He smiled a little and propped his head in his right hand. With his left, he began to move his fingers lightly from her neck to her breasts to her abdomen. "The other evening, you told me about the god Tyr."

Her eyes were open, and she looked at him warily. "The one who was supposed to treat his wife well."

He slanted her a pointed glance. "Exactly." His fingers stroked her abdomen and moved to the inside of her thighs, up to her knees, one at a time, and back down again. His hand came to rest atop the golden triangle of curls. "You told me the story of how Tyr lost his hand."

"I did." Her voice was cautious.

His fingers began to move in small circles. "You told me that the giant wolf, Fenrir—the child of the god Loki and an evil giantess, I believe—seemed harmless at first and was allowed by the gods to wander free. Is that right?"

"That's right," she said, curious.

He slipped his fingers between her legs and touched her intimately. Then, before her very wide eyes, he brought his fingers to his lips and wet them with his tongue. He touched her again, this time with very different effect.

"But then Fenrir grew so fierce," he continued, "that the Norns warned he would cause Odin's death if something was not done. Now the gods could not pollute the sacred ground of Asgard by simply killing Fenrir, so they had to devise a way to restrain him. Is that right?"

"That's right," she said again, somewhat breathless.

"So they decided to play a trick. They asked Fenrir to test the strength of an iron chain they had made. They tied it round him, hoping he would be unable to break it, but he escaped easily. So they tried with ever-stronger chains. Once, twice, three more times, and he broke them all. Then they went to the dwarves for magic. Is that right?"

She moaned an affirmative. She was responding to the delicate movement of his fingers between her thighs. They were sliding and gliding and drawing ripe, rounded desire from deep inside her.

"The dwarves made the gods a magic silken ribbon that was unbreakable, but Fenrir was suspicious by now. When he saw the strange ribbon, he refused to be tied by it. The gods promised to free him if the ribbon proved too strong, but he did not trust them. At last Fenrir agreed to the test if one of the gods would put a hand in his mouth as a sign of good faith while he made the attempt. The gods hesitated, then Tyr put his hand between Fenrir's teeth."

He was losing the threads of his own story, and it was taking all of his self-control not to respond now to the liquid desire he was producing between her legs.

He made an effort to continue. "So Fenrir was tied up and soon found that however he strained, the bonds got tighter. The wolf wanted to be released, but the gods refused to free him. So he clamped his jaws shut and bit off Tyr's hand. Is that right?"

She nodded and managed to breathe the trembling question, "What is the clarification you need?"

He stilled the work of his fingers, then withdrew his hand. "I've still got it," he said with a note of relief and desire, as if he had just removed his hand unscathed from the jaws of the raging and dangerous giant wolf. He parted her legs as he might open a sacred book—not a religious one, but rather a sorcerer's manual, full of dark secrets and black magic, one he knew he should not open, one he could not resist. He rolled on top of her and settled himself between her legs.

"What I'd really like to know," he said in a low voice, into her neck, "is whether your story was not something of a trick itself. It occurs to me that Tyr might just as easily have lost his hand between the ravenous legs of his wife as he tried to please her."

"Tyr's wife?" she asked.

"Yes, his very beautiful foreign wife," he answered. "The one who was supposedly weak and peaceful but who was, in truth, most clever, I think." He pressed his manhood against her opening. "And if that's the case, I'd like to know what happened to him when he joined, this like, with her."

He was entering her lovely liquid by degrees. "By Odin," she whispered, then tickled his ear with her tongue. "He did not make it out alive."

That was just what he wanted to hear. He entered blindly now, not caring for the danger, knowing that this was far, far different from anything he had experienced before. He sensed that some part of him was in grave peril, but did not know from which direction it was coming or how to protect himself from it. He did not even care to protect himself, but abandoned himself to the raging heat of this gentle, glorious battle. He surrendered himself to her luscious, hungry jaws. He felt his blood surging. He felt spears and arrows flying around him, whizzing past him. His shield was down, yet he felt invincible. He felt invulnerable. He felt a glorious fool.

He knew what lay over the glittering horizon, and just as he reached for that paradoxical death, he felt an arrow pierce his heart. The sensation was so startlingly intense and so real, so painful and so pleasurable that he was sure that a Valkyrie would come swooping down to claim him for Valhalla.

But as his life and seed and strength rushed into her, no magnificent warrior goddess came. Instead, when he collapsed, weak and happy, upon her, he was strangely sure that, at the very rim of the vision of his mind's eye, hovered a plump and naked male child with wings. The image made no more sense now than it had on the two previous occasions he had seen the baby boy. He drifted off on the comforting thought that the infant was harmless and that the golden bow and arrow he carried was a ridiculous toy.

Chapter Eleven

Gwyneth awoke from her drowsing to blink into pitch black. She was disoriented, as one often is upon awakening in a strange bed. In the split second as she struggled to remember where she was, she waited for that unpleasant sensation to overcome her, the one she always had upon waking from a sweet dream to realize the horrid circumstances of her life.

She knew where she was now and whom she was with. She could not yet remember anything else. Lying very still, she mentally checked her body for bruises or even soreness. She was aware of nothing but a lovely floating feeling. She searched that private space within herself that she treasured, her last line of retreat from Canute's brutality. There she discovered no trace of violation or humiliation. She let her thoughts drift. Still the unpleasant sensation did not come, and the floating feeling persisted.

She was lying on her side, her hands tucked under her cheek upon the pillow. She was aware that a man was in bed with her, lying at her back. She was certain that it was Simon of Beresford. Bits and pieces came to her. His kiss on the stairs. His challenge. His alarming nakedness when she had not even unlaced one sleeve of her kirtle. His growl of anger at her ineptitude. The hand he raised against her. His intention to rape her.

No, that wasn't right. She backed up and tried again. His alarming nakedness and readiness. His growl of impatience at her slowness. The hand he raised to help her undress. Yes, that was right. His search for knives. His intimate touch that had at first frightened, then reassured her. His hand. Yes, his hand. Now she remembered. His deep voice rumbling comfortingly. His strange story of Fenrir. And his fingers.

She closed her eyes, trading one blackness for another. His power, strength and size had overwhelmed her, but he had not hurt her or humiliated her. She did not feel ripped or torn; she felt surprisingly whole. Even hale. She wanted to sigh deeply, but she was more cautious than that. She measured her breaths slowly, getting the air she needed without a rustle of noise or the slight movement.

She felt him place his warm hand over the curve of her hip. He said into the blackness, "You're awake."

She paused, wondering whether she should go into hiding or if she could better protect herself by revealing herself. "How did you know?"

It was odd how she could feel the slight shrug of his broad shoulders on the mattress behind her. "I don't know," he said. "I can always tell."

The hand on her hip slid up to her breast and explored it, slowly. His fingers played with her nipple. She realized that she was holding her breath again, so she let it out, but too quickly. From her rapid exhalation, she feared that she had exposed herself to him, showing him either her fear or her desire. It was strange to admit to herself that she was more desirous than fearful and that his touch felt warm and good and luxurious.

His hand moved back to her hip, slipped between her thighs and caressed the flesh above her knees. It returned to her hip, where it stayed, caressing idly at first, then with more intention. After a while, he moved against her so that his front was pressed to her back. She felt the rod of his manhood against her buttocks. It felt unpleasant, or at least alien to her.

She shifted. She wanted to escape. She said, "I need to get up."

She felt the vibration of his chest when he said, "You know where the chamber pot is."

She almost smiled at that. They had wrangled over that before. She did know where the chamber pot was, and that was exactly what she wanted. She found it, used it and decided that coy embarrassment did not suit the moment. As she climbed back into bed, she asked, "And you, sire? Do you not need it?"

"I've already been out of the chamber and down the hallway for that."

She did not remember hearing him get out of bed or opening and closing the door. She had trained herself to be a light sleeper and wondered how it was that she had slept through his movements. She lay down again on her side, facing away from him. He did not put his hand on her hip. She snuggled into the pillow and said, "I can never seem to force myself to get dressed in order to leave the room."

"Neither can I."

She raised up and turned to look at him over her shoulder. She could see only the gleam of his gray eyes resting on her. From the shadowy outline of his body, she could see that he was lying on his side, his head propped in his hand. "You went out into the hallway naked?" she asked.

"I prefer leaving the room, and the guards do not pay me the least attention."

She turned back around and laughed once, quietly. It made perfect sense that he would travel abroad naked in the middle of the night. "I do not think that I would try such a thing."

"I do not think that I would let you. The guards would surely pay more attention to you than they pay to me."

"It's not just that," she said. "Even in fine weather, I imagine that going out unclothed makes one very cold."

"I suppose," he said indifferently, "but I have not really noticed."

"Not even your feet?" she asked. Leaving the bed for just these few moments, her soles had been chilled by the cold stone flooring.

"They've warmed up again." To prove his statement, he rubbed the tops of his feet against the bottoms of hers.

The effect was unexpectedly arousing, and his feet were indeed very warm. He moved against her again, and she discovered that he had lost none of his earlier desire. His arm came around her and grasped the shoulder on which she was lying. He rolled her toward him, gently but firmly. He moved across her, so that he could mount her. He was hindered only by the braiding of the bedclothes and their bodies, leg, sheet, leg, sheet, leg, leg, sheet. He untangled them and drew her into the strong circle of his arms. He was almost atop her and needed but a nudge and a stroke to be within her. He nuzzled his chin into her neck, breathing in deeply.

She felt the contradictory effects of excitement and fear. She felt his alien part against her thigh and belly and wished he would go away. Yet his arms and shoulders and chest were glorious in muscle and sinew and felt extraordinarily good against her. His skin and hair smelled unusually good to her, too. She breathed in his earthy scent, and thought of lying in a field of fresh-scythed wheat. However, the bristles of his beard burned her.

"You're hurting me," she murmured, trying to push him away.

His reflexes were always quick. He relaxed his hold on her and eased away immediately. "Where?"

"My neck. Your beard."

His hold on her reasserted itself. "That should not prove an insurmountable problem." He turned her over, away from him, so that she was lying on her side again.

The contradictions continued. She felt torn between relief and disappointment, though the disappointment was the lesser part. She thought it would be pleasant to drift back into sleep. "Good," she said.

"And my solution has the added merit of being one of the ways I like it best."

At that he turned her again, so that she was lying on her stomach. When he rose up on his knees and seemed to be positioning himself behind her, her disappointment fled completely and her relief was replaced by alarm. His hands came down on her waist, and he drew her hips up against him.

Her protesting "No!" was quiet but unmistakable. To her own ears, it held a note of panic. The next moment she could have cut out her tongue to have so betrayed herself.

She felt him pause. He held her backside against him a moment longer, then eased her down on her stomach. He stretched himself along her, wrapping himself around her as before, his front against her back, so that she could feel all his strength and desire. However, she was aware that this time he was holding himself in check.

"I have frightened you," he said. The statement was bald, his tone unapologetic.

She would not demean herself with hasty denial. He had frightened her just now, it was true, but she did not know why she should let her guard down this time, given that she had kept her composure the night before in the face of greater terror—or, rather, she had almost kept her composure. She had kept it until the moment she had flinched from him, automatically ducking away from the hand she imagined would slap her into submission or senselessness. Still, she had been proud that she had not uttered any foolish protest that he could use against her later.

Earlier, upon leaving the festivities in the hall, he had reduced her to utter helplessness with his blunt arguments against the bedding ceremony. It had seemed to her that he was telling her that he could do with her what he liked and that she had no one to protect her from him and no recourse against him now that they were wed. Based on what he had said and how he had said it, she had imagined a truly gruesome scene in the bedchamber, and had donned her

emotional armor then and there to see her through the night.
Then he had kissed her on the stairs, charming her, disarming her.

He had not charmed her or disarmed her enough to have
prevented her from flinching away from him a few minutes
later. She had thought at first that she had made a very grave
mistake with that minimal movement she could not control, but his reaction to her had not been at all what she had
expected. Nor was hers to him any more expected. Why was
the memory of her strong and positive reaction to him not
helping her now?

She knew she should yield to him. That was what a good
wife did. It would go easier for her if she was obedient. "I
was frightened at first, yes," she admitted, "but not anymore." She had to surrender her body to him in the way he
wanted. She willed herself to relax. She had her breathing
under control. "I'm all right now."

He caught her at the waist again and held her against him.
"Are you? I'm not so sure." He moved behind her, squaring himself on his knees. He raised her buttocks to meet his
hips. "And even if you're all right, I am not." The strength
and heat of his manhood startled her. "Now, my intention
is to spare you the rub of my beard against your chin. But
that is all I intend to spare you."

She imagined that now would come the humiliation. It
seemed so demeaning, this position, on her knees and elbows, her legs spread against him and around him. She
feared his unnatural appetites and knew what could happen to her, exposed and vulnerable like this. She felt her
throat constrict. She felt the channel between her legs constrict. If only she could breathe. If only she could be done
with this.

He leaned forward over her and touched his fingers to the
spot between her legs he had touched before. He stroked, he
explored, he tickled. His extended "Mmm" was appraising
and considering, ultimately dissatisfied. He withdrew his
fingers after a moment, and she realized that he was wet-

ting them with his tongue. She felt a little rush of anticipation. Sure enough, when he put his fingers again to that tiny pearl and applied sliding pressure, she felt her rush become a spurt, then a little liquid spill.

She was surprised, excited, enthralled, desirous and still a little fearful. After a moment or two of adjustment, she found the contact of her backside to his front was not humiliating, but stimulating. She might have moaned. She might have moved her hips against him. He increased the pressure of his fingers, slipped around and inside her, spreading wet lips. She felt the beginnings of pleasure and desire, like little waves lapping against a shore. Then he replaced his fingers with his manhood, filling her instantly. His penetration was deep.

Although this act of joining was not new to her, her experience of it certainly was. Before this night she had always wondered how a woman could actually want to engage in an activity as hideous as this. Now she began to understand the power and pleasure of taking him and stretching herself around him and moving against him in a way that she knew he liked and needed. The touch of his fingers combined with his penetration made her feel gloriously plowed, as if dry earth were being turned over for the rich black humidity beneath. Until tonight, she felt she must have been a fallow field left long untended, awaiting cultivation. Now her soil was being readied for his seed, and she found the fit and felt the pleasure, moving this way and that, marveling in his size and strength.

Finding, feeling, moving, marveling. The experience changed from moment to moment. His fingers pressed and caressed her slick pearl and produced swelling, swollen waves. She could feel the waves move through her to him and back to her. The waves became rhythmic and organized, gaining force. They grew to fearsome proportions, but it was a new fear. This was not the fear of anger and loss. This was a fear that edged out into exhilaration and awe.

At that teetering moment, his fingers left her lips and legs. Both his hands were clamped at her waist, guiding her hips. She wanted more, and he gave it to her. He wanted more, and she made room. She was gulping and gasping for air, not from inability to breathe, but for more life. The waves grew to monstrous proportions and swallowed her. Still he rocked her. Still he plunged into her. Rocking and plunging, plunging and rocking until she was filled, fulfilled, overflowing. Until she accepted with utter abandon a terrifying masculine force that did not hurt or kill. Until she offered him the magnificent rage of a feminine appetite that gripped and squeezed and desired and demanded every last drop of satisfaction.

With one last shuddering shove, he came forward across her, pushing her down flat against the mattress so that he was lying on her back with his full weight, still partially joined to her. Her legs were bent up, and her heels were pressed against his buttocks. The muscles of her inner thighs were stretched, but not uncomfortably. One of his hands had come down upon her shoulder. The other, spread over her head, moved jerkily, alternately mussing her hair and drawing it back from her forehead. His face was buried in her hair, which was tangled around her shoulders and trapped beneath his chest.

He was breathing heavily. She could feel his heart thumping against her back, his blood pulsating through his body, and all around her his muscles, lately tensed, now quivered with release. His hand continued to draw the hair away from her forehead, but his gesture had no particular purpose, and he seemed to get as much hair in her face as free of it. His other hand left her shoulder a moment to travel the length of her side, then he slipped his fingers under her body, which was pressed against the sheet. When he made contact with one of her nipples, she felt an unexpected and extraordinarily deep wave of desire course through her. This was followed by the reverberation of a delicious groan from her throat.

She spoke first. "It was considerate of you," she began, then had to stop. If her voice was ragged now, it was not because her throat was constricted. She was aware that there was not a constricted passage left in her body. Even her veins seemed open and flowing. "It was considerate of you," she began again, "to have spared me the burn of your beard." Her voice was low and came from deep inside her. "But it seems I'm never to be relieved of your weight."

He shifted slightly atop her, grasped a handful of her hair and tugged it away from her forehead, cheeks and neck. He placed his lips on the skin of her nape but did not kiss or rub. Instead he breathed her in. He placed his other hand under her hip and moved his still-greedy fingers as far toward the apex of her thighs as possible. The longer he lay on top of her, the more he fell out of her.

"Never," he agreed.

She felt the meaning of the word rumbling up from his chest more than she heard it. He was not going to concede a moment before necessary. She wiggled to release herself from the thorough grip of his body.

"Surely you don't object," he said lazily.

She wiggled more. "You're crushing me."

He grasped her shoulders and gave them a little shake. He lay very still atop her. His body lost its relaxed laziness. So did his voice. "Surely you don't object," he repeated into her ear. This time his low, deep voice held a note of purring, playful challenge.

She discovered an interesting new and pleasurable form of submission. "No, sire," she replied with exaggerated humility, "I do not object."

Having obtained her capitulation, he said readily, "Very well." He grunted and rolled off of her, giving her a little spank as he did so. He settled himself beside her. He stretched luxuriously, then lay on his side facing her.

She turned over slowly, trying to regain control of desire-drenched limbs. It took more of an effort than should have been necessary for such a simple movement. The floating feeling of earlier was gone, and in its place was a heavy ripeness that seemed to bloat her thoughts and slow her reactions. She got no farther than turning over heavily on her back and sinking, exhausted, against the pillows and mattress. She tried to arrange the covers around her. Her efforts were ineffectual.

His hand slipped in under the flimsy bed covers. He placed his palm possessively on the flat of her abdomen. At his touch, she rolled her head against the pillow to look at him in the dark. It was a mistake. She had underestimated the effect of looking at the man with her emotions still swirling through her. She felt his shadowy glance mingle with those surging emotions to restructure the woman who had dwelled inside her all these years and who had kept her alive.

With Canute, afterwards, she had always felt either bloodied or bruised, but always unbowed. With Beresford now, with his glance upon her, she had the distinct feeling of lying slain on a field of battle. She had never anticipated responding to a man so thoroughly. She had never anticipated allowing a man that much power over her. She closed her eyes and turned her head away from him. Still, she was aware of his hand upon her stomach. She did not dare move away from his touch. She did not want to, either. And she did not want to want it.

"There are other ways," he said at last.

His voice fell like a veil around her in the darkness, surrounding her. "Are there?" she inquired, almost at random.

"But only one other I like so well."

She dared herself to ask, "And what is that other way?"

He was very long in replying. "You'll find out."

She was not sure about this, but knew a challenge when she heard one. "Will I?"

"Yes."

She took the chance of looking at him again. This time, too, it was a mistake. She had survived her marriage to

Canute by remaining constantly on her guard. This night she had not been wary enough. She had not been wary at all. She looked away. The oddest image came into her head, of Beresford kneeling over her defeated body, his hands outspread and raised in victory. She decided that his gesture was conventional, not triumphant, for his victory over her had been too easy. That was it, then—the effect of his flat, conventionally victorious "Yes." She had no experience with this kind of surrender to interpret it as anything other than defeat.

She winced at the image, but she was too tired to rise up and fight it—fight *him* on his own terms. Or was her muddled brain misperceiving this as a battle? She did not know, and she was too tired to decide the issue. Not a weary tired, but a rather pleasant tired. A deserved tired. Yes, she deserved a little rest after the past days and weeks and months and years.

Her thoughts kept turning, but they crunched rustily, like creaky old gears. She knew that she should not let his "Yes" hang there unanswered. No, that would be a very grave mistake, and she set about to imagine every conceivable, effective response she could make. Somewhere between imagining the most banal and the most brilliant response, she drifted off to sleep.

She awoke much later when the red of dawn was filtering through the shutters. She snuffled awake with a dreamy snort, then her senses blazed to life when she realized what was happening to her. The word that formed on her lips was an immediate *No,* but with great effort she prevented herself from uttering it.

He was there beside her, seeking, exploring, demanding. He gave her little time to accept him. He gave her no time to reject him. However, he did dare her to deny him. His voice was very quiet and provocative when he said, "Surely you don't object."

This was a "No" she could submit to saying and even, perhaps, enjoy. "No, sire, I do not object."

Chapter Twelve

Half an hour later, Gwyneth decided that her best defense was to get out of bed. The light that was dribbling through the shutters was becoming brighter by the minute. According to the bells she had lately heard, it was a little past prime.

Her limbs did not move easily, and a sense of pleasurable heaviness slowed her down. She wondered if she was going to have to learn to walk all over again. Before her feet touched the floor, there came a knock at the door.

She glanced over at Beresford, who was stretched out beside her in motionless repose, one arm raised behind his head. His eyes were open, staring unblinking into the distance, and his breathing was deep. At the knock, he broke his placid pose by rising fluidly to a sitting position. He gestured for her to get back into bed with a nod of his head, then tossed off the bedclothes covering his legs. He got up, walked straight to the door, unlatched it and opened it to reveal his splendid nakedness to whomever might be standing on the other side.

From the bed, Gwyneth could not determine who had come calling at such an hour. She guessed, from the way Beresford was speaking, that it must be a page, although she was aware that her husband was as likely to speak equally rudely to one of his peers. She also guessed that the news was not particularly good—which made sense, given that the hour of the call suggested something urgent. She could not hear enough of the conversation, however, to know the nature of the bad news. Nor was she to learn what it was from Beresford, who, after a brief discussion, dismissed the messenger with a curt nod. Then he closed the door and walked to the hearth, where his clothes lay in an intimate heap with hers.

As he sorted through the clothing, she watched the movements of his naked body with fascination. She asked, "How did you know when you went to the door undressed that it was only a page come with a message?"

He raised a garment here, another there, flinging several items over his shoulder. "I didn't."

"But what if someone else had seen you? Someone more important?"

He shrugged. "What could they expect?"

He was right, of course. Anyone knocking on Beresford's door in the early morning after his wedding night could hardly expect him to be anything but undressed.

"Is aught amiss?" she asked next.

"It was serious enough to keep me from wringing the young fool's neck for the intrusion."

His tone did not invite further discussion, and she fell to watching him perform the simple task of dressing himself. The activity struck her as most extraordinary. She wondered if she would ever be able to imagine him truly dressed ever again, for her impression of his body in its nakedness was so stark that she did not think clothing would ever fully hide it from her. After he had donned his chausses and she had studied the effect of his half-clothed body, she decided that a man like Beresford, when stripped of clothing, was not really naked at all, for he had nothing to hide. Rather, he was simply in his skin.

He completed his second skin with shirt and tunic. His feet were quickly shod, and he bent to retrieve his belt, which, instead of fastening around his waist, he slung around his neck. He ran his fingers through wild, un-combed curls, hardly taming them, then picked up the tray next to the hearth and came toward the bed. She was surprised when he sat down at her side and placed the tray on the floor next to the bed. He reached over and took from her fingers the sheet that she was holding at her breasts, pushing it away so that he could look at her.

At first she was embarrassed by his scrutiny of her breasts, then curious about his intent look and finally aroused by the contemplative desire she saw awaken in his eyes and in the slight softening of his hard mouth. He reached out and touched the tip of one breast, teased it to its peak, then moved to the other and toyed with it, too, as if it were an intriguing object that he did not quite understand. He spread his hand over her left breast, and she was sure he could feel the rapid thumping of her heart. He let his hand fall. He bent to pick up the bowl of fruit and set it on the bed between them. After cutting the wine in the goblets with water from the ewer, he handed her a cup.

He said, "We never got to this last night."

She accepted the cup and took a sip to wash her mouth. "Do you have time for it now?"

"No," he said, and drank his watered wine. He selected several strawberries from the bowl, ate them in a gulp, then lifted a greenish plum. He popped this into his mouth and pursed his lips as he bit into the sourness. He made a sound of satisfaction.

She chose daintily among plump berries, red and purple. "Well, then?" she asked.

He made quick work of his wine and the fruit and put his goblet down on the tray at his feet. When he straightened, he looked at her, clasping the ends of the belt slung around his neck with his hands. He said, "I'll be leaving after midday."

"Where are you going?"

He did not choose to answer that. Instead, he said, "I don't know how long I'll be gone."

"You'll be gone more than a sennight?" she inquired.

He reflected on that, then quirked his brows. "Possibly."

"You might miss the tournament, then?"

He had apparently forgotten that detail. He reconsidered. "I'll return before the tournament." His voice was confident.

"But we shall celebrate the Trinity without you."

"Yes."

He volunteered nothing further, and she was not going to beg. He apparently thought some information was none of her business. She sipped her wine and picked out several more berries.

He said, "You can lie abed for as long as you like and descend to the hall at your leisure. I will request of Adela that you remain here at the Tower, during my absence."

She was rapidly adjusting to these new plans. She recognized this as a dangerous moment, one when the course of their marriage would be set. She put up defenses against the effect of his touch and the look in his eyes and her own nakedness. Still, she luxuriated in the feelings produced by the night they had just spent together, and her sleepy sensuousness gave her an idea of how to handle him. It was the most obvious strategy in the world for a woman to use with a man, but it seemed strikingly new to her, even daring.

She shifted her legs so that she was sitting on her heels, with the sheet pooling in her lap. She pressed her arms to her sides, framing her breasts and pushing them forward a little. "Perhaps I would like to accustom myself to my new home," she said, lowering her lashes and her voice.

"I wish to know that you are safe here at the Tower," he said.

"How can I not be safe in my own home?" she returned, looking up at him directly. She did not know how to be coy, and she did not think that coyness would work with a man like Beresford.

"I wish to know where you are."

She smiled. "But you will know exactly where I am."

"And how you go along."

She decided not to respond to that. Instead, she smiled more warmly at him, cocked her head, shrugged prettily.

His eyes left her face to fall on her bared breasts. Then he glanced away, so that his profile was to her. She could not see the expression on his face when he replied neutrally, "You may suit yourself."

It was likely that he did not truly care where she spent the next several days. Nevertheless, she felt a measure of victory, as if life were returning to her.

Her moment of victory did not last long, for he surprised her by drawing her to him. He placed his lips on hers, and she tasted wine and berry juice, both sweet and tart. The buckle of the belt around his neck pressed against her, and the cold metal stung her warm skin. The sting, his lips, the wine, her surprise and her own feminine strategy prompted her to kiss him back. Knowing that he could not stay at her side, she let her kiss promise and linger, for it would cost her nothing. Feeling his quick response of passion, she did not hesitate to let her kiss linger and promise even more. His grip on her shifted accordingly.

She was still holding her empty goblet, and his rough movement caused her fingers to loosen from the stem. The goblet fell on the bed next to her thigh, and the remaining two drops of wine spilled out onto the sheets. She broke the kiss when she realized she had dropped the cup, and looked down in dismay at the delicate red stain. Before Beresford could see what had happened, she placed her hand over the spots and leaned on her arm, as if she were simply propping herself up. She made it seem as if she had meant to end the kiss, smiling sweetly at him and letting her lids flutter down languorously.

He drew a deep breath, then rose from the bed. He looked dazed and had to shake his head once to clear it. He slid his belt from around his neck, secured it deftly at his waist and patted it, feeling for his sword, which was not there. He looked around for the blade and spied it lying before the hearth. He picked it up and held it in his upturned palms, weighing it idly. Then he bowed ever so slightly and said, his voice rough, "Perhaps I shall see you later this morning in the hall, madam, before I leave."

He left the room, and she fell back upon the pillows, letting her breath out in a whoosh. She felt as if she had kept herself in control and had gotten the better of him with that kiss. Yet the bloodred wine spots on the sheet had struck her as a sign that she had lost a particular kind of virginity to him this night, and she knew that she was playing a dangerous game of power with the risky strategy of sexuality.

Later, the same three serving women from the morning before came to her with bowls of fresh water and towels, for which she was grateful. At Adela's orders, they had brought her her dark blue kirtle and light blue linen bliaut to replace the formal clothing she had worn the previous day. They gathered her wedding finery from its heap on the hearth, helped her wash herself and brushed her greatly tangled hair. They primped and prodded her as they had the day before, giggling now at what must have occurred during the night rather than in anticipation of it. Their chatter was light and inconsequential.

When they caught sight of the spots on the sheet, they turned wide, speculative eyes on her, for everyone knew she was a widow.

"Wine," she said coolly and nodded at the tray on the floor by the bed.

One of the women felt the opportunity was ripe to ask what they were all dying to know. "So, my lady Gwyneth, tell!"

Gwyneth did not misunderstand, and had the day before prepared her response to such a demand. She smiled and said, "My husband was very kind." It amazed her to say the words, for they had the unexpected merit of being true.

"Beresford kind?" echoed one.

"How interesting," said another thoughtfully.

"Very interesting," exclaimed a third, "to imagine kindness allied to his strength!"

Gwyneth felt a blush creep up her cheeks. No voluntary action on her part could have better convinced the trio of women of the impression she wanted them to have, namely, that she was a well-satisfied wife.

When they had coiffed and dressed her, the women accompanied Gwyneth out of the bedchamber and to the stairway that would take her to the hall where she would break her fast. Before they arrived at the stairs, Gwyneth put a hand on the arm of the serving woman whom she judged to be the most friendly. She said lightly, "Prepare me for the worst, Auncilla. What, in your opinion, am I to encounter below?"

"And what would the worst be, my lady?" Auncilla replied.

"You see, it was difficult enough for me, as a foreigner, to be the center of all eyes yesterday and the preceding days, and I would like to avoid being the object of curious attention this morning, if possible." Gwyneth smiled. "Is it too much to hope that the interests of the court have turned to a subject beyond that of my marriage?"

"Oh, as to that, my lady, yes!" Auncilla chirped happily. "It seems that Duke Henry lost interest in Malmesbury, after all, and instead of heading east toward London, he has turned his forces west and south toward Bristol! It is most unexpected! So King Stephen—but we all know that it is really Adela—called for troops to be raised to meet Henry at Bristol."

"Simon of Beresford is leading those troops," Auncilla's colleague added. "But, of course, you know that."

"Of course," Gwyneth said calmly.

"But the *real* news is that reports of a traitor within the castle are circulating!" Auncilla continued with relish. "And a variety of names are being advanced, including—"

Auncilla was promptly nudged to silence by the third serving woman, who had, apparently, a greater sense of propriety than her colleagues. "Repeating idle gossip," this proper woman said, sniffing in displeasure, "leads only to mischief."

Gwyneth noted the rumors. For no reason she could name, she thought immediately of Cedric of Valmey. To the proper woman she said, "You are quite right to discourage idle gossip." The woman accepted her approbation with a superior nod. Gwyneth squeezed Auncilla's arm sympathetically and said, "But it is so enjoyable to tell stories, is it not?"

Upon arriving in the hall, she was satisfied that Auncilla's prediction that the courtiers had fresh topics to absorb their attention was, at least in part, true. Only a few curious eyes turned toward her when she entered. She scanned the hall and noted Beresford on the other side, deep in conversation with several knights. He did not look up, and she was not going to make a fool of herself by paying unseemly attention to him. She noticed Geoffrey of Senlis standing not far from Beresford. When her eye met his, he bowed ceremoniously.

She caught her breath at the expression on his face, nodded her head slightly in return and continued to survey the room. Adela was moving calmly but continuously from group to group. Cedric of Valmey was nowhere to be seen, which signified nothing at all, while Rosalyn was holding her own little court near one of the fireplaces, laughing with knights, chatting with ladies and generally dispensing her wintry charm among all.

Just as Gwyneth was completing her study of the hall and wondering what course to take next, Johanna stepped to her side. "You must be hungry, my newest cousin," she said, smiling at her kindly and gesturing her toward the table, where few people remained at their trenchers. "And so am I, for the length of morning mass always seems to raise my appetite. May I join you?"

Nothing could have pleased Gwyneth better than to see a friendly face just then and to have companionship for the

morning meal. A possibly awkward moment had been effortlessly bridged. She accepted Johanna's offer with pleasure and a trace of relief.

Johanna walked with her to the table, speaking of the
most ordinary things imaginable, the daily affairs of castle
life. She made no insinuating references to the night before, did not wink suggestively or nudge Gwyneth meaningfully. She did not treat her in any way other than a
woman worthy of friendship and respect.

They sat down together, broke their bread and dipped it
in the mild broth that was served them. Gwyneth marveled
at how Johanna could maintain easy conversation that,
nevertheless, carried the more serious message: Don't
worry! You'll make it through this day, just as you did the
previous one!

"Well, then," Johanna said at one point, "I suppose you
must be of two minds about the latest news."

Gwyneth paused. "Two minds?" she asked, always cautious.

Johanna crinkled her nose. "I am not the least interested
in politics, in the general way of things," she confessed,
"but the great affairs of kings and kingdoms can hardly be
avoided on certain occasions! Today is certainly one of
them, with the Tower so restive and the troops ready to depart."

"Yes, I've heard the king has ordered troops to Bristol."

"With Simon among them," Johanna added, "as he's no
doubt told you."

Gwyneth appreciated the way she said that without irony,
although Johanna might have guessed that Beresford had
told her nothing. Gwyneth was also aware that she had been
provided an opening to learn more information, if she
needed it. She was glad that she did not, but if she had, she
would not have had to be embarrassed before Johanna.

"Yes, I know that my husband is leading those troops,"
Gwyneth said smoothly, "which is certainly a pity, when one

is so newly married. Given that, I am of one mind only about his departure, not two.''

"The only woman I know to be of one mind only!" Johanna teased.

Gwyneth smiled a self-deprecating smile, then confided, "Except that his departure gives me a chance to adjust to my new circumstances with much breathing room, let us say, and now I will have the opportunity to put his house to rights while he is gone."

"You will reside at his house in his absence?" Johanna asked, her surprise evident.

"He has given me his permission to do so," Gwyneth stated.

"And Adela?"

"Why should she object?"

Johanna looked at her directly and said, "Let me be frank about what I meant regarding your two minds. I had imagined that you would find it difficult to decide whether you would side, as loyal wife, with Beresford or, as loyal Northumbrian, with Duke Henry."

The comment served to remind Gwyneth that she had a conflict of interest on that score. It also put her in mind of the more interesting rumor she had heard from Auncilla. The second consideration seemed the more pressing of the two.

"Which reminds me," she said with an inflection of interest, meeting Johanna's direct gaze with one of her own, "I also heard that reports of a traitor within castle walls are being circulated, and that the rumors come attached to several names. What say you to all of this?"

Johanna's brow furrowed. "I say, first of all, that they are idle, vicious and unfounded." Her voice was sad. "So you see that you needn't worry about—" Here she broke off and looked up at the person whose shadow had just fallen across the table.

Gwyneth looked up, too, and was startled to see Beresford standing before them. The way he was looking at her

was so very different from the way Canute would look at
her, and the way she was reacting to him was so very different from the way she had reacted to Canute. She attempted, from force of habit, to hold Beresford in the
familiar and magnificent contempt in which she had held
her first husband, but the attempt lacked force and failed.
She was angry at herself for not being able to remain emo-
tionally chaste now that Beresford had possessed her body.
Instead, she felt a spasm in the region of her heart. She
hoped that she was not blushing.

"What is idle, vicious and unfounded?" Beresford asked
of his cousin.

"Rumors," Johanna replied offhandedly.

"And the particular rumors in question?" he asked.

"The usual, you know, Simon," Johanna said dismissively. "Idle and vicious."

"Such is the nature of rumors," he replied. "And for
what reason should my wife not worry?"

Johanna's expression became more troubled, but she
managed to keep her voice light. "Because Gwyneth has
many friends at court, including myself, and I leave you now
so that you may discuss with her, Simon, what is necessary
before you depart." So saying, she rose, made her pretty
excuses and left Gwyneth to her husband.

When Johanna had gone, Gwyneth felt a kind of fear, or
maybe excitement, to be in Beresford's presence in public.
She said, "Do you join me, sire, as I finish my bread?"

After a meditative pause, Beresford nodded. He came
around and settled himself on the bench next to her. She
advanced a few innocuous comments, to which he replied
with palpable disinterest. Several knights drifted by, posing
questions. He answered them curtly. Or, perhaps, Gwyneth
decided, it was rather that he answered them efficiently. The
knights moved on.

Beresford turned to look at her. "And the rumors?" he
asked.

The question was abrupt, but not mysterious, and she saw no reason to evade the subject. "They concern a traitor within castle walls. Have you heard them?"

He continued to regard her. "I'm always the last to hear the gossip, and most of the time I never do."

Something about the effect of his gray eyes upon her prompted her to rashness. She considered surprising him with the conversation between Valmey and Rosalyn she had overheard the evening before. "I have my theories about who the traitor is."

Beresford looked both surprised and amused by this. "In sooth?"

"One of the least unlikely men at court." ·

His amusement overcame his surprise. "Is it not always the case with traitors?" he mused. "And a man, no less."

"Well, could it realistically be a woman?"

"Yes."

Gwyneth looked around the hall. Rosalyn came immediately to mind, but otherwise she drew a blank. "A woman. Well," she conceded, almost playfully, "I suppose that you might be right."

Beresford's gaze followed Gwyneth's around the hall. "I see a number of women whose sympathies might be suspect."

"I would not know that, sire," she said demurely, "given that I am so new to the Tower."

He grunted that this was so, and she found that she liked teasing him. She liked that he underestimated her. She liked that he thought himself so superior. It was like the kiss this morning, when he had wanted her to bow to his superior skill, but she had ended by bringing him to his knees instead.

"While we are on the subject," he said, "I spoke to Adela about my decision to allow you to remove to my house while I am absent from London."

Gwyneth turned her full attention to him. She admirably suppressed her desire to contest his phrasing, that it had been his decision to *allow* her to do as she wished. "And she saw the wisdom of such a move?" she asked.

"Not at first."

"Oh?"

"She did not want you out of her jurisdiction, with all the uncertainties of the moment," he said with a shrug of his broad shoulders, "and with all the rumors."

Gwyneth absorbed the implications of this statement, and when it dawned on her that *she* was, in fact, the object of the castle rumors, she was stunned. Aghast, she decided that her wits must have been wrapped in a misty gauze—spun during the night of lovemaking with Beresford?—for her to miscalculate the simplest of all political sums. She nearly gasped at her own stupidity at being caught in her own trap set with a sultry kiss.

"However, since I had already given you my permission to move in," he was saying, "I persuaded Adela to have several Tower guards accompany you."

Still stunned, she asked, as bluntly as he would, "I am under house arrest?"

"The guards will be there to help you," he replied mildly, as if he had not understood what she meant, "and guide you." He paused, his gray eyes warm upon her, and said, "I thought, my lady, that you would be thanking me for having secured your wishes, as a good husband should."

Gwyneth felt wild and strong emotions surge through her. She was angry at herself for having been outmaneuvered. She was angry at him for so plainly enjoying himself at her expense—for she did not for a moment believe him to be merely playing the role of kind husband. In a fit of pique, she reversed her intention to tell him anything of Valmey's potential for treachery. Hard on the heels of that decision came the realization that it was scarcely the moment to accuse someone else of treasonous plotting, when she herself was a suspect. Then, too, she knew that one Norman knight would hardly be disposed to believe ill of another, simply on the basis of a word from her.

"Thank you," she said sweetly, mastering her voice but not the fire that rushed to her cheeks.

He rose, looking very satisfied. He took her unresisting hand in his and bowed over it. "Now that I must be off, you may wish me Godspeed."

"I wish you Godspeed," she said through her teeth.

He pressed his lips to the back of her hand. He added quietly, provocatively, "And good success against Duke Henry."

She felt the tingle of his touch all the way up her arm and nearly snatched her hand away. She would *not* give him the satisfaction of wishing him good success on that score, and he could interpret her silence and her political interests any way he liked! As if she even cared!

He released her hand, bowed once perfunctorily and, without another word, turned on his heels to stride across the room.

She sat immobile, watching him depart. Her emotions, previously stirred, now spurted up inside her like a fountain. He had looked entirely too smug before he had turned away from her, as if he had her exactly where he wanted her. Well, he did not! Nor did she feel a thing except anger for the blunt, plain-speaking, graceless man who was her husband. Not a thing! She did not feel pain piercing her heart, causing her to catch her breath. Oh no, she could breathe easily, and her heart was beating just fine. She was healthy and alive and mistress of her destiny.

But what was that annoying image hovering just at the limit of her vision? It was small and seemed to have wings and was carrying a bow and arrow. What *was* it, by Odin!

She blinked and tried to shake her head clear of the hazy gauze befuddling her reason. Addled and with her anger flowing, she decided that the little winged creature must be the wily god Loki, transformed into a fly, which was the shape he often assumed to cause his trouble. Yes, that was it. The handsome, agile, cunning Loki was a fly buzzing around her head, distracting her, annoying her—although she knew of no tale in which Loki had ever carried a bow and arrow.

Satisfied by the explanation, even a little relieved by it, she decided that Loki, god of mischief, had come to play a joke on her. But why did Loki's fly look like a plump baby boy? And why did she feel a golden arrow pierce her heart?

Chapter Thirteen

Not too many hours later, Gwyneth stood in the middle of the courtyard of her new home, surveying the extent of the disaster that surrounded her. She had found an old smock and a kerchief for her hair. She had found several crippled brooms in the room on the upper story that had previously yielded the one Ermina had used to sweep out the mistress's chamber. She had found a couple of badly damaged scrub brushes as well, along with some dilapidated pails and the miracle of a block of uncut soap. She even found some slovenly serving women in the back courtyard. Into their hands she thrust the implements that would put the household next to godliness, and after the proper motivational speeches, which threatened the immediate loss of their employment, she set the women to work.

It took more skillful maneuvering to prompt the able-bodied men of the household into action. Beresford's master of the armory, for instance, had never held anything as innocent or innocuous as brush and pail, and he felt it frankly beneath him to do so. Gwyneth solved the problem by providing him with a weighty item of construction, rather than destruction. The master of the armory waved the hammer experimentally, getting the feel and balance of it. Gwyneth smiled and informed him, with a straight face, that the true test of the tool was to use it without thumping one's thumb.

She derived perverse pleasure from making similar use of the five castle guards who had come to watch over her. She discovered soon enough that they were strong and stupid and responded well to authority. They were perfect for fetching water from the well, holding ladders and moving furniture. She imagined that they would report back to the castle next week, glumly, that Gwyneth of Beresford had cleaning on her mind more than treason. She would even be sure to thank Adela some day for having provided her with such brave and brainless assistance.

Dinner was tasteless but edible, and supper not much better. She slept badly on a stale mattress and the next morning did what she had intended to do all along, which was to burn the bed curtains. On impulse, she decided to add to the fiery pile the ratty curtain that separated her chamber from Beresford's. A number of household items seemed worthy of burning along with the rotten shutters. While she was at it, she rounded up Beresford's sons, Benedict and Gilbert, stripped them naked and burned their verminous clothes as well. The two boys were dipped wriggling and protesting into warm, soapy water.

Thus went the elemental cleaning process all morning long—fire and water, water and fire. And soap.

That afternoon, in the escort of Swanilda, the least sullen of the serving women, Gwyneth left the house to familiarize herself with the neighborhood, informally known as Cornhill. She had never lived in such a large metropolis and so was not, at first, prepared for the hard bargaining that was carried out at the various stalls, all under the guise of trivial pleasantries. She wished to hire many of the local craftsmen, and since Beresford had given her no purse, she had to rely on her name for credit and her English for good bargains. Unfortunately, her ear had not accustomed itself to the peculiar cadences of the English spoken in London, and so at one booth she misheard a twenty for a two and concluded a very bad bargain that Beresford would be sure to question upon his return. Thereafter, she exercised greater caution.

In addition to the deals she argued and sealed, her ears echoed with the busy hum and mingled sounds of work: the melodious anvil, the cry of the apprentices, the songs of the retailers, as well as those of the bakers who took around the loaves and the women who sold fish. Geese tied to the poulterers' stalls honked and gabbled.

First on her list of craftsmen to engage was the glazier, and next was the carpenter. When the services of the most reputable among these were secured, she established relations with the tiler and the plasterer. Then came the vintner, the alewife, the baker, the grocer, the miller, the cheesemonger, the spicer, the knifesmith, the draper, the chandler, the chaucer (although she did not immediately need shoes), the capletmonger and the bucklesmith. On the whole, she made an excellent impression, and despite her obvious northern ancestry, was better received as a Northumbrian than as a Norman. Her beauty did not work to her disadvantage, either. The traders and goodwives generally concluded that Beresford's marriage was a boon for local business.

Gwyneth spent a strenuous few hours jostling for position and price in the warren of streets around Cornhill. At the end of the afternoon, she acknowledged that her feet had grown tired and her nose had had its fill of the tallow melting and the soap making, and the frank stink of the blood and offal that poured down the narrow lanes into the river from the nearby shambles. She and her woman returned home by way of the street that boasted The Swan.

Gwyneth had noted this tavern on her initial journey to Beresford's home the week before. It was a typical shop in that its pair of horizontal shutters opened upward and downward, top and bottom. The upper shutter was supported by two posts that converted it into an awning. The lower was dropped to rest on two short legs, and acted as a display counter. At the counter at this particular hour

lounged two men that Gwyneth recognized at a glance to be
neighborhood scoundrels. They gave her cheeky grins and
introduced themselves as Daw the Diker and Wat the Tinker. The news of her identity had quickly spread throughout the neighborhood, and so they were able to congratulate
her on her fine marriage and offer their labor for any odd
task she might have. Gwyneth walked on without more than
checking her step. They called out cheerfully, "Remember
us!" She assured them that she would.

That evening, the fare at supper after vespers was improved merely by the fact that it was fresh. Gwyneth realized, of course, that it would take many days, perhaps even
weeks, before the kitchens would be in any sort of reasonable condition and a cook properly trained. She was pleased
by the fact that she had so quickly made what was once the
boys' sleeping chamber into the solar again, and it was the
first room in which fresh rushes had been laid. That meant
that the room was available for dining, and she was determined that correct manners would be observed there. A
wide cloth was spread over the trestle table already in the
center of the room, and the places set along one side only.
On that side the cloth fell to the floor, doubling as a com-
munal napkin that Gwyneth insisted Beresford's sons,
Benedict and Gilbert, use. Because the wine cup was shared,
she explained, one must wipe one's lips free of grease before putting them to the cup.

With the boys clean and well-dressed and sitting on either side of her, Gwyneth made aggressive strides in publicly instructing them in table manners. It was her idea that
the adults in the household who also needed such lessons
could receive them indirectly. The boys were apparently well
schooled in how to properly hold a sword and shield, but
they were completely surprised to learn from Gwyneth that:
"Food is not dipped into the saltcellar. Bread is broken, not
bitten. Blowing on food to cool it is commonly practiced but
frowned upon." They were similarly surprised, and thoroughly dismayed, to learn further that: "Gentlefolk eat

slowly, take small bites, do not talk while eating, do not drink with their mouths full." They promptly wished to excuse themselves from the class of folk designated "gentle." Gwyneth merely smiled upon them pityingly and continued: "Knives are never put in the mouth. Soup must be eaten silently, and the spoon not left in the dish." They were finally horrified by their wicked new stepmother's strictures that: "One does not belch, lean on the table, hang over his dish or pick his nose, teeth or nails."

Benedict and Gilbert were inclined to think much better of their new mother when she put them to bed that night in cozy cots with clean linens. They slept for the first time in their lives without fleas and bedbugs, for Gwyneth had put in their new room trenchers of bread spread with birdlime and with a lighted candle in the middle. She tucked the boys in and kissed their cheeks in a way that brought them the sweetest of dreams.

The next day began early after prime with the arrival of various craftsmen whom Gwyneth had hired the day before. Soon the main courtyard was alive not with training exercises, but with carpenters and plasterers and sawhorses and wood shavings and tubs of water and rudimentary scaffolding. Various tradespeople came and went with their deliveries. Other misguided souls turned up at Gwyneth's door as well, along with the usual gawkers who came simply to see what all the fuss was about.

Toward midafternoon, Gwyneth received a very welcome visitor. She was in the back courtyard, standing at the door to the kitchens, wrestling with the problem of how best to attack a decade's filth within, when she happened to turn toward the person who had come up next to her.

Her face broke into a smile. "Give you good day, Johanna," she greeted Beresford's cousin happily. "What brings you to this neighborhood?"

"Why, you, of course," Johanna replied with a smile. She looked about, surveying the bustle around her. "Although now that I am here, I am wondering why I thought it necessary to come see how you are getting along. I thought that you might need cheering up, but instead I find you productively engaged!"

"Of course I need cheering up, given the wretched state of this house," Gwyneth replied. She shook her handkerchiefed head in dismay.

Johanna made a sympathetic noise. "It is quite hideous," she agreed, peering into the gloom of the kitchens, "and probably far worse two days ago than it is now."

"We are excavating through the dirt at the rate of a year's worth every three or four days, I should think. That means that in another month we should have the kitchens operating reasonably again. How were such slovenly conditions permitted to prevail, I wonder?"

Johanna shrugged. "Beresford obviously has not cared about the house since Roesia died."

"Or before she died, either, from my estimation. I am looking at ten years of dirt, not just five."

Johanna pulled a face. "I haven't been here since, perhaps, a year before Roesia died. As I recall, the house was unkempt, but it was not..." Here Johanna groped for words.

"Hideous?" Gwyneth suggested helpfully. "Horrendous?"

"Either will do, or perhaps both," Johanna conceded with a wry smile.

"But come, let us leave this open garbage pit, which is not, even under the best of conditions, the place to receive a visitor." Gwyneth led Johanna toward the main courtyard. "Let me show you what I am doing to the solar. So, tell me, what was she like, Roesia?"

"A handsome woman, really," Johanna said reflectively. "But such a temper, and such a tongue! Now, Roesia certainly had her friends and advocates, but there were those whose sympathies were firmly with Simon, for all of his lack of social graces!"

"Did he provoke her?"

Johanna laughed. "No, worse! He ignored her!"

"Did he ever beat her?" Gwyneth inquired. "Say, for mismanaging household accounts?"

Johanna slid Gwyneth a speculative glance. They had entered the main courtyard, where the neighborhood craftsmen held center stage, and were crossing to the staircase, which was undergoing a major rebuilding and reinforcement. "How much is all of this going to cost?" Johanna asked.

"Watch out for the third and the second-to-last steps," Gwyneth warned, then answered in a rather severe tone, "It will cost about tenfold what it would have taken to have maintained the property rightfully throughout the years."

Johanna cast an admiring glance at Gwyneth. "Very good!" she said. "Now, I recommend that you practice that answer in such a tone and that you say your rosary every night until Simon returns, and he will be properly chastened. Do you know when that will be?"

Gwyneth shook her head. "Several more days, I suppose. He said he would return before the tournament, in any case." She did not pursue the interesting topics of the tournament or Beresford's return, for her attention was claimed by Benedict and Gilbert.

The boys were hanging over the balcony railing, pulling up a heavy pail on pulley-rigged ropes. Although they were evidently helping in the only manner they could, they were doing so at great bodily peril to themselves, and Gwyneth caught her breath in fear that they would fall. She steadied her nerves, then called out calmly, clapping her hands, "Away from the railing, Benedict! Gilbert!"

At Gwyneth's command the boys let go of the ropes, causing the heavy bucket to fall to the ground, harming no one but angering the plasterer whose bucket it was. Taking one look at the man's face, the boys immediately pointed to Gwyneth, referring him to the true culprit. Gwyneth did what she could to soothe the plasterer and instruct the boys as to how they could safely help. They thought it less amus-

ing sport to stand so far away from the railing, but had
learned in the past few days that Gwyneth had more stami-
na than they did and that it would be less tiresome to simply obey her than to have her wear them down until they did
as she bade.

Gwyneth gestured to Johanna, and the two women
walked on around the balcony to the solar.

"I will admit freely," Johanna pronounced, "that I did
not even recognize Benedict and Gilbert. I vow, I was impressed before with what you've done, but now I am positively amazed!"

Gwyneth laughed off the high praise and said, "Yes, it is
positively amazing what a bath, trimmed hair and clean
clothes will do for a little boy. A big boy, too, come to think
of it. Now, here is the real test, Johanna." She extended her
arm with a dramatic flourish. "The solar!"

Johanna's eyebrows rose admiringly. "Not bad," she
said. "Not bad at all, given that I vaguely recall what it
looked like six or seven years ago and can imagine how far
it deteriorated in the meantime."

They stepped into the room, where the wide wooden
planking of the floors was being stripped of dirt and wax,
where the glazier was busy fitting the new casement windows and where many pairs of hands swarmed over the
fireplace facade, scrubbing off the soot.

"I retrieved the spice cupboard from an unused room,"
Gwyneth explained, pointing to the valuable piece of furniture on the interior wall adjacent to the fireplace. "Of
course, it remains empty, for I do not wish for the expense
of spices now, given everything else we need. But the true
find was this." She gestured toward the wall opposite the
fireplace, along which ran the long serving board that also
held the plate and assorted crockery. "I have managed to
assemble something resembling serving pieces to go with the
plate. They were in a rubbish heap in the kitchen. Can you
believe it? I wonder where Beresford took his meals all these
years."

Johanna shook her head in puzzlement. "My guess is that he ate with his men out in the open of the courtyard, summer and winter, at any odd moment they happened to pause in their exercise. I suspect they sat on the rain barrels and the stairs and anywhere else they could find." She sighed. "I had forgotten how very beautiful this house could be. I pray you, show me more!"

Gwyneth did so, and gladly, outlining the grand scope of her plans, which included many lengths of cloth for the sleeping chambers. For the kitchens she envisioned several decent pickling tubs along with a tank in which live fish would swim.

The two women continued to chat companionably. To Johanna's repeated expressions of amazement at her professional housewifery, Gwyneth had to remind her friend at least twice that she had been chatelaine of Castle Norham for close to five years. After nearly an hour of domestic discussion, Johanna took her leave to return to the Tower in company of the retinue in which she had come.

The following day unfolded in much the same manner as had the day before. So did the day after that, as well as the next. The dinner on that day was approaching respectability, but far from being servable to guests. Gwyneth had no intention of inviting guests yet, of course, for there was still much ground to cover in reducing the general level of slurping and slopping at the table, from children and adults alike.

The Trinity came and went and was celebrated solemnly by the entire household at the Church of Cripplegate. The day was sunny and, because June had come, it was warm.

The next day dawned even warmer, and by the late afternoon, Gwyneth was tired of her vigorous industry. She had shed her heavy smock and kerchief for a light kirtle and bliaut; she had brushed out her hair and rebraided it to pin it into a circle around her head; and she had traded the broom and the scrub brush for the needle. Because the solar was the most habitable, the most comfortable and the brightest room in the house, she went there and sat on a stool near one of the open windows. She held in her lap an old linen chemise, now washed and sun dried, to which she was applying her bodkin. A towering pile of rent garments was stacked next to her. She was deep in her own thoughts. The craftsmen orbited quietly about her, just as the stars moved around the earth.

At one moment, sensing someone watching her, Gwyneth looked up. She blinked curiously, then her air of concentration lifted from her brow. She laid aside her mending and rose, extending her hand in welcome as she crossed the room. She even smiled, though somewhat apologetically.

"No one announced you, sire," she said, "and so I am afraid that I am guilty of being a bad hostess the first time you come to visit when I am mistress."

"Not at all, my lady," Senlis said, grasping her hand and bowing over it. "When I stepped into the courtyard just now and saw all the activity, I did not wish to disturb any of the workers, who were so obviously better engaged with their projects than showing me through a house I know very well!" He released her hand and gazed around the room. "Very nice," he commented. "Very nice, indeed!"

Her eyes followed his. "Yes, the house will soon be fit for human habitation," she replied. "We may even be able to invite guests, although that seems a distant goal at the moment." She turned toward him and asked, "Have you come to see my husband? I had almost expected him yesterday, in fact, but I am afraid that he has not yet returned."

"No," Senlis said, "I did not come to see him."

Gwyneth was about to ask, "But, then, why did you come?" when she thought the better of it.

After her slight hesitation, Senlis continued, "I know that his party has not yet returned from the west, for a messenger came to the Tower this morning, reporting the news."

Gwyneth felt her heart lurch at thought of a battle or, at the very least, a skirmish. She kept her features composed as she asked, "And what, exactly, is that news?"

"Why, nothing," Senlis returned with a courteous smile. "Duke Henry prefers to rest and feast, it seems, as if he had come to England on a pleasure trip. His forces have not engaged with Simon's, and given the torrential rains in the west, he displays no desire to muddy his boots or the feet of his soldiers. It is most curious!"

"It is, indeed," Gwyneth agreed, for she had never heard that Duke Henry was shy of fighting. Quite the contrary, in fact. "In that case," she said, "may I offer you a bench and some spiced wine and a turn of conversation to less-martial topics?"

Senlis accepted this offer gallantly, and Gwyneth advanced to the sideboard, where stood a ewer of wine and several cups. She felt a grain of discomfort in receiving the handsome Geoffrey of Senlis, but his manner was so friendly and so correct that she did not think he intended anything improper. Besides, they were attended in the solar by a changing assortment of workers, and there was nothing the least objectionable that could happen to her under the eyes of a half-dozen men and women.

Senlis took a bench down from the table and set it upright. Gwyneth arranged a tray with wine, cups, a bowl of nuts and a plate of wafers. They exchanged the conversation necessary for serving these items, commenting on the pleasant breezes wafting through the windows, the work of the craftsmen and Gwyneth's pile of mending.

When these preliminaries had been covered, Senlis opened the broad topic of the tournament, which, as he pointed out, "is only a slightly less martial topic than that of Duke Henry's possible military intentions in England."

Gwyneth smiled. "Yes. However, given that the tournament is to start two days hence, it is natural enough to discuss it." The topic gave her an idea. She smiled and touched a deferential hand to her breast. "You perhaps do not know that I am fully conversant with the technicalities of tournaments, sire, and do not simply prattle in speculation about how many jousts there will be or if the weather will be fine.''

''Ah?'' Senlis answered her smile with a very charming one of his own. He teased, ''You mean the level of your conversation hovers above the general run of female imbecilities on the topic?''

Was he flirting with her? Gwyneth wondered. She decided that her very uncertainty about his intentions added just that much more piquancy to every encounter with him. Geoffrey of Senlis was a most handsome man, she had to admit, and she tried to imagine, not for the first time, what it would have been like to have married him. She could not imagine it, but that was perhaps because she was having to give her attention to the conversation and her plan.

''Far above,'' she said with mock-solemn dignity. ''For instance, I am greatly interested in the statutes, and the degree to which an event, which works best with fewest regulations, should be constrained. What say you on the statutes in general?''

Senlis entered into her mood. ''I say nothing to the statutes in general, only to the statutes in particular.'' His tone was light and challenging. ''Do you have such a one in mind?''

She considered. ''Take, for instance, the statute that no one is to assist a fallen knight except his own squires under penalty of three years imprisonment.''

''Well, yes, that statute, my lady, is most reasonable. And the others?''

She spun out the topic, weaving her web to extract the information she wanted. They spoke of horses and squires, weapons and squires, the role of spectators and squires, returning always, inevitably, to squires. When Senlis began to identify the names of various squires, Gwyneth breathed an inward sigh of relief. Her heart leapt when he began to list his own.

"Such an odd name, Breteuil," she interjected at his mention of it. "Such a strange one for me to pronounce. I believe that Beresford has a squire with this name, no?"

Senlis nodded, but said that it was common enough.

So Senlis and Beresford each were possible targets of Valmey's scheme. She was doubly glad now that she had not mentioned to Simon her suspicions concerning Valmey, given that the range of his possible victims was so wide.

"Do other knights have squires with such a name?" she inquired as casually as she could.

"Besides myself and Beresford, you mean? Why yes, perhaps five or six." Senlis considered. "Let me see now. There is Giles Breteuil, who trains with—"

He was never to finish that sentence, for from the main courtyard below came the noisy sounds of arrival and a shout announcing that the master had returned home.

Gwyneth stood up when she heard Benedict and Gilbert crying, "Papa! Papa!"

Chapter Fourteen

Beresford passed through the portal to the house, took one look at the courtyard and realized that he had made a mistake. He turned around and was about to exit again, and to command his men to do the same, when John the Porter asked him if he had left something out in the street.

Beresford fixed his regard on a man he had known for over fifteen years and wondered why his porter should be at someone else's house. The answer that came to him was so surprising that he was rendered speechless for a moment and could mumble only, "No, no, I'm all right." He turned back around and gave the courtyard a long, hard look.

He was in his house, there was no mistaking this now that his eye subtracted the scaffolding and the boxes of tools and the sawhorses and the swarming workmen finishing their tasks for the day. He recognized it, but it looked different here and there, as if the house breathed a different air. He thought it a shame that such a well-proportioned courtyard was being occupied by craftsmen who could do their work anywhere else in town, as far as he was concerned. Such a fine courtyard deserved to be occupied by a full complement of knights-in-training.

He did not dwell on the waste of the space, for his attention was claimed by two high-pitched voices exclaiming, "Papa! Papa!" He turned toward the voices and had the extremely curious notion that a few neighborhood girls had wandered into his house and had mistaken him for their father. At second glance, his eyes widened considerably, and when two small bodies flung themselves at him, he caught them automatically. He was relieved to discover that there was nothing girlish about the way his sons felt in his arms.

After greetings and gestures of affection, he set Benedict and Gilbert on the ground again and looked down into their bright, scrubbed faces. He flicked fatherly fingers at their perfectly clipped hair, now shiny clean. He asked humorously, "What happened to you, my pretty fellows?"

They were happy to tell him. "It's all her fault!" "It was Gwyneth!" "She made us take a *bath!*" "She wouldn't let us exercise in the courtyard!" "She spoiled our fun with the bucket and pulley ropes!" "She won't let us belch at the table!" "Or pick our noses!" "It's all her fault!" "Our beds are nice, though!" "Oh, yes, but the rest of it is Gwyneth's fault!"

Their wicked stepmother, who nevertheless gave them angel-sweet bedtime kisses, had descended the staircase and was crossing the courtyard. Beresford looked up at her. It was extraordinary, his reaction to the mere sight of her. He felt his eyes see. He felt his lungs fill. He felt his heart come to rest in the place where it belonged. He felt his wanderings come to their natural, desired end.

During the past several days, he had admitted to himself that he was eager to see her again, but he had not realized until setting eyes on her now that he had *lived* to see her again. She was more beautiful than he had remembered. Something about the way the golden braids encircled her head reminded him of the first time he had seen her, but he could not have said why. In the soft light of the late afternoon, her skin was flushed pale rose. Or, perhaps, her color was not affected by the slating sun but by some emotion she felt upon seeing him again, too? He could not discover the answer in her eyes, however, for she had lowered them out of modesty or respect to him.

Recalling her flush of anger at him upon his departure, when he had put her at such a delicious disadvantage, he did not think that she acted out of respect for him. Recalling the way her body had met his on their wedding night, he did not think that she acted out of modesty. He hoped she did not, in any case. No respect. No modesty. Not tonight. Only desire.

Which flashed over his skin like a warm summer's breeze, just from watching her come toward him. He saw in his mind's eye what lay beneath the fabric of her light bliaut, which molded itself to her curves as she walked calmly toward him. He could not control his reaction and was glad he did not have to. He could claim his husbandly rights now, in her chamber, for they were newlyweds, recently separated. He did not care if his men knew what was on his mind—or the porter, or the craftsmen, or the rest of his household or the neighborhood or even his children, for that matter. He was in his home. He was master, and she was his mistress.

Then she was before him, curtsying slightly, almost kneeling, and he was smiling in anticipation. He took the hand she extended and drew her to her feet.

"Good eventide, my lady," he said, permitting himself the license of kissing the back of her hand.

"Good eventide, my lord," she said, then cleared her throat. "I am happy to see you again."

"Are you?"

She looked up at him then, and he was happy to lose himself in the violet of her eyes. "Yes, of course," she said, "and I have been anticipating your return for several days now."

He released her hand and bowed slightly. "You have wrought changes, I perceive."

"Yes, I have been busy in your absence," she said. "May I point them out to you now?"

He shook his head. "Not now," he said. The look in his eyes was unmistakable.

The color in her cheeks deepened, he was pleased to note. "No, indeed, you are right. Now would not be a good time, since we have a visitor and the evening meal will be ready to serve soon. I am sure that you and your men are sharp-set. Shall we withdraw to the solar, sire, where I might offer you a cup of wine after your journey?"

He was trying to remember where the solar was and why anyone would go there. He caught the word *visitor* and was vaguely displeased, but the offer of food and wine sounded good, and as ready a substitute as any for what he really wanted. He said, "Good enough," then quickly sorted out what his attendants were to do with his horse, his gear and that of his men.

Gwyneth turned to walk back across the courtyard, and he fell into step beside her. Benedict and Gilbert tumbled along behind, eager to be with their father, while Gwyneth commented on some of the improvements being made to the house. Beresford was content to listen to her lilting voice.

They came to the stairs, and he ushered her before him. Out of habit he was going to guide her past the faulty third step, when he grasped the railing. To his surprise, the wood did not give way to his touch, but was solid under his palm. He wiggled the railing, testing it for strength.

Gwyneth looked down at his hand upon the banister, then over her shoulder at him. Her brows rose, inviting comment.

"Hmm," he said.

She smiled at him, somewhat provocatively, he thought. Then she turned and lifted her skirts slightly so that she could proceed up the stairs. When she had put her foot resolutely down on the third step, she turned back to him and said, "Of course, you have the local carpenters to thank for much of the work on the staircase. Still and all, it must be acknowledged that Robert of the Armory did his share."

Beresford blinked. His master of the armory at work on a staircase? As if conjured up by mention of his name,

Robert emerged from the back courtyard, hammer in hand, and exclaimed, "Ah, sire! I heard that you had returned!"

"Robert." Beresford ran his eye over his man's leather apron. His heavy brow lowered to see what he was holding in his hand.

Without further warning than a gleam in his eye, Robert tossed the hammer across a good ten feet of space, and Beresford caught it smartly in his left hand.

"See for yourself how it feels," Robert recommended.

Beresford did so, flexing his supple wrist, flipping the instrument over several times and catching it deftly. He tapped it against the wood of the stairs, listening to the ring of it, then tossed it back to Robert, shaking his head as he did so. He proceeded to climb the stairs behind Gwyneth. He caught up with her midflight but stayed a few steps below so that her hips were at eye level.

"Do you mean to ban all training exercises from the courtyard from now on, madam?" he inquired of her back.

"Of course not, sire," she replied sweetly without turning around. "I have no reason, and no authority, to interfere with your management of the household."

Of course, he had had no intention of allowing her to effect such a ban, but it amused him greatly to hear her defer authority to him, what with the signs of her authority all around them. He took two steps at once and came up right behind her. He put a hand on her hip, the one toward the interior of the staircase, so that no one watching could see his gesture. She paused slightly, but did not stop, when his hand moved up her waist and under her arm, where his fingers could close around her breast. He put his lips to the back of her neck and smelled her lavender freshness. He experienced an unexpected lift to be a man returning to wife and home. The pleasure was at the same time simple and extravagant.

They arrived at the top of the stairs, where Beresford's pleasure was immediately doused. He had come up behind Gwyneth and placed an arm over her shoulder casually, possessively, when he chanced to look across the balcony to see their visitor. It was none other than Geoffrey of Senlis.

His blood ran cold, then hot, then cold again. He did not like that Geoffrey of Senlis had come to see Gwyneth during his absence. He did not like that Gwyneth looked unusually beautiful this evening. Most of all, he did not like his reaction to a man he had long loved and trusted as a friend.

"Geoffrey," he said by way of greeting as he and Gwyneth walked around the balcony. He did not raise his voice, but he knew that it carried the distance.

Senlis bowed, and Beresford longed to wipe the expression—was it a smirk?—off his face.

Beresford dropped his arm from Gwyneth's shoulder when they were at the door to the solar. Now he remembered what the room had been previously used for. She went in ahead of him, saying that he should come in and sit down and she would serve him. He did not immediately obey that gentle command, but stopped instead at the threshold where Senlis was standing. He eyed his friend pointedly.

When Gwyneth was at the sideboard, Senlis said in a very low voice, "I have come to your house at Adela's orders, Simon."

Beresford's expression hinted at incredulity.

"To glean reports from the castle guards Adela assigned to her," Senlis continued.

Beresford had forgotten about the guards he had told Adela to have keep watch over Gwyneth. He did not think that his wife had much interest in politics or anything to do with plots, but he had used the rumor to make sure that Gwyneth would be safe in his home and well protected while he was away.

"Ah, yes, the guards," he said, looking down at the courtyard below. "By the by, where are they?"

"I believe that Gwyneth has put them to work," Senlis said. He nodded toward the well. "I recognize one or two of them hauling water."

Beresford's brows quirked. He was inclined to smile, but did not. "And what will you be reporting to Adela about my wife's political activities?"

"Nothing," Senlis replied. "However, I will be able to report that your house is very clean."

Beresford knew the polite smile on his handsome friend's face well enough, and he was not in the mood to be charmed by him. "Why are you telling me this, Geoffrey?" he demanded flatly.

Senlis bowed again, with a hint of self-mockery. "Merely a desire to save my skin, my friend."

Beresford laughed. "And such pretty skin it is, too."

"I know," Senlis said. "Shall I tell you now of my success this week past with the fair maiden at court who has caught my interest and perhaps my heart?"

Gwyneth was approaching them with a cup of wine in her hand and gesturing them to the table, upon which a broad white cloth had been laid.

Beresford said to Senlis, "No, you can tell me over supper."

"Oh, am I staying?" Senlis asked smoothly.

"Now that you are here," Beresford invited ungraciously.

Senlis bowed a third time. "You are too good. And this will give me an opportunity to hear how matters stand with Henry's forces in the west."

"You could return to the Tower and hear it all there, for I stopped to give my complete reports to the king before coming here."

"But I would so much rather hear it from you," Senlis said, adding slyly, "now that I am here."

Gwyneth had heard this last exchange. She said, "You are most welcome to say and sup with us, Sire Senlis." As the three walked toward the table, she continued, "Although our household is not yet ready for official entertaining, I believe we need not stand on ceremony with you. I would be

pleased if you would join us, but be prepared for a meal that
is quite plain."

So it was decided. The topic of Geoffrey of Senlis's new,
and perhaps fictitious, ladylove was not to arise during the
meal, as Beresford had suggested. First, Beresford had to
accustom himself to the mealtime ritual—that is, reaccus-
tom himself to it, for he only distantly recalled such a se-
quence of events from years past. The blowing of the horn
to announce the supper seemed familiar, as did the passing
of the napkins and the basins for washing hands. It reminded him of the high formality of the great hall at the
Tower. It vexed him to be wasting time with all the fussi-
ness when he had better things to do, but he enjoyed watching Gwyneth command the proceedings. The sight of her
must have mellowed him enough to find a further, rather
tender enjoyment in the fact that, since his household kept
no clergyman, the youngest member of the family, namely
Gilbert, said the grace.

The food was good, too, when he finally got a chance to
taste it. With Gwyneth on his left, and with Senlis to the left
of her, Beresford's attention was, at the beginning of the
meal, focused less on the food and more on the flow of
conversation, the looks and the gestures that were exchanged between his wife and his friend. Even his very attentive eye detected on Gwyneth's part not the slightest hint
of anything more than friendliness toward Senlis. As for
Senlis, whose eye he caught more than once, the handsome
courtier was a genial companion, but nothing more. He included Beresford in all his conversational gambits, and
Beresford responded to an opening or ignored it, as the
spirit moved him.

After the openers, Beresford chose to ignore the conversation and pay attention to the food. Gwyneth offered excuses, for no reason known to Beresford, for the lack of a
brewet as the first course. She was serving instead, she said,
a porray. Beresford had always liked the leek soup with

chitterlings and ham cooked in milk, and thought what was served him a particularly tasty version.

The second course was a civet of hare, which he liked even better, although Gwyneth made deprecatory noises about the dish lacking spices. To this, Senlis made some rather elaborate remarks about the subtlety of the flavors, approved of some method or other she had devised of grilling the meat and praised the onions. Beresford said that he liked his food plain but would be glad for some pepper. As for the other spices, he stated a preference for dill on fish but was just as happy when it was dressed with sorrel.

When the food was settling in his stomach, and all was being washed down with wine from the earthenware jug on the table, Beresford began to think this not a bad arrangement at all. The room was pleasant, and his eye, when it did not stray to his wife, was drawn to the bright and beautiful windowpanes, half-opened to let in the fresh breezes and the softening light and the city sounds from the street below. He felt a certain contentment to be in the room, surrounded by family and household, seeing his retainers fumble through the routines they did not know well.

He also had time to gauge his competition in Geoffrey of Senlis. For the first time, he discovered a decided advantage to being the husband. He was in command of the essential territory and did not have to fight anyone for it. He needed merely to remain in possession. The novelty of the situation appealed to him.

The meal proceeded pleasantly, the talk drifting this way and that, sometimes light and gossipy, sometimes domestic and informative. The topic of the tournament was raised and kept aloft for some time.

Senlis imparted the most delicious court news that a mysterious knight had entered the lists for the Saint Barnabas Day tourney. No one knew his real name or where he came from, but he was rumored to be the strongest man to have ever entered the lists. Adela was, reportedly, the only one to know who he was.

Beresford asked how, since no one knew the knight's name or country, it could be known that he was the strongest. Senlis had no answer to that. Beresford dismissed the topic with a smile compounded of complacency and menace and the words, "Then the matter of who is strongest will be decided soon enough in the usual manner—on the field of contest." He added reflectively, "Or perhaps his squires—they exist, I suppose—can confirm reports of his strength."

Senlis answered, "The Unknown will have squires assigned to him on the day of the tournament, so Adela has ruled." He wished to turn the topic to good account, so he added, "But speaking of squires, your wife and I were discussing them just before you arrived."

Beresford smiled indulgently. He recalled the topic from their wedding day, when he had been charmed and amused by Gwyneth's game attempt to meet him on masculine terms. It had given his desire for her a compelling, intriguing dimension, something more than the usual, impersonal desire for a woman. "She is knowledgeable about tournament regulations," he said, glancing at Gwyneth. He was pleased to see faint color scribble her cheeks.

"She knows the names of your squires," Senlis said, "and observed that one of mine has the same name as yours."

Beresford felt smug. "That must be Breteuil," he said, exaggerating the vowel sounds that were so difficult for Gwyneth to pronounce.

Gwyneth met his eye and accepted his implied challenge. "Breteuil," she repeated, matching the sounds closely enough.

Vaguely aware of the muted spark between his host and hostess, Senlis said, inadvertently playing into Gwyneth's hands, "Yes, and I was just about to tell her the names of the other knights who had engaged squires from the same family."

Gwyneth looked straight at Beresford and said, "Sire Senlis had them on the tip of his tongue when you arrived.

I believe you told me once, did you not, sire, that there were at least a half-dozen?"

Beresford felt that she was returning his challenge. He liked that. The topic was wholly trivial, and he liked that, too. "I recall something of the sort," he said, and rattled off the names of the knights concerned.

Gwyneth accepted this list with a nod he interpreted as mockingly deferential, and she lowered her gaze from his. He found her demeanor very provocative.

Senlis might have caught something of what was passing between them, for he shifted on the bench, then cleared his throat. The evening long, the talk had veered ever closer toward the heavier, more potent topic of Duke Henry's purpose on the island kingdom. Finally, Senlis decided to dance no more around the edges of it. He laid a forearm on the table and leaned forward, looking at Beresford. "So tell us, Simon," he said, "the news from Bristol."

Beresford accepted the change of topic complacently. He was in an expansive mood, and felt a desire to spar. He wanted to work himself up by degrees to the main entertainment of the evening. He slanted a glance at Gwyneth and replied to Senlis, "Do we dare discuss the topic of our moves against Duke Henry in the presence of one of his sympathizers?"

Beresford was gratified to see Gwyneth's quick flush, but it was not yet the color he was longing to fetch up. Still, the angry glare she flashed him was momentarily satisfying to him. "What harm could I possibly do, sire," she replied with a very controlled voice, "when there are five castle guards in my home to prevent me from consorting with any of your enemies?"

"But you have the guards hauling water for you," Beresford returned, "instead of watching over you."

Gwyneth's smile was exceedingly sweet and her voice remarkably submissive. "That is because the house was so very much in need of cleaning, sire. I have Adela to thank for having sent the guards along to help me." She looked up at him guilelessly. "Unless I have someone else to thank for the consideration?"

When Beresford grunted a cagily indifferent, "No," Senlis began to entertain some interesting ideas about this particular exchange. His brows had shot up at Beresford's openly outrageous insult to his wife's loyalties, then knit curiously at Gwyneth's cool reply. She did not shrink an inch from countering him move for move, and she did it all with the clever naiveté that had characterized her demeanor during that first, disastrous meeting with him in the great hall. It was almost as if Beresford had deliberately baited her, and she had bit without getting caught on his hook.

Senlis tried to imagine such a scene being played out between Beresford and the late Roesia with such interesting results, but could not. Something told him that Roesia would not now be sitting calmly at the table and reaching for a little plum in a wooden bowl that had been placed before them. Nor would Beresford be relaxed on the bench next to her, with the deceptive readiness that Senlis knew usually characterized his friend's mood before an engagement.

Beresford had not lingered over the skirmish with his wife. Before Senlis could completely calculate the effects of the exchange between husband and wife, he was answering, "It's true that Gwyneth is hardly in position to make harmful use of anything I tell you. More to the point, however, is the fact that there is nothing at all sensitive that I can tell you." Beresford shrugged. "Henry was not in the mood to fight."

Gwyneth had peeled the plum with Beresford's knife and now offered it to Senlis. She then began to prepare one for Beresford.

"That is what I heard this morning at the Tower from the messenger who preceded you," Senlis said, popping the pretty fruit into his mouth. "Henry's reluctance had something to do with the rains."

"We were knee-deep in mire," Beresford confirmed, "but I've never known a little mud to stop a good battle. My journey was a waste. We sent the messenger forward to report that Henry did not wish to sully his boots, nor those of his 'companions.'" Beresford flicked Senlis a glance. "When does a duke call soldiers 'companions,' Geoffrey?"

"When he's on a mission of peace?" Senlis suggested.

Beresford accepted the offer of the plum from Gwyneth. "Do you believe that?" he asked before biting into it.

Senlis shrugged. "It's as if Henry thinks to talk his way onto the throne."

Beresford grunted. "Can he do it?"

Senlis considered the question, then shrugged again, but not in response to the question. He perceived himself to be an unnecessary third in a conversation that was not verbal, and this unspoken conversation had little to do, he guessed, with kings or dukes or great affairs of state. He rose from the bench, made his excuses to leave and thanked Gwyneth grandly for an excellent evening and meal.

Gwyneth offered him the conventional responses. Beresford rose with him and said, "I shall miss your support, Geoffrey, when my wife and I pursue the topic of Henry's motives in England."

"You mean to pursue it?" Senlis asked, surprised.

"Yes," Beresford answered, reaching over and taking the blade from Gwyneth's hand, "and it is the very topic that requires me to check my wife for knives."

Now came exactly the flush to Gwyneth's cheeks that Beresford had been yearning all evening to see.

Chapter Fifteen

Gwyneth nearly gasped at Beresford's audacity, but was able to maintain her composure during the parting courtesies. While he walked his friend downstairs to the main portal, she remained behind. She decided that she could compose herself best by finding distracting work to do, so she busied herself between the solar and the adjacent kitchens, administering the clearing of the supper. She began the bedtime preparations for Benedict and Gilbert. She discussed with the principal retainers the duties for the morrow. Somehow this domestic activity did not seem to lower the flush that she had felt surge through her body and up her cheeks at Beresford's reference to knives.

Being honest with herself, she acknowledged that the flush had started earlier in the evening, perhaps when Beresford had toyed with her about the names of his squires and the tournament regulations. Or perhaps when they were ascending the stairs, and he had put a hand on her hip and kissed the back of her neck. Or perhaps, even before that, when she had first laid eyes on him in the courtyard, holding his sons in his arms. His obvious affection for his boys unexpectedly endeared him to her. Then he had looked up at her, and her heart had stopped for an uncounted second at sight of his strength and vitality and the look in his eyes when they came to rest on her. She had nearly melted on the spot.

She was directing one of her retainers to shake the table-cloth outside the window to free it of crumbs when two strong hands on her shoulders turned her around, and she was drawn into Beresford's arms. In front of a very interested audience of several serving maids, who hastily called in their colleagues to witness an extraordinary sight, Gwyneth was soundly and passionately kissed. Caught off guard by this public display, she responded to him fully, kissing him back. She realized that she had been wanting to feel herself in his arms since his return, just as she had been wanting his lips to touch hers.

With this kiss, he tasted familiar to her, yet exotic—a touch of her own well-prepared food and heavy wine blended anew by his body's alchemy and her desire for him. She nearly drew back when his tongue touched her lips. However, his grip was light but firm, and she did not escape. His tongue swirled around the inside edges of her lips, and the delight was so unexpected that her mouth yielded to his desire and her lips parted to receive his tongue more fully. She let herself settle into him, surrendering to him her initial reluctance, but not the part of her that met him challenge for challenge. Her tongue responded to his demand, answered him fully and asked more. She felt a thick, heavenly sweetness within her, the warm evening breezes wafting around them and their hushed and expectant audience heightening the surprise and the desire and the delight.

Just when she thought he would take her then and there on the floor of the solar, he broke the kiss and nuzzled her neck. After a moment, his hold on her, which had become a little rough, relaxed. He said indistinctly against her neck, "We'll retire," adding with a kind of low groan, "now."

She nodded and disentangled herself from his arms only partially, for he kept an arm around her shoulders as he turned to walk with her out of the solar. He must have become aware of their audience, for he looked up and growled something about everyone standing about gawking, and recommended that they go about their business. He emphasized his point with a threatening gesture of his free arm, causing the frozen line of wide-eyed serving women to break up immediately.

Although eager for what was to come, Gwyneth had not completely lost her wits. She said to Beresford saucily, "Does this count as the continuation of our discussion of Duke Henry's campaign in England?"

With a provocatively punitive spank on her rear, he propelled her out the door of the solar and onto the gallery balcony. Now that she was turned to walk down the wing that led to their bedchambers, he slung his arm around her neck. He drew her backside up against his front and said into her ear, "Be very happy that I am not asking for the reckoning for all the craftsmen you employed in my absence."

She recalled the argument she had made to Johanna—that the cost of the repairs had far exceeded what would have been the cost of maintenance—but decided that defensive indignation did not suit the mood of the moment. In fact, she far preferred the softer, flirtatious strategy that she had employed with such success on the morning after their wedding night.

She halted momentarily and looked up at him. "Do you mean that you will not ask for the reckoning, or that you are not asking for it yet?"

Beresford's eyes narrowed to gray slits, glittering attractively. "That depends," he said, putting his free hand on her hip, "on how well you persuade me of the necessity of having hired all the craftsmen."

Did she properly interpret that as a challenge to pleasure him well this evening? She dared to ask, "Do you object, sire?" She wanted from him the obedient response that she had offered him when he'd been stretched out beside her, wanting her.

"To the household repairs, do you mean?" he countered. Then, playing along nicely, he mused, "But the

question of permitting objections, wife, is one more fitting
for me to demand of you, as I recall.''

She took a step forward, and he moved with her. "So it
is up to me to persuade you of the necessity of the household repairs?''

"As a good wife, yes.''

She chose a course as blunt and outrageous as Beresford
himself had ever taken. "As a good wife,'' she said demurely, "I have already made it possible for you to finance
these repairs.''

"Ah? How so?''

"Through marriage to me, you received a vast tract of
land and the earl's third penny, so you can well afford what
I am spending.'' When Beresford did not immediately reply, she continued virtuously, "So you see, husband, it is
rather up to you to persuade me that the craftsmen are unnecessary.''

Beresford did not miss the fact that she had just issued
him a counterchallenge that he should pleasure *her* well this
evening. After a very charged pause, he said with effort,
"We had better hurry.''

They did, indeed, hurry along the balcony and across the
threshold to Gwyneth's bedchamber. Beresford kicked the
door shut with his heel. He did not pause to comment on
any of the changes she had wrought in the place, which included the cleanliness, new bed covers and a new curtain on
the doorway leading to his own chamber. He most likely did
not notice them, for he was divesting himself of his clothing in a haphazard fashion, more careless than usual and a
good deal less efficient. Nevertheless, he was stripped to the
comfort of his skin before she had had more than a chance
to unpin her hair and unlace her bliaut.

When he came toward her, he said in a low voice, "Don't
fear me.'' He waited for her to look up at him before he
touched her.

She was grateful for the consideration, for just then, in
the wake of her bravado on the balcony, she was losing her

nerve. The urgency of the undressing reminded her of the intensity of previous violence and hurt and humiliation in her married life. Despite the knowledge that this husband would treat her well, a tremor of well-remembered fear closed her throat and made her fingers fumble with her clothing.

He gently helped her with the rest of her garments, so that her skin could be next to his completely. Then he gathered her in his arms and crushed her to him, nuzzling her neck and bending her this way and that, so that he could find a better fit with her. His hands traveled up and down her body insistently and finally came to rest on her shoulders. He raised his head and looked into her eyes.

She put her hands hesitantly on his shoulders in turn, and he smiled. He dipped his head to kiss first one of her hands, then the other. He ran his palms down her arms and laced his fingers with hers, then brought them to his lips, kissing her fingertips one by one.

She watched in fascination as he kissed her fingers, causing tiny, pleasurable shocks to travel up her arms. He brought the back of her hand to his lips, and her gaze fell on his long fingers. She remembered his touch from their wedding night and must have been regarding his fingers speculatively, for when she lifted her eyes to look into his face, she saw that his heavy brows were raised and that a distinct gleam lit his gray eyes.

"Well, now," he said softly and very meaningfully. He unlaced his hands from hers and replaced the tips of her fingers on his shoulders. Then he trailed his hands down her collarbone to her breasts to her waist to her hips to her abdomen and through her curls, coming to a halt at the apex of her thighs. He cocked his head, as if considering possibilities.

He kissed her lips. He ran his tongue around the inside of her mouth, as he had earlier in the solar. He teased and tasted her. Still kissing her, he slid his fingers lightly between her legs. "Perhaps we should try something differ-

ent." He withdrew his fingers and said gruffly, "I'll show
you what I want to do."

Something in his tone caused her to brace herself and look
at him directly. She decided to be brave. "All right," she
said.

"You can tell me to stop at any time," he said, as he lowered his head to her neck. "Don't be afraid."

"I won't," she breathed.

He lowered his head further to her breasts and touched
the tip of each with his tongue. He was about to move lower
but decided against it, instead opening his mouth to take in
one nipple, then the other, sucking lightly and swirling his
tongue lavishly over their hard peaks. His hands went
around her back and slid down to her buttocks, where he
grasped her firmly, so that she would remain steady on her
feet.

As he kissed her navel, which he also swirled with his
tongue, her hands remained upon his shoulders, her fingers
flexed. Her breathing was becoming more ragged. She was
not precisely afraid of what he was doing, for the feelings
that were pulsing through her were entirely pleasurable.
Rather she was apprehensive. Of the unknown. Of the intuition that this was different. Of the knowledge that he was
going to know her in a way that was dangerously intimate.

He rubbed his lightly stubbled chin in the triangle of curls
at the juncture of her thighs. His hands were grasping her
buttocks and slightly separating them. She felt a surge of
stimulation that caused her knees to wobble, but he kept her
steady. Then he brought his hands around to the front of her
thighs. Slowly, delicately, he parted her tender, secret,
swollen lips with his thumbs, as he might open a tiny, hinged
amulet containing a gem or secret potion. His thumbs
grazed the pearl within once or twice, and dipped into the
secret potion, thereby producing more of it.

He moved his head and his mouth and his lips and his
tongue just a fraction lower, then another fraction. It was a
precious, breathless moment for both of them. He was dar-

ing her to trust him, daring himself to meet her on this pre-
carious level, to taste her essence and make it part of him.
She was daring him to do it, to be forever the man who had
braved this most extravagant kiss. She was daring herself to
allow him to kiss her thus, to spread herself to him in a way
that was well beyond embarrassment, well beyond intimacy. She feared being lost to him in a way that threatened
her own security, and she fully experienced that threat in the
strength of her desire for what was to come.

Just as she hoped and feared and dared, his thumbs
spread her lips with just that irresistible amount of inde-
cent possession, and his tongue came out to touch her pearl,
to swirl around it, to lap experimentally. Then, acquiring the
right pressure and the taste for it, his tongue became in-
quisitive and inventive.

She felt delicious with the exquisite sliding and swirling of
his tongue, trying both to accept and to resist the sensations he was creating for her. It was, finally, impossible to
resist. Under other circumstances, she might have felt embarrassed to be so exposed to him, or angry at his prying, or
indignant at his audacity, or fearful of being hurt. Under
other circumstances, she might have felt nobly regal, to have
him kneeling before her, ministering to her like a slave.
However, in these circumstances, she felt neither inferior
nor superior to him. She felt only gloriously weak and lust-
ily feminine and increasingly desirous. She wanted more:
more touch, more tongue, more exposure, more sensations, more waves. She gulped in wondrously feminine gasps
and moans.

When it seemed that he would not be able to keep her
from falling from the effects of the shuddering pleasure she
was experiencing, he lifted her up, and they toppled and
tumbled gracelessly onto her bed, where he entwined himself instantly within her arms and legs. He burrowed his
head in her neck.

In a voice edged with challenge, he said, "Now this is
what I want you to do."

She lazily opened her eyes and turned her head to regard him inquisitively. She had made the same mistake before—looking upon him while she was awash with the pleasure he had given her. She tried to mend the breached defenses within herself, the ones that kept her safe, but she was not entirely successful. When he told her what he wanted, daring her, she accepted the challenge, reasoning that, with Beresford, compliance was less risky than defiance. She hoped that his oddly tantalizing request would not cause her to lose any more of herself to him.

Later, when she awoke to gray gloom and stretched, he was awake as well and moved with her and under her, with intention.

She lazed at length, wishing to push back the faint light of dawn squeezing in and around the cracks in the door and shutters of her bedchamber. She must have moaned in protest, for the next moment a broad hand came down lightly, but with purpose, on her bare backside.

He said, "Enough of this. The day has come, and I've work to do."

"I'm not stopping you," she retorted, too smart in her half-sleeping state. She rolled over, trying to recapture full slumber, and in so doing, rolled back into his arms. She felt his erection next to her thigh, and she shot up to a sitting position.

"You're not stopping me?" he queried. He was not in the least apologetic about his state. "Remember that I am the one who announced the day and our work." He moved against her. "Consider this a promise. For later. You see, this morning I'm charged to take the useless castle guards back to the Tower first thing."

With such a good dawning to the day, Gwyneth would have never predicted that it was to end in disaster.

The household came to life. At prime the fast was broken with bread and broth. By the terce the courtyard hummed with the activity of craftsmen, and Beresford had left with the castle guards for the day, which he would spend, presumably, at the Tower, in preparation for the tournament on the morrow. Thoughts of the tourney reminded her of Beresford's squires and Valmey's potential for treachery. She decided that at supper this evening she would relate to Beresford the conversation she had overheard between Valmey and Rosalyn, letting him make of it what he could.

Sometime during the morning activity, Gwyneth received a most unexpected visitor. She was busy in a far corner of the main courtyard, dividing her attention between the carpenters on the scaffolding and the plasterers who were raising buckets of water to the balcony. She was also attempting to involve Benedict and Gilbert in the work, while keeping them safe. Two buckets of water were just being raised when one of her serving women claimed her attention and informed her that a man had come to see her. By the tone of the woman's voice, Gwyneth did not think her visitor to be a routine tradesman come with his wares.

Walking toward the shadows of the gallery where the man was waiting, Gwyneth wondered with a prick of anxiety whether it might be Geoffrey of Senlis again. Or perhaps, even worse, Cedric of Valmey. It would be just like that rat to come to her house, knowing that Beresford was away and occupied for the day.

But it was neither Senlis nor Valmey, nor anyone with anything to do with the court of King Stephen or even with the town of London. When she was close enough to discern the features of the man in the shadows, Gwyneth could hardly believe her eyes or contain her amazement.

"Gunnar? Gunnar Erickson? Is that you?" She spoke without thinking in Danish.

"It is, Gwyneth Andresdaughter," the man returned in the same language, stepping from the shadows and into the bright sunshine.

Gunnar Erickson, big and blond and blue-eyed, was all that was familiar to her, and she should have been happier to see him, this link to her past. He had been the one man from her father's employ who had gone with her to Castle Norham, as her guard and protector. He had been her father's brute, and under close supervision from her father, his volatile temper had been governed. At Castle Norham, he had had no similar check on his temper, since his lord and master there had no control over his own. Her father's brute had never harmed her at Castle Norham, but neither had he ever protected her from Canute, and she had witnessed more than once the terrifying lengths to which his temper could take him. In the past five years, she had learned to fear Gunnar Erickson.

Thus she was not wholly pleased by his presence in her new and so-far-safe household. She was justifiably puzzled to see him, as well, and even somewhat disturbed. Masking all of that in a flash, she smiled and clasped his forearms in greeting. "But what a welcome visit! Allow me first to recover from the great surprise of seeing you alive, and then I will ask you what you are doing here in London and at my door!"

Gunnar answered that, in the bloody confusion of the final hours of the siege, Gwyneth could not have known that he had not been killed by the Normans but had been taken prisoner.

"Which you are no longer?" Gwyneth ventured.

"They let me go after a few days." He lifted his broad hands to signify a fatalistic acceptance of the incomprehensibility of Norman ways. "There were so few of us left, and the Norman pigs must have thought us harmless enough or, at least, not important enough to feed."

Gwyneth felt uneasy about this explanation, but did not openly question it. Instead she asked, "Why did you come to London, of all places?"

"I was already halfway here when I was let go."

"Yes, but this is the center of support for King Stephen. Why did you not stay in Northumbria—go to York, for instance, where you might remain among the supporters of Duke Henry?"

"After the wreck of Castle Norham, I thought there was little hope for Duke Henry."

Gwyneth's unease grew. She suddenly saw dangers everywhere, but could not say why or what form the dangers took. She had to ask, "But how on earth did you find me here?"

The brute's smile crinkled his face hideously. "Now, Gwyneth Andresdaughter, that was as easy as walking into the meanest tavern and hearing the news of a Norman lord marrying a Saxon beauty from Northumbria."

Gwyneth relaxed a little. Of course, the marriage of Simon of Beresford to Gwyneth of Northumbria was newsworthy enough to have been bruited about town, and certainly Beresford's house would have been known to anyone Gunnar chanced to ask. She let out the breath she had not realized she was holding and said, "But what a lamentable hostess you find me, Gunnar Erickson! Please, come in and I will pour you some wine. Then you will tell me exactly how it goes with you and what your plans are for the future!"

At that fateful moment, a great crashing and clattering came from across the courtyard, followed by much magnificent cursing in Saxon, every word of which Gwyneth understood. She whirled and was immediately reassured that the accident had not involved Benedict and Gilbert, for the two boys were leaning over the balcony railing, looking with wide-eyed delight at the tangle of rope and spilled buckets and broken scaffolding and prostrate bodies below.

Before the confusion of servants rushing, curses flying and shouts for the surgeon-barber could reach its peak, Gwyneth turned back to Gunnar Erickson. "The wine and your story will have to wait, I'm afraid," she said, "for I must tend to this crisis, as you see."

"I will return," Gunnar Erickson assured her.

She did not want to lose contact with him. She held out her hand anxiously to stay him. "Come back tomorrow. No, not tomorrow," she amended, "for then the tournament begins."

"After the tournament then, Gwyneth Andresdaughter."

"Oh, yes, then, after the tournament!" She called out a hasty, "God be with you, Gunnar Erickson!" before hastening to sort out the mess, assuming quite rightly that the porter would see the huge, hulking Dane out the door.

The uproar in the household lasted nearly the entire day and had not completely settled down by the time Beresford returned. He entered the solar where she was directing the preparations for the evening meal. He went to the sideboard and poured himself a cup of wine, and when Gwyneth turned and first noticed him, he was leaning against the sideboard, cup in hand, regarding her silently.

"Good eventide, sire," she said, feeling a little leap of joy at sight of him.

"Good eventide, madam," he replied with a curt nod.

He was distant, and she thought he was teasing her. A small silence fell. She felt herself flush. To cover it, she smiled.

He returned no answering smile. "I thought you would tell me about the day's unexpected events."

Her smile became rueful. Of course, he was displeased by the elaborate accident in the courtyard. She explained all efficiently and summarized the damages thus: "The apprentice carpenter broke his leg but not badly, and the bone is now set. The second plasterer turned his wrist and bruised his forehead. Beyond that, there were remarkably few material damages, and I worked out a way we can all share the costs.''

"Did you?"

"Why, yes," she said, feeling a trickle of apprehension. "Shall I outline for you what I think is fair?"

He shook his head, then asked abruptly, "I would rather you tell me about the visit from the Dane."

Chapter Sixteen

"The Dane?" Gwyneth queried, bewildered. Then she remembered. She opened her mouth to speak, then closed it again.

Beresford's face took on a sardonic cast. "Did you think you could hide from me his visit to you?"

"Why, no," she said, trying to maintain a calm she did not feel. "I supposed that the porter would tell you of his visit, since he let the man in and out."

"He did not. One of the castle guards did."

"I thought you took the guards back to the Tower with you today."

His smile was not friendly. "One of them stayed behind and watched the house the entire day from across the street."

She summoned icy courage. "At Adela's urging, no doubt?"

He shook his head. "I followed my own counsel." He looked at her through hard, gray eyes. "It proved a wise precaution."

"Oh, indeed? Just what do you think I discussed with the Dane—" She broke off, then continued with tenuous control, "His name is Gunnar Erickson, by the way, and he was in my father's employ before he accompanied me to Castle Norham. He is a man I have known for most of my life." She nearly choked on her anger, but mastered it and her voice. "So, just what do you think Gunnar Erickson and I could have possibly discussed for one minute—perhaps two—in the open courtyard with the entire household surrounding us?"

"I would not know," Beresford answered slowly, "for several of my retainers mentioned that you were speaking with him in the Norse tongue."

That was true, of course, but she had not used Danish to prevent anyone from understanding an entirely straightforward conversation. She was momentarily speechless, then said coldly, "I spoke Danish to Gunnar Erickson just as you speak Norman to Geoffrey of Senlis."

Instead of responding to that, he remarked, "Apparently the Dane survived the capture of Castle Norham."

"Well, yes, he was taken prisoner."

"Ah, I did not realize that he had come to my home accompanied by Normans."

"Well, no, he came alone," Gwyneth said. "The Normans let him go free after a few days."

Beresford's heavy brows rose with frank incredulity. He repeated, "You are telling me that the Normans—we must be speaking of Cedric of Valmey—let a captured man go free after a few days?"

"That is what he told me."

"And did he tell you why?"

"Because there were so few of Canute's men left, and the Normans thought them harmless or, at least, not important enough to feed."

Beresford's expression was severe. "And once Valmey let him go, or sanctioned the order for his release, the Dane—this Gunnar Erickson—" he said, mangling the pronunciation, "came to London. Is that right?"

"Yes. He said that he was halfway here anyway, and so it seemed . . ." She could not finish the thought.

He finished it for her, savagely. "And so it seemed highly likely that, halfway to London, when Valmey released this Gunnar Erickson—for no reason that occurs to me—he would continue along on his own to London anyway. Of course, a once-captured Northumbrian Dane strolling the streets of London makes perfect sense!''

She grasped at a straw. "After the wretched defeat of Canute, Gunnar thought Duke Henry's cause to be without great hope."

"You are saying then," he blazed, "that since arriving in London, this Gunnar Erickson has heard nothing of how the Angevin Henry fares so well in the west? Without even fighting, let me remind you!"

Gunnar's explanations sounded absurd to her now, worked out in such a fashion. Everyone knew that King Stephen's hold on the throne was far from secure and that Duke Henry's threat was real. She recalled having been disturbed by Gunnar's strange appearance at her home. However, she had been so surprised to see him, and there had been such a press of activities before and after his brief visit—and during it, by Odin!—that she had spent little time sifting through the oddities of his explanations. She now realized her mistake.

One piece of the puzzle Beresford did not question. "At least it is not necessary to wonder how it was that Gunnar Erickson found you here," he said. "Even the most ordinary citizen, Saxon or Norman, could tell him where I live! That much is obvious."

Even that much had *not* been obvious to Gwyneth for, in her surprise and confusion at the Dane's visit, she had found it necessary to ask him how he had found her. She felt a physical pain at this evidence of her stupidity. "Yes," she agreed, "it was undoubtedly easy for him to find me here."

"At least," he said slowly, "you admit that."

"Of course I admit it!" she shot back. "I have no reason not to admit it! I have told you the story exactly how it happened. Gunnar Erickson arrived at my door this morning and told me just what I have told you. No more, no less!''

He was regarding her with an expression that she suspected many an enemy had seen before dying. "Do you expect me to believe any of what you have just said?"

"Why should you not believe it?"

"Because you, madam wife, are far too clever to waste your time with imperfect plotting."

"Then consider again! If I am so clever, I should have devised a story far better than this!"

A flash of admiration and a stronger emotion momentarily lit his eyes. He seemed to falter, then gave his head a slight shake. "I should have said that you are far too clever for your own good," he amended, "and that your one mistake was to have underrated me."

She saw with blinding clarity how he was interpreting Gunnar Erickson's visit. It was equally and wrenchingly clear to her that he had every reason to interpret the visit thus. She was at a loss to understand how she had let her guard down so far as to expose herself to this disaster. She was at a loss to know how to protect herself from the consequences of her misjudgment, or how to convince her husband that she was not plotting against him, that she did not want to. It was so simple, really, yet impossible to say—that she wanted to be with him, smiling at him, kissing him, lying next to him, giving herself to him.

She was without protection, without strategy, without the right words. She had only her courage—courage to face him and the danger of the situation. She stood straight before him, head high, her hands at her sides, palms out in supplication. "What can I say to make you believe me?"

She thought, from the look that flashed across his features, that he was going to kill her. She did not know that in standing before him, proud and fearless, she made him think for a moment that she was offering herself to him as a way of seducing him from his doubts about her. And he did not know, as he considered accepting her courageously flaunted invitation, whether he wished to wring her neck or make violent love to her.

She watched, terrified and fascinated, wavering between lovesick despair and morbid hope at what he might do to her. His eyes striving with hers, he visibly struggled with himself, with her, with the emotions unleashed in his breast. Finally, he thrust his cup down on the sideboard with such force that it shattered. Then he flung himself out of the room.

As he strode furiously around the balcony to the stairs, scattering retainers right and left, he was prey to emotions he had never experienced before, not even in the heat of battle. In the solar, he had just pulled himself with extraordinary effort back from the brink of complete capitulation to her, and he was shaken to the core by the previously unimaginable possibility that he would ever voluntarily lay down his arms and surrender to the enemy. He had come so death-defyingly close to it that he lost his breath all over again, just thinking about it.

He imagined crossing the room to take her in his arms. He imagined her looking up at him and smiling. He imagined abandoning himself to the violet pools of her eyes, to the cherry of her lips, to the liquid velvet between her legs. He imagined the Valkyries swooping down to take him to Valhalla.

He was at the door to the street. John the Porter was there, already lifting the bar. "I'll spend the evening at The Swan," Beresford growled, making some vague gesture that caused the man to duck.

At that, Beresford stopped dead in his tracks and eyed him in a way that did not cause the porter to think his chances of living had improved. "Do you have an objection to that?" he demanded.

"No, no, no, sire!" John assured him. "Only that, if you're to spend the evening at The Swan, you'll advertise to the entire neighborhood that you're having trouble at home. You being newly wed and all, I was thinking that—"

His master's quelling eye brought an end to that thought and a swift prayer to the porter's lips. Beresford was furious with him, with himself, with *her* all over again. "I'll be at The Boar's Head," he snapped, naming the roughest tavern at the distant Galley Quay, "in case I'm needed."

"And the curfew, sire?"

He had no choice. "I'll spend the night there as well."

The next time Gwyneth saw Beresford was across the tourney field.

Saint Barnabas Day dawned blue and beautiful and with just the right amount of breeze to keep the bright banners fluttering smartly atop their poles. The day was hot enough and sunny enough, too, to make the noble spectators grateful for the awning stretched over the wooden stands that had been erected at the sides of the lists. King Stephen did not frown on tournaments as did the Church, and because the king was so enamored of this aristocratic sport, he pronounced the usual in-town jousting area, Cheapside, to be too narrow and confined for truly grand combat maneuvers. He proclaimed instead that this day's field be established outside the walls on The Moor.

Gwyneth came to the field escorted by a retinue of retainers that she had had no difficulty assembling. As a result of the disaster with Beresford, she had consolidated her authority as absolute mistress of the household. This morning she had merely to give a quiet command to find her orders instantly obeyed. She was gratified by the power, but not ultimately consoled.

After the master had stormed out of the house, the serving men and women had regarded her with a respectful awe bordering on the reverential. They remembered vividly the blistering rows that Roesia had routinely provoked and that Beresford had won with such relish. They remembered the always-vanquished Roesia carping at them in response, finding fault and generally making their lives miserable. And they could not once recall Beresford kissing Roesia passionately the way he had kissed Gwyneth the day before.

About last evening's "incident" in the solar, it was common knowledge to everyone in the household that Beresford and Gwyneth had not shouted down the house, or broken anything more than a cup of horn, or so much as touched one another. Nevertheless, and taking into consideration the valuable information supplied by John the Porter, they reached the consensus that Gwyneth had won the contest—that is, if contest it had been. Judging from Gwyneth's behavior, they were not quite sure. After Beresford had quit the solar, the mistress had proceeded with preparations for supper, sweetly and calmly but a little distractedly, stating only that the master would not be joining them.

Gwyneth knew it had been a contest and did not feel as if she had won anything. She had slept badly and awoke in worse humor, which took the form of ice-cold detachment. In addition, she had a throbbing headache, which surprised her as much as it irritated her because she was not prone to headaches. Now, she certainly did not need the discomfort. In addition to the sheer pain, she found herself unable to think clearly or quickly, and attributed her sluggish mental state to the further mischief of Loki. On the other hand, she did need her frozen armor to face down the courtiers who, she imagined in her worst moments, would stand as a body and accuse her of traitorous activities.

This did not happen, although she became aware of a more subtle version of discrimination during the course of the tournament.

No special attention, negative or positive, was given to her upon her arrival at the field. She entered the palisade like everyone else, and like everyone else, spent the first moments admiring the stockade ornamented with tapestries and heraldic devices. The atmosphere within was hushed and expectant, the suppressed excitement heightened by the pomp. The marshals of the lists, the heralds with their trumpets and the pursuivants-at-arms were already stationed within the enclosure. The knights and their squires were milling about, creating a sea of shifting colors with their ribbons and scarves and pennons and surcoats and caparisoned horses. Helmets, lances, maces, shields and swords glinted in the sun, blinding eyes so bold as to gaze upon such magnificence.

Gwyneth soon came to realize from the variety of greetings given to her that Beresford had evidently not gone to the Tower to denounce her. She knew from the usual household sources that her husband had spent the evening and possibly the night at the most disreputable of all London taverns. However, she did not know what he had done between debauching himself at The Boar's Head and appearing on the field this morning.

Once she was standing in the shade of the awning, she scanned the area and picked out Beresford's form in a crowd of rushing squires and restless knights. She also spotted the largest man among them, who happened just then to be wearing his helmet, thus obscuring his face. Oddly, something about the way the man moved as he strode to his horse and secured the destrier's mail bard reminded her not of Beresford but of Gunnar Erickson. She closed her eyes in disgust with herself and put her hands to her throbbing temples to massage them.

When she opened her eyes again, the crowd of knights and squires had shifted, but she still easily identified Beresford, now standing away from his horse, his helmet resting in the crook of his arm. She noticed, too, his beautiful deep blue surcoat, emblazoned with the Beresford shield of argent and azure. She had not previously noted his dress, but dismissed the oversight as a product of her unwontedly dull wits.

She noted that he was speaking with several young men, obviously his squires. The name Breteuil flitted through her aching head, along with another significant detail that hovered just beyond her grasp. She was about to make some connection when her thoughts were interrupted by a gentle hand on her arm and the words, softly spoken, "It is very hot today, isn't it? Pity the poor knights, who must be sweltering in their mail and surcoats!''

Gwyneth looked up to see the kind, smiling face of Johanna. ''Oh, yes, it is very hot,'' she agreed, vaguely worried about the loss of her train of thought, ''and the contests should prove, then, all the more intense.''

''Have you chosen a place to sit yet?'' Johanna asked.

When Gwyneth shook her head, Johanna gestured to the section she had taken for herself and her women, and invited Gwyneth to join her. There was enough room for two of Gwyneth's retainers. The rest could remain standing near the benches, still in the shade of the awning.

Gwyneth and Johanna proceeded toward the benches, pausing to curtsy to Adela, who was seated front and center on a chair, making prominent the innovation of having women among the spectators at what had been until recently an exclusively male celebration. Along the way, Gwyneth became aware of suspicious glances cast at her. She missed their significance at first, so subtle were they. However, enough people lifted their eyes to her, then looked away, for her to guess that the looks concerned her relationship to Beresford and the rumors of traitors within castle walls. It occurred to her that if it had become generally known that the most loyal knight in the kingdom had spent the night apart from his new and foreign wife, all kinds of inferences could be made without Beresford having to say a word to anyone.

Yet Gwyneth knew that *someone* would have to have spread the word of Beresford's disaffection from her.

When she and Johanna settled into their places on the benches, Johanna looked out over the orchestrated chaos on the field and remarked mildly, ''But Simon wears no token of yours, my dear!'' She glanced at Gwyneth and clucked her tongue with amused disgust. ''Why can the man never seem to follow the least convention?''

Gwyneth felt stricken that the absence of a token from her was so immediately obvious. She had no ready explanation.

Johanna kindly supplied her with one. "It is perfectly obvious that the man is unused to respecting the courtesies! Now, I have never known him to wear the token of any lady before but," she teased lightly, "I was hoping that, in this instance, he would surely sport one from you!"

Gwyneth saw an opportunity to feel out her friend. "I did not give him one, I am afraid," she said.

"Oh?" Johanna's expression displayed only polite interest.

"You see, Beresford did not spend last night at home," Gwyneth said, "and he left yesterday evening before I thought to give him a scarf to wear on his sleeve."

"Ah!" Johanna said sympathetically, as if this were the most ordinary explanation in the world. "Of course, it would no doubt go better for him *not* to be with his lovely wife the night before a tournament. Such a practice is quite common, in fact!"

Gwyneth had no reason to think that marital abstinence before a tournament was at all common, but she thanked Johanna with her eyes for helping to preserve her dignity. Unfortunately, Johanna's efforts were undermined the next moment, for their brief discussion had been overheard.

"Oh, the practice is very common," Lady Chester purred delightedly, without further greeting. She laughed. "But usually only when the knight and his lady have been married a *very* long time!"

Gwyneth's heart sank to her stomach, and she turned to look at the beautiful Rosalyn, lovely in a white kirtle over which she wore a purple bliaut. The pressure in her aching temples increased when Rosalyn made a place for herself next to Johanna.

"Do you know what we are talking about?" Gwyneth asked directly.

Rosalyn smiled sweetly and condescendingly. "That Beresford spent the night away from you, my dear, and that Johanna—who is so fond of her cousin—suggests that Simon was saving his strength for the rigors of this day's activities!"

Gwyneth relied on her icy armor to see her through this encounter. It would go better for her, she knew, if her headache were less blinding. She fought against Loki's mischief and tried to keep her voice pleasant. "Do I infer that you are skeptical of such an explanation of my husband's whereabouts last night?"

Rosalyn put a delicate hand to her breast in self-defense. "Why, not at all!" she replied. "Simon's caution is entirely understandable, particularly given the reports of the prowess of the unknown knight! It is said that he is the strongest man to have ever appeared on the tourney field."

That was it, then, the detail that had eluded Gwyneth earlier: the mysterious knight whom Geoffrey of Senlis had mentioned would be entering the lists today.

"I have heard something of him," Gwyneth admitted, then quoted her husband, "but the matter of his strength will be decided in the usual manner."

"In the fifth joust, I believe," Rosalyn informed her with a smile, "where Simon will be meeting him." Her gaze moved on to Johanna. "Isn't that right?"

"So I've heard," Johanna said with reassuring indifference. She scanned the group of far-off knights and even called Rosalyn's bluff. "But I am going to assume that he has not shown up yet, for I see no one on the field to rival Simon." She turned to Lady Chester and smiled complacently. "And Simon is meeting Valmey in the—let me see, now—sixth joust, isn't it so? He'll be in form by then, no doubt."

Rosalyn's smile became a little fixed. "But the sixth is scheduled to be merely a joust *à plaisance*," she said with a pretty shrug.

Gwyneth felt a jolt of alarm. "They are all jousts *à plaisance,* are they not?" she asked. Until this moment, she had not considered that any "jousts to the death" or *à outrance* would be enacted. She had assumed they would all be *à plaisance* or "of peace."

Rosalyn looked at her directly. "I don't know," she said slowly and in a way that caused the blood to drain from Gwyneth's face. "Would you care very much, my dear, if Simon were to be... hurt?"

Gwyneth sensed a trap. *Think, silly goose, think!* she admonished herself. However, she could not. The horrible realization had come to her that if Beresford had spent the night drinking and whoring, he would hardly be in top condition to meet a vigorous rival in the fifth joust, possibly one to the death. Assuming that he could miraculously survive that, he would still have to go against Valmey in the very next round, where he could be grievously wounded, even in a joust of peace.

With a further sinking of her spirits, she realized that if anyone had wished to do Beresford in, they could do no better than to have him in bad form this day. The stray thought came to her that Beresford's possible disadvantage was all the fault of Gunnar Erickson's ill timing. Loki had, indeed, wrought his worst. Her head ached to the point of exploding.

"Well?" Rosalyn prodded.

Gwyneth turned bravely to face her tormentor. "Well, what?" she had to ask, for she was having difficulty remembering the question and working through the problem that was pounding at her temples.

"Would you care very much if Simon were to be hurt?" Rosalyn repeated.

Gwyneth turned toward her and asked, "And what would happen to me if my husband were injured?"

Rosalyn's smile was as beautiful as snowfall on a winter's day. Gwyneth looked into her face and was surprised to see the arch of her slim back brow over the secret, ugly jealousy that slumbered in the depths of her ebony eyes.

"Why, my dear," Rosalyn said, "you are so attractive and your lands are so vast that I am sure your widowhood would not last long."

Chapter Seventeen

Gwyneth's headache receded a little, and the misty gauze over her thoughts began to lift. A pattern that had previously eluded her was emerging.

Rosalyn's jealousy suggested that it was not Loki wreaking havoc in Gwyneth's life, but a mere mortal whose name was most likely Cedric of Valmey. It was Valmey who had sent Gunnar Erickson to her the day before, knowing that Beresford had a castle guard looking out for her. It was Valmey who had captured Gunnar Erickson at Castle Norham and entered into a scheme with him for Beresford's undoing. It was Valmey who was Duke Henry's man inside the Tower, but who was hedging his political bets by seeming to remain loyal to King Stephen.

Gwyneth was finally able to focus her thoughts. She asked, "When does Geoffrey of Senlis enter the jousting?"

Johanna looked startled by her question. Rosalyn turned to her, a crafty look transforming her expression from jealous to curious. "Ah, yes, the handsome Geoffrey," she commented. "Why do you wish to know?"

"No reason," Gwyneth said artlessly.

"Really?"

Gwyneth did not care if Rosalyn thought that she was suddenly imagining the possibility of a different, more attractive, more courtly husband than Simon of Beresford. In fact, if Rosalyn was misled, so much the better. But Gwyneth was sorry that Johanna had to be similarly deceived. Still, she had to eliminate Senlis as a possible target of Valmey's plotting.

"No reason, really," Gwyneth answered with a shrug. "I was simply wondering whether Sire Senlis jousts before or after the fifth and sixth rounds."

"After," was Rosalyn's response. She regarded Gwyneth with a bright, speculative eye.

Gwyneth withstood Rosalyn's gaze. She was about to ask for the jousting order of the other knights who had squires named Breteuil. Then she realized, with a further clearing of her head, that such a pointed question might make Lady Chester suspicious. Instead, she said, "Well, that is still a very long time away, and there is so much to come before! Can you tell me the matches of the first four jousts?"

Rosalyn told her.

Gwyneth's headache receded, and the pounding in her head slowed to an occasional thump. The unknown knight would appear first in the third joust, but he was not paired to a knight with a squire named Breteuil. Gwyneth guessed that his first joust would warm him up for Beresford.

"But about the unknown knight," Gwyneth said, "who is he?"

Rosalyn looked scornfully amused. "No one knows, of course, my dear. That is the point."

"Look now, the *commençailles* have begun," Johanna said, nodding toward the field.

The assembled knights were divided into two teams according to the heraldic march of their origin. They were facing off to meet one another as individuals in this prelude to the jousting of the champions, which, in turn, would eventually lead to the mock battle that would last all day, in one form or another.

"I should have rather asked," Gwyneth said, "how the unknown knight came to enter the lists, or rather how it is that he has been able to enter and remain unknown."

Rosalyn shrugged and said with convincing offhandedness, "It's Adela's doing. She knows, of course, who he is, and the introduction of an unknown into the lists was very successful at one of the tourneys last summer. It added a piquant element to the event."

Johanna added, "Yes, and although the unknown turned out to be a man as well-known as Breteuil, I confess that all of us did enjoy the mystery. However, since Breteuil is so distinctly big, many of us guessed his identity before he was unhelmeted."

"Breteuil?" Gwyneth questioned, looking at Johanna. "The name sounds vaguely familiar."

"It should be, for it's a large family," Johanna replied, "and well connected. Renaut of Breteuil is a powerful baron with three sons and a half-dozen nephews who are squires to the leading knights."

"Could it be Renaut of Breteuil who is again the unknown?" Gwyneth asked innocently, or so she hoped.

"Most likely," Rosalyn assented lightly, "simply because no one would be expecting him twice!"

Gwyneth paused, then asked reasonably, "But how could Adela condone a joust with sharp weapons, that is, *à outrance*, between two of her own knights, Breteuil and Beresford?"

Rosalyn glanced at her, a very complex and crafty look composing her features. "A joust to the death...?" she began as if she did not understand, then broke off in artful comprehension. "I am sure that there will be only blunt weapons in use today, my dear. I was only teasing you about the joust *à outrance* earlier! Just to see how you felt about...various matters."

The blare of the trumpets resounded in Gwyneth's now-clear head. Her headache had vanished. She looked at Rosalyn with limpid, implacable serenity. "And did you?"

Lady Chester did not answer, but spied instead "her dearest friend," to whom she wished to speak. She rose to

go and offered the briefest of goodbyes which was drowned
in the first call from the field of *"Laissez aller!"*

For the first few minutes after Rosalyn's departure,
Gwyneth sat straight and very still, concentrating deeply,
examining her options, fully aware of the awkward position she was in. Thus she was blind to the colorful and ac-
tive spectacle unfolding before her eyes, and she was deaf to
the repeated sound of the trumpet announcing the entrance
of each competitor, who was followed into the lists by his
squires.

At last she said quietly to Johanna, "I must ask a favor
of you."

Johanna turned to her. Between her eyes was a tiny frown
of doubt and, possibly, disappointment.

Gwyneth felt her heart twist once, knowing as she did that
her friend doubted her, and knowing that in order to secure
her assistance in helping Beresford, she would need for Johanna to believe in her. At the same time, she was a stranger
in a foreign court. For the same reason that she did not expect Beresford to accept her word against his fellow knight,
Valmey, neither could she divulge to Johanna her suspicions concerning Rosalyn. It would not increase her credi-
bility or further her cause.

She took a breath and said quickly, "It was necessary for
me to ask Rosalyn when Geoffrey of Senlis was to appear in
the jousting order. Don't ask me why I had to ask, for I
cannot explain it all. It's just that—"

Johanna's expression lost a trace of its vague doubt. Her
kind eyes held a glimmer of hope. "Yes?"

"It's just that I am worried about Beresford." Gwyneth
said, lowering her voice to a whisper. "Please believe me!"

"Is it Rosalyn who has you worried?" Johanna asked
directly. "She was very rude to you."

"Yes, she was," Gwyneth said, grateful that Johanna had
also perceived the jealous beauty's behavior as such. "But
it was not her rudeness, exactly, that has me worried. It's

rather that I have reason to believe that some mischief is planned against Beresford.''

"And you want my help."

Gwyneth's nod was minimal, but definite. "Do you know which of Beresford's squires is Langley?"

Johanna scanned the edges of the field and spotted the tree on which Beresford's shield was hung and around which his party milled, on duty. "I see him," she affirmed.

"He is Beresford's most-trusted squire, I think," Gwyneth told her. "I wish for you to seek him out and tell him that he should carefully inspect his master's weapons and armor before the fifth joust. Do you think that is possible?"

"It is not impossible," Johanna said, "but it is not the easiest thing, either."

Gwyneth felt her companion's reluctance. She did not know how much to tell, how much to withhold, and so was silent.

"Perhaps you could send a boy over to Langley with such a message," Johanna suggested after a moment.

"No," Gwyneth replied immediately. "No, I trust no one but you. And I dare not go myself, for fear that my action will be...misinterpreted. I should tell you that I suspect another of Beresford's squires of disloyalty. Or perhaps he thinks only that he is participating in a prank! I do not know, but I feel quite sure that Langley can be trusted."

"I believe that Beresford has in training," Johanna said, "one of Breteuil's nephews."

Gwyneth met her eye. "Yes, I believe he does."

Johanna regarded Gwyneth curiously. "Are you thinking that Renaut of Breteuil rides again as the unknown and means Beresford harm? I can assure you that such a strange plot is highly unlikely!"

Gwyneth shook her head. "No, I do not think that Sire Breteuil is the unknown knight."

"But I have not seen Sir Renaut yet today," Johanna reasoned, "now that I come to think on it. It could be he who has been wearing the helmet all day. Rosalyn is no doubt right that Adela has chosen him again, precisely because no one would be expecting him twice." She craned her head. "Where is he, the unknown that I spotted earlier?"

Gwyneth did not bother to look for she did not need to lay eyes again on the big, broad, helmeted man to convince herself that Gunnar Erickson was in disguise on the field, armed with an illegally sharp lance designed to *outrer*, or pierce, the enemy. She suspected, as well, that Renaut of Breteuil was probably confined, indisposed from unnatural causes, somewhere far away from the tournament field. She suspected further that Adela was not aware a switch had been made from one unknown to the other. Whether or not Beresford's squire Breteuil was party to the whole scheme, Gwyneth did not know, but she doubted it. She had a strong intuition that the foolish young man had been set up by Valmey to take the entire blame for the outcome of the joust.

Thoughts of that outcome caused Gwyneth to lay an urgent hand on Johanna's arm. She felt her throat constrict with a very real fear, and for the first time in her life, her fear was not for herself. "Just tell Langley to pay careful attention," she whispered painfully, "to all aspects of Beresford's equipment—and probably his horse, as well—before the fifth joust." When Johanna looked up at her gravely, Gwyneth managed the final words, "Please consider. This simple message can do nothing at all to harm Beresford. Only to help him."

Johanna nodded. She rose and began to excuse herself, slipping past legs and knees to leave the stands.

It took an eternity for her to make her way casually through the crowds, around the interior of the palisade, as if she had no goal in mind, and to catch Langley's attention. It was already well into the second joust when Johanna caught the young man's attention. All the while, seated in the stands, Gwyneth felt the pounding of her heart

seconded by the continuous thundering of the horses'
hooves on the field.

The second joust ended. Serried ranks of knights took the
field, riding with their lances couched in rest, passing,
avoiding, meeting. The unknown took the field for the third
joust just as Johanna ended her conversation with Langley. The helmeted knight was unpracticed but powerful, and
when came the inevitable crack of his wood breaking his
opponent's, Gwyneth felt her heart similarly splintering.

Beresford saw her almost the instant she entered the palisade with her retinue. Because he had not been looking for
her, he imagined that he was so far gone with love for her
that, despite what he now knew about her, he still had eyes
only for her. It was as if through her, because of her, he
could see.

He had achieved a strange state of equanimity for all of
that, an acceptance of the burden of his love and of this exquisite pain he had never before known. He even discerned
a pathetically aesthetic quality to his suffering. He thought
it an excellent day for the tournament. He thought it an excellent day to die.

He had, in truth, no intention of dying this day. Nor even
of being wounded. He was in fine form. Never finer. He had
not slept much the night before, but instead of feeling en-
ervated, he felt invigorated in an exceptionally clearheaded
way. It was as if he had entered in spirit the refuge of neutral ground on the field, where he could not be bodily
harmed.

The night before, at The Boar's Head, he had discovered
that the ale had no taste, so he drank less than a horn of it.
And as for the whores, he had not noticed them. Nor did he
notice that he had not. He found sport outside the tavern,
on the quay—all brute strength, no skill. Through it all, he
could think only of Gwyneth, of how he had once thought
her a beautiful, alien creature, of how he now thought her
a beautiful creature and no more alien to him than his heart.

He had misjudged her. Perhaps foolishly. Perhaps will-fully. She had told him bluntly that she was for Duke Henry, as her husband had been, as her father had been. She had not wished him good success against the Angevin usurper, either, as he had dared her to. He realized, of course, with a further wrenching of exquisite pain in his breast, that she would be no less loyal to her sovereign, Henry, than he was to King Stephen. It was a pity.

It was a further pity that he would not be able to win her love this day with a display of chivalrous skill. He recalled hearing that some men used the tournaments to vanquish every opponent before their ladylove's eyes. The pity was that Gwyneth had declared herself to be a weak and peace-able creature, one who was not afraid of violence, but who did not approve of it—or was that Tyr's wife she had de-scribed thus?

No matter. Yet it was ironic—again, beautifully so—that his extraordinary focus of mind and body this day came from the force of his love for her and from his acceptance of that love, and the certainty that all his victories would not engage her reciprocal love for him.

He had much to do, however, to insure the certainty of all his empty victories. He had Langley and Gautier and, yes, the sulking Breteuil to fashion into worthy squires. This was their training for war, just as war was their training for the games. This was their school, and he was their master.

He was not aware of the heat. He was not aware of the weight of his armor. He was not aware of time passing. He was not aware of the heralds' cries of, *"Laissez aller!"* to begin, or *"Hola!"* to stop, or *"Largesse!"* to allow the knights to seek their just rewards and booty. He was not aware of blood flowing, of resistance to the shock of im-pact, of countless blows. He was only doing, as he knew so well how to do. His horse and body were one, his shield and arm one, his sword and hand one.

A lull, a pause, a moment of not doing, a moment of be-ing. At every moment he was aware of Gwyneth. He knew that she was seated with Johanna. He knew that they had been joined by a woman. What was her name? Lady Chester? He knew that Johanna left Gwyneth's side. Or, rather, he knew at one moment that Gwyneth was alone. He did not think again of Johanna.

He had one task to do, then another. He did them. He was momentarily idle. Only idle in body, however, not idle in spirit, where he felt the flow of continuous life and love. Langley was away from his side. Gautier was tending to his horse. Breteuil was fumbling with his lance. The lad was slow today and clumsy. Beresford felt infinite patience. Such was the role of the master.

Langley approached him and wished to draw him aside, away from the tree where his shield hung. What ailed the lad? Why was he speaking so low and so quickly? And why was he speaking of Johanna, when only Gwyneth mattered?

"That is what she told me, sire," Langley said, his eyes wide and anxious.

The message sank in slowly. "She told you that you were to examine my weapons?" Beresford asked, not comprehending this extraordinary request. "That is Breteuil's task."

"I know, sire," Langley replied, also not comprehending.

Beresford shook his head and began to walk back to the tree.

Langley stopped him. "Lady Johanna told me not to allow you to dismiss this request," the squire said. "She knew you would try to shake me off."

"She knew correctly," Beresford said severely. He felt no irritation, however. Not on this day. He merely wondered briefly what ailed both Johanna and Langley.

"It concerns the unknown knight," Langley said quickly.

"Renaut?" Beresford scoffed.

"It is not Renaut of Breteuil who is the unknown," Langley returned. "At least, Lady Johanna said that it *might* not be Sir Renaut again, and because of that, you are to be sure that Robert does not disadvantage you with faulty—"

Beresford held up his hand for silence. He would not permit young Langley to fall into dishonor by falsely—and most strangely—accusing his fellow squire, Robert of Breteuil, of wrongdoing. Surely Langley was not jealous of Breteuil. Surely Langley knew that he was his master's favorite, although on this day Beresford did not favor or prefer one over the other. He was master to them all. He did not understand what all this nonsense was about, but he remained unperturbed by it.

Langley subsided.

Beresford noted that Langley was stricken, poor lad. He could embrace the young man's confusion. He put a comforting, fatherly hand on his shoulder. "You fear for me in the fifth joust, Hubert?" he asked, not unkindly.

"No," Langley admitted.

Beresford smiled. "Good boy. Could it be that you think young Breteuil wishes to embarrass me somehow when I go against his uncle? Is that it? You think, perhaps, I have been too hard on Robert these past weeks and that he will make my equipment faulty so that I cannot prevail? So that his uncle will emerge the victor?"

Langley shook his head. "No, because I am not sure that the unknown is Sir Renaut. After all, Adela played that game last time, and she would not be likely to do it again."

The logic of the situation was as evident to Beresford as it was to many another knight and spectator. "Ah, but it is the very unlikelihood of playing the same trick twice that makes it so possible!"

Again Langley shook his head. "It's the other rumors today that worry me. Castle rumors. Of traitors. I have been worried since the moment we entered the field. Watch out for a sharp lance, not a blunt one."

Beresford's smile remained. It was nearly wistful. He gave the lad's shoulder a playful shake. "Justifiable jitters, my boy," he said. Then, firmly, "You understand that I cannot undermine young Breteuil or take his task away without offering him intolerable insult."

Langley opened his mouth to speak again, then closed it, knowing there was no profit in pursuing the matter. Beresford nodded wisely and turned to finish his preparations without giving the unusual conversation further thought.

At the appropriate time, Beresford was helmeted and armed and on his charger, riding out to the far end of the palisade where he would turn to face his opponent across the length of the field. He was ready for combat, which was to say that he was already mentally within the approaching combat. He felt the absence only of a token from Gwyneth on his left sleeve.

The call was given. He lowered his visor. He put the spurs to his charger's flanks. His shield was up. His lance was couched comfortably in rest position, and he raised it as his horse gathered speed. He was certain that one well-placed blow on Renaut's shield would unhorse his opponent. It would take only this one pass to decide matters. Renaut deserved no better for attempting this obvious masquerade twice.

At the moment that the two knights met in the center of the field, three things happened at once. First, Beresford recalled that Johanna had been sitting with Gwyneth on the stands for quite a while before she had taken the extraordinary step of seeking out Langley and giving him an even more extraordinary message. He recalled, as well, Gwyneth's persistent interest in the name Breteuil. Johanna must have become suspicious of Gwyneth and tried to warn him. Second, his lance made perfect contact with his opponent's shield in a way that should have pounded Breteuil decisively to the ground. And third, his lance broke on impact in a manner that was impossible given the angle and force of his thrust. His opponent was not even shocked by the blow, much less unseated.

As Beresford thundered past on the left, he thought he took a deep breath, but perhaps it was only the collective gasp of the spectators rising to their feet in the stands. He looked down at what was left of his lance—hardly a foot of shattered wood left beyond the circular vamplate protecting his hand. He took a professional interest in the wreck, deciding that in future he would reinforce the wooden vamplates with steel. He was otherwise unconcerned by this utter disaster. He arrived at the other end of the field and wheeled his horse around so that he could engage in the second pass with his opponent.

He knew now, of course, that his lance had been faulty. He knew as well that his opponent was not Renaut of Breteuil. Johanna's suspicions were right: Gwyneth had arranged for his death. However, he did not know why young Breteuil should have betrayed him. Perhaps Gwyneth had smiled at the boy, and he had happily drowned in the limitless violet pools of her eyes. Beresford himself would certainly die for her, if he thought his death would win him her love. However, the only way he would die for her was if she was holding the knife herself and thrusting it clean and deep into his heart.

As he charged ahead in the second pass, he was prepared for his opponent's sharp lance. He was at a disadvantage, having an attacking range of a mere one foot while his opponent still had the twelve feet of his own lance. Nevertheless, he was not worried, for he had easily sized up his rival's skill on horseback and judged it low. He was prepared to take several pointed blows from the knight's shaft and knew it would now take two or three more passes in order to inflict the kind of strategic damage necessary for his eventual unhorsing.

He did not fall into the mental trap of scorning his opponent. He knew that, had their positions been reversed, the man would have been dead at the second pass with the perfect piercing of his neck. Of course, he allowed his opponent no similar opening, for his shield work far surpassed his opponent's. Certainly he would have to take wounds, and he did—one to his right shoulder, then one in his right thigh. He was aware in a dreamily abstracted way that Gwyneth was on her feet, as he guessed the rest of the spectators must be as well. He was aware that squires and knights were scurrying to and fro quite unnecessarily. He was not at all distracted by the noise and confusion around him, for he was in a transcendent state of peaceful silence.

He was prepared for his opponent's every obvious, woefully unskilled maneuver. On the fifth pass, the man deliberately dropped his lance and grabbed Beresford around his waist to pull him from his horse. This was an unchivalrous tactic at best, stupid at worst and ultimately suicidal, for Beresford was able to unhorse him at the same time.

The contest on the ground was short, decisive and little test of Beresford's skill. They rolled together once, twice, locked in murderous embrace in the dust and dirt. Then both were on their feet, swords drawn. It should have been this easy on his horse, but Beresford was indifferent to the ultimate form of his opponent's death, and he had interpreted this contest as a joust to the death from the moment his lance had broken.

The unknown knight was soon swordless and lying on the ground. Beresford knelt over him, ready to administer the coup de grace. He found the buckled straps and laces that fastened his opponent's body armor to his helmet, slit those gracefully, then sliced open his throat. The thirsty dirt drank deeply of the dying man's blood.

Beresford looked up at the gallery. He saw Gwyneth standing, her hands clasped prayerfully at her breasts. Her eyes were closed against the horror of what he had done.

Chapter Eighteen

Beresford rose to his feet. He wiped his red sword on the hem of his surcoat and resheathed it. He unbuckled the straps of his helmet and removed it. He peeled off his gauntlets. Vaguely he heard raucous cheering intermingled with the occasional wail, "Breteuil!" He was disgusted. Anyone with eyes in his head could have seen that his opponent—whoever he was—had displayed not a fraction of the skill of Renaut of Breteuil.

Senlis was instantly at his side, shaken and spouting anger at the foolish risk his boon companion had taken. Then Beresford was swarmed by other knights, squires and pursuivants-at-arms. The king of arms was there as well. He had thrown his white baton uselessly into the field.

Beresford was offered his opponent's horse and armor and arms as booty. He was unimpressed. His most singular emotion was one of dissatisfaction at having bested so unworthy an opponent. He was told that Valmey's horse had been hurt during the chaos of the fifth joust and that Valmey would be unable to meet him in the next. He demanded to speak with the king of arms and promptly berated the incompetent fool for not attending to the simplest of his duties. He received assurances that the melee to follow, for all its inherent disorganization, would be better supervised.

Great interest was taken in the dead man's identity. The helmet was removed from his nearly severed head, but no one could identify him. Beresford looked down dispassionately into the face of a perfect Northumbrian Dane. He had no great difficulty assigning to him the name Gunnar Erickson.

"Do you know the man, Simon?" Senlis asked.

Beresford shook his head. "I have never seen him before."

Young Langley was at his side. Gautier, as well. Breteuil was hanging back by the tree, white of face and withered of posture.

Beresford said casually, "Ask Breteuil. My lance was faulty."

That was the last time Beresford ever saw Robert of Breteuil. He never afterwards inquired about him, and no one mentioned him, not even later in the day when it became known that Renaut of Breteuil had had to stay behind in the castle, confined to the garderobe where he feared, as he phrased it, that he would lose his bowels. Adela would confirm that the unknown was to have been Renaut of Breteuil. Renault of Breteuil would have to admit that his nephew, Robert of Breteuil, had served him breakfast that morning.

But events had not yet proceeded that far. Young Breteuil was only being questioned as the dead man was hauled off the field. Tournaments had continued in the aftermath of far-more-important deaths than that of an unknown man—no doubt an uppity Saxon who had connived with a surprisingly evil young squire. Better the world be rid of both, without dwelling on the unpleasantness of it all.

Beresford was hailed as the unquestioned victor of a thrilling contest such as the spectators could never hope to see again in their lifetimes. He was mildly interested in this reaction from the crowd. He wondered at it a little, too, since there was more sport, of much greater magnitude, to come. Someone began to annoy him by removing parts of his clothing and armor and ministering to his shoulder and his thigh. His transcendent state of peace passed. He said that his squires would tend to him or no one would, and stated his preference for no one. He had some choice words to say about the undignified handling of this whole sloppy mess and wondered aloud if these alarms and excursions would not end by giving a healthy man a bellyache of disgust.

To his further irritation, several men within earshot laughed at that, and one offered the opinion that Beresford would live—which seemed to him an obvious comment better tolerated when uttered by a simpleton.

Gwyneth closed her eyes the moment Beresford's lance broke into toothpicks. She was on her feet, like everyone else, but unlike everyone else, she could not watch. She clasped her hands together, she unclasped them and grabbed Johanna's arm. She asked quietly, over and over, "You told Langley, did you not, Johanna? You told him, didn't you?"

She was not reassured by Johanna's repeated answers, "Yes, Gwyneth," "I told him, and he was inclined to believe me," and "Langley himself suspects that mischief is afoot."

Gwyneth relied on Johanna to tell her as well, second by second, if Beresford was still on his horse. She cracked her eyes open once and nearly cried out at the pain she felt at seeing the unknown's lance pierce Beresford's shoulder. Horrified murmurs of "Sans coronal!" went around the crowd.

Gwyneth did not know this term in Norman. "Without what? Coronal?" she whispered anxiously through a tight throat, not daring to open her eyes again.

"The coronal is the tip applied to the lance to blunt it," Johanna said, her own voice strained.

"Ah, yes, yes, yes, I know the practice, just not the term."

"It appears that Simon's opponent's lance is not blunted."

A wave of fatalism swept over Gwyneth. "Just as Rosalyn said. It's a joust to the death. He intends to kill him."

Horribly long seconds passed. Johanna said slowly, "I believe that Beresford *does* intend to kill the unknown."

Gwyneth opened her eyes just as Beresford tumbled to the ground with his assailant. He rolled over and up onto his feet, sword unsheathed in one fluid motion. She felt her fear recede when the steel of his blade glinted in the sun for a brilliant second before it began its work of terrifying beauty.

What Beresford had to do was horrible, and Gwyneth knew he would have preferred it otherwise. She felt more confident about the outcome now, but she was taking no chances in the event that Gunnar Erickson had another trick up his sleeve. So she closed her eyes and prayed to a motley pantheon: Thor and Tyr and Odin, and the One True God, including the Trinity, just to be safe. She shied away from Allah. However, from her learned grandmother, she recalled hearing delicious and heretical whispers about a host of ancient Greek gods, and she did not hesitate to send prayers to them, as well.

She heard at last Johanna saying, "You can look now." She opened her eyes and saw Beresford standing straight and steady on his feet, helmet in the crook of his arm, his clothing dirty and bloody, his face and hair streaked with sweat. Then he was swamped by knights and field marshals and squires. She breathed a profound sigh of relief and welcome air rushed to fill her lungs.

"How did you know?" Johanna asked.

Gwyneth looked at her friend without registering the question. She smiled and said, "You see, I meant Beresford no harm. I might have even provided him with an edge in the contest, but I do not think he needed any help from me. Or from anyone! Not even from his lance."

Johanna smiled in return. "Yes, but how did you know?"

Gwyneth's first wave of happiness and relief passed. Beresford was out of danger. She was not. "I overheard something at the wedding celebration almost a fortnight ago," she said cautiously.

"What did you hear?"

"Something odd, about the loyalties of a squire named Breteuil. Because so many knights have squires from that family, I had to narrow down the possibilities of mischief being perpetrated against one knight: Beresford."

"Whom did you overhear?"

Gwyneth shrugged. She did not want to draw Johanna into this, for her friend's own sake. "I did not see who was speaking, and it was very difficult for me to identify the voices I heard. I cannot be sure."

"Or won't tell."

Gwyneth gulped and said earnestly, "I may be implicated in all of this, so please ask me nothing further."

There was no more time for private discussion in any case, for information from the field was traveling through the stands like fire through dry straw. The slain man was not Renaut of Breteuil—though everyone claimed to have already known that—but a stranger. A treacherous Saxon come to spoil Norman sport, it was widely reported. How he came to enter the lists without anyone knowing it, of course, was going to be Adela's most pressing political problem for the next few days. It would have gone much worse for her had Beresford been killed. As it was, her most loyal knight had brought further glory upon himself, the tournament and his king.

When Gunnar's helmet was removed, Gwyneth imagined accusing fingers would point toward her. Thus, when word of a Saxon stranger was passed around, she realized that no one present would associate the dead man with her except Beresford and Valmey. Now Valmey was unlikely to make any claims to knowing anything about the dead man. Gwyneth noted that he was hanging about the edges of the group around Beresford, only partially participating.

Then the name of Robert of Breteuil, and his apparent guilt, crackled through the crowd, which was amazed, aghast, outraged, indignant that a squire should so betray his master. And why? Had Beresford treated him badly? Breteuil should have worshiped the ground Beresford walked on instead of faulting his lance! Everyone wanted to know more about this sorry, sniveling excuse for a human being, and although the Breteuil family was generally held in high esteem, it was agreed that evil lurks in even the best of families! But there would be time later on at the banquet to unravel the wicked schemes of young Breteuil. For now, it was more important that Beresford's health and safety be ascertained.

After that, Gwyneth noticed that sentiment toward her changed dramatically. With suspicion about a possible traitor flying to Robert of Breteuil, like iron shavings to a magnet, she was no longer treated with cautious reserve and the distant respect due her as wife to Beresford. Her acceptance among the courtiers was heartier now and more genuine.

Spectators began to shift about as a result of the stirring action they had just witnessed. Some were hungry, some thirsty. All seemed eager to pass close to Gwyneth and Johanna, to say a few words of compliment and congratulations.

Walter Fortescue passed by and paused at length. "Never seen the like!" he pronounced with great delight. "We all knew Beresford was among the finest. Today he outstripped every other knight in Stephen's court, he did! He was superior! Magnificent!"

Gwyneth made an effort to enter the spirit of the occasion. She smiled and assented, but could do no more. Unfortunately, the warm side of her spirit had been bred out of her during her years with Canute, when she had needed all her icy calm to see her through each day. Her ability to be publicly demonstrative was severely compromised.

Sir Walter teased, "Ah, now, my lady, I can see that you are still shaken from what you just witnessed! It's true, the situation looked bad for your husband when his lance broke, but when he turned his horse and made ready for the second pass, I could tell that a contest out of the ordinary was in the making. At that point, I almost felt sorry for Breteuil—not that I truly thought the unknown was he! Oh, no!"

Sir Walter was partially right. Gwyneth was still trying to recover her composure after having seen Beresford's brush with death. She was also trying to establish within herself what stance to take toward her husband when next they would meet. After his display of courage on the field, she could be no less courageous. She would not demean herself, or dishonor him, by whining or disclaiming any knowledge that his opponent had been Gunnar Erickson. She ached to tell him that she had had nothing to do with the deception on the field, but she did not think that merely telling him so would convince him. He already believed her to be clever at scheming.

Sir Walter moved on. Rosalyn came close enough to have to nod and smile. To Gwyneth's eye, Lady Chester looked confused and somewhat chastened, which was to say that her crafty confidence seemed to have deserted her. Gwyneth felt a small spurt of pity for the woman, whose only crime was to love a double-crossing rat.

The day's entertainment was exceedingly fine, although what was usually the climax of the tournament, the melee, was more of an anticlimax. Gwyneth took very little pleasure in this mock-combat exercise carried out in a spirit of comradeship. The knights had divided themselves into contending groups to fight against each other. This time she did not close her eyes to the engagement but fixed them on Beresford's form as he slashed and thrust and warded off blows. The point of the tourney was to test the strength and skill of the contestants in horsemanship, accuracy of aim and resistance to the shock of impact. In all of these,

Gwyneth saw that her husband excelled. It seemed to her that a magic circle surrounded him, preventing harm from befalling him.

The high point came when one knight's helmet became so battered he had to be escorted from the field and have his head placed on an anvil, where a blacksmith tried to beat the helmet back into shape so it could be removed. This was, naturally, taken to be outstanding proof of the knight's great valor, because it showed he had been in the thickest part of the fighting and had withstood tremendous blows. On any other day, such an occurrence would have won him top honors. This day, however, belonged to Beresford.

When the sun's rays began to slant across the earth, when the tourney field had been drubbed into a fine dust and when enough lances had been broken to satisfy the spectators' desire for extravagant waste, the victorious side was declared by Adela. The return to the Tower could begin. Escorted by her retinue, Gwyneth walked along with the other ladies, half hopeful of seeing Beresford, half fearful to be with him again. She anticipated the pain she would feel at being near him, knowing that she was estranged from his affection. She was, paradoxically, both worried and desirous.

She succeeded in convincing herself that what she felt toward Beresford was a combination of loyalty and shame that her loyalty to him should be in question. She succeeded in denying that she was experiencing new emotions, succeeded in suppressing the giddy, girlish anticipation of being with him again.

Back in the great hall, she met and mingled with her fellow courtiers. Preparations for the evening's feast and entertainment were going forward. She spoke and laughed and looked discreetly for signs of Beresford's entrance. She washed her hands and accepted a cup of wine, feeling as she did so that only half her body and soul were present.

She knew the instant he entered the hall. She was standing with her back to him, speaking with several ladies and a few knights who had already cleaned themselves up after the day's exertions. She felt his presence and turned to look at him. She could not take her eyes off him as he came toward her. The courtiers between them seemed to fall back, leaving his path clear.

His hair was still damp and destined to curl in disorder when dry. He had not shaved for the evening, so his chin was shadowed with stubble. His tunic was unadorned but clean, as were his plain linen shirt and chausses. His stride was sure as ever, making her doubt reports that he had been wounded in his thigh, for she had seen only the blow to his shoulder. As he came toward her, she perceived the rough edges of the man, so much a part of him. She did not feel them bristle her, as she had in the past. They were more like the rays of a fractured nimbus around a man satisfied with his day's work. They gave him his texture and made him come to life for her.

As he approached, she held her breath, but not from fear. If he intended to denounce her as the one who had set Gunnar Erickson against him, she was prepared. If he intended to spurn her publicly, she was prepared. But she was not prepared for what actually happened.

When he came within feet of her, he stopped. He gazed at her for a moment through hard, gray eyes that held a vast, new dimension, such that when she returned his gaze, she thought she would be lost in it. She nearly gasped when he went down on one knee before her and bowed his head. It was a signal honor to her for all to see and a magnificently submissive gesture that only the least submissive of men could afford. A breathless moment passed before he reached out and took her fingers in his. As he rose, he kissed the back of her hand. She felt his touch all the way up her arm and felt the effect of his courtly kiss like a stab to her heart.

He looked down at her and turned her hand so that he could place her fingertips on the cuff of his shirt. They began to walk. Gwyneth felt her blood beat faster just at being next to him. She basked in the glow of his rough-edged nimbus.

Looking straight ahead, he said, "I had to do it."

Her nerves were grazed by a charge in the atmosphere. She replied, "I know."

He nodded. "Perhaps we should take our places at the table." He gestured not to the central table, but to the first table on the king's left. Gwyneth could not know that he had adamantly refused Adela's request that they sit in places of honor at the head table.

They made their way forward decorously. Their conversation was equally decorous. She asked politely, "And have you recovered well, sire?"

He looked down at her with a faint question in his flinty eyes. "Recovered?" His voice, customarily gruff, was low and lazy.

"From your wounds," she clarified.

His brow lifted slightly in understanding. "My squires attended to them."

"Ah, yes, that would be Langley," she replied without thinking, "and—" She broke off.

"Gautier," he supplied.

The atmosphere crackled, causing her nerves to tingle. "Yes, of course," she said. The unmentionable name, Breteuil, hung in the air. Was it cowardice, she wondered, that prevented her from telling him the truth? Or worse, fear that he would not believe she had not conspired against him? She gathered her courage and steeled her nerves. She turned to face him. "Let me tell you that—"

The look in his eyes sliced off her words as effectively as his blade had slit Gunnar Erickson's throat. He evidently did not wish to hear any confessions from her.

The words *I had nothing to do with Gunnar Erickson's entry into the lists!* died unspoken on her tongue. She swallowed them and tasted ashes.

"Madam?" he inquired after a moment.

Her courage failed her. Her throat closed, this time from unshed tears that some longing within her might never be satisfied. She kept her eyes lowered as she said, "Let me tell you that you were magnificent today on the field."

He merely grunted. Gwyneth was spared embarrassment, for Geoffrey of Senlis accosted them. "'Magnificent' does not do justice to your performance, Simon!" he said, clapping Beresford on the back.

Beresford smiled wryly. "Ah, no, Geoffrey? That was not your opinion earlier today."

Senlis bowed gracefully. "Allow my natural love for you to have overtaken my practiced courtesies." His voice was teasing, simple and sincere. He rose and looked straight at his friend, and Gwyneth saw in his eyes the light of purest friendship. "You see, Simon, I thought you were going to die."

"You have no faith in me," Beresford complained.

"At least admit that the situation looked grave!" Senlis said.

"I will admit no such thing," Beresford returned. "The man had no skill."

"So it might have looked to you!" Senlis replied. "To us, it looked rather different! Hardly anyone has spoken of anything since. Why, not a few moments ago, Lancaster pointed out—"

Beresford eyed his friend measuringly. "Perhaps you find this subject interesting. I do not. You perceive that we are headed to this table here, at some remove from what will be the center of activity. I have no wish for idle chatter this evening."

Senlis took no offense at this rebuff. Instead, he laughed and said, "Not this evening or any evening! That is why I propose to join you for supper—to ward off idle chatter that is sure to come your way!" Senlis turned to Gwyneth and bowed. "That is, if, my lady, you are agreeable to my presence?"

When Senlis straightened, the look in his beautiful blue eyes was complex, yet communicative. Gwyneth saw in their depths a gentle retreat. She saw an acknowledgment of noble and masculine love for her husband. She saw a chivalrous regret that his interest in her could not go beyond friendship.

"Of course, Sire Senlis," she accepted graciously, "you must certainly sup with us. Here at this end, then, next to me."

The meal was soon presented. Gwyneth hardly tasted it, for she was too aware of the force of Beresford's presence to take notice of anything else. Senlis did the job he had taken upon himself and very smoothly deflected all unwanted attentions from Beresford. He maintained any number of idle, uninteresting conversations with the great variety of courtiers who passed by. Only Cedric of Valmey slipped in under Senlis's guard toward the end of the meal and got to Beresford through Gwyneth.

Leaning against the table, Valmey propped an elbow on the table and leaned close. He smiled charmingly. "And what did you think of your husband's joust, madam?"

Gwyneth tried to maintain her composure, but her smile was tight. "I told him earlier that his performance was magnificent."

"Assuredly," Valmey agreed. "However, I dare to wonder, as an admirer of your husband's—" here Valmey flicked a glance at Beresford, who was watching him lazily "—whether his opponent was not truly as unskilled as Simon made him look. The poor man displayed no trace of Norman science." Valmey paused. "Would you have an opinion on that, my lady, acquainted as you are with different practices? Did the poor man display the signs of Northumbrian science?"

"I have no eye for the fine points," Gwyneth replied. "Like many others, I thought the unknown was Renaut of Breteuil."

"Renaut would have given Simon a better contest, I am sure," Valmey said with liquid charm.

"Which is why," Beresford interrupted, "I was disappointed not to meet you in the sixth joust. Will your horse survive the injury it received?"

Valmey drew himself up and regarded Beresford. "I have every hope."

Beresford nodded. "Then we are sure to meet in the future."

Valmey bowed his head first to Beresford, accepting his stark challenge, then to Gwyneth, as he courteously withdrew from their table.

Senlis kept the others at bay. Beresford was relaxed and silently watchful of the movements in the hall. Gwyneth was breathless and expectant next to him, all jumping nerves. She was aware of his strong fingers fiddling with the wine cup, aware of his shifts upon the bench, aware of every breath he took, aware of the bones in his body and the layers of muscles covering them.

At last, Beresford turned to her and said, "We shall leave."

Gwyneth blushed and blurted aloud her thoughts. "You wish to check me for knives?"

Beresford's gaze became more focused upon her. Her jumping nerves sizzled. For one abysmal moment, she thought he would refuse her.

Chapter Nineteen

"Of course," he said, picking up her hand from the table. He brought it to his lips. "What else could I have meant?"

Her blush deepened. "I don't know."

"Don't you?"

To cover her embarrassment, she challenged, "Shall I make some suggestions as to what you might have meant?"

He shook his head. "That won't be necessary." He turned her hand over and cradled it palm up in his own. He traced the outline of her fingers with his.

Her nerves stretched taut. Her thoughts were in a whirl. Her emotions were in confusion. Her body knew just what it wanted. "But you, sire, are an advocate of plain speaking," she said brazenly. "I would be happy to name the possibilities of what I thought you might wish to do when we leave, in light of today's events."

He weighed her hand experimentally, as he had on a previous occasion. Looking at her, one heavy brow cocked, he said, "The more you talk like that, the more the possibilities narrow to one." He rose and brought her to her feet. He drew her forward so that she was standing against him, their clasped hands lodged chest high. "Which was the one I had in mind from the beginning." He put his other hand on her hip. "You, too, it seems."

A thrill shot through her. She wondered, with a surge of desire, how it happened, this evening, that he could be both blunt and subtle at the same time. Or was it always so with him, this man who knew what he wanted, but who did not always state it outright?

Anger and pique mingled with her embarrassment and her desire. She wanted to get the better of him somehow. She did not move away. She pulled her head back to look up and asked defiantly, "Do you dare?"

He smiled. "You have seen enough today to know what I dare. And this," he added, "is different."

It was her turn to ask, "Is it?"

He took the hand he held and moved it behind her back. He raised his other hand from her hip, grasped her free hand and joined it with the other. With one hand he manacled her wrists. His other hand he placed at her throat.

"My lance is not faulty for this round," he said.

Her cheeks flamed. That was blunt enough. Or subtle enough. She did not know which, for her own mind was in a whirl. Before the misty, musky gauze of desire for him veiled her reason, she decided that he must like using the flat blade of danger to whet sharp edges of his desire and hers.

"Now, if you're done discussing the matter," he said, bending toward her so he could speak low into her ear, "we shall quit the hall."

Without so much as a by-your-leave to Senlis or anyone else, he turned, drawing her with him. With one of her hands still in his, he walked ahead of her. He was taking her from the room, not ushering her out of it as would the courteous lover.

They were hardly two feet from the table when Walter Fortescue huffed, overloud, "Well, now! The most celebrated man of the hour leaves midfeast and with not a word or even a bow to his neighbors! That's Beresford start to finish, and speaking of finishes, I'm glad, don't you know, that he'll be ending the day as well as he started it! Glad to see, too, that his beautiful wife warmed up to the occasion.

Oh, she was as pale as bleached flax after the joust! Wished
to find words of praise for her husband, but was still chok-
ing from her fear. Ah, but she's loosened up now, finding
herself among Norman friends. Can't think why Beresford
was so dead set against the match when Adela first presented it to him!''

At these cheerfully insensitive comments, Gwyneth could
have died of embarrassment, if her own desire just then had
not been so strong as to drown all other emotions. As for
Beresford, he made no sign that he had heard Fortescue's
opinions other than to raise his arm dismissively, his back
still to the group. He picked up his pace, but his haste did
not spring from a wish to put distance between himself and
Fortescue.

Still holding Gwyneth's hand, he preceded her out of the
hall and along the passage to the wide stone steps. At the
foot of the spiral he stopped and ushered her before him.

She could not look at him as she passed in front of him.
The sight of him would have been too intense, for the feel of
his presence had already engulfed her, and she could not
imagine life or breath away from him. She lifted her skirts
with one hand, then placed her other against the newel post.
When she began to mount, he placed a hand on her hip and
followed her.

Feeling him behind her, feeling his hand on her hip, she
became increasingly breathless. They completed one turn of
the spiral steps, then another, and suddenly she found herself flattened against the wall, his hands on either side of
her. Her arms were flung back, hands splayed on the spiral-
ing wall behind her. A thrill flashed up her spine, produced
by the cool of the stone offset by the heat of her surprised
desire. She shivered.

"I don't want to wait," he said.

His words were blunt. So were his actions. He was poised
against her, one foot on the step below her, the other on the
step below that. Their lips were level. His hands moved from
the wall to cup her face. He leaned into her. The hilt of the

sword at his belt pressed against her stomach, the sheath against her abdomen and thigh. He bent to kiss her.

She turned her head away.

He turned it back so that she faced him. He asked provocatively, "Do you object?"

Her heart was beating furiously. She felt a strong wave of emotion wash through her. "Here?"

He nodded, then tried to kiss her once more.

Again she broke the kiss and turned her head away. "And if I do object?" she managed.

He placed his lips at her neck. "Then the nature of my pleasure in the act will change."

She was startled into looking back at him. "You mean to do it with or without my consent?"

At that, he lowered his hand to the hem of her skirt and raised it so that his palm could grasp her bare thigh. He fumbled under her clothes, seeking the immediate goal of the pearl between her thighs. No sweet words, whispered low. No tickling touch, grazing up and down the insides of her thighs. No teasing forays between soft lips and wetness. No subtlety whatsoever.

When he touched her jewel, his expression was smug. "I don't need your consent, when I have your desire."

She gasped softly. She melted against him. Her knees buckled. She was not ready to concede. "No."

"Yes."

He flipped up his tunic and released himself from his chausses. Taking advantage of their staggered positions on the stairs, he moved in under her and between her legs.

Hard muscle pressed at the soft opening of her thighs, touching off a quick spasm of pleasure inside her. A gasp, less soft this time, escaped her lips.

"The guards," she breathed, still trying to argue him out of this luscious, lascivious folly.

"You'll have to be quieter, madam, unless you want to bring them to witness."

With a smooth thrust, he folded himself into her. She accepted him easily, without constrictions, only desirous contractions and the hot-cold sensations of her spine sliding up and down the stone wall. The quick coupling was as intense as it was short. She flowered around him before he was finished, so his final pleasure extended her own. She was weak and happy, and sagged exhausted against him. She moaned sweetly into his neck. He supported her by cradling her buttocks in his hands.

Still full within her, he began to move away from her.

"No," she said, this time for a very different reason.

"Yes," he countered, withdrawing. He rearranged his clothing, smoothed her skirts, turned her and propelled her gently up the next few steps. His hands rested heavily on her hips.

"Why?" she asked, as she stumbled upward, her legs wobbly, her heart pounding and breaking and reforming itself to beat for him.

"A courtesy," he replied. "The opening salute."

She turned her head and gave him a glance filled with feminine lust. "Who won?"

"I did."

She flamed for him, melting the last cold corner within her. She completed the upward spiral of the staircase and managed better the straight length of hallway, helped by his strong, firm hands on her hips.

They clattered into his chamber. He shut the door behind them by leaning against it. He remained there, his back against the door. When she turned to face him, he folded his arms across his chest and eyed her measuringly.

He threw down the gauntlet. "Make me want you."

Her eyes widened. She felt her courage momentarily falter, but knew that her continuing desire for him was strong enough. It would have to see her through.

She took a deep breath and took the circlet and veil from her hair. She let them drop at her feet. His eyes did not follow their gentle descent. They remained pinned on her.

She took a step toward him and unlaced the ties at the sides of her bliaut. She let it, too, flutter and fall at her feet. Then came her kirtle, with more difficulty, her hands and arms and breath and heart trembling. Another step closer, and her shift was at her feet. She stepped out of it, offering him her defenseless nakedness, shuddering with fear that he would finally defeat her with humiliating violence.

He did not. He did not unfold his arms, and he did not take his eyes off her. He said, "I have always admired your courage."

The sound of his voice steadied her. He had issued her another challenge, one that turned her shuddering fear again to the poised edge of desire. She felt strong and feminine and capable of taking him again within her body, to complete his satisfaction.

She put her hands bravely on his forearms and unfolded them, so that his hands were at his sides. She put her fingers to the buckle of his belt and unclasped it. The belt and sword clattered to the floor. She worked at his tunic, and he gave her no help. The shirt was easier. She had to kneel, in supplication, to uncross his garters and remove his shoes. The chausses tricked her and got caught on the most natural of impediments as she was removing them.

She bit her lip and stepped back. "Did I hurt you?"

He reached out and brought her against him. "You'll have to try harder than that if you mean to hurt me."

"I don't."

"That's your decision, then." He nodded acceptance. "Now what?"

She considered. She put her hands lightly on his shoulders. They were wide and well muscled. She touched her fingers to the lance wound, which was clean and clotted and no threat to his life. She slid her hands down his chest to explore the smooth muscles there, seamed with old scars, and the ribbed muscles of his abdomen, similarly scarred. She slid her hands farther down and reached to touch the lance wound on his thigh. He flinched at that. She looked past his erection and saw that the second wound was not as clean. She bent to kiss the slightly swollen area around it.

When she stood up again, she slipped her arms around his neck and touched her tongue to his ear. She whispered, "I want you under me and at my mercy, but I do not think I can carry you to the bed."

He easily carried her. Soon the bed covers had been thrown back and she was straddling him, slotting him into her and working her thigh muscles around him. Nothing separated her from him, and she rode him to the tip of his desire time and again. When she had given him everything, she gave even more. Finally, she met him body and soul and lay herself generously across him.

Luxuriating against him, she wished to stay in the flow of the infinite by pouring out in words what was in her heart. With her new experience in the softer arts of speaking to a man, she decided this was the ideal moment for confession.

She shifted and placed her hand on his chest to claim his attention. She began, "I want to tell you about the visitor I received yesterday and what happened at the joust—"

"Don't," he said, covering her mouth with his hand.

Her heart lurched, then sank. She must have misjudged her moment and abused the intimacy. She felt as wretched now as she had previously felt wonderful.

She had not misjudged the moment, but rather the turmoil in Beresford's breast. He had hoped to repeat the day's victories this night in bed, but he had failed so completely that, if he could have ripped out his heart to give it to her, signaling defeat, he would have. He had challenged her. She had met his challenge, just as separate parts of him hoped and feared she would, and she had conquered him with her body so completely that the parts of him had fused, thick-thewed, with love for her. He was wed now, all of him, muscle and sinew, blood and soul, to this woman in a way he had never felt, nor ever thought possible.

He did not want to hear her lies, and so put his hand over her mouth. He could better bear the burden of his love, unmet by a reciprocal love, if she did not dishonor herself with falsehoods. He closed his eyes and surrendered himself to the whirling funnel of his emotions, which turned faster when he realized that he had prevented Langley from falsely, jealously denouncing Breteuil earlier in the day—and that Langley had been right.

The pain of his wish that Gwyneth, like Langley, was not false was so great that he thought he would die from it. With his mind's eye he searched for Valkyries, but knew they were not there. What he felt came from a new and fecund source, as fresh and generative as the beginning of the world, and far stronger than any magic wrought by the dying race of Norse gods.

The night of mingling and merging lasted an infinite second. Beresford was awakened with the news that he was to be called away, this time to the north, toward Tutbury, but not as far as Northumbria. He received his orders with indifference. He had no wish to live apart from her, yet every moment with her was magnificent agony. It was just as well that he had no choice in the matter. The love of his heart belonged to Gwyneth; the loyalty of his muscles remained always at the service of King Stephen.

He made lavish love to her one last time in the morning. He saw no reason to deny himself, for it was not as if he could rid himself of his love by spending his seed. In fact, the power of his love only seemed to increase with every mating. Yet such was the nature of his desire that he gladly accepted the possibility of more pain for the momentary satisfactions of touching her and kissing her and lodging himself within her and riding with her to the sun.

The great hall was a blur of color and movement. He was as undistracted by the chaos this morning as he had been the day before on the tourney field. This time, however, his transcendent focus was not a heightened result of the prospect of combat, but a numbing realization of love. He knew the requirements of his position and could consult with the king, call together his men and prepare for departure without having to remove Gwyneth from the center of his thoughts and being.

He was just able to discern an odd quirk in Johanna's behavior, which, if it had not been for her association with his wife, he would have missed.

When he crossed his cousin's path after breaking his fast, he noted that she was smiling at him rather broadly. He wondered why, in the face of his great pain and confusion, she should be so happy. Then, dully, he realized that she must be pleased with herself for having discovered Gwyneth's treachery.

"Well, Simon," Johanna said brightly, "I trust you rested well this night."

"Do you?" he returned, none too cordially.

She winked saucily. "Not at all!" She laughed. "I hope you did not, in fact, waste your time sleeping!"

He grunted.

Johanna's mood altered. "But, Simon..." She put a hand on his sleeve and looked up at him with a mixture of surprise and concern. "Are you vexed with me about yesterday? I assure you, I meant no harm. Quite the opposite!"

He looked down at her hand and felt its intended comfort. Johanna was excusing herself for having meddled in his affairs, but he could see that she had had no choice. Of course, she had meant him no harm. Her warning to Langley had not won the victory for him, but it had given him an edge, lessening his confusion when his lance first broke.

He pulled himself together and looked at his fond cousin. "I should thank you for your help and concern." He bowed.

Johanna's mouth hung open one fraction of a second too long. She said, "Simon, I think you may have misunderstood something of what happened yester—" But she was not destined to finish her thought. Beresford's attention was claimed by Roger Warenne, who drew him rudely aside, on the grounds that what he had to say about the day's operations was of far greater importance than any feminine silliness.

Beresford felt his heart leap at what he thought Johanna might have been about to say. He made a mental note to seek her out after he had finished with the innumerable particulars involved in moving a great many men and arms over considerable distances. He would have done so had not Gwyneth already descended to the hall by the time he and Warenne came to the end of their consultation.

He turned and saw her. It was otherworldly, he thought, how the simple sight of her could churn the splendid feelings with such aching pleasure in his breast. And it was from his breast and not his lust that these rich emotions sprang. Physical joining with her gave the spiritual feelings body, that was all—or, rather, that was everything, for the otherworldly feelings were in his body, not outside of it, in every part, in every pore, and he was happy that his body could give these feelings expression.

He watched, hovering between fatal sickness and magnificent health, as she moved through the room, pausing to chat with this lady and that knight. She smiled and nodded and gestured and listened and spoke, as he had seen no other woman smile or nod or gesture or listen or speak. She engaged in polite conversation with that dark-haired woman—what was her name?—Rosalyn. Then she moved on and spoke with Geoffrey of Senlis.

Senlis, his greatest friend. Senlis, who had counseled subtlety and had said that Gwyneth was the most beautiful woman he had ever seen. Senlis, who was handsome and charming and knew what to say to a lady and when to say it. Senlis, who—Simon could see this unmistakably, even from across the room—did not transgress the invisible line with Gwyneth and who did not suggest in stance or expression any feelings for her warmer than courtly respect. Senlis, who, when addressed by a person new to the group, did not favor Gwyneth with lingering glances or quick words, whispered low.

Gwyneth moved on again and did not cast a backward glance at Senlis. Her eyes were already on the next group of ladies to greet, her hand extended to the knights wishing to salute her. Among them was Valmey. Beresford's interest was spurred. Valmey was, perhaps, even more handsome and charming than Senlis. And now that he came to think of it, was it not Valmey who had been with Gwyneth in the gardens that evening when he had thought Senlis had tricked him? Hot, hateful jealousy flashed through him. Were there other times Valmey had been alone with his wife? And as for Gwyneth, had she ever sought Valmey out?

With blinding insight, he saw that they were a pair, Gwyneth and Valmey. They spoke the same language. They understood court business. They heard the silences. They interpreted the nuances, an ability as foreign to Beresford as setting a stitch. He could wield a sword, not a needle. He began to wonder whether a needle might not, ultimately, inflict more harm.

Gwyneth and Valmey ended their conversation, gracefully, it seemed to him. Gwyneth turned again and saw him. She started forward, smiling a little. Damn her composed serenity! He could not tell from her expression what she thought of the handsome, charming Valmey. Was that slight tinge of color in her cheeks a sign of guilt that she had been watched by her husband as she conversed with Valmey? Or could the flush have been produced by any emotion in the world that might tie her, even lightly, to him?

She approached him, his lovely wife, the woman he loved more than life itself. She spoke. She smiled. She bowed her head. She raised it again and looked at him through limitless violet eyes. She asked a question, he knew not what. He answered at random. They seemed to be speaking of his imminent departure, of the tedious details of his mission. He thought it wise to keep the details from her, but he could not think what to hide and what to expose.

She asked, in her lovely, lilting voice, "And while you are gone, sire, do I have your permission to return to our home and continue with my housecleaning?"

It was an uncomplicated request. He had granted that same request before. Just as, it seemed to him now, he had permitted her every decision and had moved to her every command. He had not questioned or called for household accounts, or laid a hand on her, or ever said a word meant to harm her. Why, he had even spoken the words she had fed him, and that at their very first meeting! She had twisted him—and everyone else at court, no doubt!—around her little finger.

She had unraveled him to the core of his being, stripped him down to his self-respect. He had been vanquished this night and, in his heart, had conceded to her his utter defeat. He knew what he had to do. It was going to be far easier now that he was fully clothed and standing next to her, rather than lying beside her in bed still aglow from the touch of her satin skin.

He shook his head and said, "No."

Chapter Twenty

Gwyneth was taken aback. "No?" She had made the request only as an excuse to prolong the conversation. She thought she had chosen an uncontroversial topic of mutual concern, not one where his approval had actually been in question.

"No," he repeated, shaking his head.

"May I ask why not?"

He did not give her an answer.

"The household is in the midst of repairs," she argued, "and I must be there to oversee them."

Again he shook his head.

She was confused. "Do you worry that I will engage in activities that extend beyond the household?"

"What activities might those be?" he inquired.

"I don't know! That is what I am asking you, sire. There must be some reason why you deny my straightforward request to return to our home during your absence."

"The reason is that I want you here at the Tower in Adela's care."

"Her care?" Gwyneth echoed, with a touch of irony. "If you are concerned about my well-being, you could kindly provide me with castle guards again—as protection."

"It is not for me to provide you with castle guards, it is up to Adela."

Gwyneth did not for a moment think that the king's consort had ordered the guards the first time. Before she could respond, he continued, "Now, I have said that I want you here at the Tower, and my guess is that Adela wants you here, as well. Thus, I see no point in you pursuing the matter with her."

"Yes, of course. However, I am not interested in Adela's wishes, sire, but rather your own."

"And I have told you that I wish you to stay here, at the Tower, during my absence."

"Yes, but—" she began, then stopped, perceiving that further protest was futile.

It seemed to her that the expression in his gray eyes had hardened to resolution. When she had approached him just now, he had looked inviting, almost as if he were glad to see her. She had been happy to see him, as well. She was even surprised by the pleasure she felt at seeing him and at her desire to catch and hold these last few moments with him before he was to leave.

It was strange and wonderful and painful to be next to him like this, apart but together, private but in public. What was even stranger and more wonderful and more painful was the familiarity of the feelings beating in her blood. She recalled how she had felt the first time she had laid eyes on him, across the hall. The only difference between then and now was that now the feelings were stronger and more recognizable.

Of course, she was not afraid of him anymore. She had even imagined, at several pleasurable moments during the past weeks, that she had power over him. Looking into his eyes now, she knew that she had foolishly played and lost this game of power and pleasure. She felt the pleasure-pain of great attachment and profound loss. She knew the word to attach to the feelings suffusing her.

When had she fallen in love with him? Last night, when he had dared her to make him want her? Before, on the tourney field, when he had prevailed so brilliantly over Gunnar Erickson? On their wedding night, when he had repeated to her the story of the hungry wolf, Fenrir? In the chapel, when he had kissed her with gentle force to seal their union? Or even—surely not—at their very first meeting, when he had turned to her and asked her whether she was carrying Canute's child?

She looked away from him. She would not ask herself the unanswerable question of why she had fallen in love with him. She did not think it was merely that he fit her so well and made her feel so good. She did not think it was simply his strength or his integrity or his blunt grace. Or even the look in his eye, the set of his shoulders or the way he spoke to his fellow knights. It must have been the mix of these elements, unique to him, that combined with an unpredictable alchemy to have affected her so powerfully and irreversibly.

She felt humbled by the realization of her love for him. She felt even, belatedly, submissive. She wished now that she had not consistently opposed him. She wished she had yielded earlier to him and more often, so that he would not have to be so hard with her, so resolute. She wanted him to look warmly upon her, to gather her into his arms and kiss her tenderly in parting. She wanted him to whisper blunt, teasing, arousing words, to tempt her as a man should tempt a woman. To trust her.

Trust. She drew a breath. He did not trust her, nor did he care to hear her acquit herself of wrongdoing. Now she understood why she had wished to lay her heart bare to him last night, awash as she had been with passion and love for him. Now she understood why he did not wish for the gift of her heart, when all he had married was her body. She blinked back a tear. In the face of defeat, she drew her courage around her like a cloak. She had made the error of prideful defiance before, but no longer.

She bowed her head in acquiescence and curtsied before him. "Yes, sire, you wish me to stay here at the Tower during your absence, and I am prepared to obey you."

"It is not your obedience I want."

Rising up, she lifted her eyes bravely to his. "No?"

His hard gaze was inscrutable. "I want your safety, as I think should be plain."

"But if it is only my safety—" She did not continue. From force of habit, she had been about to protest, to challenge, to oppose. "Yes, of course, you want my safety," she said, reversing herself. "I will stay here willingly." Then, quickly, "Do you leave on the moment?"

"Not for several more hours."

Her heart leapt. "Then I will see you again."

He shook his head. "No. I will be engaged with my men. I won't see you again."

Her heart sank. She hated the finality of that statement. "Until you return, that is."

"Until I return," he repeated slowly.

Their glances crossed and locked. Her heart—miserable, unstable organ—turned over. "So," she said. The word sounded idiotic when nothing followed it.

"So," he repeated, with that same horrible, ringing note of finality.

"So, I wish you a safe and swift return."

"You do?"

Her heart leapt again at some note she caught in his voice. "Yes," she said breathlessly.

She searched his eyes for an echo of the longing she thought she had heard in his voice. She felt desperate. Finding nothing, she felt anguished. So this was the humiliation Canute had never been capable of meting out to her, try as he might. This was the humiliation she had feared from Beresford. Of course, it was not physically hurtful, for he could never have humiliated her through violence. This was the humiliation of her pride, of the folly of thinking herself invulnerable.

Yet it was not quite humiliation that she felt, but more like humility, because he, with his uncompromising honesty and unquestioned courage, was so worthy of her love.

"Then I will make an effort to return safely and swiftly to you," he said for the sake of form.

"Oh, yes," she said. She could think of nothing clever to say. Nothing witty, enticing, magical. Nothing that would force him into a declaration. Nothing that would ward off the cramp she was sure to feel when he turned and strode out of the room.

He bowed.

She curtsied.

He took her hand in his strong fingers and brought it to his lips, but did not kiss it.

What she had earlier perceived as rough edges, she now sensed as warmth, strength, life. The vitality that was all his own radiated around him, engulfed her and intoxicated her more thoroughly than one of his kisses. She had to summon all her will to let her hand remain, unresisting, in his, and not to clutch at him. She feared that her grasp would plead with him in a way her words would not. So she let her hand rest in his that uncounted second of chaste and cherished joining and hoped that it would never end.

He released her hand. He nodded in valediction. He turned on his heels.

She watched him retreat. Then, realizing that her expression must be as naked as her emotions, she tried to shake off the effect of this bittersweet parting. She partially succeeded in bringing to order her scattered thoughts, but was never able afterwards to remember who she spoke to next or what about.

The rest of the day passed uneventfully for Gwyneth, since she did not consider being summoned to Adela's solar for an unprecedented second private audience particularly eventful when compared to the stunning realization of her newfound love for her husband.

What Adela had to say to her could be summed up in one sentence, namely that Gwyneth's presence at the Tower during Beresford's absence was to be kept a secret for the next day or two. It took Adela a full half hour to frame that idea, as if she did not want Gwyneth to sift this tiny, essential nugget from the weight of the surrounding ore. Gwyneth was given to understand further that if the courtiers thought she was removing immediately to her home in town, she was under no obligation to inform them otherwise.

Adela gave her some tasks to do for the day in a removed corner of the castle, and let her go.

Gwyneth left the solar, turning the bit of information over in her mind. It was curious and not immediately interpretable, but surely a sign of intrigue, if ever there was one. She was not certain whether Adela had planned this move, but she had the uneasy feeling that her personal safety was threatened. Throughout the day, her longings and love warred with an ill-defined fear for her life, making both experiences all the more unpleasant.

The only relatively bright spot was her encounter with Johanna, who was, predictably, surprised to see her still at the Tower. When Gwyneth had moped over her tasks long enough, she decided to circulate deliberately in the castle to see whether she could bring her vague sense of personal peril into definition. She was traveling an out-of-the-way corridor toward the end of the afternoon when she crossed Johanna's path.

"Oh, yes, I am still here," Gwyneth said to Johanna's opening comment, "although I plan to return home before too much longer, once I am through with what Adela has asked me to do. I am unusually clumsy today, it seems, for I should have been done long ago and gone home." She held up her hands. "But so it is!"

When Johanna smiled sympathetically, Gwyneth hated, even for a space of a heartbeat, to have to wonder whether she was the one within castle walls who was the source of threat.

"Well, I am sure you are anxious to return home and continue with your household repairs. But as for feeling clumsy, I suppose that must be excused as your natural feelings at Simon's departure!"

Johanna's comment was meant as harmless, Gwyneth could see, but she was unprepared for it. She must not have properly schooled her expression, for Johanna laid a concerned hand on her arm and said quickly and quietly, "What's wrong, Gwyneth?"

"Noth—"

"And don't say nothing, for I am certain that something is not right between you and Simon."

Gwyneth drew a steadying breath and countered, "What could be wrong?"

Johanna arched a brow. "Fencing with me, are you? So was Simon earlier. And speaking of which, I was not quite satisfied by my conversation with him this morning."

Gwyneth could not prevent her surge of interest, but she tried not to betray it. "Oh?" she said, affecting unconcern.

Johanna did not seem put off by this, if her penetrating gaze into Gwyneth's eyes was any indication. "Yes," she said, "and I wondered later whether he might not have realized that you were the one yesterday who originated the alert about the unknown knight. But I told myself that you and Simon must have discussed the matter last night. Now I am wondering again whether or not Simon might not be missing some part of the story."

Gwyneth asked as casually as she could, "What makes you think he is missing some part? Was it something he said?"

"In a way, yes. You see, I thought at first that he was vexed with me for having meddled with his squire at the tourney. When I assured him that I had meant no harm, only help, which would have been obvious to any other normal human being, well, instead of growling his displeasure at me, he...he *thanked* me! Very formally, in fact. It was very odd!"

"And what is so odd about..." Gwyneth did not complete the question. She did not need to be told what was odd about Beresford executing formally polite behavior. She managed, at last, the evasive response, "It was very proper of him to thank you."

"He should have thanked *you*, my dear!" Johanna's eyes narrowed with speculative concern. "And if we are to mention very odd occurrences, let me add that I have never in my life seen a more graceful bow and kiss of the hand than Simon gave you upon parting this morning in the great hall."

Gwyneth strained to recall the moment. All she could remember was blinding realization and great pain.

"He was positively courtly," Johanna continued. "Why, even Valmey remarked upon it."

"He did?"

"Said he never saw such address and was inclined to think that Simon had taken lessons from Geoffrey of Senlis!"

"Did he sneer when he said it?"

Johanna paused. "Is there some reason that you do not like Cedric of Valmey?"

"Forgive me," Gwyneth said quickly. "I meant no slur of Sire Valmey." She attempted to modulate her voice from acidic to sweet. "However, he did suggest to me once that Beresford would be unable to turn a phrase or a hand as easily as he turned his sword against an opponent. So, naturally, I wondered whether Sire Valmey was not, in fact, being ironic."

Johanna paused to reconsider the tone of Valmey's comment.

"And you will agree with me," Gwyneth pressed humorously, trying to give the topic a light turn, "that a fellow knight complimenting my husband on courtly address might well be making a joke."

Johanna conceded the point with a brief smile. "But it was not a joke in this instance. Valmey seemed serious, even surprised by Simon's attentions to you, and curiously speculative, although I certainly cannot explain why."

Gwyneth registered that information, and was about to inquire more closely into the particulars of Johanna's conversation with her husband when, as luck would have it, Rosalyn happened upon them.

Lady Chester's slim brows arched sensuously. "Are you still here, Gwyneth?" she asked. "I thought you would have left the Tower directly after Simon's departure."

It took all of Gwyneth's composure to smile and say, "I had an errand to perform for Adela here this afternoon. I am on my way home presently."

"Ah." Rosalyn shrugged prettily. She privileged Johanna with a few words, then moved on.

Gwyneth glanced at the dark beauty's retreating back. She thought that Rosalyn had seemed both genuinely surprised to see her and convincingly disinterested in her expressed intention to return home. Nevertheless, she wondered whether Rosalyn might not be privy, through Adela, to her altered plans. Something about the way she had asked, "Are you still here?" had made Gwyneth think that she would not sleep comfortably this night, surrounded by her enemies, who might or might not know where and why Adela had hidden her.

Beresford leaned forward on the pommel of his saddle and surveyed the terrain spreading out before him. Scanning the Bedford Valley, cut by its river, he mentally reviewed Duke Henry's movements since arriving in England in January. The Angevin usurper had landed, predictably enough, at Wareham, and from there had marched his small force of one hundred forty knights and three thousand infantry immediately to Devizes in order to join forces with the earls of Cornwall and Hereford, those traitors.

Then, aiming to divert Stephen from the safety of London's proximity at Wallingford, Duke Henry went west to attack Malmesbury. There, in late April, Stephen had routed the Angevin with Beresford's help; and with Valmey's surprisingly successful siege of Castle Norham in early May, Stephen's position looked good in both the west and the north. Since Duke Henry had no military bases of support in the east or south, and since he had refused to fight at Bristol, Beresford should have felt that Stephen's throne was more secure than he had thought before leaving London the week before. But he did not.

Despite Duke Henry's unopposed progress straight north, from Gloucester to Dudley to Tutbury, where they had just missed him, Beresford knew that Stephen's troops had been summoned from Northumbria, farther north, to check Duke Henry's progress in that direction. The original plan had been for the Northumbrian troops to meet Beresford, Warenne, Senlis and Lancaster at Tutbury, with reinforcements to come later, led by Valmey. However, since Beresford and Warenne, who headed this expedition, had learned upon arriving at Tutbury that Duke Henry was already on his way, incomprehensibly, to the south and east toward Leicester, Beresford had had to scatter messengers with urgent counterorders. This he did not like to do. He had a fair amount of confidence in his messengers, but the slight disarray at the need for counterorders compounded the larger disarray of Stephen's strategic resolve. Beresford recognized that getting Duke Henry to fight had already proven to be a problem. Counting on Stephen's ability to lead an attack seemed of a similar magnitude.

It was, furthermore, contrary to Beresford's nature to have to chase Duke Henry around the countryside from Tutbury to Leicester, and the lack of battle there suggested that the Earl of Leicester must have transferred his allegiance to the usurper. Then the Angevin was off to Coventry and Warwick, all without raising a sword, with Beresford in undignified pursuit.

It pained Beresford, as well, to be at odds with the Church. From the strange and bloodless path Duke Henry was pursuing, Beresford knew that a growing number of magnates were adopting an attitude of neutrality. The Church recommended that the barons and earls remain loyal to Stephen by obeying his summons to the army, but it advised as well that those same barons and earls should refuse to fight against Duke Henry as the lawful heir to the kingdom.

It was all very frustrating to Beresford, and no good for strengthening Stephen's military resolve. And it had not taken more than this stop at Bedford for Beresford to realize that Duke Henry's goal was, first and last, Wallingford, as gateway to London.

Beresford shifted in his saddle and wished he cared more about the fate of his king and his kingdom.

Warenne rode abreast and halted his horse next to Beresford. He silently contemplated the terrain a moment before he commented, "Look familiar?"

Beresford grunted his assent.

"This might as well be the Avon," Warenne continued.

"The only difference being that there has been no rain here of late," Beresford replied. "Yet you are right that the lay of the land and the troops recalls Bristol, where Duke Henry refused to engage us."

The situation at Bedford was in fact, nearly identical to that at Bristol. As before, there was only a river dividing the two armies. As before, Stephen was anxious to decide the issue in one great battle, and for that purpose he had gathered an inexpressibly large army from every part of his kingdom. As before, there were those who insisted that if the battle took place, it could only be to the general harm of the kingdom. However, this time the calls to desist came more from the king's side than the duke's.

Warenne observed, "The torrential rains did make the Avon impassable, you know."

Beresford frowned skeptically. "Or the Angevin could not yet completely trust his own army, which was greatly outnumbered by ours. But if," he continued, "Duke Henry could not trust the size and loyalty of his troops just a few weeks ago, he has done much to strengthen his position with a peaceful itinerary that is most remarkable."

"Leicester's shift of allegiance is a blow."

Again Beresford grunted his assent. "A blow, indeed. And the Angevin has accomplished all so far with words." He paused at length and repeated, "With words."

Beresford had learned the power of words—their power to hurt, their power to please. He knew a woman who was not strong of muscle, but strong of words and wise of ways, and she had power over him like no other human being before her. On the last morning he had seen her, he had refused her request to return to their home merely for the sake of withstanding her power. It was only after he had left her in the great hall that he had conceived another good reason for sequestering her in the Tower. He had gone straight to Adela to insure that Gwyneth's captivity would remain se-cret—from absolutely everyone, he insisted—so that no Northumbrian supporters of Duke Henry could seek her out again. Beresford had such belief in Gwyneth's verbal skill that he was sure she could bring Stephen's kingdom to its knees with only a shred of information and a few well-placed words.

"With many words," Warenne replied. "Do you think Duke Henry means to negotiate a peace?"

Beresford devoutly hoped that Duke Henry would not be able to maneuver himself into a position where he could negotiate a peace, for negotiation would exclude Stephen's heir from succession. "Not if I can help it," he said. "Val-mey thinks it impossible." He shifted in his saddle to look over his shoulder at the men and tents quilting the country-side around the besieged castle of Bedford. "By the way, where is Valmey? He should have caught up with us several days ago."

Warenne shook his head. "No doubt lost in the confu-sion of orders and counterorders."

Beresford grunted yet again, this time gloomily. He looked back over the valley, across the river, at the colorful dots of enemy flags and standards and the occasional mi-nute flash of metal catching the sun. He sensed a trap being set around him. He did not have words to describe the rig-gings of this trap, but he felt the sensation penetrate his muscles and settle in his bones.

Chapter Twenty-One

The day after Beresford's departure, Gwyneth stood in the main courtyard of her house and let her rage rip through her. When the rage passed its most intense surge, a great sense of violation and injustice took its place, followed swiftly by great tremors of true fear. For a while this last emotion masked the bud of a thought that the violence whose evidence surrounded her was not random.

She looked first, in anger and horror, at the smashed staircase and adjoining balcony, which had showered splinters everywhere, then at the collapsed and charred remains of the master's and mistress's bedchambers. Fortunately, the flames had not spread to the rest of the house. Roof tiles lay shattered at odd intervals, along with the scaffolding and carpenter's horses, upon which rested broken remains of the new shutters. She did not need to see inside the solar to know that the three beautiful new windows lay in shards upon the floor, glittering in the midmorning sun among pieces of broken crockery.

There was worse damage, not immediately visible. Two of the household servants had died, one of burns, one of a blow from a falling beam, and three more were hurt, one of them seriously. Her most fervent prayers went heavenward in thanks that Benedict and Gilbert remained unharmed. Upon seeing them whole and hale, she had clasped them fiercely to her breast and put them in the care of one of the household women.

She had then turned her attention to inspecting the devastation. The curious feature of it was, of course, that the master's and mistress's chambers had been torched first, and this evidence gave Gwyneth her clue that she had been the intended victim of the fire. Of course, under normal circumstances, the entire house, or a good portion of it, should have burned, thereby obscuring the place of origin of the fire. However, with the plaster of the adjoining walls still wet, the soggy gauze and limestone had effectively blocked the fire long enough for household retainers to establish a bucket chain in the dead of night.

She attempted a practical thought, wondering whether the windows in the solar might be temporarily replaced by more-affordable oiled parchments. She regretted having been extravagant with the glass in the first place, but had wanted to set the right tone for the household overhaul. She pushed aside her regret, decided on the oiled parchments and felt immediately better for having made such a practical decision. Now if she could set her mind to commanding the cleanup, she might be able to similarly organize the rest of her thoughts.

The household retainers and hired craftsmen had joined her in the courtyard to mourn their losses. Her first act had been to arrange for the burial of the dead, and the parish priest was already there when she arrived, muttering and shaking his head over the work of the devil. Gwyneth did not think it was the devil who had wrought this destruction. Nor even Loki. She knew human evil when she saw it, although she had largely avoided thinking about how that evil had intended her to be the primary victim. Finally, she could ignore it no longer. If she was to regain a measure of control over the situation, she understood that she would have to face the ugly fact.

Someone wanted her dead. Her enemy had evidently not known that she had spent the night at the Tower. Whoever it was had believed, like everyone else at court, that she was returning to her home. Adela had played a part in saving her, but her life Gwyneth now owed to Beresford. He must have known that evil was conspiring against her. He had insisted that she stay at the Tower. He had even said that it was for her own safety. He must have been the one to have told Adela to keep secret Gwyneth's presence at the Tower.

It was remarkable now to think that she had attempted to defy her husband on this issue. He had stood his ground implacably, and had thereby guaranteed her safety. It was also remarkable now to think that she had feared an enemy within castle walls last night. She was sorry that, in the rush of her summons from Adela this morning with news of the attack upon her home, she had not had the opportunity to witness the reaction of various courtiers to the news. She would have loved to have gauged Rosalyn's reaction, in particular.

She did not truly need to have seen Lady Chester's reaction to know whose hand had produced the deaths in her home and the destruction. Almost as if she had conjured him with her thoughts, she turned and saw Cedric of Valmey rush through the main portal and hasten toward her.

Guilty! was her immediate judgment, despite Valmey's intense look of concern and the serious, respectful tone of his voice as he greeted her. "My lady Gwyneth! I came as soon as I heard. I was with the reinforcement troops summoned from Wincester, and we were already outside castle walls when word of vandals within the city spread. Are you all right?"

Gwyneth had to accept the grasp of his hand, his respectful bow and the press of his lips against her fingers, along with his earnest concern. "Yes, I am all right," she replied, "but you did not need to trouble yourself."

"Ah, but I did! I will be seeing your husband at Tutbury in a matter of days. If advance word of this reaches him and he discovers that I did not assure myself of your safety before leaving London, I might not live to see another day."

Valmey's sad smile indicated that his insignificant joke could not counter the magnitude of the surrounding tragedy.

"Do you think my husband will receive advance word of this?" Gwyneth asked.

"Well, as to that, I do not know, my lady," Valmey replied. "I had simply assumed that reports of such news might well precede my departure."

"And will those reports leave London attached with the names of the possible perpetrators?"

Valmey looked around him at the shattered ruins and charred remains of sections of the house. His manner was all delicate restraint, as if he were making an effort to stifle his outrage. "Does the work of savage vandals," he asked with suppressed vehemence, "come with names attached?"

Valmey's presence had turned Gwyneth's hot rage to ice. She did not consider whether she was treading a treacherous path when she said, "The destruction looks so... deliberate to me and so—how should I say?—personal. It is surely the work of a person or persons who have names—" her glance soulfully swept the ruins and halted on Valmey "—and faces."

The baron looked creditably shocked. "Do you think...? No, surely not...but is it possible that Robert of Breteuil has managed to retaliate against his master? I know that the lad is in prison, but perhaps there are others in league with him who could have wrought such destructive revenge!"

Gwyneth had to admire him. His response sounded so spontaneous and convincing. She matched Valmey's shock. "Why, yes, I can see that this further treachery must only be the work of... but it is too horrible to discuss!" She put the back of her hand to her forehead in distress. "Adela must know of this." She removed her hand and nodded with resolution. "I will certainly speak with her."

"And when might that be?"

"When I return to the Tower tonight."

Valmey nodded mournfully. "Yes, you must return to the Tower tonight, but I wish you could tell her before then."

"You see that I have so very much to do here, sire," Gwyneth said, gesturing to her surroundings.

"Yes, of course. Well, then, allow me to speak with her first, on your behalf," Valmey offered graciously.

Gwyneth thought that he was quite predictable. "Do you have time for such an audience? Must you not be moving your troops out behind my husband and the others?"

"I must make time," Valmey replied gallantly, "and must consider that alerting Adela to possible traitors against Beresford in the castle is my first duty. I feel confident that I can see her and still lead my troops out this afternoon."

Gwyneth curtsied. "Then I would be most grateful if you could see her as soon as possible." She lifted her eyes to him. "And tell her that I will gather my retinue later today and proceed to the Tower, let us say, shortly after vespers. Will you carry that message for me?"

Valmey bowed deeply and respectfully. "I will be honored to give her that message for you."

Gwyneth could not resist asking, "And you, sire, will have left London by vespers, I expect?"

Another deep bow. "Assuredly."

He departed.

Valmey's purpose in coming held no mystery for Gwyneth. He had made his dutiful trip to her home for no other reason than to discover her whereabouts for the day. This meant, of course, that she had to get as far away as possible from the house and the Tower as quickly as she could. The morning had advanced, and it was almost the sext. She did not have time to think or to plan. She had time only to act. She had no clothes to prepare, for they had all been burned. However, she did have a little money that she would need, a few coins she had garnered and stashed in the spice cupboard, which had a small lock. So she went first to the solar, as if to survey the destruction. There she found the spice cupboard in shreds, but she was able to recoup many of the valuable pennies from the litter on the floor.

When Gwyneth had settled with the craftsmen about how to proceed and had established the mode of payment, she knew she would have to leave the house and not return. She dared not tell any of her retainers what she had in mind, for their knowledge of her movements might jeopardize them, as well. She then summoned the serving woman, Swanilda, to accompany her on her neighborhood errands. She added the highly unusual request that the woman bring along two warm shawls, "just in case the sun should go behind the clouds."

Gwyneth had to take John the Porter into her confidence. When she and Swanilda were leaving the house, she drew him into the shadows of the gallery and explained quickly what was afoot and what she had to do about it. He was surprised, but agreed to bring two horses with side-saddles through Aldgate exactly at midday and walk straight into the woods beyond the gate, where she and Swanilda would be waiting for him. She advised him to stay away from the house for the next several days to avoid being questioned by Valmey or his minions.

Swanilda was equally surprised as she walked with her mistress through the streets of London, listening to Gwyneth's plan and the reasons for it. She was certainly afraid of the world beyond city walls, but possessed enough acting skills to follow her mistress's lead by throwing her shawl over her head and playing the old woman to the gate-keeper. Her spirit of adventure was equal to the occasion, as well, which was fortunate.

The first day and night were the most difficult and dangerous for the two women, for they were still in the vicinity of London. Gwyneth envisioned Valmey's displeasure upon not finding her party in the streets of London shortly after vespers, for that was surely his prime opportunity for abducting her and doing away with her. She imagined his visit to her home and his arrogant interrogation of all the retainers. She imagined his rush to the Tower and a visit to Adela, posing similar questions, less arrogant, more obsequious, which would similarly yield no clue as to Gwyneth's whereabouts. She imagined Valmey's impotent rage, his animal fear and his calculated determination to put his hands around her neck. And he had an army at his disposal.

But she figured that the army would hinder him in finding her more than it would help him. Although she was headed to the same place as Valmey, she was not taking the same route, and in any case it would be far easier for her to avoid crossing paths with a great many men and horses and equipment than it would be for Valmey to leave his troops and track her down. She only hoped that she could get to Beresford before he did.

She did not think the task should be very difficult. Not that she had imagined it would be a physically easy one, of course, given the routine hardships of life out in the open, two women traveling alone with little money and Swanilda unaccustomed to riding. However, her strength of purpose—her love for her husband, her loyalty to him and her great sense of debt to him—kept her going.

Gwyneth's sharp wits were able to find kind old couples with whom to break bread, and sweet young peasant families willing to lend a roof to two women traveling alone. She was aiming, more or less, for Tutbury, where she expected to find Beresford, but she had chosen to angle north first, intending to head west after Huntingdon. She knew that Valmey was heading west by way of the Thames, then north around Evesham. Although her way was slightly longer, she was traveling lighter than Valmey. Thus, when she lost a day to Swanilda's sore buttocks, she did not fret. However, when she lost another to dysentery, caused no doubt by a bad piece of cheese that did not trouble Swanilda's own digestion, she began to get a little anxious. And when the next day dawned to impassable rain, she began to worry that all her efforts would be in vain.

She and Swanilda had been gone almost a sennight and were still only in the vicinity of Bedford when they heard stunning news. Gwyneth already knew from Beresford that Duke Henry had proceeded north from Bristol without fighting. At a peasant's croft she had found for the night in Bedfordshire, she learned that Duke Henry had continued that restraint in the past several weeks; and instead of going north after Tutbury, he had turned east and south, angling back, so one might guess, toward London. Normally, peasants would not be abreast of the latest political news. However, in this case, every living soul in the area knew that Duke Henry was presently camped, with an army that had grown considerably in the past fortnight, on the north side of the Great River Ouse, not five miles away.

Gwyneth slept on the news and awoke with a plan adjusted by what she perceived as clear developments in Duke Henry's favor. She cleaned herself and Swanilda as well as conditions would allow, and set off in the early morning for the river, confirming along the way that the Angevin could now count as a supporter Robert, Earl of Leicester. This shift of allegiance lent great respectability to Duke Henry's cause and added a powerful name to his list of supporters, which included already, Gwyneth knew, the earls of Worcester, Chester, Lincoln, Cornwall, Gloucester and Devon.

Night was well advanced before Gwyneth, with a combination of courage, persistence and seductive smiles, was where she wanted to be: at the entrance to Duke Henry's red-and-gold-striped pavilion in the center of his camp. While Swanilda waited outside, Gwyneth was ushered into the round tent with its peaked top and heavy cloth, woven with the lions of Anjou. In the center, standing next to the richly carved center pole, stood a young man of not more than two-and-twenty. His stance, even in repose, was energetic. His unlined, unbearded face wore an expression of eagerness and confidence combined, at the entrance of a lovely young woman, with curiosity.

Mastering her fear, Gwyneth came forward and curtsied low. "I am Gwyneth Andresdaughter, widow to Canute of Northumbria, wife to Simon of Beresford. I have come, sire, to seek your help."

Beresford wished he could shake his melancholy. It seemed the longer he was apart from Gwyneth, the more he yearned for her. The farther he was away from her, the closer she seemed. So close. Achingly close.

He had walked down into the valley, angling far from camp. He stopped at the river's edge. The night was clear, the moon full. He stood in the shadowy screen of tall water rushes, although he was hardly concerned that anyone across the river could see him. He looked up at the milky spill of stars studding the sky, feeling sick with love. He looked across the river to the opposite shore, catching the flicker of camp fires here and there, and wondered that his blood did not sing at the possibility of battle. Nor did his stomach knot with the tension necessary to lead the charge, meet the enemy, raise the sword, swing the mace. All of those familiar emotions were swamped by the unfamiliar thickening of his blood, the throbbing of his heart and the pulsing desire to see Gwyneth.

Perhaps it was not love that he felt, but doom. Valmey's reinforcements had not yet arrived and might be wandering anywhere between Tutbury and the gates of paradise. Then, omen upon ill omen, he had just learned that Warwick had, indeed, died from the shock of the news that his countess had surrendered his castle to Duke Henry while he was still in attendance on Stephen. It seemed the vital, young Angevin had only to come calling for all to surrender to him. Beresford saw little hope for military maneuvers to turn the tide of this peaceful march. In fact, a bloody battle might well further undermine Stephen's position.

So what was left? Negotiation? Beresford had no taste or skill for it. He might as well die honorably at the end of an enemy sword. He even indulged the gloomy notion that Valmey's errant reinforcements were increasingly irrelevant.

By a trick of imagination, he thought he saw Valmey crossing the river quietly in a little boat, heading for a point not far from his screen of water rushes. But, no. It could not be Valmey, because he was traveling from the opposite, enemy side of the Ouse to Stephen's camp. Beresford blinked, then frowned. The impression remained. The resemblance of the man in the boat to Valmey was remarkable.

The little boat slipped to shore. The man got out. He found a thick root to which he moored the vessel. He moved efficiently and furtively, as if he were doing something slightly wrong. Even though his back was to Beresford, his movements were unmistakably those of Cedric of Valmey. And he had just traveled in the wrong direction across the river.

Beresford's melancholy slipped from his shoulders like an unfastened cloak. He touched his hand to the hilt of his sword at his side. He stepped out from behind the water rushes into the full, flooding moonlight.

"Have you come with reinforcements, then, Cedric?" His deep voice broke the sleepy peace of the riverbank.

Valmey started reflexively, then turned very slowly. His eyes narrowed against the luminous moonlight bathing Beresford. "Why, yes, I have," he replied.

"You are a few days late with them," Beresford noted.

"I experienced a minor delay in London," Valmey replied, then waved the detail away like an annoying fly, "and, of course, we had to chase you chasing the Angevin usurper around the countryside."

"Which is how you ended up on the wrong side of the river this evening."

Valmey came forward several paces. "I was interested to determine the size and strength of the Angevin's forces," he answered. He stopped just outside of striking distance.

"I could have informed you of the numbers."

"I preferred to see for myself."

Beresford grunted. "And the reinforcements? Which side of the river are they on?"

Valmey chuckled pleasantly. He made a friendly gesture, indicating Stephen's camp. "Behind you, of course, just where they are supposed to be."

"Tell me, then. How estimate you the Angevin's chances, based on what you've just seen?"

"Fair. He's had good success of late."

"Yes. Leicester is in his camp now." Beresford paused. "Did you see him?"

"Who?"

"Robert, Earl of Leicester."

Valmey shook his head.

"Or Gloucester?" This produced another shake of Valmey's head.

"Devon? No? Lincoln or Chester or Worcester?"

Valmey responded with a consistent negative.

"Duke Henry, then," Beresford stated. "Surely you must have seen Duke Henry." He wanted to hear Valmey speak.

Valmey's response was composed. "I did not cross the river with the intention of being seen."

Beresford showed his teeth. "Evidently not. You could not have imagined that I would have seen you here, for instance."

Valmey lost his artful composure. He straightened, put his hand on his sword and asked, "And just how am I supposed to take that?"

"Exactly as you think you should take it," Beresford replied.

Valmey was not yet ready for this contest. He attempted to stall by puffing up angrily, then exhaling on a sputtery laugh. "It will not do, my friend, to have division within the ranks! Think, Simon, think of it!"

"I have thought of it, Cedric." Beresford took the crucial pace forward, to where a salute of swords was possible. One more step and it would be necessary. "And I now realize there has already been a division in the ranks of which I was previously unaware. But is Stephen's cause lost because of that? I am not sure. What do you think, Cedric?"

"Surely not, Simon," Valmey answered cautiously.

"No, surely not. I had been inclined to view Stephen's chances a bit glumly of late, I admit, but suddenly I feel more optimistic, now that I really know who is on whose side."

Valmey was silent and watchful.

Beresford continued, "Stephen can still count de Vere, you know, and Lucy, as well as Ypres and Warenne and

Senlis and Fortescue, not to mention Lancaster and North-ampton." He took the final, possibly fatal step closer to Valmey. "But he can no longer count on you."

Valmey answered Beresford's challenge with one of his own. "Stephen's chances will be greatly impoverished with the loss of his greatest, most loyal and newest earl." He drew his sword. The metal sprang to life in the moonlight.

Beresford's sword was raised and ready before Valmey had finished expressing his murderous intention. The clash of steel against steel rang out. Beresford felt good and strong. He felt purposeful. He felt like killing Valmey.

He wanted a few answers first. "Why did you do it, Val-mey? Why did you not simply make a clean break with Ste-phen if you were of a mind to change sides?"

"For the reason that you yourself have noted," Valmey answered easily. His sword work was far from contempt-ible and he, too, was in good form this night. "Stephen and Henry are evenly matched. There's naught to decide who will win in the end."

Steel met steel repeatedly. The constant ring and echo was punctuated by grunts and the padded shifting of feet on the ground. Valmey had not found his opening.

Beresford was not yet seeking his. He did not yet have all his answers. "And you must be on the winning side?"

"At all costs."

"At the price of your honor?"

"At all costs."

"At the price of your life?"

Valmey chuckled again. This time it was an unpleasant sound. "My life? Is my life in danger?"

"You have nothing to live for, Valmey."

"Unlike yourself?" Valmey jeered in response. Then the scornful expression on his handsome face was replaced by one of craftiness. "But, then, I guess you have not heard of the attack on your home and the burning of the mistress's bedchamber."

Beresford's concentration broke. The next thing he knew, Valmey's sword bit deep into his right forearm. He felt his own sword wobble in his hand, as if he were about to lose his grip.

Chapter Twenty-Two

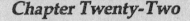

The pain in his arm seemed nothing compared to the pain in his heart, and for a moment he was dazed. Valmey advanced to take advantage of his weakness. Beresford put up his sword to ward off the blow, but had no force to counterattack. He felt himself being driven back. He was still able to defend himself, but he was not able to mount an offensive, much less gain any strategic advantage.

Valmey pressed, foolishly perhaps. "Yes, you may never see your beloved Gwyneth again, poor Simon."

Beresford was not likely to remain victim to a verbal trap any more than he would be long misled by cunning sword work. With supreme effort, he thrust aside the hideous possibility that Gwyneth had been harmed. Still, the lover's pain in his heart was more ferocious than any physical wound, and he knew that unless he could recover his concentration, he was lost.

"What makes you say that, Valmey?"

"When last I saw your house, the mistress's chamber had burned to the ground."

"And when was that?"

"On the day after you left London on this campaign."

Beresford grinned, but under the stress of wielding his sword and countering Valmey's blows, his expression looked more of a grimace. Gwyneth must be safe. Before his departure, he had refused her request that she return to the house, and he had made arrangements with Adela that

Gwyneth remain closely guarded at the Tower. He began to recognize Valmey's ploy for the ignoble stratagem it was. He noticed that his arm had begun to throb. Better to focus on Valmey's ploy and his reasons for it.

"Who was responsible for the fire?"

"I don't know. Perhaps Robert of Breteuil sent someone to wreak revenge on you."

The suggestion affected Beresford like a magic tonic. He realized that if Valmey was accusing Breteuil of torching the mistress's chambers, it would make no sense for Gwyneth to have been conspiring with his former squire. However, he did not have time to understand fully why Valmey's suggestion caused a weight to lift from his suffering heart. He knew only that the love locked there was set free to course through his body, making it solid and integral to his person, like veins in marble. He felt that not only was Gwyneth within him, giving him breath and muscle, she was also behind him, giving him strength. He focused his love on the wound in his arm. Although the throbbing did not lessen, he knew how to best synchronize it with the rhythm of Valmey's sword.

Living, breathing and loving. Beresford felt the support of Gwyneth's love behind him like the sure hands of a beautiful sea siren, turning the defensive tide into an offensive wave of attack, feint and counterattack. Through his wound bad blood was flowing, allowing fresh, clean blood to pump through his body. The sting of the pain kept him sharp, gave him courage, helped him calculate the openings.

So Valmey and Gwyneth were not entirely a pair, as he had earlier perceived when his love had wrenched his heart rather than strengthened it. Where he had once seen similarities between Valmey's abilities and Gwyneth's, he now saw only differences: where Valmey was duplicitous, Gwyneth displayed integrity; where Valmey was cowardly, Gwyneth was courageous; where Valmey connived, Gwyneth countered cleverly, but straight.

He was in love with a goddess of beauty and wisdom. He felt ancient; he felt new.

He felt his second wind. He was beginning to enjoy himself. He saw no reason to make quick work of the encounter, for Valmey had much to pay for, much more than Beresford could identify at the moment. He felt almost joyful, too, exercising his craft like a mythical master smith working in reverse, unforging the object at the end of his steel. Valmey might have begun the encounter as a man; by the end of it, Beresford was determined that his opponent would be reduced to shapeless, molten metal.

"If you're...not careful, you'll...slip in your...blood," Valmey managed.

Beresford did not bother to answer with words. He swung his sword with purpose and found the opening at Valmey's left side, making contact with his body with a force and angle that not only brought blood but also cracked several ribs. For good measure, Beresford exhaled heartily. Like a bellows, his breath made Valmey's vital flame flicker uncertainly rather than glow hotter.

"Why did you do it?" Beresford demanded. He pressed forward.

Valmey fell back. "What?"

"Play the double game."

"I've...told you."

Beresford shook his head, sprinkling his shoulders and hair with the sweat of his brow. "Because you cannot predict who will win?" He shook his head harder. "Your reason is not good enough."

"It's...good enough...for...you."

"Why me, after all?"

"Too much... You have...too much."

Beresford's contempt for his disintegrating opponent left no room for compassion and understanding. He could not see his motivations in terms of any recognizable human failing, such as jealousy or greed or the will to survive. Rather, he saw Valmey as the embodiment of evil. A man who had set himself up to determine how much another man could and could not have. A man who dared godlike judgments. A man who would kill and destroy for no reason other than personal gain. A schemer without good purpose.

"I have what I have," Beresford replied, "and you don't like it."

"I like to... win," Valmey panted.

Beresford would let the melting mass of humanity before him wind himself all he wanted. Beresford had nothing to say, and let his sword do the talking. It spoke as bluntly as he ever had, fiercely and mercilessly. The end was near, and the result was clear. Valmey's minutes on this earth were numbered.

For his final act of evil, Valmey sputtered, "And how... will... you explain... my death... by... your sword... to... Stephen? Valmey... most loyal supporter... of the... king? Greater even... than yourself?"

"I'll gladly accept the consequences."

"With... me gone... and you... discredited," Valmey continued venomously, "Henry... will... prevail." Sweat was rolling off of his head and face. It soaked his shirt and tunic and merged with the blood flowing from his side. He was panting for breath, for life. His footwork was shaky. His sword arm had become sloppy. "What... then... do you say... to... Henry... having... killed... a... most valued... man?"

Even without Valmey's comments, Beresford had already perceived that he was in a dilemma. If he could have undone this encounter, he would have.

But he could not. Nor could he turn back from what he had to do to end it. "If I'm to hang, one way or the other, as a result of your duplicity, then my death will be the only satisfaction you'll have as you roast in hell." He knocked Valmey's feet out from under him and the sword from his hand. Then he was kneeling over him. His blade glinted at Valmey's throat. "But I'll not see you there, Cedric. No dishonor damns me."

Valmey's eyes saw death. "My...death as...your fellow...knight...will stain...your...immortal...soul...nevertheless."

Beresford knew it, but bent to his bloody task. Before he could do the final deed that would seal both Valmey's fate and his own, a harsh and commanding "Halt!" rang out from behind.

Beresford stayed his hand. He looked up and over his shoulder.

As he looked upon the beautiful young woman, Duke Henry's expression was bemused and intrigued and, most importantly, indulgent.

However, Gwyneth was too anxious to be able to read the youthful duke's face properly. Too much was at stake for her to have confidence in her actions, for her to believe that she had spoken convincingly, or to hope that Duke Henry would be sympathetic to her request. Now that she was finished with her speech, her courage collapsed. She regretted having foolishly, impetuously come to plead her husband's case, but she forced herself to stand straight and unflinching, to accept his judgment.

At last Duke Henry said, "I will think about what you have just revealed, madam."

Was that a gleam in his eye, she wondered, or the tug of a smile at his lips? He nodded and turned away from her before she could decide. She understood that she had been dismissed. She turned to go and was ushered out of the pavilion by a guard at the door, who held aside the curtain for her exit.

She stepped out into the starry night and sought Swanilda, who had taken up a position at the side of the tent. Several guards had found the serving woman interesting enough to hang about her, and they achieved a remarkable amount of communication given their nonexistent English and her imperfect command of French. Gwyneth's arrival brought the guards to a sense of duty. They returned to their posts at the door of the tent.

Gwyneth touched her serving woman's arm and sighed heavily. She was about to lead her away from Duke Henry's pavilion when she caught sight of the figure of a man well known to her, sauntering away, relaxed as you please. He disappeared behind a tent.

She caught her breath. Her heart began to pound, both in triumph and in fear, and she almost rushed back into Duke Henry's tent. But she decided that discretion was the better part of valor, and that she should verify the man's identity before she acted. So she followed him around the tent, deflecting the advances of several overbold soldiers with a few choice words. She trailed the man until she could see his face clearly in the moonlight.

There was no mistaking him. It was Cedric of Valmey.

She tasted the ancient joy of having her enemy where she wanted him. But was she too late? Had he already found Beresford and done him harm? To keep her thoughts rational, she decided that he had not.

She followed Valmey a bit farther, expecting that he would go into some tent. However, when his path seemed to lead out of the camp and directly to the river, she realized that she had very little time to act. She hurried back to Duke Henry's pavilion. She would not be denied entrance, and thus caught a look of blankest surprise on the young ruler's face when he turned from his jovial conversation with several advisers to face once again the lovely Gwyneth of Beresford.

"Come!" she urged. "I beg of you, sire! I'll explain on the way." She held out her hand to him beseechingly. She nearly swooned with relief when he did not order her removed bodily from his tent.

Instead, he stepped forward with an inquiring look. "Yes, madam? Perhaps you have bethought yourself of some item you had forgot a moment ago?"

"In a way, yes," she said, gesturing faster with her arms. "I will explain on the way." As they left the tent together, she continued, "You see, when I came to you just now, I spoke merely on behalf of my husband. I had no thought of taking it upon myself to denounce anyone else or have you beware of the wicked creatures in Stephen's court. But now you must know that there is a snake who travels both gardens, and he is just now slithering from one side to the other. It is Cedric of Valmey. I assume you know him."

"Yes, of course."

"Are you aware that Valmey is just now crossing to Stephen's side this night?"

Duke Henry acknowledged that Cedric of Valmey, with whom he had had an audience some time before Gwyneth of Beresford was announced, had not mentioned his intention of crossing the river this night.

Grateful that Duke Henry was willing to listen, she poured out her tale of Cedric of Valmey's treachery. She was unaware that Henry's interest in hearing her out was accompanied by a summons to a variety of guards to follow him, in case she was leading him into a trap. He had not achieved his spectacularly peaceful results since landing in England by being susceptible to a beautiful face and falling prey to a pretty story. It was a pity, he thought, that the fair Gwyneth was so obviously in love with her husband.

She was not, of course, leading Duke Henry into a trap. She was leading him to the water's edge to show him clear evidence of the treachery of Cedric of Valmey. Once at the river, however, she saw something else that caused her heart to stop. She squinted into the moonlight. She strained her eyes to see across the river, at a far angle, hoping against hope that it was not Beresford who had stepped out from behind the water rushes once Valmey landed on the other side.

She clutched Duke Henry's arm. "By Odin," she breathed, "it's him. Or, at least, I think it must be. It's so far away that I can't be sure... yet no other man has quite the same outline. He doesn't know.... He's not yet aware.... We've got to help him. Valmey is a snake. He'll stop at nothing. Oh, where's a boat? I've got to cross. Yes, I must cross to help Beresford. Can I use one of your boats? Please don't deny me.''

Duke Henry was by now greatly interested in the drama of the two men on the opposite shore and the woman beside him. He was also curious to discover what the fair Gwyneth thought she could accomplish by crossing the river and appearing alone before two men whose stances, even from a distance, did not look entirely friendly.

He offered her not only a boat, but also his personal assistance and that of two guards. Gwyneth accepted his escort with a distracted murmur of thanks and the comment that the accompaniment of the guards was an excellent idea.

The little party was midway across the river when Beresford and Valmey drew their swords, the metal flashing wickedly in the moonlight. They had reached the thicket of water rushes when the clash of steel against steel was engaged in earnest. Gwyneth and Duke Henry were out of the boat and in the shadows of the rushes when Valmey was heard to say to his opponent, ''But, then, I guess you have not heard of the attack on your home and of the burning of the mistress's bedchamber.''

Gwyneth would have run between the two men when Valmey's sword slashed Beresford's arm had it not been for Duke Henry's restraining hand. She looked up at the young duke in horror, her eyes pleading with him to stop the contest that seemed so dire for her husband. He shook his head and put his free hand to her mouth. He made her wait in agony beside him.

She was left with no recourse but to will Beresford her faith in him. She heard Valmey's vicious taunts and disreputable lies. She was shocked anew by them and prayed Beresford would not believe them. On the wings of the love she had for him, she sent him her soul, her heart and her blood. Then, miraculously, she saw the tide of the contest begin to turn, and Duke Henry slowly released her, perceiving no further need to restrain her.

Beresford had come alive, this time against an opponent whose skill was nearly the equal of his own. His sword work was brutal poetry. His rhythm was perfect. His strokes were graceful and harmonious. His defense was brilliant, as if he knew every move Valmey would make before he did. His offense was punishing. Gwyneth heard the grunt of pain and the cracking of Valmey's ribs when the flat of Beresford's sword made contact with his side.

She winced and gasped and closed her eyes and prayed. She opened her eyes and gasped again, this time with a happy leap of her heart. She heard Valmey haltingly confess his double game, with poisonous intent and labored breaths, but unmistakable all the same. She nearly smiled when Duke Henry looked down at her, brows raised in great surprise and interest. He conveyed her a silent look that thanked her for having alerted him to the duplicity of Cedric of Valmey.

When Beresford knocked Valmey to the ground, sending his sword from his grasp, Duke Henry drew his own sword. He came out from the shadows of the rushes and called out a commanding, "Halt!"

Duke Henry walked up to Beresford, who was kneeling over his victim, and said, "I'll not stand by while you are forced to accept a stain to your honor, good knight, as this creature has suggested his death at your hands would bring you." The young ruler planted his sword neatly in a corner of Valmey's tunic, pinning the villain into the ground. To Beresford, he continued, "You may rise and sheathe your sword."

Beresford rose, amazed. First he looked up at the sky, then down again at the vital young man next to him who had put his booted foot on Valmey's chest. He was puzzled at this form of divine deliverance, for even without an introduction, he knew the man to be Duke Henry of Anjou. He sheathed his sword as he had been bid, but he did not kneel before the young ruler. He was, first and always, Stephen's man.

"I've never seen more superior sword work," Duke Henry said, meeting Beresford eye to eye, "and I'll be pleased to relieve you of the responsibility of disposing of this creature." He punctuated his statement by tapping his foot on Valmey's chest.

Beresford bit off a blunt, "Thank you."

Duke Henry smiled. He did not yet stand high on ceremony. "It is not I whom you should thank," he said, "but your wife."

Beresford's astonishment increased. He thought he was dreaming and could not quite believe his eyes when Gwyneth stepped out from behind the water rushes into the blue-white moonlight. His emotions were in turmoil in his breast. He was dazzled by her beauty; he was worried, in retrospect, by the dangers she must have run to be here in Duke Henry's company on Stephen's side of the river; he feared to interpret what her actions might mean and wished to die if they did not mean she cared for him; he loved her to distraction; he did not know why Duke Henry was involved in this extraordinary scene. Confusion settled his brow into a fierce scowl.

Even seeing his expression, Gwyneth would not let her courage fail her now. She came forward, blinking back tears of relief and of pain. "I know, sire, that you cannot be pleased with me," she said, her voice wavering. "I have interfered inexcusably, once again, in your affairs."

"Yes, you have."

His dry tone caused her shaky voice to take on a scolding edge, partly in self-defense, partly in reaction to his near brush with death. "I cannot seem to help myself, however. From the beginning, you have walked from one trap to the next like an unwary child. I am perfectly able to recognize that you slash your way out of most predicaments, but I must say that you find yourself in those predicaments because you simply do not see what should be done or how to do it!"

He did not immediately answer. She was looking up into his dear, dear face, streaked with sweat and dirt, his eyes a complex combination of continuing puzzlement and, incredibly, dawning humor. "Unwary child?" he repeated. He cocked a brow. "Is this an apology, madam?"

"Yes. No! I have no need to apologize, for it is obvious that I have rescued you once again."

"Rescued me?"

"Valmey was coming to get you," Gwyneth explained. "I knew it, even if you did not!" She gestured down at the traitor, who was still trapped under Duke Henry's boot. "It was obvious I had to find you, and when I learned along the way from London to Bedford that Duke Henry had had such good success, I saw clearly what I had to do!" Gwyneth looked at the young duke. "I knew anyway what I had to do, sire. It was only upon leaving London that I could act on that conviction."

Duke Henry, recognizing himself to be an irrelevant third in the discussion, merely nodded.

Beresford demanded clarification. "Rescued me *again?*"

Gwyneth put her hands on her hips. "Well, it was pretty obvious that evening on the Tower battlements that Rosalyn and Valmey were trying to make you look bad in Stephen's eyes by having Rosalyn trap you in an amorous embrace. And although I did not care for you then the way I do now, I was not going to let her get away with it!"

"Care for me?"

"Not to mention that absurd incident in the queen's pleasance on the evening before our wedding! You were so wrongheaded to think that your good friend Geoffrey of Senlis had stolen the march on you, when instead it was Valmey! It was so obvious, I could have strangled you!"

Beresford smiled unexpectedly at her desire to strangle him. "Yes, the evening in the pleasance. I thought that I had rescued *you* then. Ah, but that gives me an idea!"

Gwyneth did not stop to hear what it was, for her love and anger and fear for him had bubbled up through her customary composure and flushed her cheeks. "Not to mention the joust against Gunnar Erickson! I did not—and would *never*—have set that man against you. In fact, I was the one who alerted Johanna to the ruse of the unknown knight's identity and, once again, it was Valmey—not your squire directly!—who set up the outrageous scheme to have

you—" here she choked "—to have you killed that day! I
know you do not want to hear about it, any more than—"

"I do not need to hear it," Beresford interpolated calmly.

"—Any more than you want to hear my declaration, but
I feel I must tell you—"

"I have already pieced together a very strange story, you
see, and I recognize, for all my unwary childishness, that it
is as strange as it is true."

"I really must tell you that—" Gwyneth broke off, horrified.

"Tell me?" Beresford queried. "Tell me what?"

She was mortified. She had been about to declare her love
for him, but he did not want this gift that could not be returned. She had no control over her cheeks, whose color he
was surely able to discern, even in the moonlight.

Beresford gestured negligently. "You can tell me later. In
fact, I'd prefer you tell me later." At that, he unbuckled his
belt, letting it fall to the ground, and began to take off his
tunic.

"What are you doing?" she asked.

"I'm undressing," he replied, obviously.

"In front of Duke Henry and his men?"

Beresford shrugged. He was peeling his torn shirt off his
now-clotted arm wound.

Duke Henry perceived this as his moment to depart, since
it was clear what this Simon of Beresford intended. He had
been vastly entertained by this interlude. Enlightened, too.
Although he was sorry to see his part in it end, he motioned
to the two guards to pick up Valmey and carry him to the
boat, which would transport him to his doom at Henry's
camp.

Duke Henry turned back to Beresford and said, "We are
sure to meet again."

Beresford was in the act of dispensing with his shoes. The
chausses were next. He answered, "Perhaps tomorrow, on
the field of battle."

Duke Henry shook his head. "The negotiations begin tomorrow."

Beresford's mouth twisted. "Negotiations," he repeated with a touch of derision.

Duke Henry smiled. "They'll take several weeks. More, if Stephen is stubborn. Perhaps less, without the aggravating factor of Valmey. As for your future role, let's agree that you'll leave the negotiations of that in your wife's capable hands."

Standing naked before the young man who was fated to rule the island nation, Beresford said, "She'll have to convince me first."

"She'll convince you." Duke Henry bowed and withdrew.

Beresford picked up the conversation with Gwyneth where he had left off. "Now, before you tell me what you've got to tell me," he said, "I would like to point out that I've rescued you a few times, too. Admit it!"

Gwyneth was openmouthed, not from his statement, but from his actions. "What?"

"Yes, I might mention Valmey's attack on our home, for I don't suppose you have missed the significance of my order that you spend the first night of my departure at the Tower."

"No, I did not miss that."

Beresford smiled suddenly. "And for treating my wife so well, I suppose that I am entitled to the continuing protection of the three crones."

Gwyneth smiled, too, remembering the conversation from their first meal together at the Tower. "I had forgotten about the Norns. But now that you remind me of them, I wonder...."

Beresford frowned. "You don't think I deserve their protection?"

"Of course you deserve their protection," she returned, matter-of-factly, "although I don't think you need it anymore. I was wondering instead whether they still existed."

Beresford was surprised. "I had not heard that the three crones had died."

Gwyneth shook her head. "No, I mean, I wonder whether my Norse god and goddess have survived. Loki's magic seems spent, and in his place has come another little mischief-maker who, if I am not mistaken, goes by the name of Eros! And watching you fighting Valmey just now, I was put in mind of another new force. Well, not a new force exactly, more of an ancient one. Different and more powerful." She considered his magnificent nakedness. "Yes, you put me in mind of the Greek god Hephaestus, the smith."

Beresford was glad to hear that the Valkyries might no longer exist, although he had rather liked the Tyr fellow and the Norns who protected him. However, he did not know about this Eros or this Hephaestus, nor did he care. In any case, he was in no mood for a discussion of heretical gods and goddesses, Norse or Greek—nor even a pious one concerning the True God. He commanded impatiently, "Well, get undressed, woman!"

"What?"

"You're joining me in the river."

"What?"

"I've got to wash the blood off my arm," he said practically, "as well as the dirt and sweat, and I want you to join me." He stepped beside her to help her with her clothing. "More to the point, I want you naked because I saw some bramble bushes not far from here."

"Bramble bushes?"

He looked at her curiously. "Have you lost your wits, woman?"

"Yes, I think so. I don't know what you're talking about."

"I'm talking about that evening in the queen's pleasance when I rescued you from Valmey's clutches."

Gone was her bliaut. "You are?"

"There was nothing more I wanted to do that night than take you to a spot just outside the Tower walls, by the riverbank, wild with brambles. I noticed some here earlier down by the river."

As she stepped out of her kirtle, she began to catch on. "You wanted to take me to the bramble bushes that evening?"

"You threatened me with knives," he reminded her, as if this comment would make any more sense to her than anything else he had said thus far.

In a strange sort of way, his world did come into focus for her. She began to laugh. At that same moment, her undershift floated to the ground. She was as naked as he.

"I can't believe it," she breathed, shaking her head.

"You did," he insisted with relish, "you threatened me with knives."

"No, I mean that I can't believe you just undressed in front of Duke Henry," she replied, laughter still rippling through her.

"Don't change the subject," he chided, taking her hand and leading her to the riverbank.

"Is it not all the same subject, then," she wondered aloud, "your undressing and your wanting to take me to the bramble bushes that evening? After all, I threatened you with knives on the very subject of my loyalty to Duke Henry." She could not resist adding, "Which loyalty may just save your neck."

A silver ladder of moonlight stretched across the water, uniting the two shores. "Be glad," he said, easing himself into the inky water, "for my neck is connected to other parts of some interest to you."

"While we're on the subject, I will admit that it was those other parts," she said, following him into the cool waters, "that were of interest to me that evening in the pleasance."

It was Beresford's turn to laugh. "We were of the same mind, then, which, now that I think of it, probably happens more often than either of us are aware. But as for the pleasance, I did not even consider it as a possible site for lovemaking."

"No? It is, sire, generally considered the ideal site for lovemaking."

Beresford dunked his head and came up spitting water and swirling wet hair. "Is that what you want, madam, courtly bows and practiced kisses?"

"You think the bramble bushes superior to the pleasance?"

He waded over to her, put his arms around her, and drew her next to him so their slippery bodies met fully. He whispered a blunt suggestion in her ear, in terms that were far from courtly and practiced.

Though stimulated by the suggestion and the circumstances and her deep, abiding love for him, she hesitated.

He drew his head back and looked at her. He said, with a very attractive gleam in his eye, "I dare you to do that with me, snug in the dirt under the cover of bramble bushes."

Thus challenged, she accepted. To their mutual delight.

* * * * *

Author's Note

In August of 1153, the young Duke Henry of Anjou negotiated a peace with King Stephen of England, but it was not until November of that year that Stephen acknowledged Henry as his successor and heir to the kingdom by hereditary right. Stephen died in October of 1154. Henry II was crowned in Westminster Abbey two months later and reigned during a period of peace and prosperity until 1189.

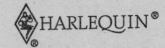

Harlequin Books requests the pleasure of your company this June in Eternity, Massachusetts, for WEDDINGS, INC.

For generations, couples have been coming to Eternity, Massachusetts, to exchange wedding vows. Legend has it that those married in Eternity's chapel are destined for a lifetime of happiness. And the residents are more than willing to give the legend a hand.

Beginning in June, you can experience the legend of Eternity. Watch for one title per month, across all of the Harlequin series.

HARLEQUIN BOOKS... NOT THE SAME OLD STORY!

Fifty red-blooded, white-hot, true-blue hunks
from every State in the Union!

Look for MEN MADE IN AMERICA! Written by some of
our most popular authors, these stories feature fifty of the
strongest, sexiest men, each from a different state in the
union!

Two titles available every month at your favorite retail
outlet.

In July, look for:

ROCKY ROAD by Anne Stuart (Maine)
THE LOVE THING by Dixie Browning (Maryland)

In August, look for:

PROS AND CONS by Bethany Campbell (Massachusetts)
TO TAME A WOLF by Anne McAllister (Michigan)

You won't be able to resist MEN MADE IN AMERICA!

DESTINY'S WOMEN

Sexy, adventurous historical romance at its best!

May 1994
ALENA #220. A veteran Roman commander battles to subdue the proud, defiant queen he takes to wife.

July 1994
SWEET SONG OF LOVE #230. Medieval is the tale of an arranged marriage that flourishes despite all odds.

September 1994
SIREN'S CALL #236. The story of a dashing Greek sea captain and the stubborn Spartan woman he carries off.

Three exciting stories from Merline Lovelace, a fresh new voice in Historical Romance.

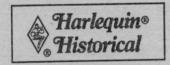

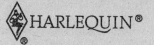

HARLEQUIN®

Don't miss these Harlequin favorites by some of our most distinguished authors!
And now you can receive a discount by ordering two or more titles!

HT #25525	THE PERFECT HUSBAND by Kristine Rolofson	$2.99	☐
HT #25554	LOVERS' SECRETS by Glenda Sanders	$2.99	☐
HP #11577	THE STONE PRINCESS by Robyn Donald	$2.99	☐
HP #11554	SECRET ADMIRER by Susan Napier	$2.99	☐
HR #03277	THE LADY AND THE TOMCAT by Bethany Campbell	$2.99	☐
HR #03283	FOREIGN AFFAIR by Eva Rutland	$2.99	☐
HS #70529	KEEPING CHRISTMAS by Marisa Carroll	$3.39	☐
HS #70578	THE LAST BUCCANEER by Lynn Erickson	$3.50	☐
HI #22256	THRICE FAMILIAR by Caroline Burnes	$2.99	☐
HI #22238	PRESUMED GUILTY by Tess Gerritsen	$2.99	☐
HAR #16496	OH, YOU BEAUTIFUL DOLL by Judith Arnold	$3.50	☐
HAR #16510	WED AGAIN by Elda Minger	$3.50	☐
HH #28719	RACHEL by Lynda Trent	$3.99	☐
HH #28795	PIECES OF SKY by Marianne Willman	$3.99	☐

Harlequin Promotional Titles

#97122	LINGERING SHADOWS by Penny Jordan	$5.99	☐
	(limited quantities available on certain titles)		

	AMOUNT	$
DEDUCT:	**10% DISCOUNT FOR 2+ BOOKS**	$
	POSTAGE & HANDLING	$
	($1.00 for one book, 50¢ for each additional)	
	APPLICABLE TAXES*	$_____
	TOTAL PAYABLE	$_____
	(check or money order—please do not send cash)	

To order, complete this form and send it, along with a check or money order for the total above, payable to Harlequin Books, to: **In the U.S.:** 3010 Walden Avenue, P.O. Box 9047, Buffalo, NY 14269-9047; **In Canada:** P.O. Box 613, Fort Erie, Ontario, L2A 5X3.

Name: _____

Address:_____City: _____

State/Prov.: _____ Zip/Postal Code: _____

*New York residents remit applicable sales taxes.
  Canadian residents remit applicable GST and provincial taxes..